MCNAMARA

BOOK SET ONE

BOOKS ONE & TWO

Mayhem on Nightingale Street

&

Scents and Shadows

ROXANA NASTASE

SCARLET LEAF

TORONTO, CANADA

2017

MCNAMARA SERIES BOX SET
BOOK 0NE & TWO

MCNAMARA SERIES BOX SET
BOOK 0NE & TWO

Scarlet Leaf Publishing House has allowed this work to remain exactly as the author intended.

ISBN: 9781988397665

PUBLISHED BY SCARLET LEAF

MCNAMARA SERIES BOX SET
BOOK 0NE & TWO

To my parents for their love and

support

TABLE OF CONTENTS

MCNAMARA SERIES BOX SET
BOOK 0NE & TWO

MAYHEM ON NIGHTINGALE STREET

MCNAMARA SERIES BOX SET
BOOK 0NE & TWO

Should we fear the dark? What about the daylight? Is life only insecurity and hell? Could we dream of heaven or at least of a piece of it?

MCNAMARA SERIES BOX SET
BOOK 0NE & TWO

CHAPTER ONE

The night air filled with the smell of fear as a sharp scream pierced its silence. The woman woke up frightened, shivering and panting, as if from a nightmare.

She turned on the light and discovered John, her lazy and chubby husband, lying next to her, with eyes wide open and horror engraved on his face. His pale knuckles clenched on the blanket wrapped over his chest.

Neither of them said or did anything as if that shout had paralyzed their minds and bodies. They only looked at each other, unable to imagine what had happened.

After several long moments of painful silence, John spoke in a low murmur, as if he had been afraid that he would awaken ghosts lurking in the dark.

"What the heck was that? Did you hear it, Doris?"

"Of course, I heard it, stupid," she spat, finally feeling safe to speak. "Why do you think I'm staring at the walls in the middle of the night? You must go out and see what's going on," she added quickly.

Her usual determination screeched in the man's ears, who looked at her in shock. He couldn't believe his ears. The daft woman actually wanted him to go out there.

Her words stirred a torrent of anger in him. Years of frustration had already painfully piled up in his chest, and the dam broke.

"You've thought about that a lot, haven't you?" he snapped at her with bitterness in his voice. "Do you think I dare to go out there, in the night, after something like that?" he shouted, waving his hand in the air. "You must be daft, woman."

She didn't say anything for a while, but the look on her face did the talking for her. After forty years of marriage, her opinions weren't a secret anymore. Not that her husband cared to know. He was aware of the shift in her feelings for him. The woman didn't harbour any warmth or delight for him in her bones.

"Oh, Lord, you're so pathetic! You're such a wimp!" she exclaimed bitingly, thinking she might make him move. She knew what buttons to push so he would do her bidding.

"This time around, you can say whatever you want, my dear... It won't work," John dragged his words. "I don't give a fig about any of that. I won't go out just to please you... you... harpy!" he stuttered. "It sounded like it had come directly from hell, and hell and I have nothing in common save for you," he repeated one of his favourite quips.

"I know, don't remind me," she snapped back, annoyed.

By now, she would know his lines by heart. They had been living together for far too long, and there wasn't anything left unsaid between them.

"But maybe someone needs help. And look at us: we're just lying here. We're wasting our time talking nonsense," the woman whined.

"Well, if you're so brave, my dove, then, maybe, you should go out there," he challenged her, more than a bit of sarcasm colouring his voice. "But I don't advise you to do that. You're crazy, old bat! I tell you."

"I don't think so," she replied grumpily. "I hear hurried steps outside, John... I think Mr Thompson's woken up... I'm sure I hear others as well... Well, what are you saying now?" she eagerly provoked him, sure that his pride would suffer if he didn't go out then.

Men were like that. They would take a dare at the snap of a finger, always willing to show that they were better, stronger, and braver than any other man in the room.

"All right, back off!" the man snapped, throwing the cover away. "If he's out there, I'll go, too. Now, shut up, back off, and let me get dressed," John bellowed, feeling cornered by his nagging wife.

He got out of bed, still springy for his age, and went to the bathroom for his bathrobe. His abrupt gestures betrayed his irritation. He tied his bathrobe and headed downstairs, all the way down, muttering a few choice words under his breath about his nosy wife.

Doris had remained in bed, content to stay there and wait for news from him. Of course, she didn't have enough courage to go and look out the window, like she usually did. Yet, she would push him out in the middle of the night just on a whim.

John opened the front door to bright lights. All the windows on the little street were lit, and that uncharacteristic illumination unsettled him. Not even at Christmas did their street display so many lights. They were Scots, and they minded their pockets after all.

John noticed three men heading with long strides towards his front lawn, talking to one another and pointing to one spot on his property. He glanced there, and his blood ran cold when his eyes fell on what they were staring at.

The moon had come out of the clouds, and a body lay sprawled in the moon's light. John needed only an instant to notice the blonde hair and the white dress, torn and stained with blood and the green of the grass. The body's right hand lay in full sight, and the crooked fingers gave the illusion that they intended to cling on to something in the air.

Then, the smell hit him — somewhat sweet and sour at the same time. John knew that the scent would linger there for days or maybe more. The lawn didn't belong to him anymore.

Overwhelmed, John suddenly felt dizzy. His body seemed to have left the material space. The relief was short-lived, though. A ruthless punch in his stomach, nausea hit him, knocking the air out of his lungs.

John bent in an awkward position and remained hunched, unable to move. His muscles screamed for oxygen as the man tried to pull air into his lungs. Yet he couldn't, and his head span faster and faster.

He saw everything as if through a dense fog. Mr Thompson had stepped on his lawn and now leaned over the body on the grass. He said something, motioning to Mr Reid, the man who lived in the third house across the street, and that one replied something back.

John thought it was strange that he couldn't make any sense of the men's words.

Then, John caught a glimpse of a shadow in the dark by the corner of the house, and the man felt threatened. However, he still had enough wits to understand it was just foolish thinking. Nothing wrong could happen to him with so many people around.

John had never been a courageous man, more evident now, in his old age when he lacked the advantage of youth's stupidity.

Crushed, the man fell on the veranda like a log. Everything went black and downright silent around him. Only that iron fist of pain, squeezing his chest tightly, remained present for another second.

Then, the peace he had longed for surrounded him. It was a safe and easy way out, even though John had never thought he would feel that way when his time would come.

From upstairs in her bed, Doris, his wife, heard Mr Reid call to the others.

"Oh, I think Mr Dobbs fainted. We should call a doctor or something, I suppose."

Doris's fingers and legs started shaking while dark thoughts piled up in her mind. She wanted to get out of bed, but her legs shook severely and didn't help her much.

The woman finally threw her legs over the edge of the bed, but she couldn't find her slippers, although they were just there, right where she would always leave them, under the bed. She couldn't pull herself together.

The woman knew John. He might have been a little lazy and sometimes too stubborn for his own good, but he wasn't the coward she had accused him of being. He had never fainted before, regardless of how bad the situation had been.

Guilt weighed on Doris. She knew that her husband wouldn't have gone outside if it had not been for her. John wasn't a curious person, and no one would have cared less about what happened in the street or in their neighbours' houses.

On her way down the stairs, Doris tried to keep her balance, leaning against the wall. She was shaking all the worse the closer she got to the hallway. Then, Doris controlled her wild panic, and the truth dawned on her — things would never be the same for her again.

That thought made her move faster down the stairs. When she reached the hallway, the front door started opening. Stunned, the woman watched the slow movement of the door, holding her breath.

A few seconds later, heavy steps sounded on the wooden floor. The woman's gaze fell on two men, but Doris didn't recognize them at first. Still, they carried John in their arms.

The woman stared at John intently, willing him to move or say something, and then she glanced at the men again. Now, she recognized her neighbours, Mr Thompson and Reid.

Thompson said, "Don't be afraid, Mrs Dobbs. I think Mr Dobbs has just fainted, that's all. He'll be back to his usual self in no time, you'll see. I do hope he doesn't have a weak heart, though," he continued, shaking his head. "That scene out there isn't for the faint of heart. Where should we put him, Mrs Dobbs? The doctor is on his way already. He'll be here in a minute. Mrs Dobbs?"

The younger man kept talking and talking, his lips moving, forming words, yet Doris couldn't perceive a sound. The woman needed a few seconds to realize that the two men were staring at her. She shook her head to clear her mind.

Understanding that the woman was in shock, Thompson repeated slowly, "Mrs Dobbs, are you feeling well? Where should we put poor Mr Dobbs?"

Doris struggled with herself. She finally pulled herself together just enough to reply softly, "On the sofa, I think."

After a few seconds, she repeated in a stronger voice, almost regaining her old composure, "Aye, on the sofa. I think it's the best place for him now. Thank you, Mr Thompson. You said the doctor was coming?"

"Aye, Mrs Dobbs, right now. I've asked Mr Brown to call him. We've called the police too. They're on their way."

"What happened, Mr Thompson?" Doris asked, somewhat reluctantly, which was peculiar.

Doris Dobbs was always the first on their street to find out what was going on. She made it her business to know if a neighbour had had a row with his wife or another neighbour. She had been the first to find out that the Porters' little Patsy had eloped with that good-looking young man, working for the Browns, or when the Davidsons had decided to divorce.

"It's best you didn't know, Mrs Dobbs. I don't think it would do you any good to know now. Here's the doctor," Thompson added after throwing a glance out the window. The doctor's car had just stopped in front of the house, and Thompson went out to greet him.

Doris sat down on an armchair near the sofa and studied her husband. John's face looked unnatural in the soft light of the living room.

All colour had left his cheeks. His left hand still clenched his bathrobe stiffly, and the other hung on one side of the sofa, lifeless.

Doris didn't hear him breathing, and she knew. The doctor needn't come anymore... At least not for John. He was gone.

The woman didn't move but merely stared at the man. Only one thought repeatedly sounded in her mind like a mantra, drowning out the sounds from the street, her heartbeat, everything. 'He's dead. Oh, God, he's dead.' Nothing bothered her anymore. Even her pain had hidden inside her mind.

***

The people living on the street had gathered in front of the Dobbs' house and noticed the doctor's arrival. A rumour passed around, whispering that poor Mr Dobbs had had a heart attack and, probably, had already passed away before the doctor got there. People couldn't understand why his wife hadn't come out yet, and why no one had heard a peep from her.

Sirens announced the police cars, and the people fell silent, watching the cars drive up Nightingale Street.

Unconsciously, they stepped farther away from the Dobbs' yard. They wanted to distance themselves and show that they were not involved in the mess on that lawn.

The police cars pulled up to the Dobbs residence, and men came out of them, some wearing police uniforms. Others wore dark coveralls, somewhat resembling the uniformed officers' clothing, and carried black cases.

A tall man in his late thirties or early forties glimpsed at the crowd in the street and then shouted to a younger policeman, "James, get their names and addresses, and send them home. We'll talk to them later in the morning. Right now, I want more room here and no on-lookers in front of the house. Too many have already trampled through this yard, probably destroying all the evidence."

"Aye, sir," said the young man, immediately heading towards the people, taking a little black book out of his pocket. The man asked for their names and addresses, and he inquired whether they had seen anything before the murder happened.

His last question remained unanswered because no one had seen anything. Everyone said the same thing: an inhuman scream woke them up. They had noticed that body on the lawn and nothing else when they came out of their houses.

Neither of them had got closer to the young woman, at Mr Thompson's request not to touch anything until the police arrived.

The people even told James of the rumours about poor Mr Dobbs, who had fainted on his own porch, and then they started back home as they had nothing left to say or spread stories about. However, they seemed somewhat reluctant to abandon the ghastly sight without getting any answers.

James returned to his colleagues to report to his boss everything he had learnt. The DCI listened to him carefully and nodded. "All right, James. Good job. Now go and see what's with that man, Mr Dobbs. I think I just saw two men go into his house. I want to talk to the three of them, too."

James nodded and walked to the Dobbs' front door, which he found ajar, so he didn't bother to knock. He just pushed it open and went inside. Whispers came from somewhere on the right, so the young man followed the voices.

Getting to the living room, his eyes fell on a man, probably the doctor, taking the pulse of a woman of uncertain age. The extreme pallor in her cheeks and the apparent toll the evening had taken on her made it difficult to tell precisely how old she was.

James's eyes scanned the room, analysing the five people. Afterwards, he knocked on the door and interrupted them. "Good evening, everyone. I'm very sorry to disturb you at such a time. I'm DS James, and I need to speak to Mr Dobbs."

His words seemed to be the signal she had been waiting for because the woman burst into tears at that precise moment. The men froze in place, surprised for one moment.

Then, the man James thought the doctor studied the old woman. "Finally, she's crying. That's good. She was bound to do it sooner or later. It's always better if the grieving starts soon," he commented with a satisfied yet sympathetic nod. Then, the man turned to James. "I'm sorry, Detective Sergeant, but I'm afraid Mr Dobbs died earlier tonight because of a massive heart attack. There was nothing I could do for him, unfortunately. Probably the shock was too much for him."

"I see," James nodded, even though he wondered why the shock had been so devastating for the old man. Yet, he continued, "All right, then. I'll leave you now to Mrs Dobbs. But sir, when you've finished here, we must talk to you. And to you, too," he said, turning to Mr Thompson. "Who are you, sir?"

"I'm Thompson. I'm Daniel Thompson," the man answered, stepping forward to shake James's hand.

"Oh, I see. I'm told you're the one who made sure the others didn't disturb the body."

"Indeed, sir," Thompson nodded. "I was in the Navy in the past. I know something about such things. There are also the movies, you know… I'll be with you shortly. I just need to finish talking to good Doctor Connolly. Is that all right?"

"No rush, sir. We still have plenty to do outside. We'll be here for a while. Come and see us before you leave," James said, going back outside.

There, his eyes found his boss, DCI McNamara, talking to one of the investigators. James stopped a few steps behind the DCI, going through his notes until the chief had finished discussing the scene with the detective. Then, the DS approached McNamara.

"I'm sorry, sir, but Mr Dobbs passed away. He had a massive heart attack. His wife is in shock right now, and I don't think we'll get much out of her. She'll probably need some time to recover. However, Mr Thompson will come out with the doctor soon, and we can talk to them."

"Oh, damn it!" McNamara swore, furious because they were too late. "Rotten bad luck! He must have seen something if he died so suddenly. We'll see," he said in a hushed voice. Then he repeated, "We'll see."

His thoughts still on the Dobbs situation and the significant piece of the puzzle they might have lost, he turned to the older man next to him and inquired, "So, doc, what do you think?"

"Well, not very much now... But, as you can see, the young woman had her throat slit – brutally too, from one side to the other. She was stabbed several times before that. You see those stab wounds there?" he showed the detective several marks with significant traces of blood.

McNamara nodded briefly, impatient to have the rest of the story.

"I can tell you she didn't go quietly," the coroner continued with a shake of his head. "Look at her hands. Scratches and broken nails. This girl fought hard to survive. I know you understand that I can't make a positive statement right now. Still, I'm almost positive the time of death is somewhere between only several minutes ago and an hour," he waved his hand.

McNamara looked at the coroner, expecting something more. Stewart sighed.

"We'll know more later. Anyway, the girl was severely beaten over several days before being killed. Notice here," he pointed to the body. "The bruises on her body are at different stages. Their colour isn't the same. These marks here are older, maybe three or four days old. They've already changed colour. As you can see, her face is beyond recognition, I'm afraid. Aye, lad, we'll have to find another way to identify her," he concluded, then looked across the lawn to the Dobbs house. He shook his head in regret again before he glanced back to the detective, "Well, I'll tell you more later. I'll have to do the post-mortem first."

"All right, David. Anyway, I think we may safely presume that she died a little over 30 minutes ago. That's when dispatch got the call, and people said they had heard the scream just minutes before the call came through," McNamara concluded.

The DCI looked around and said, "James, go see if there's an ID in her purse. They found a purse on the ground there." McNamara pointed somewhere towards the middle of the grass, several feet away from the body. "It must have been hers," he added. "I doubt there could have been more than one on this specific lawn."

James followed the path marked with numbered, yellow cards on the grass until he reached the investigator taking inventory of the personal effects found in the victim's purse.

The DS asked him for the sealed evidence bag, which, at first glance, contained several cosmetic items — lip-gloss, mascara, a compact. A closer look at the investigator's notes revealed that they had found a card inside. James felt a surge of pride looking at their first significant lead that evening. He signed on the bag, opened the seal, and carefully moved the other items inside the bag with his pen until he found the ID.

After locating the name and address on the card, he resealed the bag and signed it. Then, the DS returned to McNamara and spoke to him in a low voice, so no one else heard him.

"It's an ID for a Patsy Porter, sir. She lived right here on this street. Oh," he stopped, noticing he had missed one bit of information. "She was quite young, sir, only sixteen," he continued with dismay.

"It's good we found it, James. We'll go and see her family in the morning. They'll have to come to the coroner's office and identify the body at the morgue sometime tomorrow," DCI McNamara added and sighed. He knew how unsettling those formalities were for the families involved.

Then, McNamara signalled the two men waiting by a stretcher.

One of them was leaning on the stretcher by the van, a plastic bag hanging off his hand carelessly. He passed his boredom away with a game on his phone, and the DCI scowled. He understood their job demanded they become harder and not allow the violence they witnessed to affect them. Yet, he didn't like the complete desensitised lack of emotion either.

"You may take her now," McNamara said in a harsh tone of voice, and that snapped the two technicians out of their boredom instantly.

The men placed the body inside the black plastic bag and took it off the lawn. They carried it to the coroner's truck and left the area accessible for the forensic team. The forensic experts had already been searching the place minutely and collected what little usable evidence they found.

They didn't find the murder weapon, but, after all, they didn't hope to see it, either. It would have been too good to be true, to have the knife, and if possible, the killer's prints on it...

***

Once the police left, peace fell over the little suburb street again. However, this time, silence didn't comfort the residents. People didn't feel safe there anymore. They weren't uninformed. They read the papers and followed the news and knew such things happened in other places all the time. Yet, nothing similar had ever occurred so close to home.

Still, Doris remained there, in the middle of things. She kept looking out the window in the night, intent on finding out what had led to her husband's death.

She didn't feel any curiosity about what was going on in the street. But she thought it was her duty to find out why her husband had died. The woman felt guilty because she had pushed him out of the house. At the same time, she felt lonely, hollow, and deserted.

She hadn't been in love with her husband anymore. That was true. Too much time had passed, and life had been somewhat dull for the two of them for years now. Yet, she had cared for him.

Doris knew John was at the morgue now. She shivered at the thought that he was lying on a cold slab. The woman hadn't been aware his heart was weak to make things worse. Self-centred, she hadn't paid attention to any of his complaints about his health but just pushed them aside, as if they hadn't mattered.

The woman kept looking outside into the night and noticed someone crossing the lawn, looking for something on the ground, a small flashlight in their hand.

She didn't see who it was, but she didn't care. Doris merely presumed the police were still looking for evidence on the ground. Yet, the person moving in the shadows of the cloud-covered moon saw her looking out the window.

CHAPTER TWO

It was almost ten o'clock in the morning when McNamara, together with James, returned to Nightingale Street to question their witnesses about the murder. First, they went to the Porters and knocked on their door.

Waiting seemed such a significant part of their lives that they didn't even bother to notice it anymore. Hurried steps on the stairs, and a woman's voice shouted, "One moment, please. I'm coming."

A few seconds later, the door opened. The woman at the door looked at them, questioning their possible reason for being there.

Mrs Porter was short and a little on the plump side. She looked old, anywhere between fifty and sixty, but the detectives knew she was much younger than that. Still, her face wore signs of exhaustion.

"Oh, yes... And who are you, please?" Mrs Porter asked when she found her voice again, surprised to see two unknown people instead of the friend she expected.

"We're with the police, ma'am. Here are our badges," the tall man said. "DCI McNamara and DS James. May we come in?"

The woman hesitated for a moment, unsure that she could offer any insight into the previous night's events. In the end, she stepped aside and waved them inside. Although she didn't have any information, she couldn't just tell them to leave and slam the door in their face. Not only because they were the police, but the anxiety had been bothering her since the night's violence occurred.

Mrs Porter never went out after hearing that scream because she was alone and afraid. When she finally found the courage to glance out the window, she saw her neighbours huddled up in front of the Dobbs' house.

She had been trying to forget the rumour about a girl lying dead in the Dobbs' yard, but it still haunted her. The woman had spent most of the night lying awake in bed, frightened by her imagination.

Mrs Porter led the detectives into a living room that had seen better days. Her dark thoughts had nearly paralysed her upon the detectives' arrival, and she couldn't find her voice to invite them to take a seat. With a shaky hand, she merely showed them the sofa.

The policemen took their time sitting down. They looked over the living room, glancing at family pictures or small curiosities, willing to delay the discussion with the woman.

McNamara was still looking for a way to tell her that, probably, her daughter was at the morgue. He had been thinking about that the entire morning but couldn't decide what to say.

The detective knew there was no perfect way to break such news and make it less painful. Still, he had always felt unprepared despite his many years with the police. Besides, Mrs Porter looked highly fragile, which made him hesitate more than usual. He tried to steal some more time and delay the awful moment with routine questions.

"Where's Mr Porter, please?" The DCI thought it would be easier for her if she had someone there to comfort her after their leaving. He had hardly asked the question when tears welled up in the woman's eyes. For a few long seconds, he feared she would start crying. When she finally answered, she spoke slowly and sheepishly as if she had confessed a terrible and humiliating sin.

"What boy, ma'am? Do you know his name?" McNamara asked and shifted closer to the edge of the sofa, impatient to have finally found a lead to follow. So far, he hadn't had any idea why his victim was targeted, and his only connection to the body they found was that little street.

"Oh, aye. He was such a good-looking boy. And he was such a smooth talker... but he was a good boy. He used to work at Mr Brown's pub at the other end of the street... He left at the same time. I mean, when Patsy left home to go, God knows where. But I don't know where they are now. I haven't heard a peep from my Patsy ever since."

"But do you know his name, ma'am?" McNamara asked her again patiently, although he felt like shaking her so that she would get to the point. He hated people's blabbering, but he knew better than to interrupt.

The woman thought for a few seconds. Then, she shook her head and said, "I think... It was Peter, but I'm not sure..."

Mrs Porter tilted her head on the side and seemed thinking hard. The detectives watched her patiently.

"In the beginning, I didn't ask Patsy because I didn't know she was going out with him. I found out when she left that dreadful message and went away, but that was the name she wrote on the note. That she was leaving with Peter from the pub on the corner... And then... I was too ashamed to go to the Browns and ask them... But ... what's the matter? Has something happened to my husband or Patsy?" Her voice almost broke, and she glanced from one detective to the other as if begging them not to confirm her fears.

As dark as the shadow cast by his stubby beard, McNamara's eyes had already given her the dreadful news. McNamara cursed himself silently. He feared that neither he nor James could offer proper emotional support. Jo would have been the logical choice to send to Mrs Porter. She would have known how to comfort the woman.

The DCI searched for the right words to tell the woman that the girl found dead in the Dobbs' yard was probably her daughter because of the ID and general description. Yet, no words came to him. He was staring at her, almost without blinking, deciding what to do. The silence was dire: it scratched their skin and deafened their ears.

Finally, when she couldn't bear the silence anymore, Mrs Porter whispered, "It is bad, isn't it? Which one of them, please? I only hope it isn't Patsy. That I wouldn't bear."

Suddenly, the painful thought that her daughter was the girl from the Dobbs' yard last night penetrated the fog in her mind. She looked straight into McNamara's eyes again, and then, she knew. It was Patsy.

She thought her heart had stopped beating for a second, but she was wrong. Only her mind had stopped working. Stunned, she joined her hands in her lap, and a horrified grimace appeared in the corner of her mouth.

McNamara knew she understood. He stood up, intending to put his hand on her shoulder and comfort her. Surprised by that unusual idea, the DCI admonished himself.

He had always remained cold and detached from everything. He wasn't a psychologist but a policeman, so he sat down again. Only finding answers and convicting killers counted.

To his horror, the next moment, something broke inside the woman. First, she groaned loudly, then she burst into tears. Sobs followed. The dam broke.

Hoping for help, McNamara glanced at James but gave up, noticing the young man's expression. So, the DCI finally decided to go on with what he had to do.

"I'm sorry, Mrs Porter, but I must ask you to come down to the morgue and identify the body, just to be sure. We need someone to ID the young girl, and we only have a document that says it was Patsy," he said apologetically.

A glimpse of hope nestled in the woman's heart but died almost instantly. She knew it was wishful thinking to hope the police had made a mistake. She had already felt that her Patsy was gone. That thought had been hunting her for a few days already.

As if awakened from a trance, she said with difficulty, "When do you want me to come?"

"When you feel able to, but the sooner, the better... Do you want me to send a car to drive you to the coroner's office this afternoon?" McNamara offered.

"No, thank you, that's kind of you but... I'll come by myself... Maybe I'll ask my friend, Mary, Mary Brown, to accompany me. I don't think she'd mind...." She realised she was rambling and shut up.

"All right, Mrs Porter, we'll see you there in the afternoon. Now, I think we'd better leave you alone," McNamara stood up again. He couldn't wait to move on to the next item on his to-do list.

Mrs Porter nodded but didn't reply. She stood up with difficulty like an old woman and showed the two policemen out. The woman opened the door mechanically and nodded to them as an afterthought.

After they left, she eased the door closed. She leaned against the wall for a few seconds. Then she slid down to the floor, where she remained motionless for a while, completely numb. After a few long minutes, she burst into tears again and sobbed her heart out. Her child was gone.

***

"Come on, James. Let's go to Mrs Dobbs and see how she is. Maybe last night's shock has eased a little, and she might have something to tell us now," McNamara said.

"Aye, sir, that's an excellent idea." James agreed, following him down the street.

They strode over to Mrs Dobbs' house and knocked. They waited, but no answer came from inside. They shot each other a questioning look, then pounded on the door again... harder this time. Still no answer.

James stepped back and looked up at the windows on the first floor. "Sir, I think something isn't right here. It's ten o'clock, and the light's still on upstairs."

McNamara initially dismissed his concern but thought better and said, "Who knows why? We'd better try the back door, as well. She might be there. James, stay here and keep knocking. Maybe she'll hear you. I'm going to see at the back," McNamara continued. "I'll call you if there's something."

McNamara headed with long strides to the back of the house, glancing thoughtfully at the window James had noticed earlier.

Perhaps the woman had fallen asleep with the light on. That was one possible explanation. It was also possible she hadn't woken up yet. After all, the previous night must have exhausted her. McNamara knew he shouldn't make assumptions or think of the worst.

He arrived at the back of the house in no time. He raised his hand to knock when he noticed the door was ajar. He pushed it open and called, "Mrs Dobbs, are you at home? We're with the police."

No answer came from inside. Only the DCI's voice bounced off the walls. He didn't like it. He waited a few more moments then called to James, "James, come here."

James rushed from the front door, following the sound of McNamara's voice to the back of the house. There, he found McNamara cautiously advancing through the kitchen. McNamara pointed his index to James, his thumb to himself, and then to the inside of the house. James nodded, and both entered the house slowly, ready to fight back if anybody would have attacked.

Their eyes swept all over the kitchen. The area was clean with no recent use — no plates anywhere in sight, not even a teacup. They continued outside the kitchen, along the corridor, moving silently to surprise any intruder.

The DCI opened the door on the left only to reveal a well-stocked pantry. McNamara shook his head and closed the door.

The policemen walked on, always catlike, until they reached the hallway. Another small corridor stretched before them, and on the left, stairs led to the upper floor. There was a door on each side of the staircase, and they chose to check those rooms separately.

James tiptoed into the room on the left and discovered a small but cosy drawing room with a beige loveseat and two big armchairs in the same neutral colour.

McNamara opened the door on the right of the stairs to discover the dining room, dominated by heavy sculptured furniture in fashion decades earlier.

They quietly walked along the corridor towards another room on the left. That was the living room, which James had already seen the night before. A trace of blood beckoned to them from behind the door, but not before the strong smell of spilt blood hit them.

McNamara glanced behind the door and waved to James to look as well. Reluctantly, James did look, and as always, nausea rose in his throat. That happened to him no matter how many bodies he had seen. He had already resigned himself to suffer through it if he wanted to do the job.

Mrs Dobbs lay face down behind the door, a pool of blood almost completely coagulated under her.

The detectives looked around. The small stand that used to be near the wall had been knocked over. Last night, a vase with flowers stood there, but now, it was shattered on the wet floor, the water flirting with the edges of the pool of blood. The flowers had fallen a little further, reminding James of the flowers thrown over coffins at funerals, making him feel worse.

"I think she heard some kind of noise, and she came to the door... I can see she tried to defend herself when she was grabbed... I think she fought, but she didn't stand a chance," McNamara said, analysing the body, his hands buried deep in his pockets. "Probably, because the attacker was stronger... We can't dismiss that she was surprised," he added, glancing at James, who nodded his assent.

"I'll call the headquarters, boss. We need them to send in the coroner and the forensics," James said, digging out his phone from his front pocket.

"All right, James, you do that. Until they come, let's wait in the hallway. I don't think you want to stay around this too much, and neither do I."

***

Mrs Thompson noticed the cars crowded in front of the Dobbs' house. After what happened the night before, she was more than curious. So, the woman went outside with a determination that she didn't usually feel and headed directly to

DS James. He was speaking to a man dressed in a brown jacket.

She had already seen James the night before when he talked to them, and she felt confident approaching him.

"Do you mind, sir? What's happened now?" she asked him.

"You'd better go inside, ma'am," James replied and turned her towards her own house. "We'll stop by your house later, and we'll explain everything then."

Alice Thompson didn't want to leave, but she couldn't find an excuse or something witty to say so she could stay there and find out what was going on. She obeyed because she didn't know to refuse a direct order, even though James made it sound like a mere request. Lost in her thoughts, she returned to her house with small steps. Someone called her name.

"Alice, what's going on?" asked a woman in a summer outfit, entirely inadequate for the morning's chilly weather. The temperature wasn't as high as it used to be, and that flimsy outfit didn't offer any protection against the chill. The summer was flirting with its last days. However, autumn was already in the air and in the colour of the leaves.

The strange woman, Mary Reid, Alice's neighbour, had also heard the sirens of the police cars. As a woman who shared the imagination of two people at least, and especially after witnessing the night's events, she imagined the worst. Out of the ordinary was that she wasn't far from the truth this time.

Mary was a woman a little over thirty, but not the typical thirty-year-old. She was slightly plump, swarthy-faced, and green-eyed. Her temper was in total contradiction with the type of woman she was portraying.

Alice guessed that Mary had married one or two years before. The Reid family had moved into the area only half a year before after buying the house from Mr MacDonald's grandsons, who had been trying to push that house off the market for quite some time. Poor Mr MacDonald had died one year earlier, almost to the day.

Alice and Mary made some sort of friends, some said, but only because they stayed at home in the morning while their husbands went to town for work. They weren't very close, even though there wasn't a gap in age between them. Yet, they had completely different interests and weren't fit to be friends. Alice was the typical and obedient housewife, who had only her house and husband on her mind all day long.

Mary was nothing of the kind. She was a modern and independent woman. Understandably, Mary Reid didn't seem to need or heed her husband's opinions. She would do whatever she wanted regardless of what that poor guy would say.

Consequently, the quarrels from their house were legendary and even quite entertaining sometimes. Some neighbours craved them. After all, it was a free show and made them forget about their pesky little rows.

"I don't know, Mary," Alice finally answered. "I'm afraid, you know. I think something bad happened at the Dobbs' again. Something happened to Mrs Dobbs. That young policeman over there didn't want to tell me anything... He sent me packing quite fast. He said they were going to talk to us later," Alice shared what she knew and headed to her house, failing to see the disappointed grimace on Mary's face, who was put out by the lack of news.

Suddenly, Alice turned back and asked, "What do you think, Mary, would you come for tea? Oh, sorry, I'd better invite you to coffee. I know you don't like tea, although I don't understand why," Alice said apologetically but not feeling any remorse. She had intentionally had that 'slip' of the tongue. In reality, she didn't like Mary, but she had to pass her time somehow. Mary was as good as any.

"I don't know, Alice," Mary said pensively without paying attention to the woman's reproach. She appeared to sink deeply into her thoughts, and Alice felt like slapping her.

Mary would always think of something! She would never react like an average person and accept an invitation without pondering it.

"All right, I'll come," Mary replied. "I can't work now anyway. There's too much noise across the street, so I would think of what happened there and make speculations... All right, I'll come. At least, if I spend some time with you, I'll relax a little. Then, I'll be able to work more and even better," Mary concluded, cheerfully following Alice.

Hearing about her work, which she loathed, Alice turned up her nose, but Mary failed to see. She had learnt to ignore Alice's disapproval. Alice didn't think Mary's work was a dignified occupation for a married woman. In her opinion, Mary should have taken more care of her household instead of wasting her time with such absurd things. Obviously, she had expressed her views loudly, and not only once. But then, Mary only laughed at her and didn't care for her ideas.

Alice opened the door and invited Mary into the house, leading the way into the kitchen, where Mary sat down at the kitchen table.

Her face showed she would have liked to say something, and she was trying hard to keep her mouth shut but started making coffee for Mary and tea for herself.

Mary silently observed her. Alice's efforts amused her, and her eyes shone with glee. The young woman knew Alice well enough. She was aware her neighbour wanted to say something, probably some wife-to-wife reproach, as she usually did. However, this time, she didn't seem to have the courage to start.

Mary had had a very dull morning and needed some entertainment, so she decided to nudge Alice a little. It wasn't like she cared about what Alice had to say anyway. Mary had never paid attention to her words, but, now and then, the young woman liked to play the game. It was probably petty of her, but she enjoyed seeing Alice all worked up, only to run out of steam at the end.

"All right, Alice, say it. If you have something to say, just say it. You shouldn't hold back. You know I couldn't even get mad at you," Mary said, adding in her mind, 'You're a stupid cow, and you don't have a backbone, so why the hell would I get upset with you?'

Alice thought for a few seconds, trying to choose the most appropriate words.

"You know Mary, I heard your husband yelling at you yesterday evening. Again... You know, far from me to advise you how to run your marriage... far from me, of course... You know me. I think everyone should do whatever they want," she said, thinking precisely the opposite. "But," she continued coyly, "maybe... if you took more care of him and your household chores... A wife should always put her husband first... everything else should come second."

"I know that's what you think, Alice. But I don't," Mary replied in a determined voice. She enjoyed egging Alice. She didn't consider herself a mean person, but she liked throwing Alice's opinions back in her face.

"A husband may be here today, Alice. Tomorrow, he might be with another woman. Believe me, my dear, nothing will stop that... if it's meant to be. Even if you cook the perfect dinner and your house is spotless, Alice. But, you see, if Michael leaves me, I won't have to ask for money from him or wait for alimony every month. I won't be afraid he might want to punish me or not give me two pennies. I won't wonder whether he sends me the money on time so that I can pay rent or food or whatever. I'll have my work and make my own money. It's something I can rely on. He can stay, or he can go…"

Mary stopped for a few seconds, watching Alice through her lashes. "Anyway, I won't spend my entire day cooking his favourite dishes. I'd die in less than a week. He knows that. And he also knows he isn't everything in my life. He's not sure about me now, so he might think twice before shopping around for a new woman... And, if he does — which I don't think it's impossible, I won't join the line of those deserted women, left with nothing to their name."

"I can't believe what you're saying. I can't, you hear me," Alice exclaimed heatedly. "A husband always appreciates when his wife takes care of the small things. He appreciates her if she's there for him. When he knows he is the first and most important thing in her life, a husband appreciates and loves his wife more, and he won't desert her. I saw that with Mr Thompson. I know what I'm saying," she nodded knowingly.

'You know nothing, damn it!' Mary said to herself. She knew what the *'wonderful'* Mr Thompson did, and most people living in their neighbourhood knew too. Yet, she couldn't let her friend know. That would have been spiteful.

53

And anyway, it wouldn't do any good. Alice wouldn't believe her. She would even accuse her of being envious. So, instead, she said, "Maybe, Alice. Maybe you're right," she repeated for good measure. "But you see, I saw my mother. She was exactly like you — the caring and hardworking little housewife who didn't think of anything but her husband and his whims. When he took off, he left her behind, alone, with three children to bring up by herself because, of course, he didn't care about any of us. She didn't have money in her pockets, and she'd been left without a friend. All their friends were his, not hers. They turned their backs on her as soon as he moved out of the house. So, she had to start all over again. If you think about it, she had no training, nothing. It was a tough time for her… I'm sure you can't even imagine. The only thing she knew was to clean people's houses… So, Alice, I'm sorry, but I prefer being exactly the way I am. If Michael leaves me one day, I won't be left with no job, money, or friends. And, by the way, so you know, I prefer having my own friends, if you understand me, not his."

Alice couldn't say anything for a few moments, and then, she decided to keep her counsel, even though she still thought that Mary had it all wrong.

Maybe her mother wasn't good enough to keep her marriage strong. And after all, like mothers, like daughters. Considering Mary's aversion to household chores or heeding her husband's wishes.... Well, that said something about her mother, as well.

Alice was convinced that if she kept doing her best, her husband wouldn't desert her, unlike Mary's, who would do it in the blink of an eye.

Mary was far too lazy and didn't do anything for her spouse. She hardly cooked and preferred to buy everything already prepared from the grocer's. What man wouldn't like a nice homemade meal now and then? A man worked hard to provide for his wife, so he had the right to demand it.

Mr Reid's shirts weren't always ironed, and sometimes, even his trousers looked a little wrinkled. Alice had heard Mary telling him to start cleaning if he wanted a neat house and ironing his clothes if he wished to have unwrinkled clothes. Mary didn't care if he was tired when he returned home from work but would ask him to mow the lawn or do other things in the house, which was unacceptable.

Mary considered Alice a simpleton, even if she was a few years older. Alice lived in her own world, disconnected from reality.

Like everyone else, Mary knew that Mr Thompson was seeing Ann, the young typist residing on the same street. He wasn't as faithful as his wife believed.

Of course, having a mistress took its toll, so he was always tired when he returned home at night. Rumours said that he might have had other women stashed in town.

However, as Alice never asked him to do anything in the house, the man was living the high life, a king in his own castle.

He had Alice for cleaning, cooking, and taking care of his clothes and other boring details of his life, but, on the side, the man also had Ann for his soul and for fun. God knew how many others to entertain him in town.

Still, Mary couldn't tell that to Alice. That would have crushed the little wife, so proud of her marriage and husband. However, Mary had a moment of uncertainty. Maybe Alice wasn't as satisfied as she pretended to be. Alice's marriage was not as vocal as hers, so no one really knew what happened behind the flowery curtains carefully drawn over all the windows of their house.

Alice drank her tea in silence, lost in thought and bitter. Daniel stopped being as loving as he had been during the first months of their life together. However, the woman consoled herself. Everything was for the best because she couldn't deal with his passion, even though she sometimes longed for something different, but she couldn't say what. Alice didn't want to think of that anymore, so, with an imperceptible shudder, she turned her eyes to Mary.

"What are you writing these days?"

Alice didn't have any genuine interest in Mary's writing. She didn't read anything else but some magazines and the newspapers Daniel brought home in the evening. Nevertheless, she needed a distraction to make her forget about her restlessness.

"Oh, that. Just a little story with ghosts," Mary cheered up and laughed merrily, happy to talk about her work. There, she felt safe because she knew what she was doing. "The ghost of a man falls in love with a living woman and pursues her everywhere. It's something romantic with some comic scenes here and there. All sorts of funny things happen."

"I wouldn't like to read it," Alice exclaimed. In her way, she was a pragmatic woman, and she had no taste for things like that.

The disdain and repulsion in Alice's eyes upset Mary. "Don't worry," she snapped. "There are many other people who like to read such things. My editor told me I could make good money with it, and that's also important, don't you think? I want to visit Egypt one day, and who knows, maybe this little novella might help me see my dream come true," said Mary, winking, just to annoy Alice because she knew Alice didn't like it.

"All right, I hope you can do it," Alice grumbled. "Do you want some more coffee, Mary?" she asked, suddenly sick of Mary. She wanted her out of her house.

"No, thank you," Mary replied, aware of Alice's feelings. "I think I should go. I have a lot to write – deadlines, you know. So, I'd better go now. See you soon. Maybe we'll see each other later," she threw over her shoulder on her way out.

Alice merely nodded and closed the door behind her neighbour. Then, she washed the cups, placing them back in the cupboard in the exact spot she had chosen for them. Alice didn't like changes. She loathed seeing a thing in a different place than the one she had decided upon since the beginning.

Unwillingly, she started thinking of Mary's weird marriage with Michael Reid and their terrible fights. Even though she lived two houses away from them, their shouting matches reached her ears. The entire street heard them. Famous around there, the Reid family represented one of the entertainment outlets of the minor road where usually nothing happened. Well, at least until last night.

Alice shook her head sadly. She was convinced the Reid marriage wouldn't last, and, in a way, that was a pity.

However, Michael would definitely have enough of all that drama one day and leave her with her stupid stories. Alice would have liked to see what Mary would say then. Indeed, she would lose some of her self-confidence and some of her identity.

'A husband offers identity to a woman,' Alice decided. She thought of Daniel with fondness. The poor man came home tired to the bones in the evening because he worked hard to provide her with a better life.

MCNAMARA SERIES BOX SET
BOOK 0NE & TWO

CHAPTER THREE

Wholly absorbed by her thoughts about Mary and her own husband, Alice remained in front of the sink where she had washed the cups.

Someone knocked on the front door, and startled, she opened it to find James, the policeman she had talked to earlier, and another man waiting on the stoop.

The men greeted her and asked for a few moments of her time, so she invited them inside, leading the way to the living room.

Alice was very proud of that room. She had chosen the colours with care, and there, neutral colours complemented each other, creating a relaxing atmosphere.

"Mrs Thompson," the older man began, "I'm DCI McNamara, and you already know DS

James. I'm sorry to be so direct, but Mrs Dobbs was killed last night."

"Oh, Lord! I knew something was wrong when I saw the police. Besides, she didn't come out in her yard this morning. Well, I just thought she wasn't feeling well after what happened last night," Alice said breathlessly, stopping only when she realised she was rambling. She pulled herself together and asked, "What happened? Who killed her?"

"We don't know yet, but we'll find out, that's certain," McNamara replied with the determination of a man who never accepted defeat. "I would like to know if you or maybe your husband heard something last night. You live practically across the street, and maybe who knows...."

"Oh, I don't know if he did, but I didn't hear anything. After I heard about that girl on the Dobbs' lawn, I took a sleeping pill. I knew I would be thinking of her too much and wouldn't have slept. Usually, I don't do that. I mean, taking pills, but now I had to. I fell asleep in ten minutes, I think. I woke up only a couple of hours before you came. I'm sorry, but I can't really tell you anything. After you left last night, I don't know what happened," she rushed to say.

"When is your husband coming back home today, ma'am?" McNamara asked. "We would like to talk to him, too. Maybe he knows something."

"I'm not very sure," Alice frowned. "He might come around six... Normally, my husband should come at six but sometimes needs to stay at work till later, quite often lately. He comes home at ten or even later sometimes. There are days when I don't even see him in the evening. He says I shouldn't wait for him. He doesn't want me to get too tired," Alice replied, and pride for her husband shone on her face.

"All right, ma'am," McNamara said, already understanding how things were. "Where does he work? Maybe we'll call on him. Or phone him. We do have a few questions."

"Well, he is an accountant," Alice said proudly. "He works for the Expert Audit Company in town. He must commute every day. We've moved here because we prefer the peace and quietness of the suburbs. It is so different from the town, isn't it?"

"Hmm", grumbled McNamara. "Well, ma'am, can you tell us a few things about Patsy Porter? You must know her as she lived next door."

"Hmm", grumbled McNamara. "Well, ma'am, can you tell us a few things about Patsy Porter? You must know her as she lived next door."

"Well, I can tell you what I know, but unfortunately, I don't know much. I don't really pay attention to that kind of girl," the woman declared primly, turning off her nose. "I think she's sixteen or something like that. I hear she left school. There was a serious fight at her house that day. They shouted at each other for hours," Alice said and clapped her hands in disapproval. "Poor Mrs Porter was so upset. Patsy is a beautiful girl for her age... If you like dyed hair and very long and thin legs, that is," Alice added maliciously. "She's not very smart, and she's shallow if you know what I mean. I hear she left with that young man working in Mr Brown's pub... I didn't know him well. I believe I saw him only once or twice when he took her home if that was him... That's it. However, when I saw them together, I didn't feel they were close... Patsy didn't seem too fond of him. I don't know where she is now, and I'm sure my husband doesn't either. He isn't interested in what is going on at the neighbours'... As I've already told you, he is quite tired when he comes back home, and I don't annoy him with such trivial things."

Both men observed the woman in silence. Her long-drawn-out answer stunned them, so they couldn't react at first. Alice didn't seem that talkative at first glance, but appearances sometimes were misleading.

"I see, ma'am," McNamara said dryly, tired of the woman's judgmental and bitter opinions. "However, if you remember anything else, you can call us. Here's my card," he handed her a business card. However, the man hoped that Alice wouldn't call. He could do without a chatterbox, especially one who provided them with so little good information.

"Of course, sir," Alice said, taking the business card. "If you don't mind, sir, has anything happened to Patsy?" she asked, her voice full of curiosity.

"We don't know yet," McNamara lied. "For the time being, we can only presume things, ma'am. Thank you so much. We're leaving now, but if you remember anything, please contact us," the inspector said, pointing to the card in her hand.

"Of course, sir," Alice said, briefly nodding her head and sliding the card in her apron pocket. "But I don't think I know anything else", she warned him on the way to the front door.

When they reached the street, James glanced at McNamara. "Sir, don't you feel that Mr Thompson is playing on two fronts?"

"Aye, James. Maybe more than two. Well, I might be wrong, and Thompson might have something to do at his office. Who knows? What's interesting is the fact that the woman hasn't thought that Patsy could be the girl found on the lawn. I don't think she's too smart, or if she is, she's very absent-minded or completely disinterested, and I don't buy it. She couldn't hide her curiosity." James showed his agreement with a silent nod.

"Well, let's go and see the woman we saw visiting Mrs Thompson this morning. After we talk to her, we'll go and see the people next door. I think it's Mrs Reid," McNamara said, checking a page in his notepad. They crossed the short distance between houses and rang at the Reids' door. After a short while, Mary Reid opened the door, smiling at the sight of the two men.

"I've been waiting for you," the woman said with enthusiasm, drawing puzzled looks from the two officers. Usually, people didn't welcome them with smiles on their lips. "I was sure you would question everyone on the street," Mary continued with a wave of her hand. "I know this is the procedure. I also read thrillers now and

then. Not to speak of the telly shows, you know...
Please, do come inside," she said, showing them
into the house and leading the way to her study.
"I'm sorry I've brought you here," she apologized.
"Nevertheless, this is the most comfortable room
in the whole house, at least for me. I don't like to
spend time in the living room. It looks good,
doesn't it?" the woman said, looking around the
room as if she had seen it for the first time.

McNamara swept the room with his eyes and
noticed the computer on the desk, so he asked
their talkative hostess, "What kind of work do
you do, ma'am?"

"Oh, I write stories," she said, blushing. "I'm
not a famous writer or anything like that, and I
won't become one anytime soon, I'm afraid," she
said with a burst of self-aware laughter, waving
her hand.

The woman chewed her lips for a few
moments, and her fingers played with the collar
of her blouse.

"I don't have enough willpower, I think... I
make some money, that's all. Of course, I can't say
I don't like what I'm doing. "You understand me,
I'm sure. Your work also involves imagination, I
suppose. It's better to make your imagination
work instead of being an accountant or
something like that," she continued, pursing her

lips. "You think of various scenarios and find solutions, don't you?"

McNamara smiled at her. Even though she wasted his time with pointless small talk, he liked the woman. Although he was not good at such, the DCI thought it was a must to know the people involved in an investigation, and the woman revealed herself through her words.

She was like an open book, completely different from Mrs Thompson. Interacting with her felt like a breath of fresh air after talking to Alice Thompson, a relatively stiff woman.

"Indeed, ma'am," the man validated her assumption. "I'd like to know if you heard or saw anything last night after our departure."

"Oh," Mary blushed again. "Well, to be honest with you, I couldn't have possibly heard anything... I had a monstrous fight with my husband after you left," she admitted with some hesitation.

The woman blushed a little more, although she wanted to seem nonchalant. "You see, he was... let's say... upset with me because I'd gone out in the street in my dressing gown... Well, I must confess that my wrapper is... let's say... short and thin... Actually, it doesn't hide much, maybe almost nothing," she rushed to say with a shrug at the end.

The woman didn't seem concerned with her near-nudity, which baffled the two detectives. James blinked hard, unable to wrap his head around that notion.

"The problem is I put on the first thing I saw when I heard that scream, and that's how I went out… Imagine how furious Michael was when we got back in. I was happy he had been concerned with what happened to that girl and then to Mr Dobb. I wouldn't have liked to fight with him right there in the street. These people here talk too much, and, about us, they talk most of the time," she waved her hand, turning her nose up. "Sometimes, it seems that is their main concern. I know they listen to our quarrels with interest. They probably don't have much fun around here," she shrugged again.

"And I know my husband well. Michael wouldn't have refrained himself. He would have surely bellowed at me if he had seen me dressed like that before getting inside. Anyway, he eventually saw me, and, of course, he expressed his discontent at the top of his lungs. I had to listen to all his accusations. But then, I also told him what I thought of his behaviour. He was right in a way. I won't deny it," she tried to sound reasonable.

For a second, James wondered in what world that woman lived. She sounded like a lunatic to him.

However, Mary continued. "But he should have known I didn't do it on purpose. I didn't have enough time to choose the appropriate attire to go out under the circumstances... Would you have thought about that if you had heard such a scream? It was horrible," she opened her arms wide.

McNamara noticed that the woman had a great body, though somewhat plump. If he had been her husband, the inspector would have done the same thing as Reid. He wouldn't have liked anyone else to see that body but him.

"So, I'm sorry, but I couldn't hear a thing," Mary concluded. "We yelled at each other for at least two hours, if not more. It wasn't a great night, to tell you the truth," she grinned. "We didn't even talk this morning. Michael made breakfast for himself and left for work without a word for me," the woman explained without looking upset.

Baffled, James couldn't refrain from asking, "And don't you mind that? At all?"

"What should I mind?" Mary glanced at the DS inquiringly. "That he doesn't speak to me? Oh, no, it's nothing new. Michael does that every two days. He always finds a reason for a fight. It's either my dress, or tights, or that I've forgotten to prepare dinner, or I haven't ironed his shirts," she waved her hand dismissively. "Anyway, I never do those things, and I think he should have learnt by now. I, for one, I know I warned him from the beginning. I told him I'm not the household type," Mary said with a shrug. "He didn't listen."

Shocked, the two men stared at her. They had never encountered such a wife, or, at least, one that would admit something like that openly.

"But how can you bear it?" James insisted although he commiserated with her poor husband.

The DS wouldn't have stayed with her for one day. He wouldn't have accepted that his wife dressed that way or didn't do anything in the house. In his opinion, chores were meant to be shared, not dismissed altogether.

"But it's really thrilling, you know?" Mary explained, smiling widely. "If we got along just fine, with no quarrels, I'd die of boredom. I'm sure I'd die," she insisted dramatically. "Quarrels bring something fresh in our lives. That's my opinion, at least. And, because of them, we won't get sick of each other soon. Today I'll play my role of an upset and wounded woman, and tomorrow, Michael will try his best to make me happy. Isn't he nice?" Mary said, smiling sweetly at them. Maybe too sweetly.

Down for the count, James watched her with wide eyes. Afraid that he would burst into laughter, McNamara needed to go outside urgently.

The DCI hadn't had the chance to ask anything about Patsy but considered that there was enough time to do that later. It seemed more important not to burst into laughter in front of her, so he said, "Then we're leaving now, ma'am, but we'll keep in touch. We will surely have more questions for you and your husband."

Mary saw the detectives off and returned to her work, wondering why they hadn't asked her any pertinent questions. That did seem strange. Soon, the woman forgot about them and returned to her captivating love story. She had a deadline, and, besides, she was flirting with a new idea. The young woman couldn't wait to put it on paper.

Once out of the house, McNamara burst freely into laughter, making James watch him in bewilderment.

"Why are you laughing, sir? I don't think it's funny. Those two people, the Reids, are literally crazy, don't you think so?"

"Oh, no, James, not really," McNamara shook his head. "After all, we all have our own craziness. Mary and Michael Reid might seem somewhat out there, but I think they do have a captivating. I'm sure that there is no dull moment in their house," the man said, a grin tucked in the corner of his mouth.

McNamara pursed his lips, glancing back to Mary's house pensively. He bit his superior lip and then turned to James again.

"What's interesting, though, is that we have two interesting families involved in this case. On one side, the Thompsons, with Alice, the caring little wife, and Daniel, the skirt chaser. I'd put my money on that. We have Mary, the little relationship gambler, and Michael, jealous and possessive, in the other house. They are interesting people, aren't they? Only one thing seems out of the ordinary. They're two different families, yet they still entertain a certain relationship. I wouldn't have believed that Mary had common subjects for discussion with Alice and vice versa? They are like oil and water, James."

"Oh, no, sir. I'm sorry to disappoint you, but I think they're merely crazy, each in their way, and that's why they get along. I'm from the country, sir, and I don't have a taste for such things," he said, shaking his head with steeled determination. James hailed from a tiny village where the old ways were still the norm.

"Don't fret like an old woman, James," McNamara retorted with a snort. "Let's see the other people on this street. Still, I can't believe there's anyone more interesting than what we've seen so far. Anyway, we should talk to the Randalls now. They live exactly between the Thompsons and the Reids."

They went to the Randalls' house and rang at the door. No one came to open the door, so they persisted. However, no answer came from inside.

Alice Thompson, who had been watching them, came out of her house. "The Randalls are not at home now. They tend the grocer's shop on the corner. They own it, actually. Their children are at school probably, and they won't be back until three. I never hear them earlier, and no one can fail to hear the Randall children. They're extremely noisy."

"Thank you, ma'am. Then we'll go to the grocer's and talk to them," McNamara replied. "We'll probably see you soon," the inspector waved at Alice. Then, he watched her going back into the house and turned to James. "Have you seen, James? I do believe she was watching us from behind the curtains. What do you think?"

"I don't have an opinion anymore, sir," the DS shook his head. "I really don't have an opinion with these people," James replied, a little out of balance, and waving his hand.

The two policemen didn't usually run into ordinary people during their investigations. However, in a way or another, James could understand those people. They mainly were criminals. But the people living on Nightingale Street turned out to be out of the ordinary.

McNamara and James strode to the other end of the street, but after only a few steps, the DCI stopped in front of a small house on the left. The dwelling with blue windows and doors sported a cosy porch. Before it, a small garden with multi-coloured flowers stood proudly under the pale sun. McNamara admired the little house and flowers avidly. It must have been absolute bliss to sit on the porch at sunset, breathing in the heavy fragrance of flowers in the night.

"It's a restful house, don't you think, James?" McNamara asked, pointing with his head to the house with blue transoms, although he felt a bit wry for having noticed that.

"Aye, it is, sir. The truth is all the little houses from the suburbs have a special charm, from what I see. But at my parents', it's much more pleasant. The green is greener, and there are more birds…," James recalled nostalgically.

"I see your point, James," McNamara said, musing. He found it fascinating that such little sentimental accents lay where one didn't expect. "In the country, there's a lot of peace and serenity. It is different, James. You know, I'm curious to see the owner of this house. Soon. He must be on the list Mike drew up."

After a few moments, they walked away, failing to notice that someone watched them from behind the yellow curtain of the house on their right side. The detectives headed to the grocer's shop and, on their way, savoured the peace of the area as the children were still at school. The street might have been small but clean and restful.

The grocer's shop didn't look big. Yet, it displayed a lot of goods if one believed the advertisements on the outside wall. The policemen noticed a man with a white apron tied at his waist, arranging some oranges on the counter. The smell of spices in the air, far from unpleasant, pinched their noses.

The grocer looked up and glanced at the two men. He moved to greet them, but one of them said first, "Good day. Mr Randall, I presume."

"Aye, sir. And you are…?" Mr Randall asked.

"I'm DCI McNamara, and this is DS James. We're here to talk to you about the girl found in the Dobbs' yard last night and Mrs Dobbs."

"Has something happened to Mrs Dobbs as well?" Mr Randall asked in bafflement. He had heard about poor Mr Dobbs, but to think that something had also happened to Mrs Dobbs was downright upsetting.

"I'm afraid so, sir. She was also killed last night," McNamara replied.

"Oh, God! Alison, come here, dear," Mr Randall shouted to someone at the shop's back.

"What happened?" asked a woman, coming into the shop from the back. She was tall and thin with severe air and a lot of wrinkles. Her sharp eyes didn't conceal any trace of humour, and her pursed lips proved that she had never smiled in her lifetime.

"Listen, Mrs Dobbs was killed last night," her husband told her with anxiety.

"Oh, dear, poor Mrs Dobbs," Alison exclaimed. "She was a quite meddlesome woman, I know. Doris bothered us with her intruding nature, but I haven't ever thought she would be killed," the grocer's wife shook her head. But then, she continued in a righteous voice, "Eh, you know, curiosity killed the cat. How did she die?"

"I think she was stabbed about four times, ma'am. It wasn't pleasant to see," McNamara said bluntly, disliking the reproach in Mrs Randall's voice.

Of the dead, speak no evil, he had been taught. Most of the time, he agreed with that. They weren't talking about a villain with lots of wrongdoings under his belt but about an old and nosey woman. She hadn't deserved such a fate, in his opinion.

McNamara had already labelled Alison Randall as a narrow-minded woman, so he didn't feel like sparing her feelings. The inspector didn't like people who thought they were better than others.

"Oh, poor thing. How could we help, sir?" Mrs Randall asked, not overly concerned but just to compensate for the sting of his severe tone.

"Did you hear or see anything last night? Especially after the police left...."

"We saw only the end when the police came. We heard that scream like in a dream. We woke up with some difficulty because we had a long day yesterday. Initially, I didn't want to wake up. My husband needed even more time," the woman said with reproach in her tone, glancing at her husband.

However, the man held his tongue, knowing what was best for him.

"And I haven't heard anything from the Dobbs so far, even if they live across the street. We returned to bed after you left, and I fell asleep. I'm afraid we can't help you much," Mrs Randall said, and her husband nodded in agreement with her.

"Well, then. What do you know about Patsy Porter?" McNamara asked while James kept taking notes in his little book.

"Patsy's a very stubborn girl who didn't have the best education while growing up. That's everything I can say," Mrs Randall began in lecture mode.

The woman had a particular way of talking. She uttered the words as if they had been the absolute truth. Apparently, she was the one talking and making decisions in their family.

"She upset her poor mother to no end when she lived here. But then, her mother didn't know how to control the girl either," Alison Randall continued severely. "Poor Mrs Porter still hurts because her daughter ran away," the woman shrugged with indifference. "She took off one day a few months ago. Everyone says she left with that young man who used to work in Mr Brown's pub. He was a hardworking boy, that one if you ask me, or so he seemed before that girl stole his mind. After that, the boy saw nothing else but her."

When she stopped to breathe, which the men saluted with gratitude, McNamara asked, "Did she love him, too?"

"Pish-posh! I'm sure she didn't", Mrs Randall replied, waving her hand. "She just played with him; that's all. I was surprised they ran away together," she shook her head. "Something didn't seem quite right about that," the woman pressed her lips in dismay.

McNamara seemed confused, so she explained, "It's improbable that she had left with him. I'm sure of that," Alison Randall made a broad gesture to include the entire street. "Everyone around here thinks the same thing. If Patsy had left with a man, she would have left with an older one. A much older one," she nodded. "I remember the girl flirted with all the men over thirty on this street. So, it looked bizarre that she had left with such a young boy. That's what I think... But then, both disappeared the same day," the woman shrugged. "She even left a note for her mother to say that she was going away with Peter... So, that's it," she concluded.

"So, you never thought they would elope together," McNamara wanted to make sure he understood.

"Not at all," the woman said. "Patsy didn't care for that boy. She aimed at something more, mark my words. She used to say that she didn't date children, and only an older man would satisfy her taste. I wasn't the only one who heard her say that. Many others did. The girl even flirted with my husband," Alison accused, glancing severely at her husband.

Mr Randall blushed slightly and tried to deny it, but his wife's eyes didn't leave room for that. Reluctantly, he admitted she was right, although rage boiled in his blood.

"Aye, that's true," the man said. "She flirted with all of us. Mr Reid didn't notice her, you know. But as a rule, that man doesn't notice anyone else but his wife. I'm afraid there isn't much trust in their marriage. If you know what I mean, he's quite the jealous type, and they quarrel all day long. You hear their shouts from afar."

"Indeed," his wife approved, pursing her lips. "One day, he'll kill her, you'll see. I think they should split up. Those two aren't meant to live together. Each one would be better with someone else," she nodded with conviction.

"Don't be a dolt," Mr Randall contradicted her with a condescending voice. "They only squabble, that's all. He doesn't beat her or anything. She's a little different from what a traditional wife should be. That's why everything happens. She doesn't seem to put much stock in his needs. She couldn't care less about cooking, ironing, and such. She dresses in that way, you know," the man shrugged. "She likes it and doesn't consider what he thinks on the matter. But then, the woman also works and has a certain financial independence. That's all," he concluded.

His wife intervened at once as if something had bitten her backside. "That's not all. That poor man has the right to be upset because she dresses like a… Everyone can see her legs up to the top. She doesn't even bother to cover her breasts much. All men look at her," Alison Randall said, showing what she meant with her hands. "Her husband, of course, doesn't like it, which I think it's normal. Don't tell me you would like it if I went out and showed my legs and breasts to the entire street?" she asked, turning warlike towards her husband.

Stunned, the man stared at her. The detectives understood that he wasn't shocked because his wife would think of going out in short skirts or bare-shouldered, although even that sounded weird. His wife assumption that she could arouse his jealousy baffled him. His wife assumption that she could arouse his jealousy baffled him. He had stopped being jealous a long time ago, almost as soon as they had got married if he had ever been jealous. Nothing in her attracted him. He saw only her small and mean eyes, tight mouth, and moralizing nature. The man didn't imagine anyone else would notice anything different. That was a real pity. Someone might have taken her off his hands if they had seen something in her. Then, he would be free.

McNamara and James guessed the direction of Randall's thoughts. They tried to avert their eyes, so Mrs Randall didn't understand. Her husband's beliefs reflected in their eyes.

"Has anyone seemed interested in Patsy in a special manner?" McNamara asked, trying to change the subject.

"Mr Graham seemed to like her," Mrs Randall said evasively. "But then, he wouldn't have done anything about it. You shouldn't think of that."

"Why not?" James asked with curiosity.

"He's a teacher, you know?" Mr Randall said. "He seems a very serious lad. I don't think Graham would try to seduce a minor," the man shook his head. "He doesn't seem to have such inclinations. Anyway, the lad lacks the courage,"

Randall said, satisfied to notice his wife's displeasure. The woman narrowed her eyes to slits because he had dared to speak before her.

"Mr Thompson," Randall replied quickly. "I've got the impression that he liked her a lot. Patsy had the same colouration as his wife, you see. But then, she was younger and, obviously, much more fun. Mrs Thompson doesn't smile much and seems interested only in keeping her house clean and her husband smartly dressed. She doesn't care about dancing or anything and doesn't go out much. I've seen them going to a restaurant only once so far. They were invited to a wedding."

"Don't speak about her like that," his wife interrupted him with dismay. "Alice is a very good woman. One rarely can find such an upstanding woman these days. She knows how to take care of her house and husband. Thompson should be eternally grateful for having such a wife. He should kiss the ground she walks on. Not everyone has that luck," Mrs Randall said vehemently. "Think of Mr Reid."

Randall abandoned the subject, waving his hand with disgust. Still, James and McNamara had already understood what was going on and why Mr Thompson might have been interested in Patsy. Sometimes, a man preferred to be with a fun woman. Few were fans of having a wife concerned only with keeping the house in pristine conditions. They could hire a housekeeper, after all.

"So," McNamara interrupted the heavy silence, "have you seen Patsy or Peter lately?"

"Oh, no," Alison Randall answered. "None of them has come back or written or anything else... I think they left for good," she said with reproach for Patsy in her voice. "Ungrateful child, I've always said. Her poor mother struggled with her alone because her father rarely was home. You know, he's a salesman. And even when he was at home, he didn't care about what happened in that house. He was of no good. Maybe if he'd showed more interest in that child, the girl wouldn't have ended up a mere light skirt," she said, scowling.

"Very well, Mrs Randall, thank you. That is very helpful. Here's my card... And call me, please, if you remember anything, even if you consider it's not very important," McNamara said, offering her his card.

He tried to stop the discussion because it didn't seem to bring anything new. Alison Randall went on and on about her favourite subject without adding anything useful.

After going outside, where no one could hear them, McNamara turned to James. "I think that

Mr Thompson liked Patsy. Think about it. He could see something of his wife in the lass, but the young version must have been more amusing than his prim and hardworking wife. I think he might have enjoyed her flirt... What do you think, James?"

"Aye, sir, he might. But, you know, I also think we can put the teacher on the list and Randall. You saw how he blushed when his wife mentioned Patsy's habit of encouraging older men, associating him with that... Maybe, we could take Reid off the list, though. What do you think? He's too possessive and jealous of his wife to have cared for the lass, sir, don't you think?"

"I don't know that yet, James. I first must see and talk to him, and only then will I have an opinion. Maybe he also plays some games with his wife. Maybe he's sick of so many quarrels in the house, don't you think? No one would enjoy a continuous scandal."

"Maybe so, but don't you think Mary Reid would have smelt something if her husband had liked Patsy? She doesn't look like a simpleton. Her mind is rather sharp, even if she's the way she is."

"Maybe she is. Who knows? And Randall blushed because he's afraid of his wife, I'm telling you, not only because he likes the girl, although I think he likes her just fine. The man doesn't seem to have much joy in his life with that woman as a wife. With such an old crone at home… it would be impossible not to. Now, let's go and see the Browns, too. They are at the pub, or at least they should be."

They crossed the street to the pub, which was small, typical for suburbs. It was cosy, though, and the people inside seemed to have a great time. A massive man, about forty, with big hands and a red face, served at the counter. His red curly hair looked like it hadn't seen a comb that day. But then, his hair was always the same, with a life of its own. But for his age and height, he could have passed for a naughty boy because of his lively eyes and unruly hair. He was a merry man, and his clients liked him. The people in the pub felt at home there. It was a comfortable place to be.

McNamara could see the people coming there every day. It generally happens in such pubs located in small neighbourhoods, suburbs, or villages. There, people knew each other, and the pub was the heart of the community, a meeting place for most people, especially men.

People were talking and laughing, yet the noise wasn't unpleasant. McNamara and James strolled to the counter and took a seat on the bar stools.

Mr Brown came to them as soon as he had seen them. "Good day to both of you! What will it be?"

"Coffee, please, for both of us," McNamara ordered. He put some money on the counter to pay for the drinks.

After the man took their money, McNamara showed his badge. "We're with the police, sir, and we've got some questions for you and your wife."

"I see," Mr Brown said. He imagined their presence in the pub was related to what had happened the night before. "I can answer your questions, no problem, but my wife has just left. She went to Mrs Porter, at the other end of the street. She said she might have to stay there for a while. Mrs Porter didn't say what happened when she called, but it seemed serious enough. My Mary told me the woman was sobbing."

"Well, then, we'll ask you. We can talk to your wife later. Do you know with whom Patsy Porter would flirt around here?" McNamara asked. "We've heard she liked to encourage some men living on this street."

"Oy, that! Well, it's true. She made eyes almost at everyone on this street and, to be truthful, some of the men answered back. Now that's a girl that asks for trouble if you know what I mean. It's that kind of girl that prefers older men. A sort of father figure, I hear they call it. Now, between you and me, you know men usually are silly enough to fall for that, especially if they're of a certain age. They feel flattered and proud because they made a young girl pay attention to them, especially if they thought their days as seducers had long gone," he shook his head wisely.

"Were you also among the men she charmed, sir? Did you also respond to her encouragements?" James asked, leaning forward as if he had wanted to keep the discussion private.

"Oy, no," the man started laughing. "I might have been flattered for a while. I won't deny it," he winked at them roguishly.

McNamara liked him at first sight and understood he was an essential asset for the pub. People must have loved to talk to him.

"I'm forty-four already, and, of course, I liked to see that such a young lass paid attention to me. Who wouldn't? She's quite pretty, you know," the man said, smiling. "But, on the one hand... how could I put it so you could understand better... Well, I have a happy marriage, and I don't say that just to say it. My wife looks great, although she's twenty years older than Patsy. You'll see her, and you'll understand," he said, nodding.

There was pride in his voice. The man looked satisfied with his marriage and proud of his wife, indeed.

"She's a kind and merry woman, my Mary, and she satisfies me entirely if you know what I mean," he said, winking at them again. "On the other hand, Patsy was doing that with all the men on the street. Honestly, I don't like that kind of girl... I think a lass should be cheerful and have a little fun... Now, there's no law against that, is there? But that doesn't mean she should be a cheap flirt," the man shook his head regretfully.

"If she'd liked someone specially, I'd have understood, but she didn't. It wasn't like that. I think it was like a sport to her," he continued pensively. "She wanted to see how many men she could entice and have an older lover. You know the type... it wasn't anything serious."

Brown stared at them and seemed to think about something. Then, he added, "She probably thought she'd be admired if she'd gone out with an older man, possibly with a certain material situation... I don't know, I'm just saying."

"We've heard she left with Peter, the boy who worked for you before," James intervened.

"I heard that too, but it's odd. That's what I think," the man said, scratching his scalp. "That boy wasn't for her." Brown saw the policemen seemed doubtful, so he thought he should explain better. "For one, he was too young for her, only twenty. He used to follow her everywhere with puppy eyes. I know that. But that doesn't mean she felt the same. When I saw him like that, I told him the girl was just playing with him, fooling around, but I don't think he believed me — he was reeled in."

Brown stopped and mulled over his thoughts for a few minutes. The policemen patiently waited. Not long after, the man looked up and said, "You know, when I heard they'd left together — you know, my wife is a good friend of Mrs Porter. She told Mary about the note Patsy wrote. I couldn't be more surprised. It wasn't something I'd have thought possible. But maybe, I was wrong, who knows?" he continued. Yet, he seemed doubtful.

"Do you think it was possible that Patsy only wrote that she was leaving with Peter, but actually, she'd left with another man?"

"I don't know, to be honest... Aye, it is. But I know that Peter also left the same day. He took his weekly cheque and told us he would work in town because he would get better pay and had friends there."

"After the lad left, did you hear anything else from him?" McNamara asked Brown.

"No, nothing. The lad didn't come by here or call. I don't know anything about him now. He was a good lad, you should know. Peter never left his work unfinished, not even after falling for Patsy. We really miss him around here. We hired another lad afterwards, but we had to fire him in short order. He didn't do anything right and was interested only in having a big paycheque without any work. Many times, I had to do his job too. So, you see, that didn't work for me at all," the man said, frowning for the first time.

"But what about Patsy? Have you heard anything else ever since?" McNamara came back to the subject of interest.

"No, sir. My wife told me that Patsy didn't bother to call her mother and tell her where she was or what she was doing," the man said reproachfully. "Poor woman is sick with worry," he said, shaking his head.

"Have you heard that Mrs Dobbs was also killed last night?" McNamara asked him suddenly, watching his face closely to see his reaction.

"Oy, no, was she?" Brown exclaimed in pure shock. "I've heard that a young girl was killed in the Dobbs' yard. Nothing else. How was she killed? Mrs Dobbs, I mean," he inquired, openly curious, leaning towards them.

"Well, she was stabbed in her drawing-room," McNamara replied to him. "She might have noticed something related to the girl found earlier in the yard, and probably the killer saw her, too."

"I know we haven't had such a thing around here before," Brown shook his head with sadness. "But wasn't it a burglary?" he asked.

Things would have made more sense if the old woman had been killed during a burglary.

"No, sir," James answered, shaking his head. "Nothing was stolen from the house, in our opinion. Besides, there are only signs of a short fight in the room where she was killed."

"I see...," Brown murmured. "Poor Mrs Dobbs," he shook his head again. "She liked to pry on everyone, I know. But otherwise, the woman was really kind... good-hearted. She shouldn't have died like that," the man added, shaking his head as if he couldn't believe it.

That very moment, a man between thirty and forty came to the counter.

"I'd like a beer, Mr Brown, please."

"Of course, Mr Graham," the man replied, a professional smile on his face, despite the sadness he had shown a few seconds before. "The usual, isn't it?"

"Aye, please," the young man said absently, turning around to see if there was anyone with whom he could sit down and talk.

Brown took a beer bottle off the shelf behind him, opened it, and put it on the counter in front of the man.

When the man's name reached his ears, McNamara turned towards him. The DCI watched the younger man for a few moments, then, taking out his badge, he said, "We're with the police, sir. May we accompany you at a table there and ask you a few questions?"

Graham looked a little confused and even alarmed for a moment. He accepted the invitation, although reluctantly, and showed the two detectives to a small table in the corner.

There, the young man invited them to sit down on the bench in front of him.

"What's this about, sir?" Graham asked curiously, drinking a little from his bottle first. He needed some courage to start the conversation.

"Haven't you heard about the girl killed in the Dobbs' yard last night?" James asked him with disbelief.

The DS wondered whether the man just pretended he didn't know anything. The Sergeant thought that the people around would have expected the police to come and ask questions about the murder.

"I've heard nothing," Graham answered with bafflement. "You should know that I wasn't at home last night. I slept at my girlfriend's in town, and I've come back here just now. What girl? Do we know her?" the man asked fearfully.

"If you weren't at home, then that's understandable," James nodded, trying to get past the fear in the man's voice. "Well, last night, a lass was killed in the Dobbs' yard. Mr Dobbs died immediately after seeing her or maybe because he'd seen something else. We don't know yet. During the night, after everyone left, including the police, Mrs Dobbs was also killed in her own drawing-room."

McNamara registered the shock on Graham's face. The news came fast, and it wasn't pleasant.

"We have to fill in the official report, sir," McNamara told him. "So, could you tell us the name of the person you were with last night? I'm sorry, but we must write it down. We must verify what everyone who lives nearby did last night."

"Of course, that's not a problem," Graham said with relief. "It's just a friend in town. She teaches in the same school as me. Her name's Laura Bradshaw, and we've been going out together for a while. We were at some friends' last night because they celebrated their first year of marriage. Then, we went to her house since it was too late for me to come back here. I stayed there until this morning when we went together to school."

The man paused and sipped from his beer. Then he wiped his forehead with the back of his hand.

"If you want to talk to her, I can give you her address and phone number," Graham said, taking a little notebook out of his pocket. Tearing off a sheet of paper, the man wrote the information down.

"What could you tell us about Patsy Porter, sir?" McNamara asked him.

"Patsy Porter? Is she the girl found in the Dobbs' yard?" Graham asked, stunned. His voice shook with grief for the young girl, if not something more, but her death saddened him. Probably, he fancied her too, as did the others.

"We don't know for sure yet, but she might be Patsy. She matches the description. However, could you tell us anything about Patsy Porter?" McNamara repeated.

"Well, let's see... Patsy was my student for three years before she left school... She was a gorgeous girl, and she knew it. The boys in the school were all crazy about her," Graham said pensively. However, she wouldn't go out with them... I noticed some older men waiting for her at school...," he said, a trace of a smile in his voice. "She seemed to prefer men of a certain age... at least fifteen years older than her... You understand that I don't know who they were. Edinburgh isn't a small village... You can't possibly know everybody."

"We've heard she flirted with all the men on this street, including you... Is it true?" McNamara asked.

Graham blushed, replying reluctantly, "Aye, she did. That's true. Some men didn't care for her games, and I didn't either, even if the lass was attractive." The man sipped from his bottle again, his fingers shaking on it. "All right, I liked the girl, a little," he reckoned with a nonchalant shrug.

McNamara wondered if that shrug was only for show. The lad seemed unnerved, and his actions did not match his demeanour.

"Who wouldn't?" Graham continued. "But I couldn't think of her that way. She was my student and a minor. I had to think of her age, even after she left school and I wasn't her teacher anymore... I don't want any problems with the law. I can't afford it in my situation. As a teacher, I have a reputation to uphold... I hope you understand it," the man insisted, leaning forward, trying to press his point home.

"So, you didn't encourage her at all, sir?" James asked him.

"Of course not," Graham scowled, considering the assumption outrageous. "She'd always try to make me notice her, of course, as she did with everyone, but I didn't allow her to drag me into her game... I remember that once Patsy even wrote a letter to me. Another time, she asked me if I wanted to go with her to a dance in town, to a disco. But I didn't accept," the lad shook his head. "I don't do such things, or at least not with bairns of her age... No, I didn't encourage her," he shook his head again.

"If she hadn't been your student, would you have accepted her invitation?" McNamara considered the man was weak enough to have accepted it. The DCI read it in the line of his mouth.

"No, I've already told you so!" Graham snapped, irate, unable to keep his voice down, and the people around turned their way. "The girl was underage, not even sixteen, damn it, and I don't need any problems. I'm a teacher, for

God's sake, and I must show some decency and morality. I like the job I'm doing, even if I don't make lots of money. I can't get fired or worse because I've fancied a pretty face. And she's only that — a pretty face. She didn't have anything else to offer, or at least not to me."

"I see," McNamara replied, a smile perched on his lips. "Do you know anything about the men on the street who went out with her?"

"I can't be sure, but I think Mr Thompson did," Graham replied, thinking that it didn't matter if he gave them that. The police would have found out about Thompson's affair with Patsy because other people had seen them together. "I saw them in town once when dining out with my girlfriend. I saw Patsy and Thompson passing by the restaurant where we were. I think they were having a serious conversation, and he seemed upset."

"When did that happen?" James asked, suddenly very interested in the man's account. The DS hadn't cared much about the man's previous ramblings. Still, now, he thought they finally had a more direct line of investigation.

"Two weeks ago, or maybe two weeks and a half... I can't remember exactly... I was surprised at the time because of Mrs Dobbs... You know that Mrs Dobbs used to gossip a lot. She told me that Patsy had left with that young man working here in the Browns' pub, and she wasn't ever wrong in her gossip. I remember that I thought her infallible nose finally failed that time, which amused me."

"Knowing that Patsy preferred older men, weren't you surprised she ran away with a twenty-year-old lad?" McNamara asked with disbelief.

"I was a little surprised at that time," Graham reckoned, "but then I thought the girl might have changed her mind. And besides that, Peter was five years older than she, and he wasn't a student. I thought she'd found something interesting in him and come back somewhat to normal, I mean, to be like the other girls of her age. Things like that still happen," the man said, yet his voice sounded like he was trying to convince himself.

"I see," McNamara said. Yet, he didn't see anything. There wasn't any logic in what Graham was saying. In the detective's experience, people rarely changed, and when they did, the change was primarily superficial. Life taught him that, and he put more stock on his experience than in Graham's psychological mumbo jumbo.

"Teenagers do such things," the man explained. "Today, they love someone, and the next day, another one. At fifteen, sixteen, they're not at the age when they can develop steady relations," Graham added in teaching mode, trying to sound self-confident. However, he wasn't sure that the detectives believed him.

McNamara studied his face for a few silent moments, suppressing his amusement. The lad worked hard to make them believe his pseudo-psychological crap. The policeman didn't like Edward Graham's small dark eyes, either. They betrayed the man's duplicity.

Moreover, Graham seemed to lack willpower, and McNamara doubted that the man would have refused a young girl like Patsy. He would have found a way to be with her.

People always found a way to fulfil their darkest desires, believing that they were more intelligent than those around them. Consequently, no one would catch them in the act, and they wouldn't have to pay for their weaknesses.

The three men sipped from their drinks in silence. McNamara was thinking of his next question when his cell phone rang.

"McNamara," he answered, afterwards listening to what he was told with a scowl on his face.

The call came from the coroner. The doctor had alarming news, which changed absolutely everything he knew. Nothing made sense anymore if anything had so far, he told himself bitterly.

"We have to leave, James. Thank you, Mr Graham, for everything you've told us. We have to leave now, James," the DCI repeated, rising off the bench.

James followed suit. Both waved to Brown on their way out of the pub.

"What happened?" James asked while heading to the car parked at the end of the street, not far from the pub.

"Apparently, the girl found in the Dobbs' yard is not Patsy Porter. The coroner says her hair wasn't light brown, as we've thought, even though the lass dyed her hair. Patsy probably dyed her hair too, but hers should have been light brown, and the girl we found was dark-brown-haired at the roots. Moreover, the height doesn't match Patsy's. This one was taller…" McNamara explained in a huff.

The DCI's stride lengthened, and James tried hard to match it. McNamara would have expected that.

"Oh, and apparently, Patsy never had an appendectomy, and this one did… She wasn't beaten close to death and then had her throat slashed, as we'd initially thought. The knife did the entire job... Aye, she was beaten first and then raped repeatedly and savagely for several days... and then she was stabbed with a sharp knife — the kind used for hunting. It's similar to the knife used to kill Mrs Dobbs. Ah, and something else also of interest: the girl was four months pregnant. And apparently, she had been tied up for three or four days, if not more."

"Oh, Lord!" James said. "So, we've done nothing else but waste our time this morning. We've asked questions about a girl who's not involved in this story and where we probably shouldn't."

"Maybe not, James... The killer must have been someone who knows enough about this street and the empty house next to the Dobbs'. A stranger couldn't have pulled it off. The house has been deserted since the owner died of cancer... I'm afraid our killer wanted to kill her there, with no witnesses around, but he couldn't. Maybe the girl escaped, and she had to die in the Dobbs' yard. Indeed, the killer must have known Mrs Dobbs would go to bed at nine. He probably thought the way was clear because otherwise, I don't think he'd have taken risks. Everyone knew she was a gossiper... And he also knew Thompson would come at home late, and his wife didn't have the habit of keeping an eye on her neighbours' houses... The murderer must have also been aware the Reids had something else on their minds. They wouldn't be watching the street," McNamara reviewed pensively everything he had found out.

Getting at the car, he reached for the door handle, then turned to James again. "Aye, it must have been someone with a tight connection to this street. I bet on that," McNamara said decisively.

The detectives looked at each other for a few moments. Then, McNamara glanced along the street towards the Dobbs' house, saying, "And don't forget James, that we found Patsy's ID in the victim's purse. Why was it there, and where's the victim's ID? It's somewhat odd, isn't it? Anyway, we've found out something about Patsy and her neighbours, and I think this is important because now, at least we know the people in the play."

The two men watched each other thoughtfully again, lost in their own thoughts. Then McNamara said again, "Come on, let's go back to the office. Let's verify the past of each person living on this street. We'll come back later to question the others. First, we must find out who the dead girl is."

CHAPTER FOUR

At the police station, five men and two women were working busily. Two men talked on the phone, and the other people checked various papers. One of the two women was typing something on the computer. With James in tow, McNamara entered the office with an alert step and asked, "What's new, boys and girls?"

"Nothing, sir, I hate to tell you," one answered regretfully. "We haven't found anything to solve this case."

"Not really nothing," a woman's voice replied cheerfully.

"Got something new, Jo?" McNamara asked the young woman while putting his coat on the peg near the door.

"Indeed, sir. I've found out who the victim is, sir. I've verified if there was a record of her prints in our database, and, aye, there is. I've just got the answer. A few weeks ago, the girl was arrested for shoplifting but wasn't indicted. It was only the second time she got caught, but she had to pay a fine and has a record now, so her prints are in our database."

"All right, who was she?" McNamara cut off her impatient talk.

"Her name was McWilliams, Diane McWilliams. She was a student until a few months ago when she left school and home. According to a teacher I've talked to on the phone, she left school at the same time as Patsy Porter. But there's something more interesting, sir."

"What the hell could be more interesting? Joan, you're awful! Why can't you give me the information in the right order? Why should you make all sorts of comments besides what's important?" McNamara asked with exasperation.

"Sorry, sir, I don't know. That's me, I think," Jo smiled defensively. "I must add a little colour, or it's got no charm."

Both she and McNamara knew he couldn't get mad at her. The policeman even smiled while reprimanding her. He couldn't get upset because he knew the young woman was brilliant and she'd always find something more, while the others couldn't.

Jo had her own unique flair. No one could equal her when it came to unearthing something, even though that thing had been hidden in God knows what corner. She was tenacious and never quit.

"All right, girl, take it easy. Tell me all the facts, and if possible, only the facts," the DCI stressed the last part. The detective wanted to remind her about her habit of colouring everything with personal opinions and digressions. Sometimes, they turned out to be a waste of time.

"Well, then, I'll try to be brief and stick to the subject", Jo began. "Diane attended the same school as Patsy Porter, and, moreover, the girls were classmates. Five minutes ago, I also talked with the policeman who arrested Diane last time. He told me Diane wasn't alone in the shop when she stole those things, but with Patsy. Patsy had to make a statement too. You know how these things work," the woman waved her hand. "Anyway, apparently, the girls were good friends, and Diane defended Patsy, saying that Patsy hadn't known a thing about the shoplifting or even about her intentions to steal. Diane said it was only her idea, and she didn't bother to inform her friend about what she was going to do. She assumed the guilt, and Patsy got away."

"Well, anything else?" McNamara asked anxiously. Jo still couldn't refrain from making collateral comments.

"Well, that's it, sir. I haven't had much time, you know," Jo replied. "The doctor told us the victim couldn't be Patsy Porter only one hour ago or even less. So, I haven't had enough time to find more. Still, you know I will," she declared with conviction.

"I'm sure you will," McNamara replied with a nod and then noticed the scowls on the men's faces at his praises for the policewoman. "What's the problem, Mike? What don't you like?" the DCI started hauling Mike over the coals.

He knew that Mike was as good as Jo at his job, yet Jo was always faster.

"When you come with as much information as Jo did and in such a short time, I'll praise you too, don't worry. You know I favour no one. Until then…," he shrugged, his mouth set in a hard line. "And now, because you insist on putting yourself in the spotlight, try to find out everything you can about this girl from her teachers, but don't tell them she's dead. Find something, though. Did you tell that teacher that the girl was dead, Jo?" he turned his inquiring eyes to the young woman.

"I'm not a beginner, sir. I know when to keep my mouth shut. I assumed you'd like to inform her parents first and then the rest of the world."

"Exactly! Good job, Jo!" McNamara nodded. About to get out of the detectives' hall and go into his, he remembered something and turned back with a warning, "And, please, take care. Don't let the press get a whiff of this business. If I hear a single word about the victim's real identity, I'll chew you up and spit you out. I'm going to make some phone calls first, and then, I'm going to Diane's parents with James. Jo, find me her address, please."

"I already have it here, sir," Jo said, waving a paper before his eyes.

McNamara snatched the paper from her hand and waved to James to follow him. He started to leave the office when something else popped into his mind, "Oh, I shouldn't forget. Someone must call Mrs Porter and stop her from coming to the morgue. Tell her that the dead girl is not her daughter. She'd be glad, I'm sure. I only hope she hasn't already left."

"Aye, sir," Jo said, "I'll do it at once," she offered immediately.

After McNamara left, Jo stuck her tongue out at Mike.

"What the hell do you think you're doing? Do you think you're smarter, or what? Did all those praises get to your head and make you think you're better?"

"I'm better than you, at least. I've always told you so, love," Jo replied merrily. In a playful mood, she wanted to make Mike boil a little.

"In your dreams, sweetheart," the young man joined her game, clinging to his last traces of reason, guessing that the woman wanted to make him snap. "If you join me tonight, I'll prove I'm the best," he winked at her roguishly but wasn't kidding. He held his breath, hoping for an affirmative answer from Jo, although he should have known better than that.

"Maybe, in your dreams, love. In your dreams," the young woman repeated. "I'd rather go out with Quinn," Jo said, knowing that Mike couldn't stand Quinn.

***

"Let's go to Diane's parents first. Then, we'll go to school and see if we find something else," McNamara said after reading the coroner's report. "Something must be here. We have one girl's body and the ID of the other, and that's wrong. I'm afraid Patsy is also in trouble. Don't you get the same idea, James?"

"Maybe, sir... Or maybe she's involved in her friend's death. It's possible," the DS said defensively when he noticed McNamara's doubt.

"Aye, maybe," McNamara said without conviction. "We have only the coroner's report that mentions a hair which doesn't belong to the victim. That's all. James, we have a lot of work to do before finding the killer."

MCNAMARA SERIES BOX SET
BOOK 0NE & TWO

CHAPTER FIVE

McNamara decided to drive, and James resigned himself to the experience, knowing that his boss was an impulsive driver, quite determined not to respect the traffic rules. Consequently, James fastened his safety belt carefully. However, he feared the belt wouldn't offer him much protection, considering the DCI's driving. Anyway, it was better than nothing.

They headed to another part of Edinburgh, where Diane used to live with her parents. McNamara loved to drive fast. James insisted on watching out the window, even though everything was just a blur.

After a quarter of an hour and several traffic lights that badly tried his patience, McNamara finally stopped in front of Diane's parents' house. The policemen got out of the car under the curious eyes of some dirty little boys. Those were playing in front of a house with worn-out walls. It was in severe need of fresh paint, and the windows could have used a thorough cleaning.

McNamara glanced at the windows and realised that no one could see anything through them. The man thought that they were probably kept like that not only because of carelessness but also because it was more practical. No curtains were necessary – the dirt did the job.

They rang at the door, and before someone could come to open it, a bigger child, of about ten, with shabby clothes and dirty hair and hands, came closer to them. "Mom's not at home, you know. She's over at the neighbour's," he said, pointing to the next door.

"But where's your father?" asked McNamara, preferring to break the bad news to a man, especially after that morning's experience with Mrs Porter.

"Who knows where he is," the child shrugged. "He left a long time ago, as soon as Dennis was born," the boy pointed to a six-year-old child, playing with other children in the gutter near the sidewalk.

All of them were dirty. McNamara was positive no one had bothered to clean their faces or clothes for a few days. The DCI shook his head and turned back to the boy. "Then, can you call your mother, lad? Tell her we're from the police and have something to talk to her about."

The boy stared at him with big eyes and then asked, much like an adult in miniature, "Which one's in trouble this time? Diane or John?"

"You'd better call your mom, lad," James urged him in a kind tone of voice. "We'd better talk to her."

The child nodded and ran into the next yard. The policemen strained their ears to hear what people were talking about there. Still, only an unintelligible murmur got back to them. After a few moments, an older and slatternly woman came from the yard together with the boy.

"I'm McWilliams," the woman said, her voice unpleasant and even quarrelsome. "What's the matter? Who did what, because they wear me out, these children, I swear to God!"

"Can we go inside, ma'am?" McNamara asked, waving his hand in the direction of the curious children. "Maybe we'd better talk first, with no other ears around."

"Very well, sir. Let's get inside," the woman opened the door for them. Still, she wasn't sure it was a good idea to let them in. The woman had heard enough stories about the police coming and planting incriminating evidence when the host didn't pay attention. However, she didn't say anything. The woman was afraid that the detectives had come for something more severe at that time. It wasn't about the little pilfering her son, Richard, usually did or Diane's usual meetings with the police for shoplifting. Otherwise, this kind of coppers wouldn't have come. Usually, she would see policemen in uniform, not plain-clothed detectives.

The policemen followed her inside. The heavy smell of spoiled food, unwashed clothes and tobacco overwhelmed them. The woman showed them to a room that could have been a drawing-room. Yet, it was full of everything, reminding them of an old clothes and lumber shop.

Noticing James's disdain at the sight of the room, the woman said defensively, "I know it's not as nice as your house, but I've got only two rooms and enough children to fill them up. With only the DWP help, I can't do too much over here, can I?"

"No one said anything about that, ma'am," McNamara cut off her outburst. "We've come here for something else, not to criticise you, your house, or how you bring up your children. Though, to be honest, everything's undesirable," he said harshly, waving his hand around.

Aware that he had annoyed her, the DCI tried to appease her. "Let's leave all of that aside because we've got more serious things to talk about. We should all sit down and approach things calmly," he pointed to the dirty, stained sofa. However, the inspector decided not to sit down, though.

James looked at the sofa and then at the armchairs, which didn't inspire any trust, and he decided that he'd better stand.

"What do you know about your daughter these days, ma'am?" McNamara asked.

"Honestly, nothing," the woman replied with a shrug. "She left the house some time ago. I can't say exactly when. I was satisfied I had a mouth less to feed. It's quite difficult when you don't have much. What's she done now?"

"Don't you know with whom or why she left?" McNamara kept asking her, apparently not hearing her question.

"I didn't ask her. The girl said she was leaving. That was enough for me," the woman replied pragmatically.

"Well, but she's underage," James replied with surprise in his voice, and his scorn for the woman increased because of her indifference about the girl.

"She might be, but I have other four children to raise. I think the girl's at the age to manage by herself. I did so myself, and I didn't do too badly. After all, I've got a house at least... All my children are alive...."

"Not quite," McNamara answered curtly, unwilling to beat around the bush anymore. The man was furious. He had felt compassion for Mrs Porter and tried to treat her softly but despised the woman in front of his eyes. Her negligence and indifference had led to her only daughter's death, so he didn't think he needn't show her mercy or any kind of consideration.

"What do you mean?" the woman asked, losing something from her previous defiant air.

"Diane's dead," McNamara replied. "You'd better come to headquarters to make an official identification. We found out it was her by checking the prints on record."

The woman instantly turned white, and tears welled up in her eyes. Despite her nonchalance from before and the opinions she'd voiced so strongly, she cared for her children. She'd been quite worried since Diane left home, but she couldn't stop her. The girl hadn't been listening to her for a long while now. Neither she nor Richard had.

McNamara watched her, realising there was more to the woman than met the eye with all her misery and indifference. Despite the tears in her eyes, she tried to recover from the brutal blow.

"Don't you really know anything about what she's done since her leaving?" the inspector asked this time in a more pleasant tone.

"No, I don't," the woman shook her head and suddenly burst into tears.

The policemen waited for her sobbing to subside. After a few minutes, understanding that no improvement would come, McNamara turned to James. "Go to the kitchen and bring her a glass of water, James, please."

James strode to the kitchen, but even though he searched carefully, he found no glasses but only a few cups left on the side of the dirty sink full of dishes. He took a cup, rinsed it, and filled it with water.

The woman drank the water as if she hadn't drunk any for days. After a few minutes, she calmed down a little, and McNamara figured he could continue with his questions.

"Don't you know anything at all?"

The woman kept silent for a while, but then, with a nod, she admitted that she knew something. "Richard, my eldest son, said that he met her two weeks ago. Diane looked good: well dressed, even smartly, neat. She told Richard that she lived with a man with money. He took care of her, and maybe, he'd marry her. Diane said that she wouldn't come back to this dump, no matter what she had to do for that. She was sick of tasteless and poor food. In her opinion, it was no big deal to work hard and learn when you can have a good life without it."

"Didn't she say who the man was?" the DCI insisted.

"No, she didn't," the woman shook her head. "But Richard also told me that he saw her one day, less than a week after talking to her. Diane was with that guy. They'd just come out from a shop with expensive clothes."

"Did Richard tell you what that man looked like?" McNamara inquired.

"He said that the man was good-looking, tall and neatly dressed. Unfortunately, my son doesn't have any talent for describing people. He doesn't see anything else beyond clothes."

"When could we talk to him?" McNamara tried to find out.

"I don't know," the woman replied with a shrug. He comes when he wants. He lives somewhere in town with a friend of his. Still, he left me a phone number to call if I had something urgent. I have it somewhere in the other room," she said, rising heavily off the sofa to fetch the phone number and going into the other room.

After a few moments, the policemen heard the noise of things being slammed around. They waited for a while until the woman returned with a piece of paper that she gave to McNamara.

"This is his phone number. It's not directly to him," the woman revised her previous statement. "It's a neighbour's phone number because Richard doesn't have a phone where he lives."

"Thank you," McNamara said, copying the phone number down. He was about to leave when he turned back to her. "Did Diane have a diary or something like that?"

"Aye, she did," the woman nodded. "Do you need it? Diane used to hide it somewhere under the stove but not because of me. She knew that I respected her privacy. It's about the children. They'd found it once and laughed at her. After all, Diane's my only daughter. It's difficult for her with so many boys around," the woman explained, but then, she became aware that Diane wasn't alive and started crying again.

McNamara tried to talk to her kindly. "You need to come to the morgue, ma'am, and identify your daughter. Ah, and I also want that journal," he added, reminding her that she wanted to fetch it for him.

The woman nodded and went to the kitchen to return with a thick notebook covered with stains and the word 'Journal' written in calligraphy on the cover.

McNamara took the notebook from her hand with a quiet thanks and asked, "Do you want us to call you a car, ma'am, to drive you to the morgue?"

"Aye, I think so," she said. "It would be difficult to get there otherwise... May I take my neighbour with me?" the woman asked, almost begging. She wanted to have someone for support at her side when she was to see her daughter dead.

"Of course, ma'am," McNamara answered soothingly, knowing it was best. He remembered that the girl didn't look good. "Call a car, James," he ordered the Sergeant and waited for him to make the call before they could continue their inquiries.

"It will come at once, sir. I also called a policewoman. I think Mrs McWilliams should have another woman with her."

McNamara approved, then went outside and called the boy he had talked to earlier.

"Call your neighbour, lad. Tell her to come to your mother right away. Come on, go," he urged him when the boy stopped, glued on the spot, watching him.

The boy ran to the yard next door to find that neighbour, and McNamara came back inside, determined not to leave the woman alone until someone had come.

Unfortunately, he couldn't pry anything else from her because the woman wasn't able to say a thing. She just sat there, hunched, perched on the edge of the dirty sofa, staring into space, without seeing anything. The woman didn't realise someone was next to her — it was as if McNamara had ceased to exist. She didn't react even when her friend came with the dirty child in tow.

In a hushed tone so that the child couldn't hear him, McNamara explained to the neighbour what had happened to Diane. The huge woman with thick arms and ample bosom shook her head sadly, and her eyes brimmed with tears. She went to her friend and reached out, taking her in her thick arms, pulling her head on the generous bosom.

That was enough for Mrs McWilliams. She started weeping again and with such a force that her younger son, frightened, simply paled.

McNamara took the child's arm and led him out of the house into the street. "I think you'd better stay here and play with your friends more. You also need to take care of the younger ones," he pointed to the boy's brothers. "Your mom has to go somewhere, but she'll be back soon. You shouldn't worry."

CHAPTER SIX

The detectives stopped in front of the school, and James seemed really pleased with himself when he got out of the car. This time he had driven himself, and they hadn't been in danger for one moment. James was a prudent and responsible driver, unlike the Chief Inspector.

"James, I'm going to talk to the headmaster. You go look for Graham's girlfriend, that Laura Bradshaw, and talk to her," McNamara ordered, a scowl on his face, heading to the headmaster's office afterwards.

All those trips and interviews had exhausted him. Still, the inspector was primarily upset because he didn't have a clear starting point for his investigation. Everything was very confusing. He inclined towards Thompson but wasn't quite sure that the guy was guilty or had any connection to the events. However, McNamara had no doubt that Thompson had had a relationship with Patsy.

There was no one at the secretary's desk in the headmaster's waiting room, so the man knocked directly on the headmaster's door and entered when invited. Inside, he found a distinguished and serene woman around forty, who hadn't lost her beauty yet.

"Aye, sir, what can I do for you?" the woman asked him, raising a brow. "I don't think I've seen you before. Do you have a child in our school?"

"No, ma'am, I don't. I'm DCI McNamara," he said, showing her his ID and badge. "I came here concerning an investigation we're conducting," the man added, replacing the ID back in his coat pocket.

"I see," the woman said, although she seemed a little confused about the subject of the investigation. "What can I do for you, sir? I know we don't have any extraordinary children in our school, but, unfortunately, this is the fate of public schools at the border of the cities nowadays. However, you can't make me believe we have children that would cause serious problems. I'm talking about things requiring an investigation conducted by a DCI," she specified. "Other kind of situations we've had enough, I can't lie, especially shoplifting, breaking the peace, things like that," she added, waving her hand.

"It's not about the action of a child in the school," McNamara started, but he didn't have any chance to continue.

The headmistress simply jumped off her chair. Her eyes widened. She shouted, "Do you mean one of our teachers did something reproachable?"

McNamara cringed at the panic in her voice. It was evident that the woman couldn't accept the idea that a teacher, who should have been a model for their students, could have been involved in a police matter.

"No, ma'am. Let's calm down. I didn't mean that. If I could finish what I want to say...," the inspector raised his right brow, fixing the headmaster with his eyes. "Maybe that would help, and you'd stop making assumptions. I'm here because of two former students of yours. One was killed, and the other is considered missing for now. Her ID was found next to the body of the former."

Speechless, the woman just stared at him, unable to believe her ears. She had never had such a situation. They had children who stole from shops, fought, or got involved in various gangs. Some started trifling with drugs, doing them, or selling them to other classmates to bring their own daily dose. However, they had never had a crime connected to the school before.

The woman sat down at her desk again, keeping her eyes on McNamara. After a few moments of silence, she said, "I see. Who is this about, though?" she asked, even though her usual self-confidence had disappeared.

"It's about the two girls who dropped out of school this year, ma'am," McNamara informed her.

The headmistress laughed bitterly at his words and then said drily, "More than two girls abandoned school this year, sir. I'm afraid you must be more specific, if possible."

"Diane McWilliams and Patsy Porter, ma'am," McNamara said, gritting his teeth, feeling like a student called in the headmaster's office again. He had had his fair share of visits along his school years and never liked it.

The woman tilted her head and closed her eyes, remembering the two girls, which wasn't difficult. They had been invited into her office many times.

The girls would always do something, either minor things, like breaching the internal rules of order or something more serious, like stealing.

Diane had also managed to have a record if she remembered well. The two girls were brilliant and could have made good students, creating a safer future for themselves. Yet, they had chosen other ways to start their lives.

"Which one of them died?" the headmistress asked, her heart tight with regret for both.

"Diane, ma'am," McNamara answered, understanding the woman's feelings. It was an actual loss whenever someone lost their life. When it was a child, the loss was felt more severely than ever, regardless of their kind of people.

The headmistress tried to will away the tears brimming in her eyes. She had a reputation to uphold, and she couldn't afford to show her real feelings when she was in school or in public.

"Aye, indeed. Someone from the police phoned earlier to talk to the girls' teacher. But I didn't imagine... What can I do for you, inspector?" she asked, unwilling to deviate from the subject, assuming that the policeman had enough to deal with, and the investigation brought enough pressure on him.

"Could you tell me with whom they used to hang around here among their classmates or outside the school? If you know, obviously."

"In an ideal world, I should have known," the woman said with a bitterness she couldn't hide. "Unfortunately, we don't live in an ideal world, inspector. I can tell you that they had no relationships with the boys in the school. They didn't have a friend among them. They were part of a group of girls who preferred older men if you know what I mean... I happened, and not only once, to see them leaving with such men... Aside from two girls, who relocated to the other side of the country, the other five dropped out of school almost at the same time if I remember well. I asked to have their parents fined, but apparently, they didn't know where their girls were or what they were doing. They said they couldn't control them anymore," the woman added.

The headmaster glanced to the horizon line visible through the window, shaking her head at a loss of words. Then, she shifted her eyes towards McNamara again. Wetting her bottom lip with the tip of her tongue, she continued, "Three of the girls have only a mother. Diane had a divorced mother, and Patsy Porter's father was away almost all the time... Although, sincerely, I don't think that was the problem. We have other children in school who have only one parent in their lives, and they are quite serious and study. They try to do something with their lives. I think it's about education, a genetic fund," she lectured. "But I wouldn't like to annoy you with all my opinions. I think you understand what I mean."

"I do, ma'am," McNamara nodded, knowing what she was talking about from his own experience.

Maybe the type of family had some bearing upon a child's upbringing, but not entirely. His mother brought him up all by herself, as his father had played Houdini long before his birth. His mother had fought hard and pushed him a lot to go to school. She had worked herself to the bone for him and asked that he do his part.

Knowing how hard she fought to offer him the right house, atmosphere, and what he needed, the inspector had done his best not to disappoint her and make a better life for himself.

"So, there's no one among her friends here to talk to," the DCI went straight to the point.

"No, unfortunately," the headmistress reckoned. "I can't help you here. They didn't have any relationships with the other girls, and I don't think anyone knew whom they met or what they did. They seemed a quite exclusive group."

"Could you give me the other girls' names in their group, ma'am?"

"Aye, of course. If you want, I can also give you the names of the girls who relocated with the address for the schools where they transferred," the woman added, wanting to help.

"I'd be grateful," McNamara thanked her warmly for her effort.

The headmaster wrote everything on paper and gave it to McNamara, who stood up and thanked her for her answers again. Shaking her hand, he left her office. The Chief Inspector already thought about the possible lines of investigation opened before him. Reaching the car and noticing that James hadn't returned yet, the man called the office.

"Mike, write down the following names. Two are on the other side of the country. Please, get in touch with our colleagues there and ask them to talk to the girls and their parents," he said, relaying the information he had gathered. "Please, have people sent to each girl here," the DCI continued. "I want them to talk to their parents. Maybe you can ask Jo to verify if anything turns up about them in the database. All right?"

"Aye, sir, I've written everything down. I'll give Jo the girls' names to look into the database. I'll call Bristol and Leeds, and as soon as we hear something, we'll let you know," Mike promised.

"All right, Mike. I'll leave you to that now," McNamara said, hanging up and watching

James, who was coming towards him. "Well, James, what have you found out?" he inquired.

"It checked out, sir. Graham was where he said he was. I also talked to the two colleagues who celebrated one year of marriage. They corroborated Graham's statements, so he's all right. He couldn't have been on Nightingale Street at the same time. Have you learnt something, sir?"

"Not very much, but let's hope that Mike and Jo will bring some details later," McNamara replied.

"They'd better," James said, glancing at his watch. "It's almost five-thirty. Are we going back to question the others on the street, sir?"

"Aye, James, I think so. It is the only thing we could do. We've got no other starting point but that street."

MCNAMARA SERIES BOX SET
BOOK 0NE & TWO

CHAPTER SEVEN

"Hello, love! Have you just returned from work?" Mrs Stevens leaned on the sash, watching her neighbour Miss McNeil, who had just parked her car in front of the house.

"Oh, aye, I've had a hectic day. A new book hit the market. I think it'll become a bestseller soon. A lot of people came to the shop just to buy that book. Believe me, it was difficult to satisfy all the requests. I can't be everywhere at once, unfortunately. Now, enough about me. I don't want to annoy you with that. What have you done today? Have you had any pains?"

"A little, love," the old woman reckoned. "You're very kind to ask. Will you have tea with me, or are you having other plans in mind?"

Bryony McNeil needed to think about that because she was awfully tired. She would have liked to put her legs up somewhere and lie down. However, she knew that she still had to catch up on her work with the ledgers. So, the young woman smiled at Mrs Stevens and nodded, "Of course, why not? Wouldn't you prefer to come with me for tea? I've just bought some chocolate cakes from the teahouse near my bookshop. I'm sure you'll like them. I, for one, am madly fond of them, really. What do you think?"

"Well, then," the old woman agreed. Bryony knew her tastes very well and wouldn't have brought anything the older woman didn't like. "I'll come to you," she said. "Just let me take my walking stick."

Mrs Stevens disappeared from the window and came out after a few minutes, leaning on her walking stick as her gait was getting more difficult those days. Her younger neighbour pitied her for the aches the old woman frequently experienced.

The two women entered McNeil's house, the one painted in white, with blue windows and door, which McNamara had admired that morning. Bryony showed the older woman to the drawing-room and helped her sit down in her favourite seat. Then, the younger woman moseyed into the kitchen to prepare the tea and put the cakes onto a plate. While the water for tea was boiling, she also made the small sandwiches with butter, cucumber, and cheese they both liked.

Bryony had just returned into the drawing-room with everything when the bell at the door rang.

"Are you expecting someone, love?" her neighbour inquired with curiosity.

Since Bryony quarrelled with Ann Goddard from the end of the street, no one had called on her—just maybe Mrs Reid or Brown, but their visits were rare.

"No, I'm not. I will see who's at the door and get back at once," Bryony promised while leaving the room.

The woman opened the front door, and baffled, she stared at the two men on the stoop of her house. She hadn't expected to see any strangers. Bryony had thought that either Mary Reid or Mrs Brown came for a brief visit because they usually borrowed a book or asked her to bring something from the bookshop.

However, Bryony had never seen the two men before her eyes. The man on the right, about forty, very tall and well-built, with dark brown hair, and green eyes, looked somewhat rough around the edges. He wasn't handsome but exciting to look at. The man seemed to have lived and seen many things and knew plenty about the dark side of the world. By contrast, the one on the left was relatively young, maybe about twenty-five. He wasn't as tall as his fellow, and his hair, black with bluish reflections, reminded her of the Gaelic type. His clear blue eyes made the man look like a freshman in life. However, his smile was open and warm and reached his eyes. In contrast, the other man's smile seemed rather cold, cynical and distant, fit to match his eyes cold eyes with no shadow of a smile in them.

Bryony didn't realise she had been staring at them for a few moments without saying anything. She pulled herself together only when she noticed an ironic smile flourishing on the older man's lips.

The man had already analysed the woman. He might have just glanced at her initially but had noticed everything necessary. Although he didn't want to admit it, the man liked what he saw. Of course, he tried to hide his pleasure.

Feeling slightly embarrassed, Bryony asked them drily, "Well, who are you, and what do you want? Are you selling anything? I'm sorry for you, but I'm not buying anything."

McNamara didn't like her assumption that they were salesmen and scowled at her. McNamara didn't put much stock in people's opinions, but no one had previously mistaken him for a salesman. And he had more than his fair share of dislike for salesmen, so he didn't enjoy being mistaken for one. A deep frown appeared between his brows, making him look more foreboding.

"We're from the police, ma'am. We must ask you some questions," the Chief Inspector replied severely. In general, he was agreeable enough when he interviewed people.

His tone baffled James, as he had never heard McNamara speaking like that when they questioned someone. He tried to smile more pleasantly to compensate, hoping to sweeten McNamara's unpleasant answer and make up for his boss's apparent lack of politeness.

"I see," the young woman replied in a crisp voice, and her eyes turned cold. "What happened? Have I forgotten to pay a fine, or has someone complained about me?" she continued drily, knowing that no other explanation was possible for their visit.

Her insolence fired McNamara's anger. However, he controlled his temper, saying reproachfully, "We're not in uniform. I don't see why you would mistake us for constables. We're here to investigate two murders, ma'am, and I've got no time to exchange amiable replies with you. So..."

"Two murders!" Bryony interrupted him, and her eyebrows shot up in shock. "Lord! I don't know of any murder! Who died? And when?" she asked, unaware that her questions tumbled too fast one after the other, and they couldn't answer.

Stunned, the men looked at the woman like she had fallen from a tree. They didn't think it was possible to live practically next door and not know that two people had been murdered near your house.

Bryony guessed what they were thinking and explained apologetically, "I know you might find it bizarre. However, if the two murders you're talking about took place last night or today, it explains why I don't know about them. I didn't meet anyone this morning, either when I left for work or on my way home in the afternoon. I only came home at eight-thirty last night, and I didn't see anyone... I worked in the kitchen for a while. Afterwards, I couldn't sleep because I had a headache—the beginning of a migraine, actually, and my migraines are awful when they're full-blown. I took a sleeping pill, which I rarely do. Since I'm not used to that kind of pill, I slept like a log, and I didn't hear anything all night... Mrs Stevens, with whom I'm having tea right now, seemed to want to tell me something, but here you've come, and I haven't had a chance to hear a thing… If you want to ask me some questions, come in," Bryony said, finally taking a deep breath after her long speech.

Her tone was conciliatory now, the woman trying to attenuate somehow the harshness and irony she had shown before. She felt a little guilty for being flippant when the situation was dire. She stepped aside to allow them inside and led them to the drawing-room, where she introduced them to Mrs Stevens.

"These two gentlemen are from the police, Mrs Stevens. I'm sorry, I don't remember your names," she turned to them to make them understand they hadn't introduced themselves, as they should have.

McNamara resented her mute reproach and frowned again. Yet, he couldn't understand his sudden irritability towards the young woman because she was right. They should have shown her their IDs.

"I'm DCI McNamara, and this is DS James."

James politely shook Miss McNeil's hand and then Mrs Stevens', but McNamara didn't move a muscle. He didn't shake their hands or say anything else. The Chief Inspector still displayed that atypical air he had shown at the door, and

James felt awkward. He didn't understand what had gotten under his boss's bonnet.

McNamara disliked the young woman's behaviour and her lack of respect towards him. However, the man had no idea why he needed her respect. It wasn't like he had cared about that in the past.

Besides, it was his duty to be polite during an investigation. Yet, this time, the DCI had forgotten entirely the rules he had been following scrupulously during the years spent in the force.

Bryony McNeil didn't care for his rudeness but didn't feel like discussing it, either. Hence, she apologised for having to leave them alone for a few moments and sauntered to the kitchen to fetch cups and plates for the men. When she returned, she poured them tea and offered a cup to each one.

"Please, help yourself to sugar and milk. And have some sandwiches and cakes," the woman invited them, smiling at James.

Bryony didn't smile at McNamara, though. She didn't understand his demeanour, but the man had been driving her crazy since she opened the front door. Something about him didn't sit right with her. His presence aroused both her impatience and anxiety.

James blushed, feeling like he had been put on the spot. The DS had noticed the lass treated him differently. He liked the young woman, and her offer for tea and sandwiches flattered him. Not everyone was so kind when the police came knocking on their door.

McNamara was famished as he hadn't had a chance to have lunch that day, so he took two sandwiches and absently dropped two pieces of sugar in his tea. Then, turning to Mrs Stevens, he asked her, "Have you heard anything about the two murders on your street, ma'am?"

"Of course, I've heard," the woman said in a prim and steely voice, offended because the inspector suggested that she wasn't in touch with what was going on in their small community. "I wanted to tell Bryony about them when she came home, but I haven't had the time because you've already come to ask questions. What an awful night was last night!" she exclaimed.

"May I ask who was killed, please?" Miss McNeil asked in a small voice.

"We found a young girl murdered in the Dobbs' yard last night, and then we found Mrs Dobbs killed in her living room this morning," answered McNamara in a harsh voice, even though he wasn't aware of that.

"Oh, poor Mr Dobbs. What's he doing now?" McNeil asked, worried over Mr Dobbs' condition after the tragic events.

"Well, he's doing absolutely nothing," McNamara answered drily. "He also died last night."

Bryony jumped on her feet, pricked by his tone and blunt and deliberate brutality. As harsh as he, she said, "You might feel offended because I didn't recognise two policemen in plain clothes. Or you might disregard me because I didn't know anything about the crimes. No matter what, I don't think you are allowed to be insolent with the people you are questioning, sir. Your official position wouldn't allow it, and I won't tolerate it."

McNamara had to reckon that the woman was correct and had courage. However, he kept silent, watching her boldly, his eyes resembling those of a stealthy fox on the hunt for a hen. The DCI also reckoned that his malicious joy was due to his success in making the young woman explode. She seemed too polished, polite, and warm, and he refused to believe that she was like that for real. A cynic, the inspector didn't think such women existed outside a book or a romantic film.

On the other hand, James felt like he had been thrown into a weird parallel universe. He had never heard his boss speaking like that to a possible witness, and he didn't understand what had triggered that behaviour.

McNamara was marginally rude only when he knew that he was talking to the person he would arrest. As far as James knew, Miss McNeil wasn't a suspect in their inquiry. Besides being one of the neighbourhood residents, he couldn't fathom her connection with the case. Consequently, he didn't perceive the reason for McNamara's behaviour. After rationalising all that, the DS felt much more confused than initially.

Mrs Stevens had her own opinion about what was going on between them. She never kept her thoughts to herself, so she didn't keep her mouth shut now.

"Is Bryony a suspect, sir?"

"No, ma'am. She's not," McNamara replied briefly. He couldn't lie. Being rude was one thing. Lying during an investigation was another. "She's not a suspect for the moment. We'll see if that changes later," the inspector added meaningfully. He didn't fully understand his reasons but wanted to let Bryony know that her pretty face didn't take her name off his suspects' list automatically.

Hot lava, Bryony's fury rose a notch. She had noticed the policeman was downright mean to her, and she didn't understand why. But then a thought crossed her mind, and the young woman felt the jolt of cold fear along her spine. She feared he considered her guilty. "What answers do you need from me, sir?" she asked quickly. The woman wanted to be done with their interrogation as soon as possible and conclude that absurd duel she didn't comprehend.

"I'd like to know everything about Patsy Porter," McNamara replied.

"Patsy Porter?" Bryony asked in an astonished voice. "What relation could Pasty have with the crimes?"

"This is our business, ma'am," the inspector answered rudely. "Yours is to answer my questions as exactly as possible. By the way, your name is...." McNamara questioned her insolently again.

"I'm Bryony McNeil. Are you also interested in my daily life?" she asked, matching his insolence. The young woman found the courage to overcome the irrational fear she had felt before for a moment. As McNamara didn't bother to answer, she decided to explain. "Well, I own a small bookshop in town. And I know nothing of Patsy, or, at least, I know nothing of her now, I mean," she tried to explain herself. "She left some time ago, and I've heard nothing of her ever since," Bryony said.

The young woman forced herself to keep a calm façade, not wanting to give McNamara the satisfaction of seeing that he had upset her. Indifference was always the best weapon in such circumstances because it hurt more than anything else.

"In your opinion, what kind of girl was she?" James asked in a calming voice to counter the asperity perceived in his superior's words.

"I must reckon that I haven't paid much attention to her," Bryony answered with a shrug. "If I remember correctly, we had absolutely different interests. Besides, I didn't like what she was doing. She seemed to flirt with every man on the street. I didn't have a good opinion of her," she shook her head. "However, I must tell you that I didn't see much of her. I'm in the town where my bookshop is most of the time," she explained with a wave of her hand. "In the evening, I come home late, and most often, I see only Mrs Stevens. I don't see anyone else unless someone happens to be in front of my house.

Only sometimes, on Sundays, I meet people in the street if I don't have some work to do."

"That's true", Mrs Stevens said, interrupting her. "Bryony is a very busy girl. She opened a bookshop one year ago, and she wants to make it successful. She works long hours, too many, in my opinion. Usually, she comes home very late in the evening, and she spends most of the time here alone or with me. I happen to be a good friend of the aunt who brought her up," the old woman almost smiled. "We're very close, the two of us," she said, reaching out to Bryony, who took her hand.

"I see," McNamara said, nodding. "Maybe you have someone to spend time in town, miss?"

"I'm afraid that is not your business if it's not related to the case you're working on," the young woman replied dryly.

"I want you to answer my question, Miss McNeil. I can't have you waste my time investigating your situation. Still, I will do it," the DCI replied stubbornly in a coarse voice. "I'll decide whether there's any connection between the information you're offering and my case. Should I understand you don't like my question?" the man provoked her, staring at her through eyes narrowed to slits.

Bryony loathed the man's way of asking questions. Yet, she didn't want to have any problems with the police and didn't have anything to hide, so she answered.

"No, I don't go out with anyone in town or anywhere else. I don't have the time to date or socialise. I work alone in the shop because I can't afford to hire anyone yet. On top of that, I keep my ledgers myself too. That means I have quite a lot of work to do. And after seeing so many people all day long and talking to so many people, I prefer staying alone at home in the evening, or maybe spending some time with Mrs Stevens. But work always comes first for me. I want to pay up all my debts at the bank and make a steady situation for myself," she shrugged and waved her hand again.

Bryony and McNamara watched each other, and for a few moments, silence filled the room.

"What about you, Mrs Stevens?" McNamara asked the old lady, turning to her when he realised that Bryony wouldn't offer him any other pertinent information. He didn't want to push her too hard, as the young woman didn't seem the kind who accepted being pushed around for too long.

"What do you know about Patsy Porter and about what happened last night?" the Chief Inspector asked the old woman.

"Patsy was a very impish girl, you must know, young man," she stated vehemently. "I didn't like her much. I didn't like her at all, if I may say so. I can't walk very well," she said, covering the two men with her sharp look and pointing to her walking stick. "So, I spend most of my time reading near the window. Now, sometimes I see things. I often saw her flirting with men of a certain age on the street. She wore very short skirts and used to show too much skin. That didn't help me to like her. Girls had more common sense, education, and propriety in my time," the old woman shook her head. "Patsy would flirt with everyone. She promised to become something else, but not a good girl. Probably, a light skirt, I'd better say. She didn't seem to like either school or work. I heard people speaking about her, and I heard nothing good. Everyone would say she was a strumpet, an easy flirt. She would drive her mother crazy with all the problems she caused," she explained with a deep scowl.

"We've also heard Mr Porter left home because of her. Is it true?" James asked.

"Absurd! I don't believe such nonsense," Mrs Stevens puffed. "His wife might believe it. However, Mrs Davidson came to have tea with me last week. She told me that she'd been in town two weeks ago and seen Porter with a woman on the bus. By accident, she was seated behind them and heard what they talked about. It was clear they'd been living together. So, he lied when he said he was leaving because of Patsy," the woman waved a hand nervously.

The old woman stopped to catch her breath, tossing her head in disbelief. "The truth is he was bored with his wife and family life. When he did deign to come home," she turned her nose, conveying what she was thinking of the man. "Porter didn't care about Patsy at all. He wasn't made to be a father or a husband. That's all. That man wouldn't do anything in the house or garden, and he'd rarely come home on weekends. He would say he had travelled because of the job. I think he was a sort of salesman, but I don't know for sure. I wasn't interested in finding out," she shrugged with indifference.

James glanced at McNamara to see if he wanted to ask more questions. He had already noted down Mrs Stevens' words and wondered at the silence.

Yet, his boss was more interested in the long shapely legs of their young hostess than in the conversation, which stunned James.

"Sir, do we have any other questions?" James asked him hesitantly, unable to explain the DCI's behaviour. McNamara had a solid reputation among his subordinates. The young man had never seen his boss behave unprofessionally.

"I don't think he has any other questions," Miss McNeil replied peevishly. "He's more interested in something else, aren't you, sir?" she addressed McNamara with sarcasm. "And as you don't have any more questions and I'm quite tired, maybe you can come another time. What do you think?" she dismissed him, her voice shaking with anger. Bryony hoped that she would be luckier next time, and the policeman would find her wearing pants so that he couldn't stare at her legs.

"All right!" McNamara stood up, finally aware that he had crossed the line, something he wouldn't have typically done. "Please, get in touch with us if you remember anything else of Patsy," he asked the two women, handing them a card. "But, by the way," he remembered suddenly, "didn't you hear anything last night when Mrs Dobbs was killed?" he asked Mrs Stevens.

"I don't know. I'm not sure if it's related to that," the woman said, a thoughtful look on her face. "Around three, sometime after the police left, I think, I got out of bed and went to the kitchen to drink some milk. Milk helps me sleep better. While I was warming my milk, I looked through the window, thinking of the girl I'd heard you found in the Dobbs' yard and poor Mr Dobbs. I had heard people talking, so I knew that he had died. I saw a tall man, maybe as tall as you," she said, pointing to McNamara. "He jumped over Bryony's garden fence, heading to the gate. There I lost him from sight, of course. If I think his gait seemed familiar somewhat, you know. It was something in his posture, but I couldn't put my finger on it. However, I didn't see his face. I think he wore something over his head… a black cap," she waved her hand around her head.

"I hope you haven't said anything to anyone about that," James worried that the old woman might have been in danger. If she had said something about what she had seen, the killer might have heard about it.

"No, I haven't," the older woman shook her head. "I wanted to tell Bryony now, and that's it. I don't talk too much with the people on the street," she grimaced.

"Then, it's all right," James said again, at ease now. "I don't think there'll be any problems in that case."

"No, it's not all right," Bryony contradicted him, her mind spinning fast. "Did you turn on the light before getting into the kitchen?" she asked the old woman.

"Of course, I did. How else could I have warmed the milk?" the old woman answered with annoyance.

"And you were standing right in front of the window, weren't you?" Bryony continued with her questions. "Your stove is right by the kitchen window, isn't it?"

"Indeed, I was right in front of the window," Mrs Stevens admitted. "That's why I could see him."

"Then, he saw you too," Bryony said, almost in a whisper, clenching her hands with apprehension. Then, she turned to McNamara, white-faced already. "Don't you see, sir? She is in danger," she pointed out the obvious. "It's unlikely the man hadn't seen her. Of course, he might have thought she'd seen him coming from the back of the houses. He doesn't know she didn't recognise him if he's someone we know. That's certain," she nodded.

"Of course, Mrs Stevens. Miss McNeil is right," McNamara agreed, sitting back on the sofa. "I believe the man saw you. He might have thought he couldn't surprise you, or maybe what he'd done had been too much for one night. He might have put aside his plan to silence you for later. I think you're in real danger. I'm afraid you can't even move fast enough to fend a possible attack," McNamara said matter-of-factly, nodding meaningfully towards the old lady's stick. His eyes fell on the fingers deformed by arthritis, with no intention of sarcasm this time.

"Don't worry, love," Bryony told the old woman reassuringly, patting her older friend's arm with affection. "You can come and stay with me for a while until the police finish the investigation and arrest the criminal. I know you can't use the stairs, so I'm going to prepare you a bedroom here, in the drawing-room. I have a bed I can set up. I'll sleep in the living room on the sofa. I can hear any noise and act quickly if anything happens. What do you think?"

"I don't know, Bryony," the old woman answered with uncertainty. "You know very well I don't like leaving my house. Besides, I am against becoming an intruder, a burden, in someone else's house," she added rashly, loving her independence too much. She was afraid but also stubborn enough to push the fear away.

"Don't be daft!" Bryony snapped at her, forgetting about being polite for a moment. "You know very well you're not an intruder in my house, and you shouldn't even think you would be a burden to me. I'm glad to have you here, where I can watch over you. Don't you understand that you are in real danger?" she almost shouted to the stubborn old woman.

"Well, everything is good and fine, but when you go to work, she's still in danger," McNamara stated, bringing her back to earth in a second.

"Oh, aye, that's true. What can I do?" Bryony started to look for a solution. "I think I'd better ask Mrs Brown to stay with you while I'm not here," she decided.

"She can't, love. She's the cook at the pub, you know that. I don't think they can do without her," she shook her head. "No, they can't, especially now when they haven't had any help since they fired that boy."

"What about Mrs Randall? What do you think of her?" Bryony inquired, full of hope.

"Do you really think Mrs Randall would come to stay with me?" Mrs Stevens wondered. "She's not a very kind woman, and she doesn't like me much, from what I've seen. I had a few choice words for her once, and she couldn't forgive me. And I don't think I could stand that stuffy woman for even five minutes. So, an entire day is out of the question," she shook her head once more with determination.

"Then, I'll take you to the bookshop," Bryony decided. "It is not a problem. I've got four armchairs and a sofa in the shop, and I also have a room at the back where I keep the ledgers. I'm sure I can find an extensible armchair for you. So, you can lie down whenever you would like, or you need it. In the evening, I'll bring you here back with me. I think this is the best solution," she said and nodded with satisfaction. "We'll take lunch together and spend more time together. You'll see. It will be fantastic," Bryony told her in an excited voice.

The young woman tried to appear excited as if she had planned an outing for a picnic, not built a defence plan. She hoped her tone would convince her older friend.

"I don't know, dear. It's too much bother," Mrs Stevens argued, her voice full of doubt. She didn't have the energy to survive a day like Bryony described.

"Don't worry for any bother," Bryony argued back. "It's not a bother. You must know it. We'll feel very well, and you'll be safe. You'll see. Don't you think I'm right, inspector? What do you think?"

"Aye, it is a good solution, Mrs Stevens, even though it might be somewhat exhausting for you. However, if you prefer to remain at home, then I can send a constable to stay with you during the day. It will be less of a trial for you. What do you think?" McNamara inquired, avoiding Bryony's eyes.

"I think it's better that way," the old woman accepted at once. "Don't get upset, Bryony", she said, turning to Bryony, who was scowling. "You have a lot of work to do at the bookshop, and I'm sure you'll feel that you have to stay with me and entertain me. You know you can't set your work aside. And in the evening, you'll be twice as tired as you are now," she patted Bryony's hand. "Besides, I'm an old woman. You know me. I have my habits during the day, and one of them is to lie in bed as much as I can. But I'll move in with you overnight, all right? Then, the police won't have to send another man for me," she tried to reassure her friend.

"If that's what you want," Bryony said without inflexion, unwilling to display her anger. She was mad with McNamara for spoiling her plans. The young woman liked to be helpful whenever she had a chance. She felt the need to offer something back for what she had gotten years ago when her aunt had taken her in and offered her a life.

"Then, everything's settled," McNamara concluded. "However, I'll also send a policewoman for the night and starting right now," he said quickly to stop any opposition from Bryony. "Well, we'll leave now, and, please, be careful," the DCI ordered the old woman. "You shouldn't mention our conversation to anyone," he advised.

"I'll see you off, gentlemen," Bryony stood up.

At the door, McNamara stopped and faced her. "I might have to ask you some more questions, Miss McNeil. So, we might see each other quite soon."

The woman nodded but didn't answer. Yet, the DCI was satisfied to see a flash of anger crossing her eyes. He knew she was furious with him because he had managed to ruin her evening. Without a care in the world, he smiled at her. Waving to her, he headed to the street.

MCNAMARA SERIES BOX SET
BOOK 0NE & TWO

CHAPTER EIGHT

"I hope you won't mind, sir, but what happened there?" James asked hesitantly. He knew he should keep his mouth shut but couldn't. His curiosity had reached too high a level to rein it in.

"What do you mean?" McNamara asked absently, although he knew very well what his subordinate meant. The man was aware that he had crossed the line with Miss McNeil but hadn't been able to stop himself. Anyway, he had derived an absolute satisfaction from their mute duel in the end.

"You know, sir," James insisted, although he feared McNamara's reaction. "You talked to Miss McNeil as if you had suspected her of a connection to the crimes. As far as I know, we don't have any information like that," he thought to mention.

"Oh, no, James, I can't consider her a suspect. I can't suspect anyone yet because I haven't got enough data. I simply didn't like her behaviour towards us. She acted so superior when she opened the door that I wanted to bring her down a peg. I couldn't allow her to mock us," McNamara explained indifferently. However, he cursed himself for his lack of restraint.

"She didn't give me that impression, sir. I thought she was plain tired. She looked as if she'd needed some downtime or a good night's sleep. She didn't put on airs," James replied with a shake of his head.

"You're wrong, James," McNamara retorted sternly. "The woman made fun of us," he insisted, even though the man knew he was lying through his teeth.

The Inspector felt angry with the woman again, although a little voice in his head told him he wasn't right. Besides, he lied to a subordinate because of her, and the truth hurt.

Although he knew the woman hadn't put on airs before them, James didn't answer. He was almost sure McNamara had fancied her but didn't want to admit it. His boss had insistently watched the woman's body.

Moreover, McNamara's reaction showed he didn't believe his own words. Still, James thought he shouldn't upset his boss, even though McNamara had never mistreated his subordinates.

However, the DS preferred to keep his mouth shut because he had learnt his lessons well. His father had made that mistake in the past and had to look for another job. After two years, the man couldn't find any because he didn't have recommendations. When he couldn't stand the shame of living on his wife's money, his father had killed himself.

"What will we do now, sir?" James asked, to distance himself from his sad thoughts. He had enough on his mind. Taking trips in the past didn't help anyway.

"I'm positive there's another connection between Patsy Porter and the girl we found. They seem alike, physically and in behaviour. They belonged to the same group and had the same occupations," McNamara explained.

The man glanced up and down Nightingale Street and then turned to his DS. "In addition, I'm almost sure our killer must live on this street, James, or at least must have a close connection with someone on the street. So, we still must ask questions over here," McNamara shrugged.

The DCI glanced at his watch for a second and then continued, "I asked Mike to check out

Thompson because he seems like a real stud, and
Donna is checking out Graham and his girlfriend.
Mark must find Porter, and Jo must find Patsy
Porter. When we have all these answers, we'll
know how things are."

McNamara massaged his temples with a tired
gesture and then decided, "Meanwhile, let's talk
to Ann Goddard. She's one of Thompson's lovers
if we believe what people say. I say one because
I'm sure our man wouldn't have been content
with only one. There must be others too since he
doesn't stay home much."

**

Ann Goddard opened the door with a smile.
McNamara considered her demeanour more
appropriate to welcome two policemen than
McNeil's ironic words. Soon though, he realised
that the two women weren't anything alike.
McNeil had proven a complex and witty
personality, while Ann's wit was barely there.

The DCI showed the woman his ID, asking
her to allow them inside because they had some
questions for her. Soon, they found themselves in
a room of the same size as McNeil's drawing-

room. As expected, the Chief Inspector didn't face any opposition.

McNamara remembered well McNeil's room with its functionality and cosiness. He doubted he would forget anything related to that woman soon.

At first glance, Goddard's drawing-room drowned in cushions. Pink curtains with miniature roses on them shaded the window. Even the sofa was a shiny pink with big roses painted on the seats. Pink abounded everywhere in the room.

The room was feminine but too cluttered for his taste, and the bright pink and roses hurt his eyes. The intensity of the colour interfered with McNamara's brain functions. Ann obviously had exaggerated in her decoration efforts. McNamara glanced at James, surprising him wince at the sight of the room.

And then, it was also the smell — sweet and heavy, as the hostess had exaggerated with her perfume. The scent, overwhelming and rich, made the two detectives' heads spin. The detectives sat down, trying to breathe shallowly. The smell wasn't so bad in small doses.

Their hostess excused herself for a few moments, and while she was away, the two men glanced at each other and grinned. They thought the same thing — that was the room of a woman who hadn't grown but still lived in a sort of adolescent fantasy, despite her age. She was about thirty, if they remembered correctly.

Upon her return, both men considered her attentively. Ann Goddard surprised them because she seemed younger. Closer to twenty-five or twenty-six. With her reddish-blond hair and pale skin, the woman looked almost transparent. Golden freckles powdered her cheeks and made her look somewhat like a mischievous fairy or a playful little girl, but not a grown woman.

Ann wasn't tall, but her posture looked elegant, despite her lack of sophistication. Her dress mimicked the colours of her drawing-room, which made the woman disappear into the background.

"I think you've come to ask me about the girl from the Dobbs' yard, haven't you?"

"Indeed, Miss Goddard," James said, catching McNamara's sign to take the lead of the interview. "You live practically next door, and we thought it would have been impossible not to hear or see what happened last night."

"That's true. I live next door, but I typed something in the kitchen last night and went to bed early. I was waiting for my boyfriend to visit, you know. When he called and put our date off, I was furious and depressed, so I decided to go to bed at once. But I did wake up when I heard that awful scream. I'm not courageous, so I didn't dare to move from under the blanket. In the beginning, I didn't dare to go downstairs to see what was going on. It was only after people started talking outside that I did," she explained.

"Didn't you watch out of the window at all?" McNamara asked.

"No, I didn't," the young woman shook her head. "And even if I had, I couldn't have seen much," she shrugged daintily. "When I went out, I saw that the body lay on the other side of the yard. I couldn't have seen anything because of the Dobbs' house," Ann waved her hand.

"Did you get closer to the body?" McNamara asked her.

"Oh, no, I couldn't have," the woman said, apparently shocked by the enormity of his assumption. "I just told you I'm not very courageous. I wouldn't look at the body of someone killed. I know I couldn't," she replied defensively. "I haven't even looked at a dead person, and so far, I haven't seen someone killed."

"Did you see anyone that shouldn't have been in the street?" James asked.

"I can't say that. There was Mr Thompson, certainly. I noticed that he wore his suit, but he never goes out if he's not perfectly dressed and neat. He's a real gentleman," she explained.

The men exchanged swift glances, and McNamara raised his brows to convey his opinion to James.

"Then there was Mr Reid," the woman continued, without noticing their exchange. "I think he was wearing something brown over his pyjamas. There was also Mrs Reid, in a very light and short gown. I thought she must have been nuts. If her husband had looked at her, he'd have killed her. He makes a big fuss over a short skirt, but I don't know what he would have done over a transparent gown... Ah, and of course, Mrs Thompson came out a bit later, just after me. She probably took her time to change her pyjamas or what she usually wears at night. There were the Davidsons too. Mrs Davidson wore very ruffled sweatpants. I think she'd slept in them, although I can't figure out how she could sleep like that. Mr Davidson wore a white bathrobe... I saw no one else until the police came," Ann said after a few moments of thought. "Oh, aye," she remembered. "The Browns were also there, but the Randalls came only when the police did."

"Did you hear anything from Mrs Dobbs' house after the police left? Or did you see someone getting into the house afterwards?" McNamara asked her.

"No. I can't be sure, but I stayed at the bedroom window for a while because I couldn't sleep. I had the vague impression I saw someone sneaking on one side of the Dobbs' house to the back door. I'm sure it was a man because a woman wouldn't look like that."

"What do you mean, Miss Goddard?" McNamara asked.

"Well, the person's shoulders were too broad, and hips too narrow. No, that wasn't a woman's body. A woman would look different," she shook her head with determination.

"Did you recognise the person?" James asked.

"No, I don't know who he was, but I noticed something familiar in his posture and gait, even if he was hunching. I think he was trying to sneak around. I can't really say who he was, though," the woman opened her arms with regret.

"Did you hear anything then? A noise, a scream, or something like that?"

"Oh, no, I heard nothing like that," Ann replied in a stunned voice. Her eyes widened because she hadn't thought of the implications before. "I stayed at the window a few minutes only, and then, I went to bed because it was very late, and I usually wake up early in the morning."

"When you watched out the window, was the light on or off?" McNamara asked, remembering Bryony's logic.

"The light was off. Why?"

"Then it's all right. The man couldn't have seen you," McNamara replied. "We were afraid you might be in danger, but you aren't if the man didn't see you. Could you tell us a few things about your neighbours, especially the Thompsons, the Davidsons, Mr Graham and the Reids? Ah, and of course the Porters."

"Well, Alice Thompson is a very plain woman, in my opinion. I don't have anything to talk about with her," Ann said, turning up her nose. "She doesn't know anything else but to take care of her house and husband. Alice makes sure he has everything he could want, forgetting to offer him what he needs most, like love and physical love. She's a stupid cow, that's a fact," she shrugged, her voice reeking with scorn. "No one on the street is interested in talking to her... except for Mrs Reid. She calls on her when she has nothing else to do, although I don't understand what she could talk to her about... Ah, and there's also Mrs Randall. She's that kind of severe and pickled, narrow-minded woman,"

Ann said with a grimace. "Mrs Randall has some very firm opinions about how a wife should be. Apparently, Alice meets her expectations because she's her favourite."

"But Mr Thompson, how does he feel about his wife?" McNamara asked, curious to see what the woman would answer.

Ann blushed and seemed taken aback a little, but the men waited patiently for her answer.

"I know he's fed up with her and wants to divorce her. I know he's trying to find a better way to tell her so that she wouldn't be too hurt," the woman answered in a low voice.

"How would you know?" James asked, wanting to see if she would confess her love affair with her neighbour.

"Well...you know... Daniel and I...are involved in a relationship... we'll get married...as soon as he's divorced her. He loves me and wants to live with me," she said slowly, hesitating.

"Mrs Thompson knows that?" McNamara asked her patiently, understanding that it was difficult for her to admit to being in a relationship with a married man. She wasn't the kind of woman who changed men like socks.

"Not really... Not yet... Daniel said we should keep our relationship secret for now...

You know… He doesn't want to hurt Alice. After all, he says she's not guilty that he doesn't love her, and I agree with him," Ann said quickly, willing to support her lover. Yet, it was clear that she didn't like Thompson's idea. She would have preferred a clean break-up between Alice and Daniel.

"How long have you been together?" McNamara asked softly.

"We've been together for three years or so. They moved here five years ago, and after my mom moved out and went to live with my sister in Liverpool, I started dating him. We met in Edinburgh at first, where we both work… Then, we started to meet at my place in the evenings."

"So, Mrs Thompson knows about your affair," James concluded, leaning slightly forward.

"Only if he told her because otherwise, she couldn't have found out," Ann said, shaking her head.

"How come? Do you think she hasn't seen he was coming to you? There's only one way here," McNamara waved in the street direction. "And it passes right by their house. She couldn't have missed him," he disagreed with her. "She must have seen him, even if only once."

"Daniel comes to me twice a week. That's true. But, you see, he comes through the gardens, in the back. First, he crosses Mrs Stevens' garden. At that hour, she's either inside or at Miss McNeil's. She can't see him. It is quite easy to get into Miss McNeil's garden," she explained patiently. "The other garden doesn't have an owner here now, so there's no danger, and the Dobbs used to spend their early night in their drawing-room, which faces the other way, and they couldn't see him... So, you see, Alice couldn't have found out that he came to me. There's no way unless Daniel told her, and he didn't. I'm sure she doesn't know anything. Sometimes I wait for him, and he can't come because either Mrs Stevens or Miss McNeil is out. Mrs Dobbs was never in the kitchen when he came," she remembered pensively. "They would eat early in the evening and then watch the telly. Yesterday, Daniel couldn't come at all. I think someone might have seen him when he came back, and that's why he didn't visit me last night. Usually, he's cautious so that our neighbours don't see him. He doesn't want Alice to hear anything before he finds a way to tell her."

"I see, Miss Goddard," McNamara said flatly.

However, the DCI didn't understand how the woman could be so blind and not see that Daniel Thompson lied to her. McNamara knew that, in principle, women had more intuition and didn't let themselves be fooled for so long.

"Now, could you tell us anything about the Reids?" he asked, returning to the subject of interest.

"Reid is a nice guy, in my opinion. He leaves for work in the morning and comes back around six in the evening every day. He doesn't go anywhere without his wife. I rarely see him in the corner pub with someone else, maybe only with Mr Graham or Mr Randall. Mrs Reid is another story altogether. She's a very indolent woman when it comes to household chores. The woman is indifferent when Mr Reid gets mad with her, and he does that almost daily. I hear she writes some stories for magazines. I think they're nonsense," Ann shrugged. "I don't talk to her, and I can't say anything about her. Alice Thompson knows her better because they spend time together," the woman said.

Then, she leaned forward and continued in a low, conspirative voice, "You know, their relationship is quite odd, in my opinion. Those two women have nothing in common," Ann shook her head.

"What about Mr Graham? What could you tell us?" McNamara asked her, a smile on his lips. He noticed that Ann liked talking about her neighbours, so he decided to ask her more questions. Even if her opinions were somewhat skewed, they still could learn some new things.

"I haven't spoken to him much," she said reluctantly. "When he moved here, he tried to make friends with me, but I didn't want to have a relationship with him. I was already with Daniel, and I'm not the girl to change men like socks," she blushed. "Now, Graham doesn't speak to me at all. My attitude might have hurt him," she shrugged. "We greet each other when we meet, and that's it. I saw him in town recently. He was together with a young woman, about twenty-two, twenty-three, and they seemed very close. I am glad he found someone… However, I don't know anything else about him."

"Do you know anything about Patsy Porter?" James asked, and the woman's face turned red with anger. She didn't like the girl and didn't try to hide it.

"She's a wicked girl, very, very wicked. I don't like this kind of girl. I was glad when she left," Ann said with a lot of heat in her voice.

"Why don't you like her?" James asked, curious to see why she became so angry suddenly.

"Patsy thinks she's the most attractive girl in the world," she flipped her hand nervously. "And she flirts with all the men of a certain age. The girl tried to charm even my Daniel, but he didn't pay any attention to her," the young woman waved her hand. "Daniel says she's just a stupid girl. She isn't even marginally as beautiful as she thinks she is," Ann explained with conviction.

The detectives didn't say anything. They wanted to keep her talking as much as possible, so they couldn't annoy her by telling her about Daniel's indiscretion. Not that it would have done any good. Ann seemed wholly hooked on the man.

"I see," McNamara said softly. Ann didn't mind talking, and he didn't want to waste such a good information resource. "Now, could you tell us something about the other neighbours of yours?" he asked kindly, intent on gathering a general idea about the people living on Nightingale Street.

"I don't talk to them much. I've got my work, and I also have Daniel. I don't need more than that. I prefer reading a book over speaking to my neighbours. I don't have anything in common with them, so...," she shrugged.

"But Miss McNeil's got a bookshop, doesn't she?" McNamara asked her, curious to hear her opinion of McNeil. "If you say you like books...."

"Aye, she does. But Bryony pretends to be very busy... She comes home very late in the evening, you know...." Ann said, then kept quiet for a few moments. She looked like she was trying to make up her mind about what she wanted to say. "I haven't spoken to her since Bryony flirted with my Daniel. She was so shameless," the young woman shook her head as if she still couldn't believe what happened. "Bryony even came to warn me that Daniel had tried to ask her to become...well, you know, his lover," Ann found her words with difficulty, clenching her hands.

She focused on something on her lap, trying to control her temper. Her face was flushed, and her eyes flashed with anger when she looked back at them.

"We were friends then, but when I heard all those lies about Daniel, I couldn't stand to talk to her. She's a very mean woman," Ann shook her head and reflected a few more moments.

The policemen watched her, trying to guess what was going on in her mind.

"I'm sure Bryony is envious of my life with Daniel, and she tried to steal him from me," the woman suddenly continued. "She's got nothing so nice in hers, as we have... And Bryony even dared to say that she came to warn me because we were friends," Ann scoffed scornfully. "What a friend, huh? I'm sure she wanted me to leave him, thinking that the way might have been free then, and she might have had a chance with him. Of course, her swindle didn't last for a second. I told Daniel everything. He was so sorry that she had upset me. Daniel told me that Bryony came onto him," Ann pointed out. "But, of course, he didn't want to have anything to do with her. He told me that I was enough for him," she nodded, stopping to breathe.

After a few more moments of silence, she continued, "Daniel didn't even find her pretty. He told me that Bryony was probably angry because he hadn't responded to her flirt, and that's why she came to me with all those lies... Of course, I believed him," Ann waved her hand. "After all, we have been together for some time, and I trust him... So you see, I can't tell you anything about her because I don't know anything about her anymore. We broke our friendship and for good. She wasn't too much of a friend. Maybe these days, she's trying to break another relationship because she doesn't have one of her own," the young woman added maliciously, turning her nose up. "Bryony is too harsh, and she's got no feminine traits, so she can't get a boyfriend for herself."

Ann's accusations rendered James speechless. He had just seen Bryony and would have said that she was one of the most feminine women he had ever seen. That woman didn't need artifices to entice a man, and indeed, she didn't seem the kind of woman who needed or wanted a man like Thompson.

"All right, Miss Goddard," McNamara said, already sick of her defending the vicious Mr Thompson. "Maybe we'll come back later or tomorrow to talk to you again. However, please, don't tell anyone that you saw something last night," he urged her.

"Of course," Ann agreed but didn't look like she would take his advice. "However, I wanted to tell only Daniel, but I haven't seen him yet. Of course, when I see him, I'll tell him," she decided. "I don't think women should hold things back from their men," Ann shook her head. "And, anyway, Daniel isn't involved in this mess. He's too kind and loving to do such a horrible thing," she flipped her hand.

"Please, don't tell him either," McNamara urged her. "It's better if no one knows. You could be in danger, you know."

The woman nodded but not convincingly. McNamara knew that she would tell her lover, and the detective didn't know what to believe of Thompson's innocence. Still, he couldn't force her to heed his warning, so he decided to propose something else. "What would you say if we put a policeman here, with you, to protect you? Overnight, I mean."

"No, no, out of the question," Ann replied vehemently. "I won't accept that. I like my privacy, and anyway, I don't think anyone would attack me." Ann thought that Daniel wouldn't come to her if he saw a policeman in the house, and she didn't want to be without him for another night.

McNamara understood it was pointless to argue with her, so he nodded, stood up, and left with James in tow.

Outside, James turned to McNamara. "I'm sure that Daniel Thompson tried to make some moves on Miss McNeil, and she didn't accept him, not the other way around. She told her friend the truth."

"Maybe," McNamara shrugged. "But she might have tried to reel Thompson in a relationship. I recall his face from last night, and he's a handsome man. Women like that kind of face," he said with sarcasm. "Besides, we know the man already has two loyal women here on this street, Goddard and his wife, and God knows how many others in town."

"Do you really think Miss McNeil would do that?" James asked him in disbelief, baffled by McNamara's assumption.

"Maybe she would," McNamara answered thoughtfully. Yet, the woman didn't seem a simpleton that men like Daniel Thompson could have wrapped around their little finger.

However, James recalled the meeting with Miss McNeil and started suspecting his boss of something else. McNamara probably liked the woman but wanted to keep his reputation as a tough man, which was a reasonable explanation for his inappropriate behaviour towards Miss McNeil.

McNamara guessed what thoughts crossed James's mind, and it bothered him. He was afraid that James wasn't far from the truth, so, disappointed in himself, the Chief Inspector scowled at James, "Stop dreaming, James. We still have a lot of work to do. I don't want any unpleasant surprises. You'd better call the police station and ask them to send two policemen for protection, one to McNeil's house and the other to Goddard's. Both constables must be here in half an hour. A policewoman will stay with McNeil in the house because I'm sure she won't be against that. She knows better. The other will guard Goddard's house at the back of those

181

trees," he pointed to the trees across from Goddard's house. "Then, we'll see if Thompson or Reid has already come home. We have to talk to them too."

James turned his eyes downward, keeping his mouth shut. The man wanted to stay on McNamara's good side, so he made the calls and followed McNamara across the street, where he knocked on the Thompsons' door.

Unfortunately, the same Mrs Thompson appeared in the doorway with a smile for the two policemen again.

"Is Mr Thompson at home, ma'am?" McNamara asked her.

"I'm afraid he isn't," the woman replied regretfully. "Daniel has just called to tell me that he would be late because he's got something urgent to solve at the office."

"Then excuse us, ma'am. Probably, we'll have to go and see him at work tomorrow," McNamara nodded with frustration, realising that they couldn't find Thompson at home early in the evening. Probably, the man returned home only around midnight.

CHAPTER NINE

The detectives headed to the Reids' house, but when they reached the door, an angry voice, belonging to a man in the climax of rage, bellowed from inside.

The detectives exchanged a swift glance, and McNamara grinned widely, guessing that they stumbled upon one of the Reids' famous quarrels, everyone talked about. They had the chance to experience it first-hand now. "Let's stop this great domestic dispute. What are you saying, James?" the Chief Inspector asked drily.

"And ruin their pleasure, sir?" James inquired, a mischievous light shining in his eyes.

"Indeed, my dear friend. Let's spoil their pleasure. Why should they have all the fun when we've had an exhausting day and two bodies on our hands?" McNamara wondered with a wink for James.

James chuckled, knowing that his boss was merely joking. Besides, he liked to see McNamara relaxed and carefree.

At the Chief's invitation, James rang the bell, and a melodious tune, in total discord with what they'd heard from the house earlier, reached their ears. The policemen looked at each other and snickered again.

Almost instantly, the shouting inside ceased. After a few seconds, a tall and solid man practically pulled the door off its hinges. He was still fuming, his face scarlet because of his rage.

"What the hell do you want?" the man asked with barely suppressed anger, staring fiercely at McNamara, instinctively labelling him as the man in charge. The man didn't even bother to spare a glance at James.

"Imagine, we're the police," McNamara answered in a quiet voice, a grin still tucked at the corner of his mouth.

"And why would you care about our personal life? Has anyone complained about our arguments?" Michael Reid asked, both furious and stunned. He knew that nobody on the street cared about what other neighbours were doing in their houses. Besides, he couldn't imagine that Randall or Thompson would pick up the phone and call the police if they were at home at that hour by any chance.

"Not really," McNamara shook his head. "No one called us for your domestic dispute. We're here on another business."

The man stared at the inspector with a blank face for a few seconds, not understanding what the detective was saying. Still trying to comprehend, Reid finally glanced at James and suddenly recalled the sergeant's face from the Dobbs' drawing-room the previous night. Slapping his forehead, the man exclaimed, "Now I get it! You've come for what happened last night. The poor girl in the Dobbs' yard," he said with compassion, and his anger subsided.

"Not only," McNamara replied, enjoying the changes in the man's demeanour.

The giant seemed puzzled, and a frown appeared between his bushy brows.

"You see, sir, Mrs Dobbs was also killed last night. We have questions on both matters," McNamara waved his hand, deciding to help the man, whose emotions played openly on his face.

The man wasn't good at hiding what he felt or thought, and obviously, the news surprised him.

"Hasn't your wife told you anything about that, sir?" the DCI asked Reid, lifting a brow inquiringly.

"She didn't have a chance," the man confessed, mumbling somewhat contritely, and the detectives assumed that Reid had started his argument as soon as he had got home.

"Aye, I see," McNamara replied scathingly, his upper lip lifting in a sneer. "You've been in quite a hurry to start your favourite domestic activity, sir," he shook his head. "You didn't give your wife a chance to tell you anything."

Michael Reid blushed intensely but couldn't refute McNamara's words. Yet, he knew that the policeman wasn't allowed to speak to him that way, but the man felt ashamed, so he showed the detectives inside without another word.

McNamara and James followed him into the living room, where Mary Reid sat on the sofa, browsing a magazine peacefully as if nothing had happened. She didn't seem to share her husband's embarrassment.

"Would you like tea or coffee?" she stood gracefully, leaving the magazine on the coffee table.

"Anything you want to drink, Mrs Reid, will be welcome," McNamara answered courteously, with a slight nod, even though he preferred coffee. Tea wasn't so bad, either.

"I think I would like to have some coffee," the woman mentioned, reading the detective's mood.

She sashayed out of the room, followed by her husband's fierce eyes.

Michael Reid burnt with jealousy, feeling that his wife showed more kindness to the policemen than she had for him. Focused on his wife's exits, he didn't notice the detectives' looks.

Both McNamara and James had noted her kindness and that the woman didn't make her offer just to be polite. Mary Reid played a dangerous game: riling her husband.

Indeed, the woman loved to see the steely chips in her husband's eyes whenever she teased him. She knew that he wasn't a violent man, so playing with him only made life more enjoyable. The young woman turned her head to Michael right before stepping into the hallway with a roguish smile to show her husband she knew what he was thinking.

Reid grounded his teeth, and McNamara's brows shot up. The detective bit his lower lip to suppress a chuckle. Dumbfounded, James widened his eyes, wondering if such a relationship could be called love. The daft woman liked yanking the man's chain, and the sergeant couldn't understand why the Reids loved to torment each other.

McNamara waved to the sofa and armchairs, throwing an inquiring glance to Reid. The man shook his thoughts and invited them to sit.

"We spoke with your wife this morning," McNamara told Michael Reid while taking a seat in an armchair. The detective wasn't so sure that Reid wouldn't act violently, despite what Randall had said. He wanted to chase away the murderous thoughts reflected in the man's eyes.

"And did you learn anything interesting?" Reid asked with sarcasm, sitting in the opposite armchair.

James had no other choice but to sit on the sofa. He refused to imagine what their host would do when his wife returned to the room and sat next to him.

"I'd be amazed," Michael continued with a snicker. "As far as I know, my wife does nothing else but sit in front of that damn computer all day long. At night, once she falls asleep, you need the entire artillery to wake her up."

"No, we didn't," McNamara admitted with a nod. Yet, the DCI knew that they hadn't learnt anything because he hadn't been able to ask Mary Reid anything. He had been excessively amused at the Reids' expense, but it wouldn't have been a good idea to tell Reid. So, with a broad gesture, he preferred to say, "But maybe we'll hear from you. What could you tell us about the previous night?"

"Not much," Michael shrugged. "I heard that brutal scream and woke up... That scream made my blood run cold," he shook his head. "Anyway, I put on my bathrobe and went out. I understood that a woman was screaming, which shocked the hell out of me. Women are safe around here, normally. I haven't heard of any attack so far. We chose this area because of that," he opened his arms.

"Was there anyone else outside when you came out? Neighbours or unknown people?"

"The neighbour — Thompson. I think he had just arrived home. He still had that damn tie around his neck. Then his wife came out, and the others. I can't tell you in what order. What I saw in the yard across the street shocked me, so I didn't pay much attention to the other people. I only know I noticed Mr Dobbs a few seconds before he fainted or had a heart attack, better said."

"Mr Thompson called the doctor, didn't he? Does he know him well?" James inquired.

"Well, Alice Thompson always thinks she's got a disease or another," Reid gesticulated. "I think it's a tactic to draw her husband's attention.

189

She doesn't seem sick, in my opinion. She's just in a sort of rut," the man shrugged.

"And does she succeed in drawing his attention with her tactics?" McNamara asked with curiosity.

"Not really," Reid admitted grudgingly. "The truth is that guy is a Casanova," he said, opening his arms again. "All day long, I see him with all sorts of women, and all of them younger than him, almost half his age. He's got a fixation," he shrugged, showing little interest in Thompson's affairs.

"I see," McNamara said. "And do you often happen to see him?"

"Not very often. Once or twice a week I must go to the architect's office. Sometimes I have lunch with him in town. On such occasions, I also see Thompson. Once, we found ourselves in the same restaurant. When I was about to leave, he came after me. Man to man, he asked me that I didn't say anything to his wife. As if I'd been going to run immediately to tell on him," Reid scowled with derision. "The guy is plain stupid if you ask me," he concluded with a snort.

Meanwhile, Mary returned with the coffee and a cup of tea for her husband, whose eyes widened.

"Has something happened?" McNamara asked, leaning forward. The DCI wondered if Mary had placed something in the cup. Maybe a bug. It wouldn't have been farfetched.

"No. Not really," Michael answered evasively, shaking his head.

"I think that my husband is just a bit perplexed right now, detective and can't answer you. I rarely take his preferences into account, you know. And now, here I recalled that he prefers tea. That shocked you, right, love?" she turned to Michael with a devilish smile.

The man closed his eyes with dismay. Mary managed to spoil everything for him. And the fool in him still hoped that his wife would show him a real sign of affection one day. He should have believed his wife when she had told him that, if he married her, he only asked for trouble. Yet, it hadn't been easy to forget his feelings for her, and he had taken a risk. Now, he had to go through with it to the bitter end, at least not to give Mary the satisfaction to run him away, as she always said she would.

Watching him, Mary felt a tinge of regret. She didn't know why she was so determined to annoy Michael. The woman didn't see the point in changing her ways, as she knew well that men weren't steadfast. At least, that way, Michael would understand that leaving her wouldn't be a significant loss. Nevertheless, Mary always felt acute loneliness at the thought of Michael's going away, which reflected in her eyes.

Michael didn't know what hurt her but felt her pain in his heart. One couldn't care about someone as much as he cared for her and not feel their anxieties. The man grasped her hand, his fingers lacing around hers.

McNamara had recognised the look in Mary's eyes. His mother used to look like that whenever she would remember his father's betrayal. He tried to shake off the unpleasant deja-vu and come back to his questions. "Did you see anything after the police left last night?"

Michael felt as if someone shook his shoulder when he was dozing off. McNamara's voice pulled him from contemplating his wife, but he didn't understand the question. Mary had heard him perfectly, though.

"I told you I saw nothing. Michael was furious and accusing, so I couldn't pay attention to anything else but his voice. I think he bellowed louder than just now, didn't you, love? "

Michael blushed again. "No," Michael said after a few moments of silence. "I didn't hear anything, and, as my lovely wife has just remarked," he added sharply, glancing at her, "I was busy with something else. I'm sorry, inspector, but I don't see how I could help you. I don't know the people on this street very well, even though we've lived here for quite some time. We greet each other as neighbours, but nothing more. We don't visit each other or anything like that. We either go out by ourselves, my colleagues, or Mary's friend from college."

McNamara looked at Mary, and she agreed with her husband's words. "Aye, that's true. The only one I talk to is Alice Thompson, but I don't talk much to her, either. I'd like to make friends with the girl living in the house next door to Mrs Stevens. Bryony, I think her name is. But she's always at work and doesn't socialise either. Of course, we all know the Randalls from the grocer's... That woman is awful," Mary grimaced. "She's got her mouth in a tight and thin line. The woman is awfully moralising. At least, she despised me from the very beginning. I don't know how her husband stands her, but I don't think he has a choice. I understand that everything belongs to her."

"The Browns are nicer," her husband continued when she stopped. "We go to them to the pub now and then. They're kind, nice people. However, we don't visit with them or anything, either."

"All right," McNamara said and stood up. "If you remember that something unusual happened in the area or to your neighbours, call me. Here's my card," he gave his card to Michael.

CHAPTER TEN

The constable hid in the darkness, cursing the storm, which had been raging for some time. The man was cold, and the hot coffee in the thermos didn't help much, even though his guard had started only at midnight, half an hour before. The young policeman felt that hours had passed, and dampness had sunk into his pores despite his thick raincoat. He lit a cigarette, concealing it in his palm so that no one could see it.

The man grumbled under his beard, upset that 'that stupid woman' had refused a guard in the house. Otherwise, he could have been warm, like McKay, not out in the rain and wind.

A twig cracked behind him, and the policeman snapped out of his distracting thoughts, listening intently. Turning his eyes in the direction from where the crack came, he took a few silent steps, but something hit the back of his head. The pain shot deep in his skull. A subtle scent of aftershave and mint chewing gum tickled his nostrils for a few seconds. The man collapsed on the wet ground, enveloped in the smell of wet leaves and faded grass.

***

The wind hit the window. The whistling noise startled the woman, and she turned to look outside. The storm raged intensely, and the lightning slashed the night and hurt her eyes. Irritating, raindrops hit the roof rhythmically. Cold seeped into her bones, making her shiver.

Ann laid the magazine on the night table to close the window in the next room. She remembered that she had forgotten about it and was content that the glass hadn't broken.

Getting inside the room, the young woman turned the switch on. The light blinded her for a second. Ann blinked a couple of times before striding to the window, where she stopped, watching the night for a while.

The pounding rain brought an ominous feeling of sadness and loneliness. The woman felt the burden of her age, and her aunt Martha's words came to her mind, 'You didn't get married by twenty-eight, let's say thirty, a spinster you'll stay. No one will take you. You'll be like me: old and a burden in other people's houses.'

It was the first time Ann felt some doubt. What the heck was she thinking about getting entangled in a relationship with a married man? Daniel promised to divorce Alice and marry her, but what if those were only words in the wind? At least Graham was free when he approached her, but she didn't know if he was serious, either.

Ann shook the dark thoughts away and tried to regain some of her earlier self-confidence. Daniel wouldn't cheat or lie to her. He must have loved her and would marry her.

The man had just repeated that a few hours earlier when he visited, more loving than ever. Daniel worried for her when Ann told him what she had seen the night before. He implored her not to say anything to anyone. He feared the killer might want to kill her and swore that he couldn't live without her, which touched her heart.

Ann smiled, recalling that Daniel looked so sincere that her heart grew warm at that memory even then. The young woman felt appreciated, wanted, and needed.

She threw a last look out the window, deciding to go back to her bedroom. Out in the hallway, something seemed wrong. Confused, the woman looked up and practically jumped out of her skin. The light had gone out, and she knew it wasn't her doing.

Fear seeped into her mind. The switch was on the wall at the other end of the corridor, but that looked like miles away. Ann started shaking, her heart beating quickly, nearly jumping out of her chest. Her legs turned to jelly, and panicked, the woman remembered the policeman's warning and Daniel's words.

The woman had talked about it, damn it. She had told Mrs Reid about what she saw, and Graham also heard her as he was passing by. Earlier that day, she had also told Alison Randall.

Ann thought of going to the study to grab a vase or something so that she would have a weapon of sorts. The woman regretted not having accepted a policeman to guard her, but she had done it because of Daniel. The man wouldn't have come to visit her if someone had been there.

Ann clenched her fists with anxiety. Then, she left her slippers behind not to make a noise. On the way to the other end of the landing, the woman had to pass by her bedroom, and the lightning struck the half-open door, which Ann had left wide open. Her heart cringed.

The woman prayed not to die, and with a shaky hand, she pushed the door open slowly.

The silhouette in the shadow waited, ready to attack. The door moved slowly, yet adrenaline ran through the intruder's veins faster. A muscular hand raised, and the lightning reflected in the blade, driven down with force. Thunder ripped through the night, covering Ann's soft scream when she fell to her knees. The woman clung to life and turned her head. The black mask confused her, but then, she recognised the eyes and the mouth.

Her lips uttered a stunned, mute no. The darkness descended in her mind, erasing thoughts and memories. Her last thought echoed in the emptiness, 'It can't be you!'

Before the dark covered her eyes, the criminal knew the young woman had recognised him. His fingers itched, tempted to close her eyes, but the man controlled himself. He couldn't make mistakes.

He left Ann lying on her rose-decorated carpet, blood-red now, and snuck out. He still had one more problem to solve that night.

***

The constable struggled to open his eyes. Pain pounded in his head with the force of ten drums when the lightning reached his pupils. The man lowered his eyelids for a few more seconds with a groan, tightening his teeth. Then, he attempted to open his eyes again, but slowly.

The young man touched the top of his head gingerly, getting his fingers wet and sticky, and he realised that his hair was matted with blood. The constable tried to stand up and got dizzy but still tried to think and understand what he needed to do. Then he remembered that his mobile phone was in his pocket and dialled McNamara's number with shaky fingers, terrified. The man knew what was going to happen.

The ringing drilled into the man's brain, making him groan again, and he rubbed his temples in a half-hearted effort to ease the throbbing pain.

"McNamara," the DCI's voice barked in his ear, and the man's mouth went dry instantly. He couldn't say anything for a few seconds. The constable knew the Chief Inspector and didn't doubt that he was in trouble now.

"McEwan, is that you? Answer now, damn it!" McNamara boomed, irritated that nothing else but a man's heavy breathing came from the other end of the line.

"A... aye," McEwan stuttered. "It's me, sir."

"What happened?" McNamara barked again. He wasn't a patient man on a good day, but that hadn't been a good day.

His voice warned McEwan that his boss's famous short patience had just run out. Everyone was aware of McNamara's legendary temper, and the people in the department knew not to anger him. Messing things up drove him mad the most.

"I've been hit, sir," the constable whispered, his voice hardly heard.

"What the hell?" McNamara bellowed. "What were you doing, McEwan? Sleeping? Why did I send you there?"

"He... he hit me from behind, sir," McEwan stuttered again, propping his head with his hand. His boss's shouts had penetrated his skull like a knife. "I didn't hear him, sir," he explained.

"What kind of a policeman are you?" McNamara shouted again, showing no compassion for the constable's sorry state.

McEwan squeezed his eyes tighter when the sharp shouts pierced his throbbing brain again. "No, sir. I'm sorry, sir, but the storm... You know," he tried to excuse himself.

"All right, all right," McNamara said. "At least, have you gone to see Goddard? Is she alive?"

"I know you'll be very angry with me, sir," the constable said, almost sobbing. "But I can't stand up... My head's spinning, sir. I don't think I'll be conscious for long. No, I haven't checked on Goddard," he finally remembered to answer the DCI's question.

"All right, stay there and don't stand up," McNamara admitted defeat. "I'll send James to you with Mike and Jo. I'll also come," he said, disconnecting the call just in time because McEwan slipped to the ground unconscious, despite the cold rain splashing his face.

CHAPTER ELEVEN

The man watched from the back of McNeil's house. The police had chosen not to use the sirens this time, looking to surprise. They couldn't surprise him. He scoffed.

DS James got out of the car and headed to the trees where McEwan was lying on the ground. A man and a woman got out of the other vehicle, looking around, but they didn't see the murderer. James switched on his flashlight to search for his colleague.

The sergeant finally spotted McEwan under a tree and bent to verify the man's pulse. It was weak, but it was steady enough to feel it. James shook McEwan but couldn't wake him up, so the DS looked at the top of the man's head to discover that his wound was severe and needed an ambulance. James dialled 999 to call for one and remained with the constable, surveying the other detectives' actions.

Mike Johnson and Jo Critchet strode purposefully to Goddard's house, where Jo rang the bell and waited. As no one answered, the woman rang once more, holding the button for a longer time that second time around. The house kept obstinately silent and dark.

"I'm going to the back door, Mike," Jo announced. "Stay here. Count to twenty and then break the door if you don't hear anything from me."

Mike nodded and put himself in position. On the count of twenty, the man broke inside, and at the same time, Jo attacked the back door, which splintered, echoing the noise coming from the front door.

Jo sneaked carefully along the corridor until she met Mike in front of the stairs.

"Everything's all right there," Mike whispered, pointing with his thumb to the left.

"All right, let's go upstairs," Jo whispered in turn, and they tiptoed up the stairs.

The entire floor was shadowed, as the killer had also turned off the light in the bedroom. The inspectors reached the bedroom, and the lightning slashed the room's darkness, showing that the door was open.

Jo snuck inside first, and her foot touched something. She leaned in carefully, and her fingers felt the place next to her foot. When she touched the delicate and still slightly warm hand, she understood they found Ann Goddard.

"Mike, the woman's here," Jo whispered at first. "I think you should turn on your flashlight so we can see inside. The bird has already flown the cage," she said in a normal voice.

Mike turned on his flashlight and looked over Jo's head to the woman on the floor. Ann had fallen on her stomach, her head turned to the side. The tense expression of her face betrayed the terror she had felt before death. The inspector searched for the light switcher and pushed it using his sleeve, not to leave prints. "Do you want to call it in, or should I?" Mike asked Jo.

"You do it," Jo replied with a tinge of tiredness in her voice. "I don't feel like explaining the crime scene right now."

The young woman disliked that aspect of her work. She liked gathering information and building up a case, discovering causes and motives. Evidently, she felt an enormous joy in catching the criminals, but she hated to look at victims. Their faces had the bad habit of haunting her for days.

"Talk to me, Mike," McNamara's voice thundered over the line.

"We found Goddard, sir. I think she's been stabbed twice. I haven't touched her, of course. Anyway, she's dead," Mike explained, and the line went silent. The inspector didn't push for an answer but waited patiently, knowing that his boss loathed losing a witness.

"All right," McNamara's answer came after a few moments. "Stay where you are. I'll come now. I'll call the prosecutor and the coroner. You call the forensics," he ordered.

"Very well, sir," Mike replied, but McNamara had already hung up.

CHAPTER TWELVE

Bryony stood and winced when her stiff muscles complained. She stretched and then turned off her laptop, tired to the bones. The rain pounding on the roof tiles encouraged her to go to bed.

The woman strode to the window and looked outside for a few moments, trying to distinguish something in the dark, but nothing seemed to move. She didn't notice the silhouette hidden in the corner of the house by the tree, watching her. A few minutes later, she left the room and turned off the light.

Bryony sauntered into the kitchen where the constable, Claire McKay, was browsing a magazine. A pile of magazines was stashed on the table in front of her. The young policewoman had brought them to keep her awake over the night. When Bryony came in, Claire looked up.

"Haven't you gone to bed yet, Miss?" she inquired.

"No, I've had some work to do," Bryony waved her hand. "I'll go to bed now, though. But I think we agreed not to be so formal," the young woman smiled at the constable.

"I know," Claire said, returning the smile. "But it isn't easy to get used to that. Not everyone is as kind as you are. Usually, we get a different treatment," she shrugged.

"Really? I'm sorry to hear that. I'd have thought that people would appreciate your effort," Bryony replied, raising her brows. "You defend their lives, after all, don't you?"

"Aye, we do, but they aren't always aware of that," Claire smiled wryly. "For instance, two months ago, I had a nightmare of a night. I had to stay with an older lady, and I had no peace at all," she shook her head bitterly. "It was so uncomfortable. The woman watched me continuously like a hawk, afraid that I would steal from her. You should have heard some of the things she said," she tossed her head in disbelief.

Bryony remained silent for a moment, too stunned to form words. Then, she burst into laughter. "It can't be! You must be joking. You were representing the police. How could you steal from her?"

"Oh, aye, it can!" Claire answered, amused. "The woman stated that there weren't any honest people left in this world, and she couldn't be cautious enough. She didn't trust anyone, and especially the police."

"I see," Bryony replied flatly, even though she found it absurd. She shook her head dumbfounded. "Would you like some more tea?" she decided to ask the constable.

"Don't bother. I'll make it," Claire replied. "You seem tired. You'd better go to bed."

"If you want to make it yourself, it would be great. I feel run down. It's tough to run a business alone, no matter how small it is," Bryony pursed her lips.

"I believe you. I couldn't do it. I think I wouldn't have enough courage to take the risk. Now you'd better go to bed, love. Good night," Claire waved her out of the kitchen, smiling.

"Good night. If you need anything, you're free to look in the fridge or cupboards, anywhere," Bryony said with a grin as she left.

Bryony tiptoed to Mrs Stevens room and knocked softly on the door, but no one answered. Although she disliked invading someone's privacy, she pushed the door open to make sure that everything was all right. For a few moments, she watched the old woman, who had fallen asleep with the light on the night table turned on. Bryony shook her head, knowing that the woman had had a difficult evening with much pain. Then, she stepped back, closing the door behind.

She went upstairs to her room. She was exhausted and didn't bother to turn on the light but took off her robe and slipped under the blanket, closing her eyes with relief. Despite her weariness, the young woman couldn't fall asleep quickly. Bryony was too fatigued. Lots of thoughts raced through her brain, and she couldn't focus on only one.

First, she thought of Mrs Stevens, sleeping in her drawing-room downstairs, and of her aches. Then, she thought of Claire, downstairs, in the kitchen, browsing her magazines and guarding them. Bryony shook her head with dismay remembering the woman Claire had told her about. Next, McNamara's face popped into her mind. The man had annoyed her, but the young woman couldn't stop a smile perching on her lips when she thought of him. The DCI was an arresting man. No other had caught her eye for a while. Of course, she had to like exactly the one she couldn't do anything about.

When Bryony thought she would fall asleep, a muffled thud from downstairs reached her ears. The woman merely shrugged, too tired to get out of bed and see what it was.

She assumed that Claire would take care of everything. But then, a door slammed against the wall, and Bryony couldn't imagine that the constable had started to make a racket in her house at night.

Although afraid, the young woman got out of bed and rushed to the door barefoot. Her mind searched frantically for something to use as a weapon, but she had nothing like that at hand in the house. Maybe just the knives in the kitchen, but Bryony supposed that the kitchen might have already been out of bounds, so she forgot about getting a knife.

The young woman looked around anxiously when she remembered the scissors on the shelf in the bathroom. On tiptoe and barely breathing, Bryony slipped into the bathroom and searched for the scissors with the tip of her fingers, afraid that she would drop something, alerting the intruder. When her fingers touched the scissors, she grabbed them with a relieved sigh.

Then, the woman snuck downstairs, holding her breath and listening intently when she reached the bottom of the stairs. Her hand went ice-cold on the scissors, her shaky fingers tightening on the metal, afraid that she would drop them. A distinct gasp came from the kitchen, so she started that way. However, a creak on the opposite side of the hallway, where Mrs Steven was sleeping, stopped her.

Bryony knew that she couldn't do anything in the kitchen, so she decided to look at her neighbour. The woman tiptoed, as fast as she could, trying to remember which part of the floor creaked, and she reached the room without any incident.

The young woman leaned against the doorframe, the emotion seizing her breath. She leaned in for a closer look and noticed the silhouette of a man advancing, already halfway through the room.

The man looked like he was keeping an ear out for any sounds, and apparently, the lack of noise appeased him. In an instant, he closed the distance to the bed. The little light in the room reflected on the blade in his hand. At the sight of the sharp edge, Bryony rushed forward, forgetting everything about keeping quiet. However, she was unsure that her legs would support her.

The woman didn't think she would have time to reason with the intruder. She knew he would stab her friend in a few seconds, so Bryony didn't think of anything else but struck quickly. The man didn't even have the time to turn entirely. The scissors pierced his shoulder, and he screamed in agony. The knife fell from his fingers and rolled under the bed. Yet Bryony dashed again.

MCNAMARA SERIES BOX SET
BOOK 0NE & TWO

CHAPTER THIRTEEN

"Go and check on Mrs Stevens, James. McKay isn't answering," McNamara said harshly, afraid that something had happened at the McNeill house. Otherwise, the constable would have answered his call. She knew better than that.

The Sergeant started to McNeil's house without saying a word. Still, he had hardly taken a few steps, that McNamara stomped behind him, livid with fury.

"I'd better come with you," the DCI explained briefly, matching James's stride.

The younger man just nodded. Another time, he would have smiled, knowing why McNamara had decided to come along. But he couldn't now, being so afraid for McKay. Claire was a good girl, maybe too good for that job. Fear lengthened his stride, and McNamara could hardly keep up.

If the Chief Inspector hadn't been deep in his own thoughts, he would have noticed that

something was going on with James. But
McNamara tried to assure himself that what
happened at Goddard's house didn't necessarily
occur at McNeil's. Still, the man worried because
the criminal had become too bold and hadn't
been shy about striking a policeman. Now the
killer could murder one.

McNamara reached out to ring the bell when
the door opened in his face, and Bryony appeared
in the doorway, stepping out onto the porch.

Her strawberry hair was dishevelled, and her
eyes shifted around frantically, searching
something or maybe someone along the street.
Although they were right under her nose, it took
the woman a few seconds to notice the
policemen.

Stunned, the men stared at her in disbelief.
The lass's face was paper white, and an ugly
bruise was taking shape on her right cheek while
blood trickled down from her nose and from the
corner of her swollen lip.

The young woman didn't recognise them at
first. A weak smile flickered on her lips when she
did, but her busted lip hurt, and she whimpered,
lifting a shaky hand to McNamara, who was still
in shock. Bryony tried to say something but
couldn't because of the knot in her throat, afraid
not to burst into tears.

The man couldn't reconcile the vulnerable and pleading woman before his eyes with that afternoon's slightly ironical and spiritual lass. However, he grasped her hand and squeezed her fingers, trying to transfer some of his strength to the woman. The lass finally pulled herself together and squared her shoulders.

Bryony started talking in a raspy voice, which echoed through McNamara's blood, reminding him of forgotten sensations. The words tumbled one after the other, and the men had to make an effort to keep up with them.

"How did you know to come? My phone's dead. I think he cut the line first. I'm afraid I hurt him badly. I think I stabbed him. But, really, I couldn't do otherwise. Oh, and Claire's on the floor in the kitchen, I'm afraid. She hasn't recovered yet. She's still unconscious and hurt."

The woman looked in pain, but she kept talking. She needed to voice her concerns, and the men discerned the despair in her voice.

"Shush, now," McNamara tried to soothe her. "Let's go inside."

The woman noticed that the storm was still raging, and the men were soaking wet. She stepped back to let them inside.

"Come on," McNamara said, always holding her hand. "Let's go inside and see to everything.

Once the door closed behind them, the DCI threw an arm around her shoulders, pulling her on his side. He looked into her eyes and asked, "You said you hit him?"

"With scissors. I stabbed the man in the shoulder first," Bryony's voice trembled, and the woman shivered again when she remembered everything. Nausea lodged into her throat, and she suddenly broke free from McNamara's embrace. Surprisingly steady on her feet, she ran to the bathroom, hardly getting to the bowl, before throwing up.

Her dash had surprised McNamara, so the man remained behind, staring after the woman. Only after a few seconds, he understood what happened and felt sorry for her.

"Sir, I will see what McKay's doing," James said in a tense voice. "Shall I call the forensics?"

"Aye," McNamara answered absently. But then, he glanced sideways at James, and something on the Sergeant's face made him change his decision. Even if his men believed the DCI was focused only on the job, the man still noticed other things. He knew James needed to do something else before making any calls.

"Forget about it. I'll call the forensics," the Chief Inspector decided, waving his hand. "You'd better go and see to McKay. "

The Sergeant nodded briefly, relief etched on his face. The young man didn't think he could have waited anymore. He hurried into the kitchen, leaving McNamara alone in the hallway.

McNamara headed to the room prepared for Mrs Stevens, and relieved, he noticed the old lady was sleeping like a log. Her breathing was heavy but steady. A few snores made his lips twitch, and the man thought that the old woman had probably taken something to sleep or for the pain.

The DCI looked around the room, shaking his head. A chair lay knocked down, and moonlight reflected in a blood pool near the bed, where the bloody scissors lay. His eyes fell on the scissors, and Bryony's devastated face appeared in his mind.

"I'm sorry," Bryony's voice came from behind. "I couldn't stop myself."

McNamara turned and looked at her. The woman seemed to recover little by little and didn't have that lost look anymore.

"Did your friend sleep all this time?" the man asked, baffled.

"Mrs Stevens had some awful pains this evening," Bryony said. "You know, when it rains, her aches become more intense. So, she took some stronger painkillers and a sleeping pill.

Otherwise, she wouldn't have slept," the young woman explained.

"I hope you realise that I must wake her up. The forensic team must come to collect the evidence," McNamara waved his hand to encompass the entire room. Still, he kept his eyes on the young woman. He couldn't believe that she had recovered so much. Bryony might have seemed fragile but had a lot of strength.

"Of course... I mean... I think so," Bryony stammered. "I'll try to wake her up," she headed to the bed.

"Take care not to disturb the scene too much," McNamara warned her, taking his phone out of his pocket. "I need it the way it is."

Bryony nodded and leaned over Mrs Stevens, shaking her and calling her name reassuringly. The woman knew it was vital that the police could do their job. She, for one, didn't intend to let that intruder get off the hook after everything he had done, especially after he had forced her to hurt him.

CHAPTER FOURTEEN

Steven, a massive man, said, "Lads, Georgie and I are going to Miss McNeil's house, a little down the street. It seems to have been a circus there, too. Bloody night!" the man exclaimed angrily. "Tom, Lisa, and Joe, you remain here and collect every bit of evidence," he said, packing his kit carefully. Taking his gloves off, he crumpled them and threw them in a plastic bag prepared for that. Then, the man waved to Georgie to come with him.

The two men exited the house, and Steven took his cigarettes out of his pocket. He lit one, protecting the flame of the lighter with his hand. The wind still blew, even though the rain had stopped. After the first smoke, Steven looked up at the sky and noticed it was clear.

"Steven, do you think we have another body there?" Georgie asked, slightly chilled by the night's air, rubbing his hands.

"I hope not," Steven replied, smoking eagerly. "I've heard McKay was in the house. I hope nothing happened to the lass. I don't know what James would do. I've seen them together in town, and they seem fond of each other. The Chief didn't seem as tense as he is when he has a body on his hands, and he didn't say anything about the coroner, either."

They passed by the yellow tape surrounding the Dobbs' house. In front of the McNeil house, Steven finished his cigarette, put it out, and threw it in a small bag.

"Bad habit," the man said, knowing that his friend wholly approved. "I know I have to give up, Georgie," he surprised Georgie's accusing look. "Don't bother me, too. I have a wife for that. Come on inside."

The men went through the unlocked door into the hallway, where Steven looked for McNamara.

"Where to, boss?" Steven called out, not seeing the detective around.

"Over here, Steven," the answer came from somewhere on the right side of the house, so the two men headed down the corridor to the room from where McNamara's voice came. When they reached the door, a young woman came out of the room, carefully leading an older woman with a walking stick. As they passed by the forensic experts, the young woman greeted them with a warm smile, despite the awful way she looked.

"Good evening, gentlemen," she said quietly, but Steven and Georgie were so surprised that they couldn't answer. Usually, they didn't meet such polite people in their line of work.

McNamara's angry voice interrupted their contemplation. "Are you coming inside, lads, or will you stare after her until the cows come home?"

"Now, sir," Steven's rushed answer came. Noticing the blood on the carpet, he asked, "Where's the body, sir?"

"Fortunately, no one was killed here," McNamara replied harshly. "Most of the blood you see is the killer's."

"And he's still alive? With all that blood, that must have been some wound. Who did it?"

"The young lady you just passed. With those scissors over there," McNamara pointed to them. He had left them in the exact spot where they had fallen.

"Brave girl, sir," murmured Georgie in his beard.

"Brave, but no brains," McNamara replied sharply. "She should have gone out for help, not fight a guy with a knife in his hand," the DCI snapped, looking at the disaster on the floor. "But what's done is done," he said drily. "Do your job, gentlemen. I'm going to talk to the lass and see how everything went down."

"We need at least one or two other people for the exterior," Steven said thoughtfully. "Georgie, call them while I'm taking a look around."

***

McNamara headed to the kitchen, where the Sergeant had succeeded in bringing McKay around. Now the Sergeant looked at her head, and his hand shook. The policewoman groaned in pain. Dried blood matted her hair, and her face lost any colour. McNamara studied the woman's eyes, which were glassy, the sign of a bad concussion.

Claire could hardly keep her eyes open. It looked like her chest had sustained a severe wound, which McNamara couldn't see, but the bleeding didn't stop. The DCI feared that the constable had lost too much blood already.

"Have you called an ambulance?" McNamara asked James, aware that only in a hospital they would keep McKay.

"Aye, sir! I told them that we had two people hurt. I thought Miss McNeil should be seen to, as well. She doesn't look as bad as Claire, but she doesn't look too good either," the Sergeant explained.

Nodding, McNamara agreed with him and then turned to Bryony, who was just coming into the kitchen. The young woman kept her back straight, trying to smile at Mrs Stevens, whom she had helped to sit on one of the chairs at the table earlier. The old woman was dozing, still under the influence of the pills. Now, Bryony brought her a sweater to put around her shoulders to protect the older woman from the night's chill. Pain smouldered in Bryony's eyes. Her hand throbbed now and then, and the smile on her lips looked forced.

"Would you like some tea?" the woman asked the policemen. "I know I'd like some," she said, turning to the stove.

"Sit down," McNamara said harshly, almost ready to make her sit forcefully. "I'll make that bloody tea if you need one," he snapped, standing up to go to the stove.

"What happened?" Bryony asked quietly, thinking that the man might calm then.

"Nothing," McNamara replied, but his eyes contradicted his own words. "Whoever tamed you, tamed you well," he continued.

"What do you mean?" Bryony asked, a little hurt, rubbing her temples, as the throbbing in her head had worsened, and she had the feeling that her head would explode soon. The young woman recognised the signs from the beginning of a migraine, which she hated. She didn't have migraines often, but the headaches lasted for days when they came. That was the last thing she needed right then.

"I think you would offer us tea even if you were the one lying on the kitchen floor instead of McKay," the DCI noted. "You won't ask for help and have someone else make it," he shook his head in dismay.

McNamara avoided her eyes artfully, afraid not to read something else than pain there. The man knew he had been mean. However, he couldn't refrain when she looked like that.

The silence, a spring, ready to pop loose and hit everyone, grew unnaturally long and intense in the room, and Mrs Stevens' heavy breathing didn't help things either.

"You'd better tell me what happened," McNamara demanded in a matter-of-fact voice, without looking at her. He waited for a few moments, but no answer came, and his brows climbed onto his forehead. The man turned around, staring at Bryony. Her eyes told him that the stubborn lass merely refused to speak. The Chief Inspector held her gaze for a while, but, despite her exhaustion, Bryony didn't turn her eyes away. Neither of them wanted to lose the battle of wills.

Wide-eyed, the people in the room glanced from Bryony to McNamara and back, aware that something was happening but not knowing what.

Bryony understood that McNamara intended to make her yield. The young woman wouldn't have but knew that what she had to say was more important than their childish game.

Still holding his gaze, Bryony started speaking, and McNamara turned to the stove, a grin on his lips. He got her message. Nevertheless, the inspector knew that the lass was going to talk. A responsible person, she wouldn't have persisted in her stubbornness when more important things came first. It was still difficult for her to speak, but she went on.

"After stabbing him with the scissors in the shoulder, I pulled them out fast. I couldn't afford to lose them... Then the knife fell from his hand. I think I heard it hitting the floor... Then, he slapped me with the back of his hand. He threw me down, and I think I hit my right hand because it hurt terribly. It hurts right now," the young woman said, trying to move her hand with ease, but failing. "Then the man jumped on me", she shook the memories off with horror... "He tried to strangle me... I hit him with the scissors again but in his arm this time. The intruder punched me ... To be honest, I think I blacked out for a few moments... I started to regain consciousness when he tried to pry the scissors from my fingers... I lifted my knee and hit him in... you know... his groin... hard. He bellowed and slapped me again... Then, he scrambled off me with difficulty. I noticed that he was in pain. I clenched the scissors tighter, but the man went out the window."

"You must have seen his face because it was some light in the room, wasn't it?" asked McNamara, turning off the stove once the water boiled.

"Aye, the night light was on. But I couldn't see his face. He wore a ski mask."

McNamara grew angry, cursing the missed chance to solve their case. However, the man calmed down and only then turned back to the woman.

"Still, I think you can tell me something about the attacker, he insisted."

Bryony felt his frustration and regretted that she couldn't say more to help him. The guy hadn't even talked. "It was a man, and I'm not saying that because of the stature and body shape. You understand, I hope," she blushed slightly. "When he … he came over me, I …. I felt he was a man," she stuttered.

She drank a little of the tea McNamara put in front of her to mask her expression, embarrassed and not knowing how to hide it.

Mrs Stevens had awoken during Bryony's speech and listened to everything she said. Now, she looked at the young woman worriedly. "I hope he didn't do anything else to you," she said harshly.

"Oh, no," Bryony denied vehemently. "I don't think he had such intentions. He wanted only to kill me."

"The eyes, you must have seen his eyes," intervened the Sergeant.

"I was too scared and busy trying to stay alive," came her dry answer.

James blushed with embarrassment, knowing that the girl had been alone with a criminal, and no one protected her even though the police had placed someone in her house.

"They were hazel or brown," Bryony said quickly, suddenly realising what James was thinking. She knew that no one was guilty of what had happened. "I'm not sure, though," she added.

"No problem, I'm sure. Later, you might recall," Mrs Stevens petted her hand to soothe her.

"Has McKay regained consciousness?" McNamara asked James, glossing over the moment. Nevertheless, the DCI doubted that McKay would recover, considering the bleeding. She might have had a chance if they had taken her to a hospital in time.

But the Sergeant didn't have the time to answer. An ambulance siren distracted them, and soon enough, the paramedics rushed in with a gurney.

"We have two women hurt," McNamara informed them. "A policewoman and a civil. The policewoman is in a worse condition, though."

One team dashed to McKay, who was still unconscious. The towel pressed on the chest wound was already soaked in blood. The other team checked on Bryony, whose eyes had a glassy shine. Physical and mental exhaustion marred the features of the otherwise young and energetic woman, whose fingers shook on the cup now.

CHAPTER FIFTEEN

The tech people had already placed Ann Goddard in a bag and pulled the zipper, covering her face. The coroner had finished his work at the scene and had only to do the post-mortem. However, he already knew the cause of death — a stab wound in the back. It hit too close to the heart and with extreme precision. The killer had gained either experience or confidence. Besides, he had probably surprised the woman, which had helped too.

The forensic team sprayed the walls and floor to identify the slightest traces of blood and determine the exact position of the aggressor. They powdered the door handle and the light switch in the room to draw prints. The technicians also noticed the wet pattern of a shoe on the floorboard behind the door. They lifted it carefully, photographing the spot afterwards.

They found a thread from a black sweater caught in the wooden door and assumed that the killer had leaned against the door before the attack. That piece of evidence also found its way in a small bag, which was sealed and sent for analysis.

"We finished," an older, short man said. "I don't think there's anything left here that we could use. Ned, have you verified the other room?"

"Aye, sir! There, we found only a half shoe print. Probably he stepped with the other half of the shoe on the carpet."

"The entries? Have you checked them all? Including the windows?" the short man, who seemed to be the boss, asked again. That was his habit, even though his men knew their job.

"Aye, sir! There's no trace. The intruder wore gloves," a middle-aged woman replied.

"All right, then. We can leave," the short man concluded. Despite his small stature, no one could deny that he dominated everyone with his authority.

The man had hardly left the room when steps came up the stairs. He glanced in that direction to notice McNamara, who inquired, "Have we got anything, Shorty?"

"Oy, aye, sir. Of course, we have. If you catch him, we've got enough evidence to nail him, don't worry." The man loathed having a criminal released because of lack of tangible evidence or sloppy work. "Are there other people needed over there?" he asked, tilting his head towards Miss McNeil's house.

"No, we've covered everything. You may go now," McNamara said. "The night is almost over. You might still catch a few hours of sleep, though."

Shorty accepted his encouragement with a slight nod, as tired as McNamara, who had been up for far too long.

The DCI's workday hadn't ended yet, though. While Shorty gathered his people to leave, McNamara massaged the base of his nose, needing to get rid of the stress and exhaustion. The man was furious because many people had already been hurt or killed. The thought that he couldn't do anything to prevent the last two deaths bothered him. It had never happened to have so many successive victims in a case without any idea about the killer's identity or his reasons.

McNamara knew why Ann Goddard had to die and why Mrs Stevens was attacked. But he didn't see the reason for Diane's or Doris Dobbs' death, although the inspector suspected that the latter saw the killer.

The man shook off the bothering thoughts and left the room, turning off the lights. He left the house and, lifting the yellow stripe the policemen had put there, he passed under it, heading towards McNeil's house. Arriving there, he knocked on the door, which the Sergeant opened after a few moments.

"How's she doing?" he asked James, pointing to the woman in the house.

"Bryony's still sitting in the kitchen, sir. She refused to leave by ambulance, saying that she needed only a cold compress."

"I expected that. No problem. Did the woman put that compress?"

"No, she didn't. The lass seems to lack the strength to go to the fridge. I offered, and Mrs Stevens offered, too. I'm afraid that either McNeil didn't hear any of us, or she didn't want to hear. The woman doesn't seem like the kind who lets others take care of her."

"I see," McNamara said, too tired to stress over that. "Would you take Mrs Stevens to her house? She can't sleep in that room now. I hope you can stay with her until morning. Then we'll see what we can do."

"Aye, sir," James said. "Of course, I'll stay with her. I wouldn't like any other unpleasant surprises. We've already had enough. What about Miss McNeil? Is she going to stay alone, or should I take her with me?"

"I'll stay with her. Don't worry about it," McNamara said, admitting no further discussion on the topic. He entered the kitchen, and James followed.

There, Mrs Stevens tried comforting Bryony by petting her hand. As if it helped, the man thought.

Bryony was already beyond exhaustion. She didn't seem to have any energy left in her. The young woman didn't notice the two men, looking wholly detached from reality.

"Mrs Stevens," the DCI addressed the old woman. "DS James will show you to your house and stay with you until morning."

Mrs Stevens approved, nodding, and standing up, she hobbled to the door. Suddenly, the older woman stopped and turned to McNamara. "What about Bryony? I don't want her alone. She'd better come with me."

"I'll stay with her," the Chief Inspector answered coldly, not leaving room for discussion.

The old woman observed him. "I see," she said, disliking the situation. She scrutinised McNamara carefully, evaluating him with a sharp gaze. "I hope there'll be no problems, young man," the woman said harshly. "I hope you realise that she's very vulnerable now."

"I don't think we need to talk about that now," McNamara replied, matching her tone. "It's not appropriate. I'm a policeman, for God's sake!" His eyes lit with boiling fury and indignation, and his fists clenched. The man was too tired and frustrated to take a moral lesson from Mrs Stevens.

McNamara had offered to stay with Bryony because he didn't have any other available people to send to her house. He needed them the next day. It isn't as if I liked the girl, the DCI thought. He preferred more flexible girls, who asked for help when needed, rather than suffering quietly to appease their pride.

The Chief Inspector glanced at Bryony, who didn't seem so self-confident now, but small and helpless. Yet, he knew better. That state of things was only temporary.

Mrs Stevens knew when she lost the battle, but Bryony ignored the conversation. Otherwise, she would have said something. The young woman wouldn't have let others fight for her.

James and Mrs Stevens left, and McNamara remained alone with Bryony, knowing that the latch at the front door locked automatically. The man approached Bryony and lifted her chin, looking into her eyes. Surprised, he noticed that the woman also studied him attentively. She still had some strength in her but couldn't speak yet.

However, the woman proved him wrong again. "You needn't have stayed," she said in a low and tired voice. "I'm sure the criminal's not coming back tonight. I don't think he's got the force or courage to repeat the experience."

"You might be right, and I think you are, but I don't want to take any risks. You realise you're on the killer's blacklist now. You've probably just made the top of that list. Any man defeated by a woman hates her, especially this kind of man. He killed only women so far," the inspector pointed out.

"Maybe, but now he's hurt, and I don't think he wants to mess with anyone tonight," she argued in a weak voice.

"Don't waste your time, Bryony. I'm staying. Don't worry. Tomorrow, I'll send someone else, and I won't bother you with my presence," the DCI added in a mean voice.

"All right, then… I think you should take the opposite bedroom, in this case. You shouldn't stay in the kitchen. I'm going to make your bed."

"No. I'll stay here. Go upstairs, and I'll bring you a compress for your face."

"You don't need to. I can take it myself," Bryony shook her head.

"Aye, I know. You've been taking it for half an hour already. Try to do what you're told. At least for once. It won't kill you. I assure you."

"All right, but you'll also sleep upstairs, in the guest bedroom. All right?"

"We'll see, don't worry, I'll manage somehow."

Bryony frowned but gave up and tried to stand up. When she did, she felt dizzy again, but McNamara caught her.

"I'd better carry you," he decided.

"No, I can climb the stairs", the girl replied after a moment of hesitation.

"I'm sure you can, but let's say you'll do it for my sake," he said drily and lifted her.

"I'm not very light, you know," Bryony complained.

"I know now, but don't be afraid, we'll get upstairs somehow," the man replied, with a grin she didn't see.

Bryony closed her eyes and leaned against his shoulder. McNamara carried her upstairs and laid her on the bed. After pulling the blanket over her, he said, "I'll bring you a compress. Stay here and be good." The man was almost to the door when he realised that she hadn't answered. He turned and glanced at the woman only to notice that she had already fallen asleep.

Amused, McNamara grinned. The woman had stubbornly insisted she was alright, only to fall asleep in his arms. He regretted bothering her, but he had to wake her up. That compress was necessary.

Downstairs, the man took some ice cubes from the freezer and wrapped them in a towel, afterwards returning. Approaching the bed, McNamara noticed that her sleep was agitated. The woman murmured something, and he brushed the hair away off her face, gently caressing her temple and the cheek where a darkening bruise had already appeared. Bryony groaned and slapped his hand aside.

Feeling mean, the man put the towel wrapped around the ice onto the bruise, and she woke up with a wince. McNamara chuckled and then soothed her gently. "Be good. I just put the compress on your face. If I don't, tomorrow, you'll look worse than now."

"All right," she grumbled. "But it's awful. This must be your revenge."

"Don't be silly. I gain nothing if you keep this on your face, but instead, you'll look better tomorrow," the inspector snapped.

"I prefer to look awful and sleep now," the young woman replied in the same tone.

"All right, then. I'll take this downstairs, and I'll leave you alone," McNamara growled, leaving the room.

Bryony tried to look after his silhouette, but she couldn't keep her eyes open.

CHAPTER SIXTEEN

The man tried to stop the bleeding but failed. 'Bloody woman! Next time I'll kill her!' It hadn't been enough that he had so many problems with the other two.

He didn't have any explanation for his appearance. At least his wife was sleeping. Otherwise, he would have been doomed.

His eyes followed the cars leaving the street, and the man realised that neither McNamara nor James had left. Probably they remained with the two women. 'Stupid people! How can they think that I would go back there tonight?'

The killer expected a second chance because he must be given one. He had been lucky so far.

If those tiny parasites had been satisfied with what he gave them, everything would have been fine. But then, they wanted more, and he didn't have more. The man had been caught in the net and just defended himself, even though he knew what he had done wasn't right. He wasn't mad, after all. Still, he hadn't had any other choice.

The man felt sorry for Diane because she had satisfied his needs. But the girl had become greedy and had to pay for that. That bitch had also stolen Patsy's bag when she ran away. But he got the better of her.

The man chuckled, recalling everything. That proud Patsy wasn't so proud now after he had wiped that smirk off her face. Now, she couldn't make a fool of him anymore.

Those policemen weren't very smart. They didn't know where to look for Patsy, and she was right under their nose. It would have been better if Diane had also remained there and hadn't tried to escape.

The killer wanted to know what Mrs Stevens saw that night, though. He didn't know whether she had recognised him or seen from where he was coming. The man thought better and concluded that she couldn't have. The police would have arrested him already. But the old shrew might still remember.

The bleeding had just stopped, but the man became agitated, and it started again. He pressed the compress onto the wound in his shoulder harder. The vein throbbed under his fingers, and he hissed.

The man feared losing consciousness. Then, his wife would find him in the morning, and everything would be lost.

He took two more strong painkillers and felt better after a quarter of an hour. He promised himself to get his revenge and not let the bitch, who had stabbed him, live. 'And to think I have respected and even liked her,' the man scowled. Now, she had to die.

The murderer hoped that his wife wouldn't notice the missing clothes, which he wrapped and hid in a safe place. It wasn't safe to throw them in the garbage with the police swarming around. Yet, he couldn't keep them in the house either. His wife had the bad habit of rummaging everywhere and would find them. 'Damned woman! She always must know everything. I'm not allowed to have a thing of my own.'

The man dozed and woke up after half an hour. The bleeding had stopped, but he was in constant pain. Still, the discomfort had subdued now because of the pills.

He was grateful that, at least, the scissors hadn't burrowed deep. McNeil hadn't had enough force to drive them in his body.

He wrapped the remaining stained clothes in the plastic bag on which he lied, making a ball of everything. He needed to find a place to hide

them. With the police still in the area, he couldn't
go to his hiding place.

CHAPTER SEVENTEEN

The phone rang, and McNamara woke up groggily, looking around. He ran his fingers through his hair and over his face and rubbed his eyes. Then, the DCI answered the phone left on the night table next to the bed. "McNamara," he said in a voice heavy with sleep.

"Sir, it's me, Jo," his subordinate voice came from the other end of the line. "Did I wake you up?" she inquired, surprised to find him sleeping.

"No, problem, Jo. I should have woken up, anyway. Tell me if there's anything new. What time is it?"

"Sir, it's ten already. Didn't you know?" Jo replied, and bewilderment rang in her voice.

McNamara grimaced. He had slept only a few hours — three, more precisely. The man had tried to stay awake, and the last time the inspector had looked at the clock, it was past six. He must have fallen asleep afterwards.

"All right, Jo, tell me what's the problem," the DCI said harshly, disliking the woman's reminder that it was late. He hadn't had fun all night long.

"Noticing that you didn't contact the team today, I decided to call you," Jo explained. "We've got information from the country, and I've also discovered something in the database."

"Go on," McNamara ordered, hoping they would finally have a breakthrough.

"The lads in the country visited the two girls and spoke to them and their parents. Apparently, their parents decided to move out of town because they discovered that the girls had joined an escort organisation. They said a man, Daniel, runs it. One of the girls, who seems to have changed lately for the better, let it slip that his last name is Thompson. The name rang a bell. Anyway, it looks like Patsy got them into the business."

"Good girl, you've found out some interesting things. We must take care of this individual, Thompson. He's managed to elude us so far. What have you found out from the database?"

"Another girl on the list, Linda Peterson, has also disappeared. She's been on the missing persons' list for two weeks already. We couldn't find the other two at their addresses, and their parents know nothing about them, but they don't seem to care much. I have them looked for, sir."

"Well done, Jo."

"Mike helped me, sir," the girl reckoned. "Now he's at one of the addresses we've got from a lad who lives in the neighbourhood. The lad saw one of the girls there quite often. He always sells newspapers on the same street corner, so it seems credible to think the girl's living there if he's seen her so often."

"All right, Jo. James and I are coming later. I want to see what's with this Thompson. Call me if you hear anything, " McNamara said, putting then the phone down and heading to the bathroom to wash.

He looked at his bloodshot eyes and told himself it had already become a habit. His cases required fast investigations, so sleepless nights were not unusual.

Anyway, the inspector didn't have a reason to rush home. No one was waiting for him. His mother had passed away a year ago, and he hadn't found anyone to share his life with, not that he had tried to find someone. When it came to commitment in a relationship, the man ran in the opposite direction.

Suddenly, the girl, lying in bed next door, popped into his mind, but, with determination, he pushed the thought of her away. The man couldn't think of her like that as long as she was part of an investigation.

McNamara strode to her room and opened the door. Bryony was still sleeping, but there were signs that she had fretted throughout the night. The blanket was on the floor, and the sheets wrinkled. The man grinned, heading downstairs. The lass wasn't bad to look at, and he did a lot of watching. Besides, she was smart and had a backbone. He liked that he couldn't intimidate her.

The inspector put water on the stove to boil for coffee and tea in the kitchen. He thought that Bryony might want tea when she woke up.

***

Upstairs, in her bedroom, Bryony opened her eyes. She had felt someone watching her and woken up. The young woman barely smothered a scream before her eyes fell on McNamara's back on his way out, and she wondered what the man might have wanted from her.

Still exhausted and feeling like someone had beaten her up, Bryony closed her eyes again. However, the woman couldn't sleep anymore, so she glanced at the clock. With a head shake, she noticed that it was already past ten. She didn't sleep so late, even on a Sunday.

The young woman got out of bed and moseyed to the bathroom. Every bone in her body hurt. She looked at herself in the mirror and gasped. 'Oh, Lord! I should have listened to McNamara.'

Bryony looked awful. She couldn't open the bookshop looking like that unless she wanted to run all the customers away. Resignedly, the woman decided to hire someone part-time and remembered the student who had come into her shop the previous week. She had promised the girl to call her if she decided to hire someone.

The woman headed downstairs a few moments later. She stopped halfway down the hallway when a merry whistle reached her ears. Apparently, McNamara was in a good mood. Bryony grinned, enjoying the image taking shape in her mind.

The young woman arrived at the kitchen door and stopped and watched the detective prepare coffee and teacups. He had already made some toast and placed the butter and jam on the table.

"Interesting, detective," Bryony noticed. "You seem very efficient in the kitchen. I wouldn't have thought you were."

McNamara crushed a curse on his tongue before turning around. He had felt so comfortable in the small, bright, and clean kitchen, so different from his kitchenette at home, that he had let his guard down. The man didn't like it when people saw him without the invisible rigid wall around him.

"So, you're up," the Chief Inspector noticed. "Too early, but whatever. You could have slept a little more," he shook his head.

"Aye. If you hadn't come into my room, I might have," the lass replied. "My sleep is very light," she continued, heading to the kitchen bench where she had left her purse.

McNamara looked after her, a scowl on his face, but didn't comment on her words. "Coffee or tea? What would you like?" he asked instead.

"I think I'll have coffee first," Bryony said. "I'm not entirely awake. I'm pretty grumpy until I've drunk my first cup of coffee," she explained in a throaty voice, without looking at him but searching for something in her purse. "I don't think you would like to see me like that," she added. "It might be unpleasant. An unforgettable experience, as my roommate from university would say."

"What are you doing?" the DCI asked, slightly alarmed when she picked up the phone.

"I'm making a phone call. Can't you see?" the young woman mumbled, dialling a number.

"Who would you call? I hope you don't want to wake Mrs Stevens. I assure you she's all right. She's with James, isn't she? And James is competent," the man hasted to say.

McNamara wasn't in a hurry to see the old woman that morning. He knew she didn't like him, not that he cared about that, but the old woman also wanted to yap a lot and come with unwanted advice and opinions.

"I know, don't worry. James seems very good at his job, and he's also kind. I'm sure Mrs Stevens is fine," Bryony waved his concerns away.

McNamara took some offence at her words but decided not to let her see she had affected him. "Then, who do you want to call?" he insisted.

The woman didn't answer but put up her hand to stop his talking. He would know when he heard her conversation, she decided.

"Hallo, Meg. Bryony McNeil here, from the bookshop. I need a shop assistant full time for a few days, and then, I promise to keep you half time, what are you saying? ... Good, then. But you must come to my house and take the keys... Aye, right now, if you can... Write down my address," she gave her address to the girl. "All right, I'll wait."

"Are you hiring someone?" McNamara asked once she hung up.

"Aye, of course. You can't believe that I can deal with customers as long as I look like this," she pointed to her face. "No one will buy anything. Everyone will run away," she said, sipping from her coffee. "You make good coffee, McNamara. By the way, don't you have another name? Everyone has a first name usually. What happened to yours?"

"My first name's not your business," the man snapped. "Maybe you haven't noticed, but this is not a social visit. I've just been your nanny for the night."

"You're rude again, McNamara, and I'm already furious because of the last night's idiot. He's costing me a lot of money," she scowled at the inspector.

"You won't go broke if you pay a poor girl a salary," the man mumbled grumpily.

"You can't know that. You don't run a business to know how difficult it is to deal with everything," the lass retorted with dismay. "However, now I have to hire someone. I'd lose too much otherwise. Including my credibility."

McNamara shrugged, and silence fell between them, as both were too tired to continue arguing. They focused on their coffee and toast until his phone rang.

"McNamara!"

"It's James, sir. I've called the police station to send a man to stay with the two women. They'll stay together until nightfall, I presume?"

"Aye, James, they'll stay together. When is the constable coming?"

"Maybe in an hour. There wasn't anyone available now. Maybe an hour and a half."

"All right, James. When Mrs Stevens wakes up, fetch her here. Then you can go to the hospital and see McKay."

"Thank you, sir," James replied warmly, as that was the real reason for his call. Mrs Stevens hadn't woken up yet, but he was sure she wouldn't sleep much longer.

McNamara disconnected the call and poured himself some more coffee. He was stuck there for a while and wasn't happy about it.

"James has some feelings for McKay, doesn't he?"

"What's your interest in his feelings?" the policeman's rough answer came.

"It was just mere curiosity, McNamara. It was an attempt to make conversation. I haven't ever happened to have breakfast with someone as taciturn as you," Bryony replied quietly, taken aback by the harshness of his words.

"Do you often have breakfast with men?" he asked with disdain.

"Not that concerns you, McNamara, but usually I have breakfast alone."

McNamara didn't have time to answer because the doorbell rang. McNeil stood to get the door, but McNamara stopped her and went to open it himself.

A young woman with glasses and hair falling down her shoulders looked at him curiously.

"Aye," he said. "Who are you looking for?"

The unexpected hostile welcome intimidated the woman, but she answered, "Miss McNeil. I'm Meg McPherson. She called me earlier and invited me here."

"Oh, aye, come in," McNamara showed her to the kitchen.

At the sound of their steps on the wooden floors, Bryony looked up and smiled at the girl. "You got here fast. That's good. You must go and open the bookshop for me. You'll manage alone, I hope. As you can see, I've had a little accident."

"I think you need to change your boyfriend," Meg said brashly, pointing to McNamara. She wasn't the kind of girl who accepted physical abuse from men and wasn't too scared not to say anything.

At her words, McNamara blushed with anger. "Listen here, lass," he bellowed, but he couldn't continue because Bryony interrupted him.

"Calm down, please," she asked him. "Meg, McNamara didn't hit me. He's a policeman, and he's here to defend me. I was attacked."

"I'm sorry," Meg said contritely. "I'm sorry, sir. I didn't know, and you seem to be at home here," she started explaining but stopped when red anger stormed the man's eyes.

Bryony couldn't resist and burst into laughter. "Oh, Lord, McNamara, if you could see your face... Calm down. No one has proposed to you. But let's finish playing around. We have serious things to talk about," she said to the girl, inviting her to sit down, waving her hand.

"Let me explain to you briefly what you have to do. McNamara, would you be so kind as to pour a cup of coffee for Meg, please?"

McNamara looked sideways at her, expecting to see that she was mocking him. Realising that the woman was serious and already wrapped up in explanations, he said nothing but poured another cup of coffee. Then, he also filled their cups and went to look out the window.

Then he noticed something. He turned suddenly and asked. "McNeil, does anyone live next door?"

With a flash of irritation in her eyes, Bryony wanted to snap at him because of the interruption. But then, observing the severe line of his mouth, she realised that the man was just doing his job.

"No, of course! The house has been empty for five months already. I haven't seen anyone there ever since," she said in a rush, feeling the man's tension. "What's the matter?"

"Finish your explanations because I have to go and call James. I don't want indiscreet ears around," he nodded towards Meg.

Meg felt the burn of his dismissal, but she didn't find any come back. The lass didn't know what to reply, so she said, "Leave it, Miss McNeil. I've understood everything, and I've already seen how you work. I'm sure I'll manage."

"All right. All my hopes are on you. And I've asked you not to be so formal. My name's Bryony, all right?" she said, seeing the girl off.

When she opened the door, the young woman found James on the stoop, just fetching Mrs Stevens. "You've already come, James. Good morning. You too, Mrs Stevens."

"Hallo, girl," the old woman replied, not letting James answer. "That policeman had just called when we were at the gate," she said, tilting her head to the house. "This lad here rushed me, with no respect for my arthritis," she continued, making poor James blush and mumble some apologies.

Bryony smiled because she knew Mrs Stevens well. She imagined that the old woman had made the Sergeant's life a living hell that morning.

"Who's the girl?" asked the old woman suspiciously.

"I have just hired her at the bookshop," Bryony answered, smiling at the confused young girl. "I can't go to work like that," she pointed to her face.

"Aye, you're a little colourful," the old lady snapped roughly, in complete contradiction with the tears in her eyes. The woman really cared for her young friend and felt guilty. She should have been in her place.

Bryony guessed her older friend's thoughts. "Don't you dare blame yourself! Do you hear me? You're not guilty of that, but the scum that came after you," she continued but suddenly stopped, seeing Meg's curiosity.

Bryony didn't want that everyone knew what had happened to her. More importantly,

McNamara had already told her it wasn't a good idea to let the truth be known outside the house. "However, Meg, once again, I'm counting on you. Tonight, please, just call me. You shouldn't make the drive over here. All right?"

"Don't worry! I'll take care of everything. I'm grateful to you. You've offered me a chance to have a job. You know, I've had some hard time so far."

"No problem," Bryony said, but her heart tightened nervously, as it was the first time she had left her business in another one's hands.

CHAPTER EIGHTEEN

"You've come, James. That's good. I saw that the door at the other house, the one opening to the garden, is half-open. We know that the house should be empty. Yesterday we didn't think to check the inside. Let's do it now," McNamara said.

"Of course, sir. Do you think we could leave the ladies alone for a while?"

"I think so," the inspector said, glancing at Bryony, who nodded in agreement. "However, we won't be gone for long. All right?" he asked her.

"Aye, it's not a problem," Bryony agreed. "It's daytime, and I don't think the killer will repeat last night's experience so soon. He must be slowed down because of the two wounds I inflicted on him."

McNamara agreed with her estimation and waved at James to follow him. They went out through the back entrance and jumped over the fence in the neighbour's garden. They reached the back door there, and McNamara signalled James to wait.

The policemen listened, but no sound came from inside, so McNamara opened the door wider and entered carefully, his senses sharpened. He didn't want any surprises.

The men strode towards the kitchen when a strong smell hit them, and they turned back. A door opened on the left, and McNamara recalled seeing a similar one at Bryony's when they had searched the house the previous night. He remembered that it led to the basement.

The DCI opened the door carefully, James covering his back, and a powerful foul stench punched them in the face, arousing their nausea. Although mixed with the odour of dampness and mould from the basement, the detectives knew that smell.

McNamara lit his flashlight and waved at James to stay put and watch the door. The man climbed down the stairs, where he swept the space from one end to the other with his flashlight, revealing an indistinct shape in the left far corner, which was likely the source of the pestilential smell.

The inspector headed towards that corner. His eyes fell on something similar to a body, wrapped in plastic bags, stuck together with tape. He noticed another package a little longer than the first one, a little farther. The DCI assumed that the bodies' height was different. Next to them, his light swept over some blood-covered clothes gathered into a ball. Shifting his light to the left, he uncovered drops of blood and down, on the ground near the wall, a kind of improvised bloodied bunk.

McNamara analysed the basement carefully and concluded that it must have been soundproof. Still, he wanted to make sure of that, so he went back upstairs to test that theory.

At the top of the stairs, the Chief Inspector told the Sergeant, "Stay here, James. I'll close the door. Keep your ears open and tell me what you've heard when I get back. All right?"

"Aye, sir," James nodded.

McNamara returned to the cellar, shutting the door behind him. He strode to the left wall and shouted 'help' five times, but James didn't rush down the stairs.

He returned upstairs again, opening the heavy metallic door of the basement. "Did you hear anything, James?"

"No, sir. Why, what should I have heard?"

"I shouted 'help' five times. Didn't you hear anything?"

"No, sir, I swear," James said earnestly.

"Well, if you didn't hear anything from here, you can imagine that the people outside couldn't have heard anything either," McNamara said. "We have to call the team, James. There are two bodies downstairs. I suppose that one belongs to the girl that disappeared — Jo told me about her. The other might be Patsy. Besides that, we have a lot of bloodied clothes and a miserable bunk. I think we've stumbled upon our killer's nest."

McNamara decided to leave the foul stench behind and headed outside before making the call. Once out in the fresh air, James called the station to send for the forensics and the coroner.

"I think you can go to the hospital and see McKay, James," the DCI ordered the DS. He didn't need James to wait there with him anymore. He could stand watch until the team arrived.

"Someone must ask the constable what she saw. I suppose you can do it," the man continued, slightly embarrassed, noticing the Sergeant's stunned and grateful eyes.

The DS smiled and wanted to say something but decided against that. He nodded and headed to the car he had left near Ann Goddard's house the previous night.

Behind him, McNamara grinned. He didn't think McKay had seen much, as she was hit from the back, and the blow must have rendered her unconscious.

Yet, the DCI knew he couldn't rely on James all day long if he didn't let him go to the hospital to make sure that McKay was all right.

MCNAMARA SERIES BOX SET
BOOK 0NE & TWO

CHAPTER NINETEEN

"What do you think, doc?" the DCI asked.

"These two young women were also beaten and raped, like the other one. One died more recently, the red-haired one on the right," the coroner said, pointing to one of the bodies. "I can't tell you for sure now, but both were killed a few days ago. After performing the post-mortem, I'll know more and tell you exactly when they died. Of course, he used the same knife on both of them. It's that knife the lads found at McNeil's last night. It matches the shapes and dimensions of the wounds on Diane's body. I'm sure it will also match these two girls' wounds."

McNamara thanked the doctor and went to Shorty, who, together with his people, was ransacking the basement systematically for the slightest trace.

"Have you found something we can use, lads?"

"Enough, but the case won't be solved only with this evidence, and you know it," Shortly replied in a huff, tired after the previous night. Besides, they already had a lot of evidence to process at headquarters. Anyway, the man knew that he had chosen that job, so he had to do it. No one had pushed him, and his mother warned him not to expect an everyday life. His father had been a copper until the day he died, so he had known what kind of life to expect.

Tired and nervous as his people, McNamara understood Shorty and his reproach. The inspector knew it was his duty to find the killer. Shorty could only help him build a case for the court.

McNamara left his people to do their job and went back to Bryony's, jumping over the fence into her garden. He went inside through the back door to shorten his trip. The man got into the kitchen and found the two women very silent and thoughtful.

"What was it, McNamara?" asked Bryony. "What did you see there? I heard the sirens."

"We found two more bodies," the policeman told her directly, knowing that she would have heard the news from her neighbours sooner or later. "Apparently, that was our killer's favourite playground — his nest. Have any of you seen anything suspicious over the last two weeks? Maybe you saw someone who doesn't belong on this street."

Bryony gave it some thought, but nothing came to her mind. Mrs Stevens recalled something. "I saw a girl two weeks ago, at night. I think she was red-haired and tall. The lass caught my eye because she was looking for a house number. She passed by my house, and then I lost her from sight. I haven't seen anyone else."

"Well, that night, before or after the girl passed by, who did you see?" McNamara insisted.

"Graham passed first. I think," the old woman tried to remember. "Oh, aye, and Mr Reid, indeed. Afterwards, a few seconds later, I heard shouts from their house. I don't know what the man didn't like that time," she turned her nose. "However, it was an uglier fight than usual. You must remember, Bryony. You told me that you heard it too, even though you were working in the kitchen," she addressed the young girl.

"You were in the kitchen and saw no one?" McNamara wondered. "He must have passed by your windows."

"I noticed Daniel Thompson, going to Ann Goddard that evening Mrs Stevens is talking about. That time, he visited Ann almost daily and rarely skipped an evening. I saw him all the time, even though they were sure that no one knew about their affair. Earlier that evening, I saw one of the Randall children. Mr Randall shouted at the boy, telling his son that he would skin him alive if he went there again."

"Why?" McNamara asked, hoping that he had found something.

"He's a man who fears God and his wife," Mrs Stevens answered. "That's why. Even his own shadow frightens him if you must know."

"Oh, I see," McNamara chuckled, and Bryony's skin tingled. "By the way, haven't you ever seen anything? For instance, someone getting into the house next door?" he asked the lass.

"No, I didn't, but I didn't watch specifically for that either, did I?" she answered dryly, disliking his effect on her.

"Usually, this girl doesn't look at anything that doesn't interest her," Mrs Stevens remarked. "I've told you, love. Sometimes, you should look around you. You can't know what or whom you might see."

"If I had the time, I would do it. But for now, I have other things on my mind," Bryony replied in a prim voice. She would have liked to tell her friend to mind her own business but knew it was a waste of time. The young woman understood what the old woman implied. Mrs Stevens was vocal enough when she wanted to let Bryony know something.

McNamara figured out what the girl meant and felt amused. Still, the man wondered how the lass bore such discussions that, probably, took place daily. He didn't see Mrs Stevens capable of keeping her mouth shut. The woman was a stubborn mule. Apparently, the old woman was determined to see Bryony with someone, at the very least, if not married.

Part of the old guard, Mrs Stevens thought that a husband ensured security and, possibly, wealth. Women in her generation didn't know anything beyond that. Usually, they married early, and most of them left their jobs and stayed at home to take care of their husband and children. Making a career didn't make sense for them.

After all, a man was supposed to take care of the wife and provide everything she needed while pursuing a career that would help him provide better.

Nevertheless, McNeil was a different type of woman. She wanted to make her own way, like Mrs Reid. Still, Bryony didn't seem to be against men, unlike Mary Reid, probably because she hadn't started her life with particular baggage or prejudices. Bryony didn't consider a man automatically unfaithful, ready to leave his wife and house at the drop of a hat. However, the young woman believed that she had to stand on her own two feet first and then start a relationship as a partnership on an equal basis.

The DCI knew that the lass would never become a victim. Although the woman tried hard to avoid precisely that, McNamara could see Mary in that position. But Mary didn't know to let things be and pushed, and as a result, she might have found herself in a bad situation sooner than she thought.

The inspector didn't think that Michael Reid would bear that daily treatment for long. Love would surely vanish one day, leaving bitterness behind. McNamara wasn't an expert, but he didn't rule out that the Reid marriage might end in a few years.

Bryony would fight to make her marriage work if she got married, the same way she was fighting for her small business now. She wouldn't give up before the end of the fight like Mary Reid.

The girl's voice brought him back to reality. "No, I'm sorry, but I didn't see anyone. And to be honest, I didn't hear anything from the house next door either," she shook her head with astonishment.

"You couldn't have," McNamara said, waving her concern away. "The basement is soundproof."

"It's awful. I wouldn't have expected something like that," Bryony said with a frown. "Our street seemed so peaceful. On Sundays or in the evenings, you hear only the neighbours' children or the song of birds. It's so quiet that it's like we weren't even on the outskirts of the town," she shook her head again.

"You can't say that it's been too quiet these days," Mrs Stevens replied drily. "We've heard nothing but sirens, and people are suspicious. They want to think someone who doesn't live here is guilty, but they still fear evil lives here on this very street."

"Possibly," McNamara replied without getting involved in that discussion. "Well, I'm leaving now. I must ask some questions to the people on the street."

Bryony stood to see him off. "I'll be here," she said. "I work easier in the kitchen. If I can't go to the shop, at least I can catch up on the books."

"Don't you think you should sleep a little more? You can't say you've had a peaceful night," Mrs Stevens replied peevishly.

"No, I wouldn't sleep. I'm too energized after so much coffee," the young woman replied. "But if you want, you may go and rest in my room. I'll help you upstairs."

"No, I don't feel like tormenting my legs now," the old woman retorted. "I prefer to remain here with you."

"As you wish," Bryony replied calmly, although she was boiling inside. The young woman wanted a little peace to do her work, and she feared she wouldn't have any. Mrs Stevens didn't seem in a good mood that morning, and Bryony knew that the old woman would bother her with all her ideas. Usually, the lass took it in stride, but that day she was tired, and a horrible headache tried her patience.

McNamara let himself seen out to the door, reading her thoughts perfectly. He knew she wouldn't have a peaceful day with the old woman by her side. At the door, he turned to her and looked straight into her eyes. The headache reflected in her pupils, and his heart cringed.

"I think you'd better lie down. If you want, I'll send two constables, one for you and one for her, so that you could have a little peace. She'll be able then to go to her house."

"No, it's not necessary," Bryony refused the offer. "I'll handle her. I'm sure you need all your people. Don't worry. I'll manage."

"I'm not worrying. I wanted only to be helpful," the man retorted, harsher than he wanted. Still, he didn't want to leave the lass with the feeling that he cared for her.

"You shouldn't get angry again," Bryony said tactfully, rubbing her temple to ease the pain intensified by his voice. "You've done that enough this morning. You may calm down. I never get any wrong ideas if you feared that," she continued, inferring McNamara's thoughts perfectly. "I'm just interested in seeing you punish the one who's taken so many lives."

"Well, then," he tried to smoothen things. "I'll probably call later to see if you're all right."

"You don't have to," she refused him drily. "If we have an emergency, I'll call you. You've given me your number, you know."

McNamara nodded shortly, understanding that the woman had effectively dismissed him. He left with a slight tinge of regret and anger directed towards himself.

Bryony watched his tense back, and a grin appeared in the corner of her mouth, despite her headache. She returned to the kitchen, unaware that the smile hadn't left her lips.

"You smile for nothing, lass," Mrs Stevens snapped, startling her. "I don't think you've chosen well if you want to know my opinion. That's a man who doesn't spend much time at home. You can see for yourself. He's out there in the street all the time. Nothing's worse than a salesman or a policeman. You need someone who leaves for work in the morning and comes back home in the evening, not one who goes, God knows where."

"You shouldn't think of that," Bryony replied. "Besides, I'm not going to have a relationship with anyone now. I have other things on my mind. I haven't even thought of him in that context."

"Nonsense! You can't fool me. I've seen the sparks between you two. But that might be only because the situation is what it is. Don't pawn your heart now! Wait and see what comes next! Maybe when he finishes here, the man disappears and never comes back again."

"You needn't tell me that. I'm not a simpleton. I know very well how things are. And I repeat it for the last time: I'm not interested."

The old woman wanted to say something more. Still, Bryony took some documents out of her bag and pretended to be reading so that the old woman would keep her opinions to herself.

Mrs Stevens still had things to say. A woman needed a steady man, and McNamara was far from that. She thought Bryony shouldn't fall for that man.

Bryony regretted the toughness of her words and gestures. The old woman drove her crazy, getting involved in her business and giving advice. She also expected Bryony to follow her advice, and she wasn't always right.

Aye, maybe McNamara attracted her a little. Tough and taciturn, he appealed to her on a fundamental level. However, the woman felt that she could rely on him. The man wasn't shallow but thoughtful and took his duty seriously. In Bryony's opinion, being responsible was very important. Not many men were like that, especially the twenty or thirty-something. They dreamt of sex conquests and didn't take any responsibility.

MCNAMARA SERIES BOX SET
BOOK 0NE & TWO

CHAPTER TWENTY

McNamara had just come out of McNeil's house when he noticed James heading in his direction. Judging after his expression, McNamara assumed that McKay was doing fine. "How's McKay, James?" he asked.

"She's well, sir. They stabilised her, and amazingly, she hadn't lost as much blood as we thought. Claire will recover. I asked her what she saw last night, sir, but, unfortunately, the poor girl didn't have the time to see anything. At least, she's tough. After the guy had hit her over the head, the lass still had the strength to stand up once more and fight back. Unfortunately, the knife stopped her."

"So, McKay didn't see the aggressor's face," McNamara concluded.

"No, sir. She told me about the same mask that McNeil told us about. Brave girl, McNeil. Too bad she couldn't see more. By the way, you should know I've just heard from headquarters. They found Peter."

"Good. And what's the lad saying?"

"He says that Patsy invited him to elope together. She came up with the idea. They stayed together for only a few days, but the girl was mostly away without explanations. Then, the lass told him she had someone else who wasn't an 'unfledged lad.' This is an exact quote, by the way. Anyway, Patsy left Peter. The lad says the girl used him as a cover, but Peter realised that too late."

"Did she say who she was with?" McNamara asked, rubbing his eyes.

"Aye, the girl told Peter that Thompson had rented a flat in town for her, and she would live there with him. Thompson promised to divorce his wife and marry Patsy."

"Interesting! Very active this Thompson! He promised Ann to marry her, and now Patsy. He probably said something to Diane, as well. Anything else?"

"Nothing special, sir. The coroner's report shows exactly what he said this morning with the mention that one of the girls died two days before the other one. Patsy was the second, sir. Imagine how awful it was for her to lie there with her friend's body around! I can't even begin to imagine what she felt. The lass probably went slowly crazy."

"I see. Let's go and tour the neighbours first, and then we'll go and see Thompson. So far, he fits the role of the killer if we consider the connections. Still, the man doesn't seem to match the profile," McNamara replied, going up the street to Graham's house. However, no one was at home there.

The detectives decided to leave when they noticed Mrs Porter on her way back from the morgue. A lady in an elegant outfit held her arm. The woman looked around forty, but time had been gentle with her.

Noting that the men came from Graham's house, she commented, "He's not at home at this hour. You should try in the evening."

"We're from the police, ma'am," McNamara said, showing her his badge. "And you are?"

"Oh, aye! We haven't seen each other so far. I'm Mary Brown. You talked to my husband when I was at Mrs Porter's," she said, pointing to her friend, who seemed to be in her own world.

"I'm afraid this is not the appropriate moment to talk," McNamara remarked.

"No, unfortunately," the woman replied, smiling sadly. "I'm sorry, but I must get Mrs Porter inside and take care of her for a while. I'll call her sister to come. She should be here in half an hour, at the most. Then, I'll go to the bar, because it's almost lunchtime. You may find me there. You can also have lunch," Mary said kindly. "I don't want to boast, but everyone likes my food, and I'm sure you need something warm now and then. What are you saying?"

"Thank you, ma'am," McNamara nodded, already charmed. Mr Brown knew what he was saying when he bragged about his wife. He didn't have any reason to want other women. "We accept your invitation, ma'am. We'll come in an hour, maybe an hour and a half," he specified.

"Perfectly, sir. I have time to prepare one of my famous chicken pies," she let him know, showing Mrs Porter inside.

The grieving mother hadn't reacted to the exchange of replies and hadn't even noticed that Mary had talked to someone.

Touched by the woman's tragedy, James shook his head regretfully. "What a waste, aye, sir? Such a young life! The only child, too," he turned to McNamara.

"What can you do, James? That's the result of bad guidance and education. I don't think there's an excuse for that, James. My poor mom managed by herself, but she'd never allowed me to go wrong. And I would lie if I said that she restricted me with many rules."

"I see your point, sir, but apparently not everyone has the same talent," James said, thinking of the girls who had chosen to walk the wrong path with Patsy.

"That's it. Anyway, it's pointless to think of all that right now. Let's do our job, and then we'll see," the DCI decided.

If McNamara had to believe Bryony's words, the street had been peaceful before. But, now, the neighbourhood was awfully silent. Not even the song of birds broke the silence.

MCNAMARA SERIES BOX SET
BOOK 0NE & TWO

CHAPTER TWENTY-ONE

Mary Reid came to the door only after they had already rung four times. They knew she couldn't be anywhere else, but at home at that hour, and after their failure at the Thompsons', they refused to believe they had the same bad luck.

"Oh, good day, gentlemen! I knew we would see each other today again," Mary said. "For a few days now, many things have been happening on this street. Before, you had to wait for a long time for something to shake the stillness of the street."

"Does all this fret make you happy?" James expressed his shock.

"You misunderstand me, sir," the woman replied harshly. "I haven't meant this kind of fun. I don't like the meaningless loss of human lives. No more than you do... I can't stand unwarranted violence. I enjoy my quarrels with my husband, but we don't hurt anybody else, and

283

I know he wouldn't lay one finger on me. Michael bellows at the drop of a hat; that's true. But every time he is mean to me, he regrets it immediately. The man doesn't even curse but only speaks in a louder voice. Oh, look at me, keeping you at the door! I'm sorry! Come in," the woman stepped aside to let them in.

Her sudden seriousness made the two men understand she was something more than a mere moony woman who liked to rile her husband. After all, she had some social values and principles, even though she hid them under the mask of frivolity.

Reid probably knew that side of hers. That was why he didn't give up on his marriage, even if it didn't seem to bring him much joy at times. Or maybe it did. They couldn't judge that.

The detectives followed her into the same room she had shown them to the previous morning. Soft music filled the room, and they understood why she hadn't heard the bell. A pile of printed pages lay on the desk. Her work seemed to have advanced.

"Have you made progress with your story, ma'am?" McNamara asked, indicating the pile of papers.

"Aye, quite well. I've just finished now. I'll ask my husband to take it to my editor tomorrow."

"Do you trust him to do it?" James asked with disbelief and then glanced at McNamara to see what he thought of his blunt question. However, the DCI seemed only interested in hearing the answer.

"Of course, I trust him," Mary grinned and shook her head. "It isn't a big deal. Michael wouldn't solve anything by sabotaging my work. And quite the opposite, he encourages me all the time. My husband doesn't mind my writing. He minds my clothes and behaviour," she replied matter-of-factly.

"And then, why don't you change, ma'am?" McNamara asked, his curiosity aroused.

"Because I don't want to give him the satisfaction of doing what he wants," the woman answered bluntly.

"But don't you think that now and then you should do what he wants too?" the DCI insisted.

"Of course, when it's something important. I don't see why to bother otherwise," Mary shook her head, shrugging.

The detectives couldn't follow her logic and abandoned the topic. McNamara said, "So, I gather you heard what had happened last night."

"Well, it was difficult not to hear. I was here downstairs, and I was writing when the cars came. Michael also came downstairs. The noise woke him up. He even said that two nights in a row was a bit over the top. And then, when he was about to leave this morning because Michael left later today, he saw a lot of cars again. He said that either this criminal is a maniac or all the criminals had started prowling this very street. My husband already regrets we bought the house here. We thought it was a quiet area, you know. We never thought such things would happen."

"If you were still working here, did you see anyone or anything?" McNamara continued with his questions.

"Nothing unusual," Mary shrugged. "Mr Graham passed by at eleven, maybe eleven-thirty. Usually, he comes late. I think he's got someone in town. The man has got a junk car, and it's impossible not to hear it. Of course, that made me lift my eyes. As my desk faces the street, I saw him. Mr Thompson came by twelve, a little after or before. However, not much later after Mr Graham's arrival. I hadn't turned back to work yet. I heard his car and then saw him parking. Who knows where he was because the man wanders a lot. Then, Mr Randall passed by the house. I think he made an inventory or something. His wife asks him to make inventories almost all the time. She keeps him henpecked, and the man doesn't dare to make a move without her approval. Then, no one passed by until you came."

"All right, ma'am. Your husband didn't see anything until we came?"

"No, Michael was sleeping because he was exhausted. He had had a hard day at work. He hadn't had a peaceful evening at home either," she said, biting her lower lip. She regretted what she had done the day before, although it was now pointless.

"By the way, do you know where Alice Thompson is? She didn't answer the door." James inquired.

"Alice came by an hour ago, maybe an hour and so. She said she wasn't feeling well and went to the doctor. Well, it's perfectly normal for her," Mary shrugged. "At least once a week, she goes to the doctor or calls him here."

"Aye, I see," McNamara said. "When was the house across the street put on the market?"

"Some time ago, after the owner died. However, the heirs' asking price is steep, and it didn't sell. They left it in waiting, hoping the prices would go up. The heirs are in Africa or Australia somewhere. They left two or three months ago, maybe. With their job, if I remember correctly."

"Do you remember if a stranger to this street passed by during the last two weeks?" McNamara asked.

"I don't think so...." the woman said thoughtfully. "Oh, aye, there was a young woman. I saw her turning around the empty house across the street. I thought she'd be a buyer, although I doubted that she could afford the house. The woman was well dressed. That's true. But not enough for how much they asked for that house. Besides, she looked awfully young."

"How did she look like?" McNamara asked.

"Tall, red-haired, the coquettish type, I think... Pretty young... I'm sorry, I can't remember anything else about the young woman," Mary waved her hand with regret.

"All right, ma'am, thank you," McNamara said. "We'll go and speak to the Randalls at the store."

"Mr Randall isn't there," Mary warned him. "I saw him driving away early this morning. He takes out his car only when he must go to town. Probably, they need supplies. They don't have all their goods delivered here."

"Thank you, ma'am! Good luck with your writing," the DCI said on his way to the front door.

Mary smiled and thanked him. When she opened the door, she found Michael with his key in his hand, unpleasantly surprised to see McNamara. He worried the detective would be a potential rival because of his looks. Then he spotted James behind the DCI and calmed down.

"Good day, sir," McNamara said, enjoying reading Michael's thoughts on his face. "I have a question for you. Did you see or hear anything before the police came last night?"

"I went to bed only after twelve, maybe at one or a little after one, I think, even if I went upstairs earlier," he said. "I thought to shut the window so that the rain wouldn't get inside. It was pattering quite hard, and the thunder was loud. I saw a shadow in front of the house across the street, the one that is empty now. The person was trying to hide behind the trees. It looked like a tall man. But I think it was your man, wasn't it?"

"No, sir, it wasn't our man. If you could recall anything about him, anything at all...." McNamara replied.

"Unfortunately, I don't recall much," Michael answered. "I saw him only for a fraction of a second when the lightning struck. It was clearly a man — tall and massive, but he didn't resemble Graham, for instance... I'm sure of that. I can't tell you more," the man apologized. "I know he was

289

in black and was leaning against the tree, almost half hidden," Michael Reid tried hard to remember.

"All right, sir," McNamara said. "I hope you won't think it's too much, but may I ask you what you're doing at home at this hour?" he asked Reid. McNamara admitted that curiosity got the best of him, but he needed to know.

"I didn't have much to do at work, so I thought to invite my wife to lunch at the pub on the corner. I know Mary doesn't eat when she's alone, and she's got work to do. So, I knew she could use a good meal. Couldn't you, sweetheart?"

The woman, sincerely flattered, nodded. "I'll come right now," she said, forgetting about the detectives. "Wait only until I get a sweater. It's too chilly for this blouse."

Her blouse was light and sleeveless, and it was cold for it even in the house. McNamara had wondered that the woman dressed like that but put it on the fact that Mary was a strange woman.

McNamara brushed off his thoughts about Mary Reid and took his leave from Michael.

"I think it's one of the three, sir," James said. "Graham, Thompson, or Randall. But I still think it's Thompson. Graham seems too much of a coward, and Randall doesn't seem to have a reason."

"You're right, James, but we must verify them all and see who could have done it, even though everything leads to Thompson."

Pensively, the policemen strolled down the street, keeping silent. After a few moments, McNamara broke the silence.

"You know what, let's have a good meal at the Browns' pub, and then we'll go to the station and see what's new. Afterwards, you can go and see McKay once more. Maybe she remembered something."

James agreed more than gladly. He didn't know if the Chief Inspector sent him to see Claire because he had noticed his feelings for her or hoped to hear something new, but the DS didn't care. He wanted to see Claire, and any pretext worked for him.

Suddenly, McNamara changed his mind. "You know what? We haven't asked the two Davidsons any questions. We've forgotten about them. Let's see them," he said, changing direction to their house.

James followed, already regretting the lunch the DCI had promised.

A dark-haired, attractive woman answered the door when McNamara rang at the Davidsons' house. "You're the police, aren't you?" she said. "I kept seeing you on the street and wondered when you might come by our house."

"We have a lot of things to verify, ma'am," McNamara replied. "Are you alone at home, or is your husband here too?"

"I'm alone. Davidson travelled to Plymouth yesterday and left the hotel's phone number so that you could reach him. He left it for you because I have no reason to talk to him," the woman added, leading them inside. "And by the way," she turned to McNamara. "He's not my husband anymore. We divorced some time ago."

"But you still live together?" James asked with astonishment. The residents of Nightingale Street surprised him again.

"Aye, we haven't finished with dividing the property. I'm afraid we must sell the house and split the money. He doesn't want to leave it to me, although I have the children's custody."

"Where are your children?" McNamara asked her curiously.

"I drove them to my parents' yesterday. I didn't want them here. They would have listened to what people were saying. Mrs Randall also called her mother in the morning to take her children. It is not a safe place for them now," the woman shook her head.

"I don't think they were in any danger," McNamara said, but he couldn't be sure. A child might be too nosey and find something about the killer. They didn't have a very scrupulous killer on their hands.

"Did you see anything related to the murders, ma'am?" the DCI thought to ask.

"I'm afraid I didn't. I don't have the habit of spying on people. If poor Mrs Dobbs had lived, she could have told you everything you needed. But now...," she shrugged with sadness. "I haven't seen anything these two days."

"But before? During the last two weeks?"

"I don't think so. I didn't see any strangers. I saw only Patsy, Mrs Porter's daughter," the woman flipped her hand as if it hadn't been significant.

"When?" McNamara became alert.

"A week, maybe a week and a half, I think. I went out with the children for ice cream. It was around seven in the evening, maybe seven and a half. She was with another lass, a little taller than her. Patsy pointed to me and said something to the other girl. They started to giggle. I think they made fun of me because of the house, but I don't have where to go for now. I can't get around too much with my salary," the young woman shook her head.

"Didn't you see anything else, ma'am? Where they went, or what they did?" McNamara insisted.

"They went up the street, and I remember there wasn't anyone else in the street. In the beginning, I thought the girls went to Patsy's house, but Mrs Porter didn't say a word, and I didn't think it was appropriate to ask questions."

"But do you know what the people on the street were doing or where they were then?" McNamara insisted.

"Mrs Stevens was at the window. I spotted her," she frowned, making an effort to remember. "I think Bryony was somewhere in the house. I didn't see her, just her car. I didn't see the Reids or the Thompsons. I know nothing of Goddard, the Dobbs, or Mrs Porter. I passed by the grocer's and spoke to Mrs Randall," she said thoughtfully. "Her husband had left to see a supplier. That's what she told me. About the Browns, I can only presume they were at the pub. After six, a lot of people go there. Really, I don't know what else to say."

"It's enough, ma'am," McNamara smiled at her with gratitude. "You offered us a good image of the general picture. We should have come to you yesterday."

His words made the woman feel important, and she blushed. She had been missing that feeling for some time. The young woman led the two men to the door and remained there, watching them heading to the bar.

McNamara sensed her eyes on his back but didn't say anything. After a few moments, in a quiet voice so only James could hear him, he noted, "She knows a lot. If we had questioned her yesterday, we'd have known Patsy had been here with her friend. Damn it!" The man shook his head, getting into the bar with James in tow.

MCNAMARA SERIES BOX SET
BOOK 0NE & TWO

CHAPTER TWENTY-TWO

After giving their order, the two young people sat down at a table and expected someone to bring them the food. For a few moments, they kept silent, not knowing what to say to each other. Michael watched Mary with sad eyes. He didn't understand why they treated each other the way they were.

Mary looked out the window, although she didn't have anything to see. The pub was precisely on the corner. Beyond the corner, there was a square, and after that, the madness of the city started. People wouldn't pass by there often, only those living on the street. But trees stood in front of the pub and across the street, on one side of the grocer's. The autumn colours bloomed, livelier after the previous night's rain.

The young woman turned and looked at Michael. She noticed the intense way the man was watching her and asked him, "Why are you upset now?"

"I'm not," Michael answered with a soft smile. "I was only thinking of us and our endless quarrels. You know, I think I'd like a more peaceful life. When I think of the people who died, I realise that life is too short. We shouldn't make such a mess of it."

Mary watched him closely, trying to understand what he was thinking, afraid that Michael had decided to end their relationship. Despite everything she said, the young woman loathed the perspective.

"You mean to say you're going to leave me, don't you?" Mary asked in a quarrelsome voice.

"Oh, no," her husband replied in a rush, shaking his head. He reached for her hand and squeezed her fingers. "Just the opposite. I'm not thinking about leaving you. I think I should give you more space and take things with a grain of salt. I should stop letting everything bother me. But no, I'm not thinking of leaving," Michael shook his head again. "If I had wanted that, I'd have done it long ago. We've been playing this silly game for some time," he noticed with surprise, and his brows rose on his forehead.

The woman relaxed a little but kept her guard up. She had never learnt to take anything for granted.

"You want to say you won't yell at me anymore? No matter what I wear or what I do?"

"Not really," the man grimaced, struggling with his pride. "I was thinking of a sort of compromise," he confessed.

Mary Brown brought their order then and put their conversation on hold. The weight of his words started to sink in. They began eating, and after a few moments, Mary nudged him to continue.

"So, you said you thought of a compromise."

The woman didn't like the idea of a compromise. She thought the man wanted to make her do something she didn't like, which didn't sit well with her.

"I was just thinking... I make good money now," Michael explained, forgetting his chicken pie on the plate. "You know my income has increased lately," he waved his hand.

Mary listened attentively, watching her husband.

"And anyway, you also make good money. So, I was thinking we afford to hire someone for cleaning, washing, ironing, and cooking. I know you don't like doing any of it, and I understand that," the man added very matter-of-factly. "I talked to Larry the other day, and he recommended one of his housekeeper's cousins, who's trustful and hardworking. I think she'd be a real help. What are you saying?"

"And what should I do in exchange for that?" Mary replied, doubt sounding in her voice.

"Not very much," his answer came. "I'd like you not to wear such bare-shouldered and short clothes. Not all the time," the man explained. "But if possible, only now and then." He waited a few seconds and asked, "Do you think we could make a deal?"

Mary thought for a few moments and reckoned that his request seemed reasonable enough. She wasn't sure it was wise to compromise, but the man didn't ask much. Besides, it was getting colder lately, and she had been freezing to death only to spite him.

"All right," the woman said, and her agreement surprised Michael, who had already given up waiting for her answer. "However, if you want that, I'll have to go to town tomorrow. I need new clothes. You know what kind of clothes I have," she pointed out.

The woman had always taken care to buy very short skirts and revealing blouses. "And by the way, as variation, I thought to start wearing slacks. What do you think?"

Michael smiled happily, and again, he reached over the table to take her hand and kissed it. "That's brilliant," he exclaimed like a child in front of the Christmas tree. "Truly brilliant."

A few tables away, McNamara and James watched the scene on the opposite side of the room.

"Sir," James said. "These two are a walking disaster. Either they quarrel or kiss each other happily," he shook his head.

"Something like that, James. I'm afraid their marriage is meant to resist, despite its weirdness. Yet, they must get along in their strange way. Meanwhile, Mrs Thompson's will fail, even though the people around think she's the perfect little wife," McNamara replied cynically.

"I wouldn't be surprised," James agreed. "If we think of the 'wonderful' Mr Thompson...."

"Oh, aye, our 'wonderful' Mr Thompson," McNamara scowled. "We do have to go and talk to him in his office. Do you realise we haven't seen him or heard from him since the first night we came here?"

"Aye, it's quite strange. Thompson is somewhere else all the time. People don't hear noises or fights from their house because his wife doesn't have anyone to quarrel with. I'm not surprised everyone thinks they have a good marriage. Don't you think so, sir?"

"Oh, aye, I do," McNamara said. He intended to say something more, but Mrs Brown came with their order and made him stop. She put the plates before them and smiled.

"How's Mrs Porter?" McNamara asked her.

"Not very well," Mary. Brown said sadly. "Her sister came, but I'm afraid my friend is completely down. She can't imagine how Patsy could have died on this street without her seeing or hearing anything. I understand her, really," Mary pitied the woman. "I think I would go crazy if something happened to my children."

"Do you have children, ma'am?" McNamara inquired curiously.

"Aye, I have two boys," the woman said proudly. "One is at college, at Oxford. He didn't want to stay here, and he won a scholarship. The boy is a good student," she said proudly. "The younger one became a pilot and lives in London now. I have good boys. The problem is that we haven't got anyone to run the pub once we're gone," Mary said sadly. "Only if Mark, my older son, comes back, but I don't think so," she shook her head.

"Don't worry, ma'am, things have a way to work out in the end," James tried comforting her.

"Aye, maybe," the woman admitted softly. "Anyway, enjoy, and come to have a meal here anytime. I hope you'll like it."

The men thanked her and started eating.

"James," McNamara raised his head suddenly. "I don't think it's the case, but let's check where the Brown boys were during the last three weeks."

MCNAMARA SERIES BOX SET
BOOK 0NE & TWO

CHAPTER TWENTY-THREE

"Mike, I found something interesting here," Jo said.

"What?"

"I verified what you said. I found out that the lads from Vice had their sights on Daniel Thompson for some time. He seems to have a neat network of escort girls, and all of them are underage. And listen here. Thompson has also got a similar small company on the Internet. For that, he's got five girls, apparently. The lads say that he makes quite a profit. They've been shocked to see how much. It seems that many people prefer picking up girls that way instead of picking up prostitutes on the street. Well, it's the age of information," Jo shrugged. "The inspectors from Vice said that they have a thick file with everything, already having gathered more than enough evidence for a conviction. So, they are moving to arrest Thompson," the young woman, waving broadly.

"Interesting," Mike replied. "But I'm sure there's something else besides the minor girls."

"Of course, love, what did you think?" Jo glanced sideways at Mike.

The man grinned, knowing that Jo had something good under her sleeve. She didn't disappoint him.

"Of course, there's something more. Our man also likes good blackmail. It's more efficient than only pimping the girls. Everything started with one 'client' who couldn't pay anymore. The sod filed a complaint with police and told our lads everything. In detail. Another complaint came from a businessman afterwards. He'd been blackmailed because he had sexual relations with an underage girl. Thompson told him to pay, or his wife and the police would get photos with him and the girl in question. Of course, the man only bluffed by mentioning the police. I don't see Thompson putting himself in our hands. But the businessman got scared and preferred to step forward himself. He also sent his wife on vacation in France as a birthday present," Jo winked at her colleague.

"So kind of him, don't you think?" Mike noted with sarcasm. "Anyway, the man's smart, in his way. I'll give him that. He won't have problems with his wife if anything comes by mail. He gets the letters or the pictures, and the little wife is not aware of what's going on. I'm afraid our story here is also related to blackmail or something like that, Jo," Mike said.

"Of course, Mike. It must be," Jo said. "In most of the cases, the blackmailed people have the tendency to kill the blackmailer. But he should have killed Thompson, not the girls."

"Not if the girls blackmailed him, though. And that, without Thompson's knowledge. The lasses might have decided to make some money on their own. Who knows?" Mike shrugged.

McNamara and James happened to come into the office right then. The DCI surveyed the entire room, and his gaze fell on Jo and Mike, huddled in a corner talking. The other inspectors were hard at work at their desks. When the Chief Inspector greeted them, people's eyes turned to him.

"What's new?" the man asked. "Have you made any progress? Anything new come up?"

"Aye, sir," Jo said. "I've got something new. Actually, we do," she said, including Mike, with a broad gesture, as the detective had started that line of investigation.

The woman recounted to McNamara what she had just told Mike about Daniel Thompson's side business.

"We've also got documents, sir. This Mr Thompson seems to be a real tart, sir," Jo said fiercely.

"What a language, Jo," Mike chided her. "You should watch it a little, don't you think so, love?"

"Mike, I don't feel like playing now," McNamara snapped. "You have fun with Jo on your own time, not when we have so many problems to solve. I've got a lot of murders here, and we aren't closer to the killer than we were yesterday. It might be Thompson, but there's no guarantee. The girls could have been killed by someone they blackmailed. Don't you think?"

Jo blushed because of McNamara's words, but both detectives nodded. They had been thinking of the same thing, even if they still saw Thompson in the role of the killer. Yet, everything seemed to point to him, which meant he might not be the killer. That was often the case.

"Think that everyone said that Thompson immediately arrived at the crime scene in the Dobbs' yard. He was the first," McNamara said, leaning against a desk. "Thompson wore a suit — all witnesses say the same thing. If he'd been the killer, the man wouldn't have had time to change clothes, but neither James nor anyone else saw any blood on his suit, did they?" he turned to James.

"Indeed, sir," the DS said. "It was spotless, sir, although a little wrinkled because he had carried Mr Dobbs in the house. He hadn't even taken off his tie. Thompson can't be the killer. If the man had killed that girl, I would say he'd have had at least some bloodstains on him."

"So, we must find one of the girls' clients," McNamara concluded, confident in his man. "The lasses probably blackmailed the client without Thompson's permission, thinking it was easy to do, but, obviously, they were amateurs. If Thompson learnt about it, then he knows who killed them. Have you found out where's the flat he rented for Patsy?"

"Aye, sir, just now," Jo said. "I was thinking of going there with the operative team. I've already asked for the search warrant. I thought we shouldn't waste time, and I was positive you'd want us to go."

"Of course! You've done well. Good, I'll come too," McNamara said. "Let me see what's piled on my desk. We'll leave in five minutes," the man said, leaving the squad room.

Meanwhile, James went to one of the other guys to pursue the line of investigation he and McNamara had discussed at the pub.

"Listen, Jay. Please, investigate the Browns' boys. I understand one would be at Oxford, a student, and the other one would live in London. He's a pilot. Please, see where the lads have been this month. If you find out something useful, call us. All right? At least we want to ensure that they have no connection to this business."

Meanwhile, McNamara left his office and gestured towards James, Mike, and Jo to follow him. "Have you called the operative team, Jo?" he asked on his way out.

"Aye, sir, they're waiting outside in the car," she confirmed.

"Good, you'll come with Mike, and I'll be with James so that we can move freely. We might have to go somewhere else afterwards. James will be off duty tonight. During the last twenty-four hours, he had a difficult time," McNamara said.

"And you, sir?"

"I'll manage, Jo. No worries, no one's pining for me. By the way, who did you send to McNeil's and Stevens?"

"Clarence will stay with them until tonight. I thought the women should stay in their own homes like last night, so I assigned Phelps and

Dulgon. If something happens, at least we don't have two victims simultaneously, sir," Jo said matter-of-factly.

"It sounds cynical but true," McNamara said pensively. "We'd better limit the losses. Although I don't think the man will attack tonight. The attacker is hurt, and we know that he didn't go to any hospital or doctor. So, he didn't get any medical assistance. The man can't be in a good state," the DCI said, turning to the door.

About to go out, the DCI turned and asked, "Has anyone read Diane's diary?"

"Aye, sir," Mike said. "I have. That's where I read about Thompson and his funny business. Jo verified with the lads from Vice to see if they knew about it, and that's how we learnt what we've just told you."

"Haven't you found anything related to the murder?" the DCI insisted.

"No, sir. However, the diary entries stopped the day Diane left home. She might have met her killer afterwards. In the diary, the girl only praises Thompson for how smart and good-looking he is. The lass wrote that she would make a lot of money, have a good life, and have fun. She also wrote about Patsy. Apparently, Patsy introduced her to Thompson. Patsy seemed convinced that the man would marry her after he'd divorced 'that cow.'

McNamara scowled, so Mike hurried to mention, "That's a quote, by the way. That's what Thompson called his wife before his little friends."

"All right then," McNamara grimaced. It disgusted him to hear someone talking that way about their life partner, no matter what. "Come on, maybe we'll find something in Patsy's flat," he said, leading his men out.

The Chief Inspector disliked Thompson more and more. The man had his petty affairs, but he also used girls to make money, and in the process, he would also disparage Alice.

McNamara was sorry for the poor woman, but he also despised her for believing blindly in her husband. The inspector would have shown some consideration if he had had a good woman in his corner.

Still, the man couldn't see himself marrying a woman like Alice. She was too charmless and prim for his taste. And her old-fashioned ideas were better suited for another century.

McNamara couldn't stop comparing her to Bryony, who had much more life and willpower in her little finger than Alice had in her entire body. He couldn't imagine someone would dupe Bryony like Alice had been duped.

***

The police entered the flat in the presence of witnesses — the superintendent and a cleaning lady. The other people in the building were either at work or still on vacation.

The flat was in a very stylish block. The staircases were bright, and the lobby reflected perfectly the luxurious interior of the building. Probably, it was pretty expensive to live there, what with the security guard and its extreme cleanliness.

Apparently, Thompson's business went well. McNamara presumed that the man must have had flats for the other girls, not only for Patsy.

Jo had told McNamara the network involved over fifteen girls. So, there was a lot of money involved.

Thompson wouldn't have persuaded the girls to work for him if he had brought them into a dump. Probably, his fees were high. The girls were underage, and besides that, such films on the Internet were well paid, and a specific type of public enjoyed them.

Considering the blackmail the man used to practice, Thompson made quite a quid, so he could afford to rent pleasant flats for the girls working for him.

The police sifted through the flat but didn't find much to help them with their case.

They didn't find any kind of documents, not even a piece of paper with one line written down, which seemed off. No newspapers or an agenda lay on sight or inside the drawers. Such things could be found everywhere unless people were illiterate, and Patsy wasn't.

Noticing that the police didn't have any success, the superintendent stepped forward. He hesitated to disturb McNamara but thought he'd better share what he knew.

"DCI McNamara," he said, "you should know something. Yesterday, the man who rented the flat left here with a bag stuffed with many things. He paid the rent in advance for six months only three weeks before, so I didn't panic. It wasn't my place to inquire about what he was doing. Nothing seemed illegal, and he didn't disturb the other people in the building. The girl, you know, I thought she went back home. Probably, she didn't like something. They didn't fool me when they said that the lass was his niece from the country," the man scoffed.

"So that's how it is. Thompson cleaned the flat. That's why it looks as if nobody had lived here," McNamara said with resignation in his voice. Yet, fury thundered in his eyes.

The police turned out only a few clothes, too few for a girl like Patsy. She worked in the world's oldest profession, which required specific garments.

The forensic experts didn't find a newspaper or magazine. Thompson must have been afraid that the girl had noted something down, so he had preferred to make everything disappear.

McNamara turned to Jo. "Do the guys from Vice have people following Thompson and his clients?"

"Aye, they put him under surveillance the day after we found that girl across the street. It's a pity they didn't do it earlier. At least we'd have known exactly where he was and what he did that day."

"Aye," McNamara replied dryly. "It's a pity. Call and tell them I don't care about their plans, but I want them to arrest him at once. I can't afford to wait. We must investigate his office and all the places where he might have hidden something, and possibly, the places where he kept the girls. The lads from Vice know where those places are if they have monitored his movements for a while. And I want to interrogate him myself. If they don't know that already and complain that I'm spoiling their case, explain that murder always comes first. And we don't have only one," the DCI continued bitterly.

"Aye, sir."

CHAPTER TWENTY-FOUR

Mary and Michael's coming back from the pub together, holding hands, surprised Alice and stole her breath. A tight knot chocked her. That wasn't what she had expected after the fights heard from their house lately.

Alice Thompson wasted time with Mary now and then, but only because she didn't have anything else to do. She would have thrown that evil woman out of the house on her ear if she had been in Michael Reid's place. However, she didn't have to live with Mary and bear her laziness and slutty behaviour.

Alice waited for them, and when they got closer, she came out in the street as if she hadn't seen them before.

"Mary, hello," Alice shouted, pretending to be surprised. The woman wanted to be heard and interrupt the couple's conversation. "I'm sorry. I didn't know you were with your husband," she lied, wanting to make Michael believe that Mary could have gone out with someone else. "Never mind, I'll come another time," she said in a sad voice.

"It isn't necessary, Mrs Thompson," Michael replied to her, a small smile tucked in the corner of his mouth.

The man refused to take the bait. He knew his wife was more intelligent than Alice thought.

Mary had her flaws, but stupidity wasn't one. She wouldn't have been so stupid as to bring someone on Nightingale Street. If she had cheated on him, the woman would have done it somewhere else where no one would have told on her.

"I have to go," Michael continued. "I only came to take Mary out for lunch," he said, squeezing Mary's fingers with affection.

To his satisfaction, Alice turned green with envy. The man assumed that she would be jealous because he knew her kind of woman, dissatisfied with her life, even if she tried to prove the opposite. Alice tried to hide her misery and unhappiness under the mask of a responsible person. In the process, she judged everyone else.

Michael hid his smile. That was his little revenge for Alice's evil thoughts about his marriage. Besides, the woman had been nagging at his wife all the time.

The man was right, and Alice felt as if she had been choking. That wasn't right at all. She did her best and tried to be a good wife, but Daniel never came to invite her to lunch.

At the beginning of their marriage, the man would phone and ask her what she was doing and if she needed him to buy something. She had never heard anything from him during the day for a long time now.

Alice knew that Daniel was still living there, in the same house with her, only because food or clean clothes ran out. Otherwise, she didn't see him for days in a row.

They had even been sleeping separately for a long while now. Daniel said that he didn't want to disturb her when he came home late at night, and she accepted.

Alice didn't know what to think. She was afraid, although she had hidden her fears. The young woman tried to call Daniel at the office in the past, but lately, he had always been away. So, she stopped. Daniel started coming home so late in the evening that she would fall asleep before seeing her husband.

And there was Mary, who didn't care a fig about anything concerning her husband's comfort, and yet, Michael Reid came to invite her to lunch during the week. He was attentive and tender with her, which wasn't right. The injustice of everything made her sick, and Alice felt like screaming.

Instead, the woman smiled and said warmly to Mary, "I wanted to invite you for coffee. That's all."

"You'd better come to my house, Alice," Mary replied. "I visited you last time," she explained, but she didn't want to be on Alice's territory again. The woman preferred to have battles on her own ground. The thunder in Alice's eyes warned that a fight with her neighbour seemed imminent.

Alice accepted somewhat reluctantly. Michael said goodbye to them and leaned over his wife, whispering something in her ear that made her smile. Then, the man kissed her, but not perfunctorily, as Alice thought.

That devastated Alice, who choked on her own emotions once more. The sight of Michael Reid kissing his wife as if they had still been on their honeymoon sickened her. Daniel hadn't kissed her for a long time — maybe on her cheek occasionally when he left for work. Otherwise, they were two strangers living in the same house.

Alice didn't want the Reids to understand her feelings, so she smiled. Yet, they noticed that her smile was somewhat bitter.

After Michael left, Mary invited Alice inside the house, feeling sorry for her, in a way, but not very sorry. Alice had nagged her too much, and she couldn't have genuine compassion for her.

Mary let people do whatever they wanted. Obviously, if they let her be. She didn't like people who pushed her to change, as Alice did.

The young woman prepared coffee for both of them, even though she knew that Alice would have preferred tea. But then, Mary also had her little wickedness. She put the cups on the table and lit one of the three or four cigarettes she would smoke every day.

Her neighbour's reproachful look amused her. She had expected it, and Alice never disappointed. She was predictable.

Alice thought it was undignified for a woman to smoke, but Mary didn't care for that opinion. She only thought it wasn't healthy and tried to quit, but she didn't think of saying anything to Alice about her goal. The woman would have thought that her pestering had made Mary stop smoking, and she refused to give Alice reasons to gloat.

"Have you seen, Mary, how full of life our little street has become lately?" Alice tried to make small talk, although what she had just seen still bothered her.

"I think it rather became full of death," Mary replied dryly. "As far as I know, only bodies have been taken from here these days. How could you say such a thing, Alice? Don't you have a little compassion for the killed women?"

'Even though one of them was your husband's lover?' Mary thought. Although, that didn't explain making light of murder, either.

"I was talking about the cars and people coming here," Alice said with a blush, resenting Mary's reproach. "I didn't mean to minimize what happened," she explained apologetically.

"All right," Mary replied softly. "I didn't want to snap at you like that. I resent what's going on and that such young lives were wasted. Obviously, I also have a selfish reason. Everything disturbs me from my writing," she tried to appease Alice with a joke.

Alice didn't comment. Because curiosity gnawed at her, she decided to ask Mary about what had happened with her husband.

"Yesterday evening, you and your husband had a bad fight, and everyone heard you. How come he invited you to lunch today? I noticed he's usually mad for a few days after one of your discussions."

"I don't know," Mary shrugged. "Probably because he wanted to give me some important news."

"What news?" Alice asked, thirsty to hear about new things, even if they didn't concern her directly. Her life had become so dull lately that she tried to live vicariously through others.

"He wants to hire me a permanent housekeeper so that I wouldn't get tired working in the house," replied Mary. Her tone implied it wasn't a big deal.

'As if you had ever tired,' Alice thought spitefully. Moreover, Mary's indifference about her husband's gesture shocked her.

"How kind of him! He's so full of consideration," Alice remarked sweetly.

"Nonsense," Mary replied. She didn't like pretences and knew that Alice wasn't happy for her, but the opposite. Her neighbour would have preferred to hear that Michael had come to tell her that he would pack his things and take his leave.

Watching Alice closely to better enjoy her expression, the woman said maliciously, "I think he just got sick of cold food and ironing his shirts by himself, Alice. I think he thought about his own comfort when he made that decision."

"But you don't do anything in the house?" Alice asked with astonishment. She had noticed that Mary wasn't the perfect housewife, but she hadn't thought that the woman didn't do anything. After all, it was her house, and she had to take care of it somehow.

Alice didn't think that a man would overlook something like that. Michael Reid worked and brought money into the house. Alice didn't believe Mary made much from what she wrote.

As if she hadn't noticed Alice's expression, Mary replied, "Only if I can't do without." The woman shrugged. "I don't have a domestic streak, like you. I prefer working on my computer all day long than passing the vacuum cleaner or peeling potatoes," Mary continued, indifferent to her neighbour's horror.

The woman hadn't cared about what people said for a long while. Mainly, she hadn't cared about her neighbour's words, considering Alice was a stupid snob who didn't see what happened right under her nose.

On the other hand, Alice never believed that a woman could be so careless with her house. Now she understood why she had always seen dust on Mary's furniture and things all over the place. Their kitchen looked unused. Yet, Alice had assumed that Mary did something. She couldn't get away without doing anything.

"How's Mr Thompson these days?" Mary asked, deciding that some payback was in order.

"He's at work, you know that," Alice answered stiffly. The topic had become more sensitive for her since she had seen Mary with Michael. "Daniel works hard to get a promotion. You know, he is a critical person there, and they need him. They give him most of the accounts, especially if they're difficult and other people can't manage them," Alice answered, beaming with pride. "But people know that my Daniel is the best in the company, and he can't say no, you see, even if he's sick of that. But he promised to take me on vacation soon. We'll go to a wonderful place to compensate for all the lost time," Alice said, but the woman knew that she was lying to herself. She didn't think Daniel would take her anywhere.

"Aye, I see," Mary said, even though she didn't believe a word. She knew that Daniel Thompson was no good at accounting and was sure he didn't have any intention to take his little wife on vacation.

Thompson wouldn't go with Alice anywhere. The man would have taken one of his little sweethearts if he had left. Mary suspected that her neighbour didn't work but earned his money otherwise.

She had a friend who was a bookkeeper in the company which employed Thompson. The woman had told Mary that their boss disliked the man and was on the verge of firing him. Daniel had lost many accounts because of his incompetence. Their boss had decided to let him go at the beginning of the following month. Daniel had already received the termination notice.

Again, Mary was annoyed with Alice. She never had anything important to say and frustrated her invariably. Silence filled the room while they drank their coffee. After a while, Alice felt she had to say something.

"I think I'm going home. I bought a lamb chop, and I was thinking to cook it with mint sauce. Daniel is crazy about that, and I make it wonderfully. Everything is in the spice."

"I'm not very fond of meat," Mary said with indifference, unwilling to listen to Alice's recipe for lamb. "I prefer salads. It's easier to prepare and easier to digest."

Alice made a face but said nothing. She smiled softly, stood up, and moseyed to the door. Mary followed her — she couldn't wait to see her out. "See you later," Mary said with a smile when Alice went out.

After closing the door, Mary scowled. 'Dull woman, Oh, Lord! I can even nap when she visits. What the hell did Thompson see in her in the beginning? Maybe he knew she was one of the few women who would say nothing about his extracurricular activities. He could have as many lovers as he wanted. Aye, that's got to be it!"

The woman snapped her fingers as if she had reached an essential conclusion and returned to her desk to work. She forgot everything about Alice when Michael's gesture popped back into her mind.

Mary was afraid that the man had taken advantage of her somehow. Her mistrustful nature got in her way of thinking. She couldn't let herself believe in someone else.

Since very young, Mary had learnt to protect her heart and never wear it on her sleeve. She wanted to avoid any disappointment and preferred to take people as they were. The woman didn't invest much in them, so her pain was close to the surface when they left.

Shrugging, Mary started work, determined to forget about all of that. She couldn't know Michael's precise intentions. What was meant to happen would happen anyway.

***

Alice busied herself in the kitchen after she had finally calmed down. She knew what to do there, and no one could upset her. Yet, the woman couldn't stop thinking that something wasn't quite all right. She had had that feeling for days. Still, she chased her dark thoughts away and got lost in her cooking.

The doorbell rang and made her angry. Alice didn't feel like seeing anyone, so she thought to ignore it. However, the person at the door insisted.

With a scoff, the woman rinsed her hands, dried them on a towel, and went to see who didn't want to go away. The sight of the policemen shocked her, and frightened, she opened the door. "Aye, what is it?"

"We have a search warrant, ma'am," a short and plump woman said. "For the entire house."

Alice fainted.

CHAPTER TWENTY-FIVE

McNamara monitored Thompson through the interrogation room window and noticed that the man seemed confident, convinced that the police brought him in for questioning because of the crimes on Nightingale Street. That meant that he didn't have a direct connection to them.

Yet, the connection existed. Thompson had taught blackmail tactics to the girls, which led to their deaths.

"We'll leave him in there for a while. Maybe an hour or two. He'll lose some of that confidence," McNamara said to his people and assigned Mike to Thompson's surveillance before returning to his office. The papers on his desk needed his attention.

The DCI had already received the forensic reports about the findings in the basement that morning. They had enough incriminating evidence, and, more important, they had his

DNA. The inspector still had to wait for some details, but now, he was confident that the killer wouldn't get free once they caught him.

After about fifteen minutes, McNamara left the papers on his desk and sauntered to the window, overlooking a square. The view was attractive, and not many people passed by there at that hour. It was almost deserted. Afternoons were peaceful in the area. Two streets farther away, he would find the haven of the underground world — pimps and prostitutes.

A young woman with golden-blond hair crossed the alley and sat on a bench, still, her hands in her lap, deep in thought. She reminded the DCI of another girl, but with strawberry-blond hair. McNamara liked both her apparent calm and her hot fury.

Now that he was alone, the man could admit it to himself, even though he wouldn't have confessed that to anyone else, fearing the show of weakness. The detective had seen how feelings weakened people.

McNamara had never allowed his heart to get involved in any of his relationships. At almost forty, the man doubted that it would ever happen to him.

Still, something in that lass, Bryony, inspired trust, stability, and longing and made him have crazy thoughts, like asking her to belong to him. Obviously, that might have been a consequence of the previous night. The young woman had seemed vulnerable, small, and hurt, which made him want to hold her. He had tried to tell her he was there, and she needn't be afraid anymore. But he couldn't do it then, and he couldn't do it now. Probably, he wouldn't ever be able to do it.

He might offer his friendship to her in the end, and if Bryony accepted, then it would be fine. If not, it would be fine, as well. 'It wouldn't be a big loss,' he murmured. Yet, something told him that he was just lying to himself.

McNamara had always entertained temporary relationships. He broke off any affairs before women believed that he might get serious. It had been a good ride for him, at least so far. 'It would be good now, too,' the man whispered, leaving the window.

The Chief Inspector sat at his work desk again and started to browse the papers, looking for a new line of investigation. Still distracted, the man couldn't focus only on the case. He needed something but didn't know what and was restless. McNamara thought that probably he needed to sleep an entire night again and spend some time in the office instead of running all over the place.

The man had hardly finished that thought, that James came into the room. "I think it's time, boss," he said with a nod. "Thompson's lost his temper and is making a big fuss downstairs."

"Then, let's go, James," McNamara said, happy to set his disturbing thoughts aside. He feared the conclusion he might have reached and decided to keep his distance from such reflections for a while.

Downstairs, the DCI watched the man through the one-way mirror. Thompson had lost his temper, indeed. Panic marred his traits, and fear shone in his eyes. He was afraid that the police knew about his business. Otherwise, it wouldn't have made sense to keep him in there.

Deep lines on his forehead, Thompson wondered if he should call for a solicitor. But then, he didn't have one. The man had never thought he would need one, being confident that he would never see a police interrogation room in his lifetime. Besides, his business wasn't legal, so he hadn't needed a solicitor in his organisation before.

Thompson was almost sure that Patsy was one of the girls found that morning because, otherwise, the police hadn't bothered him. No one of the men he had blackmailed threatened him or seemed unwilling to pay.

Suddenly, the feeling that someone watched him from the other side of the wall on his right made his skin crawl. The man tried to compose himself but failed. He had panicked, but he had never functioned well in small and close spaces. Anyway, it was too late after he had lost his temper earlier.

McNamara and James entered the room and interrupted the man's thoughts. Thompson tried to smile at them. "May I know why I've been brought here?" he thought to attack first.

"Don't you really know?" McNamara asked, sitting across from him while James sat on his left.

Mike remained on the other side of the mirror, as McNamara had told him, to survey the evolution of the interview.

"No, I don't know," Thompson said, staring at the DCI through narrowed eyes, trying to find out how much the police knew.

McNamara didn't answer and didn't even glance at the man but busied himself with the preparations for recording the interview. He turned on the recording camera and announced the date and the hour for the record. Then, the inspector mentioned the names of the people present in the room and turned to Thompson.

"We'll record the interview with Daniel Thompson. Sir, you must know that you don't have to answer our questions. You're entitled to have your solicitor or a solicitor appointed by the court present for this interview. If you refuse to benefit from this right, you must know that everything you say will be used against you in court."

Thompson thought whether he should ask for a solicitor appointed by the court for a few moments but concluded that a solicitor couldn't be more competent than he was, so he refused.

"All right, then," McNamara said. "What can you tell us about Diane McWilliams, Patsy Porter, and Anna McDower?"

Thompson understood they knew a lot if they had found out about his connection with the three girls. However, he decided to give an evasive answer. "I'm not sure, but I think I met Patsy in town once. By accident, you know. I was coming from a client, and she was with some friends. She introduced them to me. I can't be sure, but I think I heard those names."

"So, there's no other connection between you and them?" McNamara asked drily.

"Of course not," Thompson tried to smile charmingly. "How could there be?"

"For instance, by paying the rent for their flats," McNamara attacked in force and opened the file he had brought and placed before him on the table.

Instantly, beads of sweat covered Daniel Thompson's forehead. The man hunched over the table but still tried to deny their statement.

"Me? I didn't rent any flat for anyone. For God's sake, where would I get such money?" he asked, dumbfounded. "Everything I make I bring home. I've taken a hit with the penalties, and I can't say I bring much at home. Business is not very good," he tried to explain away his incompetence and disinterest in his job.

"Then, how would you explain these lease contracts?" McNamara asked, removing a few pages from the file and showing them to the man. "It isn't only one, and the leases aren't cheap, either. The flats are situated in good areas and have amenities. Anyway, you didn't pay for them from your salary. You couldn't have paid for them with your salary, even if you had kept working. So, you have another source of income," McNamara concluded.

"Where could I have found another source of income?" Thompson bellowed, losing his temper. "Do you really think I could make so much money even if I had two jobs?"

"Of course not," McNamara grinned at him sarcastically. "But when you have your own business and other people work for you, you can," he nodded knowingly.

Suddenly, Thompson understood that he had gambled and lost. Yet, he decided not to abandon the fight so quickly. "I don't want to answer any more questions now. The interview ends here," he knocked his fist on the top of the table.

McNamara turned off the camera and said, "Pity, you could have exonerated yourself of murder. If you don't want to, it's your business. The rest is easy for us. Everything we have pointed to you." The DCI turned around and left Thompson at the table. The man had turned white when the implications of the Chief Inspector's words hit their mark.

Thompson couldn't utter a single word, although he would have wanted to shout after the detective. As McNamara had thought, Thompson was essentially a coward and couldn't face the consequences of his actions.

CHAPTER TWENTY-SIX

"Bryony, it's quite late, and I'd like to go back home," Mrs Stevens said harshly, and her request interrupted Bryony's thoughts.

"You can't," the girl practically jumped off her chair. She worried that the old lady might be a target that night again. "You can go only when the constable assigned to stay with you arrives. Isn't that right, sir?" she turned to the policeman who had stayed with them that afternoon.

The man had remained silent, noticing the determination in the old woman's voice.

"I'm sorry, love," the woman said in a steely voice, not allowing the constable to answer. "I can't stay one moment more. I want to go home and be among my own things. You're a nice girl, but I don't like to stay away from home much, which you know. I'm not afraid of that murderer. I will lock the doors, and he won't do anything to me."

"I'm afraid he could harm you, love," Bryony replied in a calm but determined voice.

The young constable's respect for her increased. He had seen her sparring with the old lady all day long.

"So, if you really want to go, and believe me, I understand you want to, you'll take him with you," the lass continued, pointing to the constable, who froze. To spend an entire evening in the crone's company didn't represent his idea of a pleasant evening.

"What about you?" the older woman asked. "I don't even think to leave you alone with no guard. The attacker has more against you than against me," she emphasised. "You are the one who hurt him, literally and figuratively."

"I won't even discuss it," Bryony said decisively. "You want to leave, then you take him with you."

The old woman felt selfish to take the police officer with her and leave Bryony alone. However, the woman realised that the lass wouldn't make easy prey for anyone. Not even for McNamara, who would watch her in that particular way when he thought no one observed him.

"Very well, love," the woman accepted. "But only if you promise that you'll be careful and let no one inside, woman or man, whether you know the person. When the constable's shift arrives, you call this young man here to come and see if he recognised the person, and only then do you let them in."

"All right, mom," Bryony smiled. "I'll do that. Now, go on. I see you can't wait anymore."

The old woman hesitated for a few moments but told herself that nothing would happen to the lass and headed for the door. The constable followed her, his heart in his boots, thinking of what McNamara would say for not respecting his orders. Still, he consoled himself with the thought that he had remained with one of the women.

Bryony returned to her ledgers. She had already made significant strides in her work but worried about what happened at the bookshop that day. She couldn't be sure that everything was all right. After thinking of that for a while, she glanced at her watch. She decided to call, seeing it was just a little before closing time.

"Bryony's bookshop," a pleasant voice answered her call.

"Hallo, Meg, is that you?" she asked. "Bryony here."

"How nice you called. I've done a good job today, and everything is all right. I had enough clients and cashed in a lot. You won't be sorry you hired me," the girl announced in a cheerful voice.

Bryony smiled, the girl's youthful optimism working wonders on her own mood. If she had to temporarily hand over the shop's management to someone else, she was happy she had that girl to take care of things.

"I'm happy you've had a good day," Bryony said, her voice betraying her smile. "Was there anything you might need some help with?"

"Not really," Meg answered thoughtfully. "Oh, aye, there was something. A bloke about fifty, a stocky, limping man, bothered me asking where you were and when you would come at the shop."

"Oh, Lord," said Bryony. "What did he look like?" a bell rang in her head, hearing about the limping.

"I don't know what to say," Meg replied with regret. "I couldn't get a good look at him. He came when it was very crowded, you know. I told him he couldn't find you for a few days because you were sick. Have I done something wrong?" she asked in a small voice.

"No, you haven't," Bryony reassured her. "Don't worry! However, if he comes back, pay attention to his face. The police would like to know what he looks like. But I don't think he will be back."

"Well, Bryony, I'll do that. What should I do after closing the shop?"

"Take the money to the bank as I told you and deposit it. You keep the deposit note with you, and tomorrow, you record it in the log you can find in the left drawer."

"All right, I got it. Should I call you back?"

"No, call me tomorrow. Bye."

Meg thanked her once more for the job and trust and hung up.

Bryony had made herself some tea and toast as she didn't feel like eating anything else and had just laid them on the table when the phone rang. She reached out for the receiver, putting some sugar in her tea simultaneously.

"Aye," she said.

"Put Clarence on," McNamara's voice thundered in the receiver.

"I would, but he's not here," the lass replied.

"What?" McNamara's voice thundered. "What do you mean? Where the hell is he? I've assigned him to stay there with you."

"Aye, but Mrs Stevens couldn't stay here anymore and had to go home. So, I asked him to go with her."

"You, stupid, little woman," McNamara bellowed again and disconnected the call.

Bryony scowled at the receiver and then hung up. "Happy to hear from you too," she murmured, sitting down at the table. She drank her tea, browsing a magazine but couldn't focus. McNamara's way of talking to her bothered her. Everything related to him troubled her — everything that had happened the previous night and that morning.

Something about that man drew her towards him. Yet, there was something else that made her reticent. The detective was as changeable as the weather and very hard to comprehend. He knew how to hurt her but also had a unique way to make her feel safe and carefree around him.

CHAPTER TWENTY-SEVEN

The man was sitting in his car, thinking. He had looked for Bryony everywhere. She wasn't at the bookshop, so the woman had probably stayed at home.

The intruder knew precisely what she would do as he had liked the woman and followed her a few times. He had liked her more than he liked the stupid bitches he had killed. He had wanted her and decided to have her in the end.

But now, the man had to get rid of her if he wanted to keep his self-esteem. The woman had hurt him and had to pay for that.

He had decided not to take anything from any woman anymore. He had had enough of that in his lifetime. The man was sick of being told what to do and when to do it.

His mother was the first, nagging him and preaching about the punishment he deserved for looking where he shouldn't or doing something she didn't like.

Unfortunately, the hag didn't pass away soon enough, amazingly, surviving her constant drinking. It took her years to die, but the day the woman died was his first day of happiness, and he had thought that the time to take care of his own life had come.

So, the man left the village where he had lived for twenty-seven years and hoped to see the world. He needed to feel that the world belonged to him, and it did for a little while.

He didn't have much money because he didn't have what to sell. They had rented a miser cottage, as his mother called it. It was more of a shed that she had divided in two with plywood to have her own space. So, the man left only with the clothes on his back. He worked on his way to London, a few days here, a few there. He chopped and carried logs and dug gardens but saved money and headed to the capital, thinking he would make something of himself. Something big. For that, he went to evening school and studied hard.

But, in the end, he ran out of money, always because of women. He didn't know what they were able to do to a man. Then, he learnt. He needed to keep them on a leash, or they would make a fool out of him and suck every penny out of his pockets.

Left with nothing again, the man thought of what he had to do. The choices were few, so he decided to marry a woman with money, being sick of hard work and miser dwellings. He needed someone to take care of him. And he found her. Aye, she really cared for him!

The man became a servant in his own house. Well, actually, hers. Nothing inside belonged to him. Sometimes he felt as if he had lived with his mother again. Only the smell of the booze and men his mother used to bring into the house each night were missing.

His wife didn't listen to him, as if he hadn't had a brain to think. Yet, he was the one who had attended college. He had got a college diploma, for God's sake!

It was like the man hadn't even existed in the house. Her way was the only way. She knew better what to say and do and the place for everything. He had to work all the time. Everything suffocated him.

Then, those stupid girls came and asked for money from him. As if he had had more money to give them. He had already paid for the fun he had with them. That was right and understandable. He hadn't thought he would have to pay for something else.

All his painfully saved money was gone, and he couldn't touch the family money because the crone would have noticed.

But he paid the girls for everything. He had picked them up one by one, and they came to the cage willingly. It had been so easy.

The man had fun with them for a few days and would have liked to still have them in his hands for a while, but it wasn't possible. He had to lie to them and asked each of them to lie. But they did because the stupid cows hadn't understood that he couldn't let them go.

And now, that McNeill woman had to spoil everything. She had a lovely face, but he couldn't forgive her. She didn't know what he could do.

Bryony didn't know who he was because, otherwise, the police would have arrested him already. But she still had to pay for having hurt him.

He would wait a few more days, maybe two or three. Just so that the police would think that he had given up. Then, he would make his move.

It was a pity that he had lost his hiding place. He could have kept Bryony there for a while and enjoyed it. It had been fun with those lasses, but it could have been spectacular with her.

Well, now he had to forget about that. He would just kill the woman. Then, he would take care of the old crone, although he was afraid that he would do her a favour by sparing her any future pains. In compensation, he would make her suffer now.

He had heard the old woman saying that he was a puppy on a leash. Such words deserved punishment. The old hag would die knowing that he couldn't be duped or ordered around.

At first, the man thought that he was killing those girls to keep his marriage. Afterwards, he realised that he had power and didn't need his marriage. He could do whatever he wanted. He had proven his manhood so many times over! His eyes sparkled with pride at that thought.

Unfortunately, the man couldn't give up his servitude now. He had to keep appearances and come back home. But only for a little while.

MCNAMARA SERIES BOX SET
BOOK 0NE & TWO

CHAPTER TWENTY-EIGHT

The furious knocks on the door made Bryony's heart practically jump out of her chest. She was afraid to go and open it, but the banging on the door didn't seem to stop. The woman dashed there, with angry steps, forgetting about her fear.

She looked through the peephole and noticed McNamara scowling ferociously. His eyes had turned hard. He started bellowing by the time she reached for the doorknob.

"Open the door at once, Bryony. I know you're in there."

"Only if you calm down," the woman replied in a steely voice. "I've had enough today, and I won't take your mood now. Consider that I'm not at my best either," she added, quarrelsome as ever when it came to him.

"I'm calm," the man said quietly. "Now open the damned door."

Bryony sighed but opened the door. A smile perched on her lips when she thought that McNamara wasn't included in Mrs Stevens' indications. However, it would have been fun to see his face if she had called the constable to vouch for him first.

McNamara shoved past her furiously. "Are you alone?" he asked.

"Of course, I am," the woman replied. "Who could I be with?"

"I don't know, but I don't see why you'd have let me knock like an idiot, the eyes of the entire street on me."

"I'm sure it's not the entire street," Bryony said. "It's only Mary Reid and Mrs Randall. You exaggerate, McNamara, and it doesn't suit you, really," she said, closing the door.

McNamara scowled at her and then followed her to the kitchen, where, apparently, she had set up her operational centre.

"I wonder why Alice Thompson hasn't come out. You did make enough noise to rouse the entire street," Bryony said, amused. "She doesn't have much fun at home, and your shouts must have been entertaining."

"You shouldn't laugh at me. This is actually the thanks I get for coming to see if you're all right," the inspector noticed with bitter reproach.

"Sorry," Bryony murmured remorsefully.

Yet, McNamara's gesture still amused her. The lass wouldn't have expected that from a man like him. She could see him sending someone when he had found out she was alone. But Bryony hadn't imagined he would come himself, probably leaving his work unfinished. She was sure he had enough to do.

"By the way," he passed over her excuses as if she had never said anything. "Alice Thompson has been very busy today and probably doesn't need any supplementary fun."

"What do you mean?" Bryony asked breathlessly, and her voice shook with fear. She hadn't thought Alice was in any danger.

"Don't worry," McNamara said, waving her fears away. "She wasn't attacked. I wouldn't make a joke about something like that. She just had her house searched, and I'm afraid it was unpleasant," he added. "No one likes such things."

"Do you think that Thompson did it?" the woman raised her brows. "I would be surprised," she shook her head. "He doesn't dare to do something like that. He's just a lame Casanova."

"You're wrong," McNamara retorted. "He's capable of more than you think. Now, I can't tell you what because you're still part of the

351

investigation, but take my word for that," he nodded.

"So, I'm a suspect," Bryony exclaimed in a shocked voice, getting angry. "Do you really think I hurt myself last night? Could you tell me how I could have done it? I'm really curious," she replied with sarcasm.

"Don't be silly," McNamara replied, suddenly annoyed again. "Of course, I don't think you're guilty. When I said you were part of the investigation, I meant you're one of the victims."

"Oh, thanks for reassuring me," Bryony replied, always in the same sarcastic voice.

"Do you really have to be so acid all the time?" McNamara asked, lifting his left brow.

"As long as you behave like a caveman when you come into my house, yes. You've never come here without getting furious for no reason, being cynical, or yelling."

"I've always had reasons," the man defended himself. "Every time, something happened."

"Not really," Bryony replied and started making tea without asking him what he would like. She thought the man could use some sleep. "That first day when you came, you had no reason to be nasty with me, yet you were," she pointed out.

"You can't get over that, I see," he said drily.

The woman turned back and stared at him. The man tensed under her gaze. After a while, she said, "Oh, aye, I can. If I couldn't, I wouldn't have behaved nicely with you, as I am now, by the way." Bryony smiled, turning her attention back to the kettle.

Behind her, McNamara scowled because she had touched a nerve. He reckoned that the lass was correct, though. She had always behaved nicely with him. However, he couldn't change what had happened before though.

Bryony turned her head to him again. "I've made you some tea, not coffee. I think you want to sleep tonight after all the sleepless nights you've had lately."

"No problem, I'll manage," the man replied evasively. "By the way, if you want, I can stay with you again tonight. Instead of the assigned policeman," the inspector thought to specify.

Bryony turned and gazed at him closely, not knowing what to make of his offer.

"Don't look at me like that," the man reacted defensively. "I haven't asked you to be my lover, and I have no such an intention. I hope you know that. I have already come out here, and I don't think it makes sense to have someone else make the trip. Besides, no one expects me at home. I have no family or animals to miss me,"

McNamara continued, indifferently waving his hand.

Suddenly, he stopped, realising that he had already revealed too much about himself. "That being said," he pointed out so that she didn't get any ideas, "I can sleep anywhere. So, I can try your guest room once more. It's quite comfortable."

Bryony still didn't say a thing but kept looking at him. After a few more seconds, McNamara, sick of waiting for an answer that didn't seem to come, changed his mind.

"All right, I got the message. After I drink my tea, I'll leave. By then, your protection detail will have come. I understand you prefer someone else with you here, not me."

"No," Bryony said quickly, even too quickly, surprising McNamara with her reaction. He hadn't expected such a vehement answer. "You'd better call the station and tell the respective constable he shouldn't come," the lass continued. "I prefer you. I know what to expect with you," she said in a playful voice as if she had wanted to make her decision sound unimportant. "Who knows how that bloke will be."

McNamara looked at her and tried to understand the sparkle in her eyes but gave up, deciding to take things as they came.

Bryony had the feeling that the inspector knew what was going on behind her blue-dark eyes. She thought it wasn't a good idea to tell him that she preferred him, so she sauntered to the fridge.

"If you want, I can make you bacon and eggs and cheese. I'm afraid I don't have anything else here, and I really can't see you eating just toast like me. I'm sure you're starving," the woman said.

If what she had read in crime stories was true, then the man had gone hungry all day long, although she remembered that he had gone to the Browns' pub around noon. Mrs Stevens, who surveyed the street from behind the window, said he had been in there long enough to have had lunch.

"Aye," McNamara said, taking his phone out of pocket. "I'm famished. I haven't had time to eat since lunch. So, if you can make me a huge helping, it would be brilliant," he added. "I'm going outside to call the station, all right?"

"Aye, I know, I'm not allowed to hear how the investigation's going," Bryony said drily, and McNamara scowled again. "You know, you look good with that frown on your face. You should give it up if you really don't want me to fall for

355

you," she teased him and almost burst into laughter when his eyes went wide.

Her words surprised him, and McNamara stopped on his way out, ready to give her a blistering reply, but he thought better. The lass seemed confident that she would make him shout again, and he didn't want to be predictable. So, after a slight hesitation, the man went out of the kitchen without bothering to answer.

Behind him, Bryony's smile bloomed. Yet, she hadn't expected him to do that. 'Well, people can be wrong now and then,' she told herself.

CHAPTER TWENTY-NINE

Long after the police had left, Alice Thompson still stood in the middle of her house. She was dizzy, and a terrible headache drummed in her temples. The woman still couldn't believe that something like that had happened in her home. That Daniel had been put under arrest was unbelievable as well.

Alice looked around bitterly — her tidy house was in shambles. Almost mechanically, she started putting things back. She had lost any hope that things could be better one day. From that moment on, they could only get worse.

The woman thought of what the police had found inside Daniel's desk. She knew he had some documents there, and he worked on them on Sundays. She didn't think they were accounting logs.

The police must have laughed at her when they realised that she knew nothing about her husband's business. Alice couldn't even breathe when they told her what kind of business Daniel handled. She wondered how she could have been so blind.

'Her husband! What a good joke,' she told herself with pain and bitter irony. Tears started running down her cheeks again. Alice had thought she had a good marriage, and she had done her best for that. Suddenly, her thoughts wandered to Mary, her neighbour. 'Oh, God, what a satisfaction that bitch would have now!'

Mary had never been kind to her husband and had everything while here she was. Alice had worked so hard and was left with nothing. She had been an exemplary wife, damn it. She knew that. But that bastard of a husband of hers hadn't cared a bit.

Mary would laugh at Alice now and ask what she had been left with after putting that jerk of Daniel first.

The bell rang, and at first, Alice thought that she shouldn't open the door to anyone. Then, the image of the police breaking the door made her rush with heavy steps to open it herself.

When her eyes fell on Mary, the wish to attack the woman and scratch her face overwhelmed Alice. The woman put her arm around Alice's shoulders to direct her to the kitchen, closing the door quietly behind her.

"Come on, Alice. I'll make you some tea, and everything will be all right then. I'll help you put everything in order," the woman said, her eyes sweeping over the ravaged house. "You will see, you won't even notice anything once everything is where it should be. Damn the police! They've left a disaster behind," Mary shook her head in disbelief.

Shocked, Alice just watched her neighbour, unable to say anything, letting herself be driven as if she had been a puppet. The woman couldn't believe her ears — Mary wanted to help her clean.

The house Alice had been so proud of looked terrible with things thrown everywhere. Even the kitchen had been ransacked. Mary helped her sit on a stool in the kitchen and started on the tea, feeling immense compassion for the poor woman.

'Fools! They should have known they wouldn't find anything in here. This is Alice's domain, to be sure.'

If Daniel had had something to hide, and probably he had — otherwise the police wouldn't have come — he wouldn't have hidden it in the kitchen. There Alice knew everything.

After a few minutes, Mary put a cup of strong tea in front of Alice on the table. "If it's too strong, I apologise," Mary said. "I've never been good at that. But it's good for you anyway. I'm sure. You'll grow stronger, have a bit of energy and help me around here. It's not nice of me, but I'm not good at cleaning up, either," Mary shrugged to excuse herself.

Alice expected her to make some ironic remarks and to mock her. But Mary didn't do any of that.

After Alice drank half of her cup of tea, Mary rubbed her hands. "All right, we'll start over here. Where should these be?" she pointed to a pile of dishes.

Alice showed her with a shaky finger, and Mary started working. In a few minutes, she replaced the dishes, stunning Alice with her efficiency and speed. The other woman didn't expect that of her. Mary seemed to know her way around cleaning up, after all.

While Alice drank two more cups of tea, watching Mary, always surprised, the woman cleaned her kitchen. Suddenly, everything seemed back to normal.

Then, Alice had the strength to stand up and accompany Mary through the other rooms. In a couple of hours, with more effort from Mary than Alice, everything was back in the right place.

By then, Alice had recovered, but her bitterness had increased. She had started hating Daniel that afternoon, and her hatred grew while she cleaned together with Mary. Now, the woman resembled a kettle under pressure.

"Alice, I don't want to hear any objections," Mary said when they finished cleaning. I've already talked with Michael and decided you'll have dinner with us tonight. I know it's well over dinnertime, but I don't care."

Alice tried to refuse, but Mary interrupted her.

"I've told you I don't want to hear a thing, Alice. While I was here, Michael made dinner. He cooked just for you, so you can't refuse."

Baffled, Alice stared at her neighbour, having a hard time believing that help had come from where she expected the least. It was unconscionable that Mary, who never did anything in her home, had come to clean her house. It baffled her that Michael would cook, only to make her feel better.

However, Alice accepted Mary's invitation and went out with her, locking the door behind. It felt like closing the door over an unpleasant chapter of her life.

Alice had no idea about how her life would be from that moment on, but she was sure that her life with Daniel had ended.

CHAPTER THIRTY

McNamara lay in bed, although he knew that his dress pants would be wrinkled the next day. Yet, he was exhausted after working the previous night and day.

The man folded his arms under his head and thought of the case. He hadn't solved it yet, but he knew the elusive solution was hiding in the corner of his mind. He couldn't see it yet because everything was messy.

He couldn't eliminate at least one suspect from his list. Maybe only Thompson. He certainly couldn't have been in Bryony's house because he was already under the Vice Squad's surveillance at the time.

Thompson wasn't hurt even if they had lost him and didn't want to admit their failure. There wasn't any sign that the man had been stabbed with a pair of scissors.

If the man had been hurt, he would have shown signs of discomfort. Thompson didn't have enough strength to resist the pain. The policemen had kept him in the interrogation room for a long time.

Reid couldn't be exonerated entirely, either. However, McNamara was almost convinced that Michael was the kind of man who shared the bed with his wife. Mary could be considered anything but air-headed. If the man had been hurt, the woman would have noticed. The detectives would have seen something on her face when they talked to them, even if Mary had wanted to protect her husband.

Still, McNamara was positive that Mary wouldn't have forgiven those crimes, even if she had loved Michael something fierce.

It was another story altogether with Graham, though. McNamara knew they must arrest him the following day. Thompson had given them enough information to indict Graham, who had also been involved in Thompson's business. The teacher had supplied the girls to Thompson, as he worked in the perfect place to enlist them.

Graham had implied Thompson's fault because he had thought the man was guilty of Patsy's death and had been afraid that he would be the next on the death list.

That was why the teacher hadn't stayed at home lately. Thompson had guessed what Graham was thinking and had been highly amused at his expense. When Daniel Thompson couldn't get rid of the accusation of underage human trafficking, he used the first chance to throw Graham to the wolves.

The next day, the police would interview Graham's girlfriend to make sure that she wasn't involved in that story, although McNamara doubted that she was.

The DCI didn't see Graham capable of murder either, but he didn't want to exclude him from the equation yet. Enough people didn't look capable of killing and still did it.

Then Randall popped into his mind. The man would have matched the profile. McNamara didn't doubt that Randall had strong resentments towards women. In general, if someone was under someone else's domination, the instinct was to escape it in one way or another. Randall displayed a calm façade, which meant that he definitely harboured many resentments that would eventually make him act.

His situation was somewhat similar to Michael Reid's, but in Reid's case, hatred could replace love. If someone's heart and pride were constantly crushed, they would react in the end.

Mary didn't do anything to keep her husband's feelings intact. Reid was a passionate man who wouldn't take the emotional abuse for long.

Worn-out and sick of everyone, McNamara decided to stop thinking of the people involved in the case. He also needed sleep, so he closed his eyes.

As he was sliding into sleep, the inspector heard a door open and someone sneaking out onto the corridor. The man quickly became fully alert and got out of bed. He tiptoed to the door he had left a tad open, glancing outside. Because of the darkness in the corridor, he distinguished only a silhouette silently walking towards the stairs.

The person's height didn't match the alleged one of the attacker's if Bryony hadn't been wrong. It was someone shorter, but the DCI didn't want to take any risks.

The man jumped over the silhouette and immobilized the person who groaned. His fingers touched the curve of a woman's breasts, which drove the truth home. That and the fact that he breathed in Bryony's scent.

McNamara barely stopped his fingers from rubbing the roundness of her breast and tried to make her believe it was only an accident. Under his hand, the woman's heart thumped quickly, practically ready to jump into his palm.

Bryony felt the man's musky smell, which had become almost familiar during the last couple of days.

After the first moment of fright and surprise, the lass said in a slightly strangled voice, "Now, what do you want to do? Finish what the killer started last night? Let me go, you idiot," she snapped.

"Calm down," the man whispered softly and let her go suddenly. Her hoarse voice had made its way under his skin, awakening all his nerves. "I couldn't have known it was you," he replied in a harsh voice now.

McNamara was upset because of his strong reaction to her voice and because he couldn't control himself better.

"What the hell are you doing here at this hour? Why aren't you sleeping?" he snapped. He turned her to him with an abrupt and unkind move. "Why aren't you sleeping?" he repeated. The man looked straight into her eyes even though he didn't really see them in the darkness. "It must be over two o'clock already," he added through tight teeth.

"I can't," the young woman replied. "I'm afraid to close my eyes. I keep seeing what happened last night, and believe me, it isn't something you'd remember with pleasure," she answered wryly.

"Why? Don't tell me you're afraid he's coming back. You know I'm here for that, and as you've just experienced, I react promptly," McNamara replied teasingly.

"Aye, I have, thank you," Bryony said dryly and then paused. "But it's not only that," she added with some hesitation, turning her head away because she couldn't look into his eyes. Despite the darkness in the corridor, their eyes had become accustomed, and they both saw each other well.

"What?" the man inquired after a few moments, irritated with her hesitation.

Bryony didn't say anything and thanked providence that it was dark enough, and he couldn't see her blushing.

McNamara lost his temper, lifted her chin, and snapped, "Come on! What's all this about?"

"Oh, Lord, how quickly you get angry, McNamara!" Bryony noticed, smiling shyly. Yet, she was relieved to see the man he had been earlier.

"All right, then," he said. "If you feel like joking and have nothing serious to say, you'd better go back to sleep. Remember, I'm in your guest room. Nothing could happen to you tonight," the detective added, leading the woman to her room.

When they reached her door, Bryony stopped and didn't want to go inside. She put her shaky fingers on his arm.

"What now?" he snapped, trying to hide his telling reaction to her touch.

Bryony winced, and he took her hand, lightly running his fingers over her arm, soothing her. She seized his wrist with her fingers tightly as if she didn't want to let him go. Frustrated because he couldn't see the expression on her face with clarity, the man pushed the door open with his shoulder and pulled her inside, turning on the light. McNamara's eyes searched the woman's face hungrily. He was shocked and hurt seeing fear in her eyes.

"Don't tell me you're afraid of me," he snapped and released her hand.

Bryony quickly shook her head vehemently and said with hesitation, "What would you say if... I asked you to stay with me tonight?"

"But I'm with you, aren't I?" the man replied with exasperation.

"I mean, here, in this room," she specified, blushing again. Bryony knew she was bold, and her request might leave room for interpretation.

She also feared that the man would reject her. "I mean to stay with me. That's all," she said quickly.

"With you? Do you mean, with you, in your bed?" McNamara inquired with a catch in his breath.

Her request surprised and intrigued him at the same time. When he came to stay with her overnight, he hadn't thought he would get into her bed.

"Aye," the lass repeated, nodding vehemently. "But only to stay with me," she stressed her last words. "Nothing more... Or, maybe, you could also hold me," she added.

'So that I wouldn't feel so lonely and unsure of what happens to me. So that I feel a little tenderness and feel these strong arms around me,' Bryony thought, and her fingers brushed over the length of his forearm.

"Why?" McNamara asked, interrupting her thoughts and staring into her eyes, impatiently waiting for an answer.

"Because," she replied. They watched each other in silence, trying to read each other's thoughts. Bryony wanted him to understand that they couldn't have that discussion.

McNamara finally understood what she wanted and said with unexpected kindness, "All right, then. Get into bed, and I'll be there in a second. I'm taking my things from the other room, and I'll return to you."

She smiled shyly, and after thanking him, squeezing his arm, she ran to the bed. He waited for her to get under the blanket. Her breasts moved under her pyjama blouse, and the man ran his fingers through his thick and coarse hair, wondering what he got himself into that time.

Somehow rigid because of the suddenly tight pants, McNamara turned on his heels and went to take his things from the other room. He returned with his coat and mobile phone in his hand, making visible efforts to relax the tense muscles in his face and back. Still, a metallic light shone in his eyes.

Silently, the man placed his coat onto the chair in front of the vanity table and then laid his phone on the night table. He glanced into the mirror — Bryony was watching his movements closely. She seemed apprehensive, and he wondered if the woman thought he would jump on her now. True enough, his instincts, now awake, demanded just that.

The woman stared at him and wondered what McNamara thought of her request. Bryony didn't have any experience with men. She had always been careful to end all her relationships before sharing the bed with anyone.

McNamara lay down on the blanket next to Bryony and looked at her. He tried understanding what was going on in her mind.

The lass glanced back shyly and whispered in a thick voice, making him hard with need, "Why don't you get under the blanket? Nothing will happen to you, I promise."

"It's not that," the man replied, annoyed, rolling his eyes at her coyness. "I simply can't. My dress pants will be wrinkled anyway, but they'll be worse tomorrow if I lay underneath the blanket."

"Oh, I haven't thought of that," the woman said. "Don't move," she jumped out of bed and disappeared out of the room so fast that he could only blink in surprise.

Bryony returned a few minutes later with some sweatpants and a t-shirt. She found McNamara at the door, ready to come after her and bring her back to bed. The woman burst into laughter at the usual wrinkle between his eyebrows. 'It fits him so well,' she thought.

"Here you are," the woman said quickly, noticing that the man was ready to shout at her. "These belonged to my aunt," she said, putting the clothes in his hands. "She was almost as big as you," she added.

Bryony liked his scowls but still hoped to make the frown between his eyebrows disappear. She didn't want him angry that night.

"I'm sorry I haven't thought you couldn't sleep in that. I'll get into bed and cover my head with the blanket so that you can get dressed here."

She left him with the clothes in his hand and dashed into the bed. McNamara noticed that the simple blue cotton pyjamas suited her. They hugged and caressed her body, giving him an idea of how it would feel to touch her skin with his hands.

The man shook the thought away while waiting for her to get under the blanket. Then, he undressed quickly and put the sweatpants on. They fit him, and he grinned. Bryony had had a big aunt. He tried the t-shirt as well but heard a tear and gave up. Apparently, Bryony's aunt wasn't as broad-shouldered as he was.

McNamara turned off the light and climbed into bed next to Bryony under the blanket. As she had asked earlier, he pulled her into his arms to hold her.

Bryony burrowed into him. Not very close at first, but after a short hesitation, she slid her arms around him and got closer.

McNamara found enticing the apparent contradiction between the woman's earlier boldness when she invited him to share her bed and her present shyness when they shared the same blanket. He found her hesitation endearing and amusing at the same time. A grin appeared on his lips, but she couldn't see it in the dark.

He pulled her tighter against him and pushed her head on his shoulder. When she felt his arms holding her tight, Bryony sighed and closed her eyes, feeling genuinely safe. His smell teased her nose and gradually overwhelmed her. It made her feel good and protected. After a few moments, the lass fell deeply asleep, very close to him. In her sleep, she moved even closer, and her half-open mouth caressed his chest, her hot breath making his skin shiver.

McNamara couldn't sleep anymore. His arms were too full of a warm woman, and unwanted sensations teased his skin. He had never held a woman in her sleep. The man had always avoided such intimacy because he didn't want to mislead anyone.

He hadn't been ready to commit in the past, so he kept his distance. However, McNamara couldn't find any reasons against getting close to Bryony. Moreover, the man knew he would feel like a jerk the next day if he let go of her and went back to his own bed because of his usual anxiety. Besides, it felt good holding Bryony quietly in his arms. The lass showed she trusted him enough to fall asleep with him.

His body felt very alive holding her, but in the end, McNamara gave in and fell asleep, a smile constantly tugging at the corner of his mouth. He didn't register that it was the first time he had fallen asleep with a smile on his lips since his childhood.

MCNAMARA SERIES BOX SET
BOOK 0NE & TWO

CHAPTER THIRTY-ONE

Teasing sunrays woke McNamara, and the man breathed deeply. The woman's scent made him aware of their closeness, and he looked down at Bryony, bracing on an elbow.

His movement woke the woman, and her bright dark blue eyes opened, widening at the sight of the pure green of the man's pupils. Her lips moved, but no sound came out.

Desire clenched McNamara's belly. Bryony's face and full lips, half-opened and inviting him for a taste, looked far too tempting. Not entirely awake, the man leaned over, touching her mouth with his.

Almost brutally, McNamara took Bryony's mouth hungrily and deepened his kiss more and more, using his teeth and tongue to tantalise and appease her. Her lips trembled and opened more. A soft sigh escaped from her throat, and the man tensed, his control slipping.

Suddenly, Bryony slid her arm around his neck, pulling him to her. The man dragged her closer, possessively, burning her with his passion. His kiss was intense, McNamara giving as much as he took, and he took insistently.

Something in her mind warned the woman that his kiss was dangerous, but she couldn't deny him. She didn't want to.

McNamara abandoned her swollen mouth to brush his lips along her neck, arched in abandon under the brush of his lips. His teeth scratched her skin, and Bryony trembled, holding him tighter.

McNamara opened her blouse. His fingers spread over her skin when the bell at the door rang, startling them both. They watched each other for a few moments, willing to ignore the bell, but it became more insistent.

"Damn it!" McNamara snapped, his curse blasting her ears. "I'll kill whoever's at that door," the man bellowed, jumping out of bed and running downstairs.

Bryony grinned and stretched, satisfied, still feeling the warmth McNamara had ignited in her body. Then, finally, McNamara's fury registered in her mind. The woman shot out of bed and ran after him, afraid of what he would do, catching up with the man just when he opened the door.

"And what the hell do you want?" the man shouted.

Mrs Stevens stood in front of the door with her lips pursed in a tight line. The woman glanced at Bryony, who came behind McNamara, and understood what had happened before her arrival. With her swollen and wet lips, Bryony looked very well kissed, and McNamara's stubble beard had irritated the skin on her neck.

The girl blushed under the accusation in the old woman's eyes. Mrs Stevens stared deliberately at her gaping blouse, and red-faced, Bryony buttoned it at once.

The constable who had guarded Mrs Stevens kept very still and silent. He knew his boss well, so he didn't dare talk to McNamara when he was visibly angry.

McNamara barked at the constable before Mrs Stevens could open her mouth and admonish them, "Well! You can leave now. We'll talk later. Now go and get some sleep."

The man thanked the Chief Inspector and hurried away. Then, McNamara glanced at the old woman, who looked like she wanted to say something. He knew he wouldn't have liked what she had to tell them, so he stepped aside and said, "Come in, Mrs Stevens. I doubt you'd like to have the entire street as a witness."

His calm voice didn't match his bleak frown, and the old woman didn't miss the steel behind his words. She obeyed the man's order but still pinned the two young people with her narrowed eyes.

McNamara closed the door, glancing at her with indifference. He didn't care whether she thought he slept with Bryony. However, Bryony blushed to the top of her ears under the old woman's accusing eyes. The girl did not realise that her red cheeks made her neighbour imagine much more than it happened.

In daylight, Bryony understood that asking McNamara to sleep with her and hold her during the night had been inappropriate. The young woman refused to think about his kiss because whenever she remembered it, her stomach grew taut, and she shivered.

"Would you go to the kitchen and wait for us to get dressed?" McNamara asked the old woman formally, but the firmness in his voice turned the invitation into an order.

The woman wanted to reply, but one gaze into the man's hard eyes told her she had better do what he said.

McNamara grabbed Bryony's hand in his and pulled her after him upstairs. The girl didn't like it and tried to pull her hand back, but he squeezed her hand stubbornly, unaware that he hurt her, and refused to let go.

"Please, let me go," the girl whispered, afraid that she might be heard from downstairs. She imagined Mrs Stevens coming after them ready to make a fuss.

Yet, the man understood how the woman felt about his Neanderthal manners.

"No," McNamara said and didn't allow her to answer. "You will come with me now. After getting dressed, you may go downstairs and talk with your neighbour. But, if you want my opinion, you shouldn't let her dominate you. The old bat's got the impression that she can run your life, woman. One reproachful look and you immediately cower, as if you had done something wrong. And you blush like a schoolgirl," the man snapped.

His fury singed Bryony, and the woman leaned against a wall, shivering under the thunder in his green eyes. She stared at him for a few seconds and then said, "But I made a mistake, McNamara. I'm sure you think that too. I shouldn't have asked you to sleep with me. I behaved like a slut," she said morosely, shaking her head.

"Not really," the man replied angrily. "Don't be stupid! You just wanted to be with someone. I understood that. Otherwise, I wouldn't have come to your bed. Damn it!" he hit the wall with his palm, startling her. "Why do women always have to complicate things?".

"Well, that might be correct for last night," Bryony found the courage to say. "But what about this morning?"

"I'm to blame because of what happened this morning if you want to blame someone. Tell the old crone I couldn't control myself. You did nothing wrong," McNamara said, pulling her into the room.

The woman pulled back, her cheeks in flames. "Oh aye, I did. I pulled you into my arms and responded to your kiss."

"Don't flatter yourself," the man interrupted her in a sarcastic voice. "If you want to believe that, it's your business. But, I advise you not to tell that to her," he said, pointing into the general direction of downstairs. "She'll make mincemeat out of you, and, as far I can see, you're stupid enough to let her do it."

"You know, if I let you kiss me, it doesn't mean I'm stupid," the young woman retorted.

"I haven't said that," he shook his head. "Anyway, you should know I like doing it, not talking about it," he added sardonically, pulling her into his arms.

The man kissed her deeply to prevent any continuation of the discussion. But not only because of that. After a few moments, he let her go but had to support her because her legs shook.

Shaking his head, McNamara chuckled. He picked up his clothes and mobile phone and headed to the door, where he stopped, turning back to her.

"If you didn't know it, we're in the twenty-first century. Now, a man and a woman may kiss if they want that. And, actually, they can do much more," the man added, his eyes sweeping over her body. Then, he left the room, letting her ponder on the implications of his words.

His unpredictable kiss and acid words petrified Bryony. Her blood boiled with repressed fury, especially because she had allowed him to have the last word. Frustrated, the woman stomped into the bathroom.

MCNAMARA SERIES BOX SET
BOOK 0NE & TWO

CHAPTER THIRTY-TWO

Bryony stepped into the kitchen, where the wave of hostility between Mrs Stevens and McNamara whirled around her. It was so thick that the young woman even stepped back.

Suddenly a coward, she thought of running back to her room but gathered her courage to go inside. Bryony avoided her neighbour's reproachful eyes and instinctively made a beeline towards McNamara, who had already made coffee. He was her only ally despite everything.

Without a word, McNamara offered her a hot and strong coffee cup. Then, he put one before the old woman, visibly smouldering with anger.

Mrs Stevens started to add sugar and milk to her coffee but couldn't finish, slamming the cup onto the table so angrily that some coffee spilt. McNamara merely lifted his left brow, unintimidated.

The old woman spoke with authority as if she had talked to two teenagers found fooling around on the sofa, "Could you tell me what you two were doing before I came?"

"No," McNamara answered, his steely eyes zeroed in on her, showing that he wasn't afraid of her. "And I've already told you that. It's none of your business."

Offended, the old woman glanced at Bryony with reproach. Bryony opened her mouth to say something, but McNamara turned to her and pinned her down with his stormy eyes. He knew the lass would start making excuses.

When she felt his eyes on her, Bryony couldn't say anything, so she just sipped from her cup and then sat down across from Mrs Stevens.

They drank their coffee in silence. McNamara glanced at his watch — the constable who was supposed to watch them that morning was due to arrive. He asked Bryony to accompany him to the door because he had to go.

At the front door, McNamara stopped and stared at her for a few moments. "I hope you're not sorry. I honestly don't regret anything. Maybe only that we stopped too soon. Please, don't let that damned woman make you feel guilty. You aren't guilty... of anything, believe me," he said and unconsciously brushed a finger along her jaw.

Looking at him with those big, shiny eyes of hers, Bryony didn't answer for a moment but shivered under his caress. The man didn't know what she felt or thought, and he didn't like it, so he decided to leave.

"We'll talk," McNamara said and opened the door, ready to go out, still, swiftly, turned back and pulled her into his arms, crushing her to his chest. The man kissed her lips hard, forcing them open, deepening his kiss, tasting her with his tongue. He bit her lower lip softly before letting her go.

Looking at her intently, McNamara whispered, "We'll talk later. I promise you." Then, he left, pulling the door closed behind himself and leaving her alone in the hallway.

Bryony remained there, completely still. Only after a few moments was she able to go to the kitchen, breathing deeply on her way.

When the young woman entered the kitchen, Mrs Stevens opened her mouth to speak. However, Bryony forgot everything about being polite and stopped her for the first time in her lifetime. She put her hand up and said harshly, "I'm sorry for you, but it's my business, as McNamara said."

Miffed and surprised, the old woman couldn't reply for a few seconds. When the surprise faded, Mrs Stevens exploded. However, her voice shook with frustration. "I was your aunt's friend and confidante for twenty years, Bryony. She always respected my opinion. You know that. I thought you respected me too, but I see I was wrong," the woman said, tears pooling in her eyes.

Bryony felt bad but held her position. She knew McNamara was right, so she replied, "It's not like that, Mrs Stevens. But you must understand that my private life should remain private, and my decisions are mine to make."

"Why don't you understand that this man could be here today and somewhere else tomorrow? Do you really believe he'll stay with you?" the woman asked in a baffled voice, opening her arms. "Girl," she shouted, "that happens only in films, not real life."

"I don't know where McNamara will be tomorrow, and honestly, I don't care. He didn't make any promises if you were afraid of that. I know, though, that he was here last night when I needed him. That is enough for the moment," Bryony replied, pouring herself another cup of coffee with abrupt gestures, even though she didn't want anymore. However, she needed to do something with her hands.

The old woman wasn't willing to drop the discussion, though. She wanted to make Bryony see reason and said with exasperation, "Really, girl, I don't understand why you won't find yourself a good lad. Someone to be with you all the time, help you with everything, with the bookshop."

"Because I'm not interested," Bryony interrupted her. "Really, I don't want to talk about that. Let's eat something. I'm hungry," she said and went to the fridge, even though she had lost appetite.

***

Mrs Stevens reminded the constable of a kettle under pressure. The man didn't know what to do and fidgeted, pretending to read. Although the young woman calmly verified the bills and invoices a girl had brought fifteen minutes before, the tension was tangible.

After another ten minutes of heavy silence, the old woman said in a determined voice, "We can't go on like that, Bryony." She slapped her palm on the table, startling Bryony and the policeman. "We must talk. You must get your feet back to the ground."

"I'm sorry," Bryony said, leaving the documents aside. "I've already told you we won't discuss this subject. Not now or ever. However, if you want to talk about something else, you're welcome to."

The constable thought to leave the room. He considered they couldn't speak because of him, but Bryony stopped him with a gesture.

"You needn't leave, Mr Mackie. It's not you. Mrs Stevens wants to discuss a matter which doesn't concern her," she explained. "I don't want to talk about that, and really, I don't see why we should quarrel on this topic," Bryony added, glancing at the old woman.

Mrs Stevens frowned and stood up. "Then, I'd better leave if I'm not wanted here."

"You know it's not like that," Bryony said. "You are always welcome here. You're only exaggerating now. There's nothing to talk about. That's all. And if there is, I decide in matters concerning me. I don't have to accept every piece of advice."

Her words didn't have the effect she wanted.

"Then I really must go," the old woman stubbornly said, heading towards the door, limping.

"If you really want to go, you can take the constable. I'll be fine by myself," Bryony said with conviction, although she was far from being confident.

The old woman nodded briefly and left the kitchen, the constable following her but feeling desperate. Horror filled him at the thought of McNamara's reaction to the news. He decided to call him as soon as they got to Mrs Stevens' house.

MCNAMARA SERIES BOX SET
BOOK 0NE & TWO

CHAPTER THIRTY-THREE

The woman discovered that the boys had eaten in bed again, although forbidden, and spilt the food. She descended to the basement, looking for something to wipe the stains on the boys' sheets.

The basement was her husband's domain, and she would have sent him to bring what she needed, but the man still slept. He had started skipping work lately, getting lazy. Angered, the woman shook her head. She should have woken him to go to the basement in her stead.

She turned on the light and looked on the left shelves but found nothing. So, she headed to the right corner of the basement, where a dark plastic bag drew her attention. Something white-stained poked out of it, and curious, the woman opened the bag to take out a bloody sheet wrapped around some clothes with broad and ugly bloodstains. Disgusted, she threw the clothes on

393

the floor, and a big hunting knife fell out, clattering noisily.

The woman gasped but covered her mouth with her hands, afraid that someone had heard. She saw the shadow of an arm, which swiftly grabbed her throat. She tried to break free when a man's chuckles filled her ears. With a flicker of his wrist, the man threw her to the floor.

"Bitch!" he shouted, and the woman recognised her husband's voice. "You couldn't leave this place untouched. I'm not allowed to have anything of mine."

Scared, the woman flinched, unable to utter a sound, which wasn't like her. She could talk for hours, lecturing everyone in earshot. But now, fear suffocated her, and her throat hurt.

"You won't say anything now. Don't be afraid. You won't speak anymore. I'm sick of you, as everyone is on this street. I want to live without having you under my eyes," the man said, leaning to take the knife.

The woman tried to rise and run, but the blade stabbed her hand. Screaming, she backed away, her heart beating wildly in her chest. The knife struck and knocked her down once more. Still, the blade pierced her again, taking her last breath.

The man threw the knife next to her body and left the basement quietly, taking care to close the door behind. He returned to the kitchen and made some tea, feeling lighter than usual.

He knew that he controlled his fate and would also escape from the police. They didn't prove wise enough to catch him, especially the inspector who cosied up with McNeil. They deserved each other, the man thought. That stupid bitch hadn't even looked at him twice. 'Probably, she doesn't know what she's missing,' he laughed aloud. 'But I could show her, couldn't I?'

He had just seen the crone leaving McNeil's house, taking the constable with her, so the way was free now. The man decided to drink his tea quietly and then go to Bryony. The woman would surely be glad to see him, even though she pretended not to be interested. However, the man needed to defend the honour he had lost the night McNeil attacked him with the scissors.

MCNAMARA SERIES BOX SET
BOOK 0NE & TWO

CHAPTER THIRTY-FOUR

McNamara strode into the squad room, and everyone glanced at him. The man looked even grumpier than usual, and his stubby beard made him look tougher. His face was far from pleasant that morning.

"Good morning, boss," Mike dared to greet him. He thought things couldn't be so grim. "It's good you came. Your phone has been going off the hook for two hours. It's the big boss," the detective said, pointing to the ceiling. "It seems important, but he wants to talk only to you."

"All right," McNamara replied. "Anything new?"

"Jo went to Vice. They arrested Graham forty-five minutes ago and also brought his lass for an interview. When Jo inquired why, they just replied they had already gathered all the data, and it was their collar."

"Damn it!" McNamara exploded. "We should have made that arrest, not them. Tell them to bring them here at once."

'They can't, boss! The order came from high up."

"How high?"

"McCullen," Mike said, understanding the frustration on McNamara's face.

"Why?"

"He didn't tell me but said he would speak to you directly. But Jo went to Vice. She charmed a bloke there and made him let her lead the interview with Graham. So, don't worry, boss," Mike chirped. "You know Jo. If there's something to find out, she will."

"At least that," McNamara snapped. "Have you verified the others?"

"Of course, sir. We're almost finished. Just a little more time, and we'll have finished with them. The Brown boys weren't in the area. The eldest one was on campus during the entire period we're interested in. The youngest had flights on the days of the murders."

"So, they're off the list. That's good. The others?"

"Reid's past is common. His parents died in a car accident in Surrey shortly after Reid married. He inherited something but not much. His wife got something more from an aunt of hers. That is how they afforded the house and car. They both earn well, so they don't have any financial problems."

"Have you found anything to prove that he's our man?"

"No," Mike said, shaking his head. "We haven't. He might be, but I think his wife would have known if he were the killer."

"That makes two of us. Randall?"

"That man had a bad past and worked hard to get where he's now. We couldn't find out what he did yesterday. His wife has got the blunt, though. His situation seems just a bit more complicated," Mike said, slightly frustrated.

"I see. Well, persevere. When James comes, send him to me."

***

The door was wide open. James wanted to knock but changed his mind. His boss looked deep in his thoughts, so the DS thought he'd better just leave.

He turned away when McNamara said, "Come in, James. It isn't a problem."

"Did something happen, sir?"

"Unfortunately, aye," McNamara said, leaving the window and sitting down at his desk. "McCullen called, agitated because we arrested Thompson."

"Any connection to him?"

"No, not him personally. He didn't get into the details, but I understand that his brother was one of Thompson's clients. Of course, the man said that it was a minor mistake. He wasn't a constant client, but he didn't want his name in reports. You know the law for sexual relations with a girl underage."

"What did you say, sir?" James asked curiously.

"I advised him to speak to the blokes from Vice because I didn't believe his brother was connected to our crimes. But I'll still ask Jo to investigate him discreetly. She knows how to deal with delicate situations. If I sent Mike, he would go to McCullen with the entire cavalry."

"I'm afraid so, sir," James grinned, knowing his colleague well. "The lad is as delicate as a herd of buffalos."

"Exactly... Have you learnt anything else from Thompson?"

"No, and I don't think he knows anything about the crimes. He confessed to the blackmails.

He had also recognised the girl on the Dobbs' lawn. He's been under stress ever since, especially because two other girls were missing, including his favourite. Patsy's other friends are in Bath for a month with some clients. We've sent for them."

"And didn't Thompson suspect anything when his girls went missing?"

"Oh aye, but he didn't do anything. He was afraid."

"All right, James. How's McKay?"

"She's recovered well, sir. I think they'll discharge her from the hospital next week," James replied with visible relief.

"That's good, very good," McNamara said. "All right, James, see what you can find out and then we'll talk."

***

"Lads, meeting! Now, everyone in my office," McNamara ordered and then returned to his office.

In a few moments, all the inspectors gathered in his office. Jo and Donna sat on the two chairs across from McNamara's desk while Mike, James, and Mark stood.

'I definitely have to order more chairs for my office,' McNamara thought.

"Well, I understand the two Brown boys aren't suspects anymore, and Jo eliminated McCullen's brother off the list. Now, I want to hear your opinions on the others. Jo, you start," McNamara said.

"In my opinion, sir, Thompson can't be the criminal. He didn't have either opportunity or motive," Jo said.

"Indeed," Mike interrupted her. "And if we think about it, the girls brought him a lot of money. It wouldn't have made sense for him to kill them."

"And Reid?" McNamara asked, his eyes sweeping the team.

"Reid seems to have only one objective, sir: to watch his wife," Jo said maliciously.

"Aye," James approved with a nod. "He wouldn't have spared a look at Patsy or any other woman."

"So, I would say that he didn't have a motive for the murder," Mark concluded. "I've researched him well."

"Brown?" McNamara asked.

"No, sir. It's not him," Mike shook his head. "Brown's got only two interests: his wife and the pub. He didn't have any relation with the girls, except to Patsy, whom he knew because she lived on the same street. He can't go onto the shortlist."

"All right, then," McNamara said. "Who checked Davidson?"

"I did, sir," Mike replied. "When the two girls died, the man wasn't in the area but in Leeds. And by the way, I also investigated the women, as you told me. However, we both knew it was a waste of time," he added, and McNamara singed him with a brutal glare.

The DCI didn't think that a woman was connected to the murders but didn't want to leave any stone unturned. So, he had asked Mike to look into them.

"McNeil didn't have a motive, sir, or the necessary force to knock two girls down and tie them. She's a delicate woman," Mike started to explain but stopped when McNamara threw him a sharp look.

Like the others, Mike suspected that McNamara had fallen for the girl, although it didn't seem possible. McNamara left the impression of a cold man with cynical views about women.

Reading his subordinate's line of thought correctly, McNamara tensed. His mouth tightened, and the man demanded severely, "Go on. Anything else?"

"McNeil was at the bookshop, sir, from morning till evening if we believe the woman from the tea shop next door. McNeil is not involved with a man, and she should have had an accomplice because the girls were repeatedly raped," Mike reminded him.

McNamara nodded and turned his inquisitive glance to Mark.

"We can't take Mrs Stevens into consideration, sir," Mark reported. "The woman has low mobility. No man visits her. From what I could gather, she apparently despises everyone, especially us, the police, and the salesmen."

"Aye, I've noticed," said McNamara dryly, recalling that morning's events. "Alice Thompson?" he asked.

"She didn't have a motive, sir. Maybe only for Goddard and Patsy Porter, although we couldn't prove that the woman knew about her husband's affairs. Hearing about her husband's occupations shocked her," Mark explained.

"Aye, sir," James intervened. "She effectively had a nervous breakdown when she found out. We had a hard time reviving her. The other women can't be included on our lists of suspects, either. Mark and I investigated all of them and found no motive, opportunity or complicity with a man," the DS decided to shorten the discussion.

"Sir," Donna interrupted the discussion shyly. The woman hated standing out in a crowd and rarely volunteered any information. "From what I read in the reports and what I found out myself, Randall is the only one that could be the criminal. The motive might be blackmail. The man had the opportunity because no one saw or talked to him when he supposedly visited his suppliers. He usually solved things by phone, even though his wife thought differently."

"Aye, you're right," McNamara approved. "I also think he is our man, but we need to find out where he was yesterday or if someone saw him. I heard he was limping, and McNeil said that she planted the scissors into her attacker's shoulder and into his leg. However, the leg wound was superficial."

"No, sir," Jo said. "No one saw him. Mark discussed with all his suppliers, and Randall didn't visit them yesterday".

"Mark?" McNamara turned to him.

"I looked into his past, sir. Some of his former school friends told me that he liked women a lot until he married. I'm afraid his tastes didn't change after marriage. His wife is ugly as sin, and Thompson claims that she's also frigid."

"When did Thompson say that?" McNamara jumped off his chair.

"This morning, sir," Mark stuttered, noticing the DCI's anger. "We interrogated him once more before the blokes from Vice took him. The man said Randall was his client too, but he didn't blackmail him because they were neighbours."

"Do you think he is the one?" Jo asked, suddenly aware of what the Chief Inspector was thinking.

"Of course!" McNamara sneered. "He is the one. Why the hell haven't I seen it so far? There were enough signs. Besides, we knew about his limping yesterday. That's it," he said. "We're arresting him. The motive is clear enough. The girls tried to blackmail him on their own, and they didn't know how to do it. We search his house and get something for a DNA test. We have enough samples from McNeil's house to test it against. Come on, let's go," McNamara rushed them, clapping. "Meanwhile, I'll get a search warrant," the inspector added, reaching for the phone.

That very moment, the phone went off, and McNamara answered. A deep line appeared between his brows, and his eyes changed, a metallic shine of cold steel storming the green pupils.

"Good, I got it," the man snapped, slamming the receiver. "McNeil is alone again," he told the inspectors, watching him with open curiosity. "That crone went back home with the constable and left Bryony alone. Get me patrol cars, James. Jo, go get the search warrant. I'll call now and ask for it. You'll take it and get it to Randall's, where the others will wait for you. I'll leave after I make the call and then go to McNeil," McNamara decided, failing to see the suggestive looks exchanged among his inspectors.

James and Jo went to take the search warrant, McNamara was just asking for over the phone, and Mike called the forensic team to go with them to the Randall house.

MCNAMARA SERIES BOX SET
BOOK 0NE & TWO

CHAPTER THIRTY-FIVE

Five minutes into their drive to Nightingale Street, Jo's phone rang, and the woman answered McNamara's angry voice.

"Jo, you must make a turn North-East. There was a severe collision here, and the road is completely blocked. I'm afraid I'll need at least ten minutes to get out of here, so I'll catch up with you after that," the DCI said. He didn't expect an answer but disconnected the call.

Jo put the phone back into her pocket. The woman relayed the conversation to James, who was driving. "That was the boss. He's pissed off. He is stuck in traffic because of an accident and told us to turn North-East. I'll let the others know," she said, turning on the police car radio.

It took them nearly twenty minutes more, but they finally got to Nightingale Street. They passed by the Randalls' grocery store, but it was closed, so they drove on to their house.

James and Jo, armed with the search warrant, rang at the door and waited. As no answer came from inside, they insisted once more.

Recognising James, Mary Reid came out from the Thompsons' house.

"You shouldn't bother to try the Randalls. I came to visit Alice, and I met Mr Randall, who was just leaving the house. He told me that his wife left early this morning to see her children, although I wouldn't have expected that from her. Anyway, Mr Randall is down the street. I think he went to the shop, but I'm not sure. This is the day when they usually open late."

"Thank you, ma'am," James said obligingly. "How's Mrs Thompson?" he inquired.

"Not very well, I'm afraid, but she'll recover eventually. Although she looks weak, she isn't. She's got enough strength inside," Mary replied, but noticing that Jo was tapping her foot impatiently, she said, "I'd better leave you now."

"What now?" Mike asked. "Should we break the door down?"

"I think so," Jo said pensively, measuring the sturdy panels of the door.

A second later, they turned around when tires screeched on the pavement behind them. McNamara got out of the car, shouting.

"What the hell are you doing?" "Why have I sent you here? To gossip or what?" he chided them harshly.

"There's no one home, sir," James tried to explain why they were still in front of the door.

"And what? Are you waiting for someone to come back home? Break down that damned door! Or maybe you expect me to do it?" he barked.

Mike nodded and kicked the door right in the lock, and the door broke open. Jo's mouth hung open, her baffled eyes wide.

***

Bryony poured herself another cup of coffee, although she was aware that she had already drunk too much. She sat again at the table where she had spread her ledgers and sighed. The woman hated that work, but she couldn't afford to pay anyone to do it for her.

That morning's tension still clung to her. Bryony was also upset because she hadn't been nicer to her older neighbour.

Besides, the thought that she had been about to do something irreparable that morning nudged at her. She had almost given in to McNamara, and she had never felt inclined to do

411

so with another man before. Her reactions confused the young woman.

Although her thoughts were unsettling, something startled her, and Bryony listened carefully. Someone was trying to pry open the backdoor, and a cold shiver ran up her spine. Her hands shook, and the woman spilt coffee on the tablecloth and on her hand. So, she put the cup down, unable to hold it anymore.

Bryony knew she had to keep her head to get out of trouble in one piece. Determined, despite her wobbly legs, she quietly walked to the rack of knives and chose the sharpest blade.

She listened intently. Someone snuck along the wall, careful enough not to make much noise. Bryony hid behind the door, holding still. She held her breath and closed her eyes so that she could picture the intruder's movements in her mind. She sensed when he came into the kitchen and slashed at him, but the blade only nicked the intruder's arm.

The next second, with a beastly scream, Randall knocked the knife out of her hand, and a broad grin sprawled on his lips.

Bryony attempted to escape and pass by him, but the man slapped her hard and banged her head against the door, which slammed shut upon impact.

A weak scream flew off Bryony's lips, her arm hurt, but the blow had made her dizzy, and her eyes grew dim. Pain radiated everywhere in her body, and tears trickled down her face.

The young woman felt fainting but recovered when she felt the man's hands on her blouse. Randall pulled hard, and buttons flew around the room. The tearing cloth hurt her ears, and Bryony tried to knee him in the crotch, but the man had already learned his lesson and snickered at her efforts. So, the woman raised her unharmed hand and scratched the man's face deeply. Randall shouted, forgetting about her blouse for a moment.

Bryony immediately crawled away from him. She almost managed to stand and, lightheaded, leaned on the table, but the man jumped on her again. Putting his hands on her waist, he threw the woman onto the table and tore off her pants.

The woman flailed her legs, shrieking and hitting him with her fists, but busy removing what was left of her pants, the man ignored her efforts to escape. However, when Bryony punched his nose hard, making him bleed, Randall stopped and backhanded her. Her vision blurred, and she felt the sting of tears in her eyes.

Randall got closer to her face, warning her, "Be careful, bitch. No one can help you now.

Maybe, if I like you enough, I'll let you live a little longer." Bursting into unnatural laughter, he repeated, "Maybe," and the woman shivered.

Suddenly, steely fingers knotted in the man's hair and pulled his head backwards, stopping his glee.

With a roar, Randall turned, intent on murdering the intruder. He reached for the knife he had taken off the basement floor and secured behind the belt of his trousers before coming for Bryony. However, his fingers didn't reach it because a fist in the temple knocked him down.

McNamara knelt and bound the man's hands with handcuffs, and then, standing, he used his mobile phone to ask James to come and remove Randall.

Afraid he would shout at her for having sent the constable away, the man couldn't look at Bryony right then. He didn't want to frighten her more than she already was, so he didn't say anything to the woman and avoided her gaze carefully. However, he felt her wary look on his back.

Bryony had grabbed her torn blouse with shaky fingers, but noticing that McNamara's eyes avoided hers, she froze on the table in shock. She imagined that what had happened disgusted him deeply.

Randall came to his senses and started writing on the floor, trying to stand and kick McNamara, confident that

he could kill the detective with his hands tied at his back.

McNamara caught Randall by the shoulders and pulled him up, trying to control his rage.

Screeching like a trapped animal, Randall thrust his head into the detective's chin, and McNamara leaned back. Then, he shook Randall, smothering the urge of killing him, and warned him harshly, "Stop it if you don't want me to beat you senseless."

Still, Randall didn't heed the man's advice and jumped forward, but McNamara planted his fist in the man's temple once more, and Randall fell at his feet with a deafening sound.

James showed up, having used the door that McNamara had broken down when Bryony screamed. The DS stared at Bryony, who was still on the table, shaking and clinging to the torn blouse. Afterwards, he noticed Randall on the floor.

"Take him," McNamara said curtly. "Take him to the station and lock him up. Too bad you can't throw the key afterwards. If he causes you any problems, you're free to do whatever you think is right. I'll take full responsibility."

"Aye, sir," James nodded and struggled to pull Randall up. The man was as limp and heavy as a potato sack.

"Have you found anything there?" McNamara asked.

"Aye, unfortunately," James started, but his voice warned McNamara, and the DCI stopped him, waving towards Bryony. She didn't need to hear that.

"James, you and Mike take this bloke," the Chief Inspector indicated to Randall. "Jo will prepare the report with what you've found. I'll stay here with her," he said, pointing to McNeil. "Ah, and by the way, tomorrow, send someone to fix the door. I don't think it locks anymore."

James nodded again and pushed Randall to the door. Suddenly recovered, Randall tried to escape from his hands. Still, McNamara furiously grabbed one of his arms while James held the other. They pulled him to the door without noticing Randall's curses and threats.

Outside, McNamara spotted Mike coming out of the Randalls' house and called him over.

While Randal continued his struggle, Mike sprinted towards them. The prisoner fought to break free from the hands of the two men, threatening them.

"Calm down," McNamara growled and shook the man. "I'm looking forward to having a reason to seriously kick you. So, please, oblige me."

As McNamara's voice betrayed the man's willingness to follow through with his threat, Randall became apathetic, giving up his fight. Anyway, he couldn't win, which he hadn't believed possible. But McNeil had stolen his mind, so he didn't finish her when he had her in his hands. The bitch deserved to die in the worst way possible. At that thought, his eyes turned savage.

McNamara noticed the change in the prisoner and suspected what thoughts crossed Randall's mind. The line between his brows deepened, and the man leaned over Randall, pinned him with his hard eyes, and whispered, "I advise you to forget that this woman exists. If not, I swear to make your life a living hell."

Randall glanced at him with hatred but didn't dare to reply. Suddenly, he considered it wiser to hide his thoughts, even though he loathed McNamara even more than before.

Mike and James led Randall to one of the police cars when Mary Reid and Alice Thompson, who had been watching out of the window, came out. The women shared whispers, watching Randall placed in the back of a car. Still, the man didn't pay any attention to anything or anyone.

McNamara remained in front of Bryony's house, gazing at his inspectors until Randall had been secured inside the car. He noticed the two women and supposed they were curious and probably puzzled by the arrest, but then Jo came out of the Randalls' house, and the DCI signalled her to come to him.

"Tell me briefly what's in there," he said when the policewoman approached.

"We've got another body, sir. I think it's his wife. We found her in the basement, stabbed twice. The lads are still searching the house. We've already found the clothes he wore the night when he attacked McNeil, or at least that's what we think."

"Good, Jo. When you here, you may leave. I must stay here with McNeil. She needs someone now, and I'm as good as any. Besides, I broke her lock, and the door won't close now."

Jo, who knew more than her boss let on, nodded with a serious mien and returned to her colleagues. The woman hid her grin until she got out of the DCI's sight.

McNamara was just about to go inside Bryony's house when Mrs Stevens called to him. With a scowl, the man turned to face her.

The old woman had witnessed the events in front of Bryony's door and couldn't force herself to stay inside anymore. She limped towards the Chief Inspector with determination.

Mackie, the constable, watched McNamara with guilty eyes, but McNamara knew the poor man wasn't to blame. It wasn't easy to deal with the old woman when she wanted something.

"Aye, ma'am, what's now?" the DCI asked her without caring about the worry swimming in the woman's eyes.

"What happened?" she asked. "Where's Bryony? How is she? I want to see her at once, young man," she asked.

"We've just arrested the criminal, so you don't need the constable to guard you, ma'am," McNamara said, glossing over her words. "You may leave now, Mackie," he tilted his head in the constable's direction. Relieved, the man couldn't wait to get rid of the old bat. She had driven him mad until then.

"And Bryony?" Mrs Stevens didn't give up. "I'm going to see her," she told McNamara, in a harsh voice that didn't leave place for discussion or refusal.

However, angry with the woman for everything that had happened, McNamara didn't yield but barred her way, determined not to let her into the house. If the old woman hadn't left, taking the constable with her, Randall wouldn't have dared to attack the young woman in broad daylight.

"Not now, ma'am," he replied firmly. "You can come tomorrow to see her, but not too early in the morning," he pointed out, pleased to see her frowning. "I'll take care of her, so you can relax."

"But I want to see her now," the old woman exploded, trying to pass by him.

"No, you can't see her now," he stopped her. "She must rest. She had quite a tough day, don't you think?" he turned to go inside and show that the conversation had ended.

The old woman had wanted to say something, but the determined look on the man's face made her hesitate. However, she didn't give up and grabbed his arm. McNamara shook her hand off and turned to her.

He took advantage of her hesitation and decided to tell her exactly what he was thinking. "If you hadn't left with Mackie, Randall wouldn't have attacked her. She was attacked because of you. So, have the decency to leave her alone for the day," he said with resentment.

The old woman stepped back as if he had slept her over the face. She also thought that her leaving had led to Randall's attack but tried to push the bothering thought somewhere far at the back of her mind. The woman frowned and left, her heavy movements showing her biting frustration, but McNamara didn't care.

The DCI glanced looked at Mackie, who had remained on the stairs. The constable's face betrayed his astonishment. The man knew that the Chief Inspector was a harsh and direct person, but he didn't expect to see him hurting an old woman, even though he was right. McNamara understood what the man was thinking but shrugged.

***

He found Bryony still on the table where he had left her. Her face lacked colour, and her eyes had grown wide and glossy. She held herself, swinging absently.

McNamara's heart reacted to her pain, aching to see her without the vitality he had enjoyed so much. He came closer to her and cupped her cheek with his right hand. Then, the man slid his other arm around her and drew her to his chest, holding her tight and kissing her ruffled strawberry-blond hair. His lips trailed down her cheek like an illusion and stopped over her trembling lips. A sigh left her lips when he touched her mouth, and her body moved closer to him. She was coming back to life again.

McNamara lifted her in his arms and headed to the bedroom with her. He thought Bryony had said something on the stairs. However, the man hadn't understood her words but had only felt her lips moving against his neck, making him tremble with desire. He knew it was the most inappropriate moment for something like that and clenched his teeth. Then, the man stopped and asked, "What did you say?"

"I said," she answered in a stronger voice now, "that I thought you didn't want to speak to me after what just happened."

"Don't be silly," he replied with impatience, squeezing her tighter, and she cried out. Her ribs still hurt from Randall's abuse. He chuckled and loosened his grip on her, striding into the bedroom. He laid her on the bed and took the blanket to cover her, but she stopped him.

"No, please. I want to wash first, to get rid of that man's smell. It feels like it's in my skin already, and I can't stand it."

McNamara nodded, understanding how she felt and asked her reluctantly, "Can you do it alone?"

"Aye, don't worry. I'll be back soon," Bryony said, heading to the bathroom.

The man thanked providence for small favours. He didn't think he could have kept his blood cool and his hands to himself if he had had to help her get undressed.

While waiting for her to come back, McNamara looked out the window at the little street that seemed peaceful again.

After fifteen minutes, Bryony returned from the bathroom, dressed in the same comfortable cotton pyjamas she had worn the previous night. McNamara felt her presence and turned to her, watching her with expectation.

"Do you want to stay with me tonight?" she asked him, almost begging, and her words seemed to echo the words she had said the night before.

"Tonight, aye," the man answered, avoiding making any commitments or promising something he couldn't deliver.

However, Bryony understood what he wanted to say. She got into bed, waiting for him to come next to her under the blanket.

McNamara changed in the sweatpants he had left on the chair of the vanity table that morning. Then, he strode to the bed and slipped under the blanket.

The man pulled the young woman in his arms and put her head on his shoulder, holding her tight. Kissing the top of her head, he whispered, "Sleep now. We'll talk later."

SCENTS AND SHADOWS

MCNAMARA SERIES BOX SET
BOOK 0NE & TWO

PROLOGUE - MAUDE IS IN FOR A HARSH SURPRISE

The little beagle growled and pulled on the leash, making old Maude jump ahead and almost fall on her face. The abrupt move came as a surprise to Maude.

Going out with Missy meant she would just drone along, wrapped up in her thoughts. The sedate stroll helped Maude order her ideas, make plans, or think of something she had read or seen on TV.

Her old beagle had never reacted so unpredictably before or, at least, never during the last six years. She was never excited, even when she was around playful or hostile dogs.

In the morning, they would saunter leisurely along the shore, and at night, they would take the trail near the ravine close to their house. Their strolls always followed the same pattern. Missy would trot a little ahead, neither too fast nor too slow, and Maude would stroll along at a comfortable pace. Maude had gotten somewhat brittle along those last years, and she didn't have the strength to wrestle with a dog, even though her beagle was not a giant hound.

Maude had been pleased to see that her dog quieted down once she had reached a certain age. The woman had her doubts in the beginning and feared that she wouldn't be able to control her once her age and arthritis advanced.

"Missy, calm down, girl," Maude commanded with all the authority she could muster after her fright.

Those days, the old woman couldn't rely on her knees anymore. The woman had practically seen herself thrown to the ground for a moment, and that scared her. She didn't know if she would have been able to stand up again.

The woman tried to yank the leash so that Missy understood to go back to the peaceful pace they both enjoyed. It was just wishful thinking, though. Missy had sniffed a strong scent, and her primal instincts overcame all her training. That instinct urged the old dog forward now. It made her forget the aches and stiffness the unforgivable time had brought.

Maude's commands fell on deaf ears. The scent trail was compelling, and the hunting dog, lurking inside Missy, had woken up. The dog had already reached a particular zone, and a new spring appeared in her walk.

The beagle growled fiercely again, and the sound was frightening. A shiver of fear crept down Maude's back. The ferocious sound that came from her sweet, well-behaved dog made the hair on her neck stand, and hairy spider legs dragged along her spine.

Maude glanced around with apprehension, and her fingers shook on the leash when her eyes swept over the vast wooded area on her right.

The midnight glow drowned the trees in an unreal light. Maude had been walking her dog in that wooden area for years and knew it as well as the back of her hand. Yet, that night, it was as if she had noticed its menacing midnight appearance for the first time.

Missy broke into a run, which didn't sit well with Maude. Her arthritis had restricted her movements for some time now, and there were days when she couldn't do more than drag her feet. That was one of those days. Maude cursed the beagle under her breath.

The old woman began shouting and demanded the dog to stop, but with no effect. The dog seemed very intent on getting to a specific destination.

Then, the old woman realised that Missy had hurried toward her favourite hydrant, which confused her. Missy had to know she would get to that hydrant sooner or later, as it was one of the main attraction spots of their walks, after all.

"Easy, girl, easy," Maude tried to soothe the dog and make her walk slower, but to no avail. Missy continued her forced race, and in the process, she dragged a cursing and aching Maude in tow.

The woman had great respect for exercising. Her doctor had advised her repeatedly that she needed to keep moving, or her joints would grow more painful and stiff. She had heeded his advice. However, her exercising was limited to fairly-paced strolls, not sprints. Maude hadn't been too fond of sprinting even in her youth, and she had never understood the logic of jogging with no destination in mind. Now, her knees were not accustomed to taking such abuse and began to protest loudly to the effort.

Again, the old woman cursed the little dog and what might have turned her obedient companion into a beast. Maude had a hard time keeping up with the now running dog. She couldn't ignore either the gruelling rhythm or her tortured knees, and she wasn't even aware that tears were running down her face, let alone wipe them off. Yet, the thought of letting the leash go never crossed her mind.

Maude felt deep gratitude when Missy finally stopped in front of the blasted hydrant and closed her eyes in relief. The woman breathed deeply for a minute or two, taking her time to rest her mistreated knees, unaware of anything else.

Now, the dog started howling and snarling. To be truthful, Maude had never heard anything like that from her dog before, and her heart pumped faster.

Yet, the old woman needed to catch her breath, so she still took her time. No other sound reached her ears. Maude didn't believe that they were in any danger, and at that moment, she didn't even care if they were. Other things were taking precedence in her mind, like the stabbing pain in her joints and laboured breath.

Only when the piercing pain in her knees subsided and became more bearable, Maude decided to see why her lovely pet had turned into a primal being. The howling was gone, but the dog's snarl had turned deep and vicious now, and the old woman couldn't ignore the real world anymore.

When she finally opened her eyes, Maude froze, unable to do anything else but stare, riveted in place. Her gnarled fingers turned into stone on the leash.

Maude opened her mouth to scream, but no sound came out, her shouts remaining trapped at the back of her throat, even though she could still hear them reverberate inside her head.

The woman's eyes had widened with shock, and the skin on her face tightened over her bones as the blood receded. The spiders crawling on her back earlier multiplied, and their hairy legs left traces of fright in their wake. Her legs began to shake, and the old woman wondered if she would still be able to stand for a split second.

The moon had just come out of the clouds, and Maude had a clear view of the hydrant. There, a severed human head basked in the moonlight.

Maude's terrified eyes stared at the slashed skin that once might have covered a pretty graceful neck. Traces of blood smeared what was left of the once-long neck.

Blood was still dripping, and Maude's shocked gaze followed the downward direction of the blood drops with morbid fascination. The droplets fell in the dark, nearly coagulated pool, which covered the now sticky grass at the foot of the hydrant.

The woman shifted her gaze back to the head. Open and lifeless eyes stared back at her, and Maude noticed their unusual violet colour, which gradually faded right there in front of her eyes. Still, the immobile gaze mesmerised her.

The old woman made a considerable effort, but she could finally shift her eyes off those cold, hypnotic pupils. She moved her sight above the head, and only then, she noticed the knot of hair fastened to the hydrant.

A fog bubble had enveloped her mind, and Maude shook her head to clear it, knowing that she had to do something or call someone because she couldn't just leave that head alone there. The woman couldn't just avert her eyes and be on her merry way. Her generation had been brought up with a sense of justice and responsibility.

She remembered the cell phone her niece had made her carry with her everywhere. She took it out of her pocket with a shaking hand and started dialling 999.

The old woman had become aware that she was alone with her beagle near the ravine. The closest building was quite a distance away, maybe even more than five hundred yards.

If anything happened, Maude didn't believe that Missy would be able to protect her. The dog had already used all her energy running to catch the scent she was hunting and growling ferociously. Now, the dog merely panted, and apparently, had lost interest in the severed head, which did seem curious.

Waiting for the call to go through, Maude's eyes swept the surrounding area with dread. The tree shadows, the woman had loved so much before, suddenly seemed to hide dangers that Maude had never imagined before. The thought that someone was lurking and stalking her from afar crept into her mind, and her lips quivered.

The voice of the 999-operator startled Maude, and she almost dropped the phone. The woman recovered fast, though, and related what laid before her eyes with a hesitant voice. Fear that the operator wouldn't believe her seized her throat, even though Maude couldn't have condemned the agent. The scene did echo a horror film.

Knowing when to express her gratitude, Maude said a silent prayer. The woman was thankful that Halloween wouldn't be there for a few more weeks. Otherwise, the emergency operator would have advised her to have a nice cup of hot milk, go to bed, and stop looking at the neighbours' decorations.

CHAPTER 1 - MCNAMARA DECIDES TO TAKE ACTION

McNamara rubbed his forehead and then glanced at his watch impatiently. Noticing it was almost eight in the evening, the man scowled in dismay.

The man had worked another long day, despite his promise to stop staying in the office after five and working overtime, especially when he didn't have an active case. He knew he would do a lot of overtime then, and such a harsh regimen wouldn't work forever.

Everybody had their limits. The DCI was realistic enough to reckon that the time would also come for him. One day, he would have to pay the price for the lack of respect he showed for his own body. That thought made the man grimace. He shook his head and muttered a few choice words under his breath.

The Chief Inspector stood up and stretched to eliminate the tension in his muscles, whose knotted fibres had objected loudly. He grimaced again when he felt sharp stabs in his lower limbs and knots in his neck. In such moments, the man would feel old, older than his age, and he loathed the most thinking of that.

The detective strode to the window where he glanced at the square on the corner, burrowing his hands deep in his pockets. He looked out the window, as he would do at least once a day to enjoy the life outside that room. The man would enjoy looking at the people and guessing what life they had. However, this time, his eyes didn't notice the couples strolling hand in hand or the proud young mother pushing a blue pram.

McNamara's mind was far-off, wandering other trails. His green eyes looked remote and cold as if the man had been trying to make up his mind about something.

Being alone in the office, the man didn't bother to control his features. Suddenly, a metallic sparkle shone in his eyes, betraying his resolution.

He had decided to call Bryony again, and even more, to go and visit her. It was high time he had done it. McNamara had been thinking of the young woman for the last couple of weeks and quite constantly, which had bothered him enough, but he couldn't take the young woman out of his mind.

When the police closed the Nightingale Street case, the Chief Inspector thought he would forget about Bryony soon enough. He would be able to go on with his life, as dull and dry as it might have appeared at times. As the detective wasn't a very social person, the man liked it that way. A loner, he functioned well on his own. Problems appeared only when he interacted with others outside of his work.

McNamara's romantic involvements didn't last enough to grow into intimacy, and the man knew it was quite a stretch to use the word romantic when it came to his affairs. He had always avoided any romantic tangles, and all his male acquaintances envied his skills in evading unwilling connections.

McNamara had spent a second night in Bryony's house when the Nightingale Street case closed. He had spent that night in her bed right from the beginning. There wasn't anyone there to stop him, after all. However, the man had felt compelled to refrain from enjoying the moment. He would have felt like a cad only for thinking of taking advantage of their proximity so soon after the woman had survived a killer's vicious attack.

As the policeman liked to think of the murderer on Nightingale Street, that creature had tried to rape and kill Bryony, and the dire circumstances had dictated the detective's behaviour. At that moment, McNamara had thought only about protecting the young woman, even if only from the memory of the savage attack.

He had believed that he would have his chance later. Nonetheless, that window of opportunity closed to his total dismay the following day. The Cerberus, Bryony's older neighbour, Mrs Stevens, had appeared at the girl's door early in the morning. She had wanted to make sure nothing inappropriate would happen between the young woman and McNamara.

Then, the detective chose to go to the police station and leave the two women alone. He couldn't forgive the old woman's selfishness, which had led to the attack on the lass, and he knew that he would have been unkind to her, if not worse if he had stayed.

The man knew himself well enough, and he wasn't a forgiving person. He also kept a very accurate account when it came to wrongdoings. McNamara couldn't forgive or forget. He wasn't built that way. Everything had to go in two columns: right and wrong. Grey areas represented a complex concept for him, and the man had not succeeded to grasp it yet.

McNamara had pretended that he merely wanted to check on Bryony and avoided looking too deep into his own reasons. Still, he had phoned Bryony a few times afterwards. The inspector was afraid that he was trying to deceive either himself or her. The man didn't like either of the two options. He wasn't a coward as a rule, but now he felt like one, and that feeling bothered him the most.

The man preferred to play everything close to his vest and was painfully aware that he couldn't be entirely open with Bryony. That was one of the reasons he had avoided her. Yet, after a few sleepless nights, McNamara reckoned that his feelings surpassed a temporary attraction for the contrary lass. To his dismay, she had wormed her way into his heart and mind, and he couldn't shake the memory of her.

Dismayed, McNamara frowned and shook his head. He reckoned his defeat, at least for the moment, so, with determination, the man returned to his desk and sat down.

He picked his cell phone off the desk and swiftly dialled the young woman's number as if he had been afraid that he would change his mind. Then, with his characteristic impatience, the man waited to hear her voice over the phone.

His fingers tapped the top of the desk in an increasing staccato. The man became aware of the meaningful gesture and stopped his fingers with a glower.

The woman took her sweet time to answer, and all that time, McNamara clenched and unclenched his fists, irate. The phone ring sounded ominous in his ears, and his eyes narrowed to slits. He didn't even realise that a smile perched on his lips when Bryony's cheerful voice came on the line.

"Hullo," the woman said breathlessly as if she had run to get to the phone, and the man's heart skipped a beat.

"It's me, McNamara," he replied, and then he paused for a few seconds.

To his horror, the detective couldn't remember what he had wanted to say or the reason for that call. So, he struggled to find his words.

"I've been wondering how you were," the detective said the first thing that came to mind, suddenly unsure of himself, something new for him. He was never uncertain of himself, so he scowled at his stupidity. Stunned, the man realised that he had never experienced anything similar, not even when he had tried to get his first date, back at the age of thirteen, and he didn't like it.

McNamara waited a few long seconds, straining his hearing, but only the static on the line buzzed in his ears. That made him wonder if the woman had already disconnected the call, and he felt cold inside at the thought that she wouldn't welcome his call.

With a steely resolution, he decided to count to five. If Bryony hadn't answered by then, he would terminate the connection. Looking around with feigned disinterest, McNamara counted the seconds in his mind. He had got only to three when a soft sigh reached his ear.

"I've been fine," the young woman said gently. "And you?" she inquired, and now, her hesitation filled the line.

"Just work, you know how it is," the man replied automatically, and then, another pause ensued for a few seconds. "Are you busy tonight?" he asked once he had regained his determination.

"Not really," her soft voice replied. "Do you have anything in mind?"

"I haven't planned anything," the man admitted. "I was just thinking that we could have a drink or... a coffee, maybe...."

McNamara hated himself when he perceived the defensiveness in his voice, and he flexed his fist on the top of the table. He didn't like the thought that a mere slip of a woman could make him so insecure that he wouldn't be able to gather his ideas and articulate a coherent sentence.

"That would be nice," Bryony answered. "I've already got home, though...."

"I see," McNamara replied. This time, there was no mistake. The steel was there back in his voice. He assumed that the woman was brushing him off, and his pride couldn't take it graciously. His expectations had leaned onto another result to his invitation, and her soft refusal bruised his ego.

"No, you've misunderstood me," Bryony hurried to say, and he grinned, catching the haste in her voice.

McNamara knew Bryony had a pretty clear idea about the kind of man he was. Probably, she had thought that he would disconnect the call immediately.

"I wasn't saying that I wasn't available tonight," Bryony specified. She wanted to brush off any misunderstanding from his mind, and her slight reproach brought a twinge of guilt in the man's mind. "I was just saying that I'd like you to come here to my place for that drink. But I'm already home, and I don't feel like going out into town again. Still, I'd like to spend the evening with you if you could make the trip here," she clarified her statement patiently as if she had been talking to a child.

McNamara chose to disregard her tone and merely exulted hearing that she wanted to spend the evening with him. Nevertheless, whenever he thought of her house, Mrs Stevens would also come into his mind. The man had no doubt that he could live without seeing her again.

"And will Mrs Stevens be part of the company for the evening?" he inquired in a crisp voice, although the man would have liked to sound more pleasant or, if not, at least, indifferent. Still, the old bat raised strong feelings in him, and the man couldn't act otherwise. His last memories about the woman were vivid enough to make him grind his teeth to powder.

Bryony burst into laughter, saying, "Oh, no, don't worry about her. I've already had her over for tea this afternoon, and she was saying that she wanted to go to bed early tonight. The poor woman was a bit under the weather if you know what I mean. She's been like that for the last few days. What, with the chill in the air and the humidity, you know... I'm pretty sure that we won't be hearing from Mrs Stevens tonight," the young woman reassured him in a soothing voice.

"All right, then," McNamara made up his mind. He couldn't care less about the chill in the air and the old bat. Yet, the man was satisfied having the green light to see Bryony. "I'll be there in about fifteen minutes, depending on the traffic," he informed the woman in a grave voice.

"I'll wait by the window, but take your time," she said jokingly, surprising the man that even such a trite joke coming from Bryony had the power to put a smile on his lips.

"I'll keep that in mind," he replied mildly and hung up, without noticing that he had forgotten to say goodbye or anything similar.

Anyway, it wasn't in his nature. Most social conventions eluded him, but it wasn't like the man had missed any of them. He never lost sleep over the niceties he would forego daily. It made for briefer and more purposeful discussions.

CHAPTER 2 – EXPECTATIONS AND ASSUMPTIONS

McNamara impatiently snatched his coat off the peg hidden in the corner of his office and left the room in such a hurry that everyone looked after him in awe. He had forgotten to hold the door in his rush, and it had closed with a resonant bang.

The Chief Inspector had thought about having it fixed several times, but it hadn't become a priority for him yet. Now, he reconsidered the matter and made a note in his mind to call the maintenance guy the following day early in the morning.

As if nothing had happened, McNamara glanced at the people in the squad room. He threw over the shoulder, to everyone and no one in particular, "I'm on my mobile phone if you have an emergency."

He didn't expect an answer but continued towards the exit, mumbling to himself, 'I hope you won't, at least for one blasted evening.'

Then, the man headed to the underground garage taking the stairs by storm, in a rush to take his car out and drive to Bryony.

On his way to Bryony's house, the detective chastised himself for behaving like a teenager, eager to get in time for his first date. The man found his reaction irrational, and as a rule, he preferred that things made sense. He got lost when encountering the unknown.

She might have been somewhat different than other women he had encountered, but the man was sure that their date that evening didn't deserve all that fuss. After all, Bryony was nothing else but another woman, and he had dated his share of women over the years. His relationships might have had a short span of life, but that was worked well enough for him.

For a moment, McNamara's hand froze on the steering wheel. He had no idea if Bryony saw his visit in the same light. It was very possible that she merely expected to meet a friend, not a man who was thinking of dates and what that would entail. The thought frustrated him, and a deep line burrowed between his brows.

Besides, McNamara was already furious with himself for having broken one of his golden rules, which was gnawing at him. His entire professional life, he had tried hard not to let his subordinates see when something happened in his life or with him. The inspector liked to believe that he had successfully separated his professional life from his private one until then. He had never let anyone see beyond what he wanted to let them perceive and even perfected that art. Nevertheless, he had given his people a reason to wonder about his behaviour that evening.

The detective knew that he had to find a better way to deal with that matter and Bryony because he couldn't continue turning his life upside-down. That wouldn't do at all, as his acute sense of order didn't allow that, and if the man didn't have order in his life, he couldn't function.

***

After an infuriating ride through the evening rush hour, a frustrated McNamara stopped his car in front of Bryony's house. There, simmering, the man needed a few seconds to calm down. He couldn't understand how so many incapable drivers might have got their licenses. They represented a nuisance he couldn't avoid on the road, and one thing he loved was driving. The man didn't even stop to consider that his driving style represented a more significant challenge for the others on the road. He liked fast and risky driving and didn't see anything wrong with that.

The detective breathed a few times deeply, and when he considered that he was calm enough, he took the key out of the ignition.

Bryony's blue and white house, he liked so much, drew his eyes as soon as he got out of the car. From the first moment he had laid eyes on it, the contrast between the sparkling blue of the windows and door and the shiny white of the walls made him feel at ease.

Involuntarily, McNamara glanced at her neighbour's house just in time to notice a hand in the shadow, pushing the curtain aside. The old bat wanted to sneak a look at him.

Mrs Stevens's inquisitive eyes probed him insistently. Still, the man pretended that he wasn't aware of her spying on him. He didn't feel like starting his evening confronting the old crone and only hoped that the woman wouldn't come by Bryony's that evening to spoil his party.

McNamara didn't doubt that the old woman could do that only to spite him. He had had enough bad experiences with Mrs Stevens in the past, after all, and was wary of her.

The thought of her presence intruding into his brief time with Bryony made him grind his teeth, which was a habit he was aware of, but which he chose to ignore.

McNamara was a master at ignoring what he didn't want to see or think of, as long as it wasn't related to a criminal case. There, he didn't discount anything.

The man had hardly climbed up the flight of stairs to Bryony's front door that it opened before him. McNamara was pleased to notice that the young woman had been waiting for his arrival with some impatience. Apparently, the lass had been watching the street for him, as she had promised. A huge smile flitted on her lips when she gazed at him.

Relief washed over McNamara when he noticed her pleasure to see him. He had been afraid that her behaviour towards him was merely a result of his role during her ordeal. The man couldn't accept the thought that Bryony had turned to him simply because he was the only one available at that time.

That was actually why he had already avoided the woman for a few weeks. Except for a couple of calls to check whether Bryony was all right or not, the man hadn't attempted to reach the woman since leaving her house after concluding the Nightingale Street case.

It hadn't been easy for him to do so, but McNamara had kept his distance, nonetheless. Several times, he had surprised himself reaching out for the phone to call her, and he had to squash the thought on the spot.

"I was sure you would forget everything about us once you closed your case, detective," the young woman greeted him. That soft voice the man had been thinking so much about lately found its way into his heart, making him feel good.

"I called you, didn't I?" the man replied morosely, and her smile widened at the sound of his sullen voice, which she knew so well.

McNamara closed the distance between them and touched her face with an absent gesture, his eyes softening. The tight line of his mouth relaxed somewhat, and the man inquired quietly, "Shall we go inside?"

Bryony nodded and led the way into the hallway. McNamara followed her, closing the door behind and keeping his eyes on the discreet movement of the woman's hips. He also monitored her other actions so that he could glance somewhere else if she turned around. The man knew the young woman wouldn't have been happy to notice his eyes fixated on her lower body.

The smell of the house felt familiar and welcomed him. McNamara was confident that nothing had changed since his last visit and felt as if the house had accepted his presence, which confused him. He didn't pine for hearth and home, and the direction of his thoughts discombobulated him.

Disturbed, McNamara chose to gaze at Bryony and chase everything else out of his mind. That evening, Bryony wore a knee-long blue dress, which exposed her shapely legs. The pale colour of the cloth lit her curvy strawberry hair. McNamara remembered well how those soft locks had felt on his skin but tried to push the memory aside. He shouldn't have thought about certain things if that evening didn't have a positive result.

MCNAMARA SERIES BOX SET
BOOK 0NE & TWO

CHAPTER 3 – AN INTERESTING BEGINNING FOR AN EVENING

"May I take your coat, detective?" Bryony asked, turning back to him when they reached the hallway closet.

"Why so formal?" the man asked while taking his coat off. "If I remember correctly, you were using my name the last time we met," he continued in a scolding voice, a frown between his brows while taking off his coat and handing it to her.

"Yes, I remember," the woman replied quietly while carefully putting the coat on a hanger and closing the closet. Then, she turned back to him. "And I also recall you didn't want to give me your first name," Bryony mentioned, tilting her head to the right as if she had challenged him.

The playful lights in her eyes told McNamara that the woman was just teasing him. It was nothing else but pleasant banter, not reproach for his inflexibility at that time.

Yet, that didn't seem incentive enough for him to give her his first name. 'McNamara' had worked fine for other women in the past, so it should also have worked for her.

The silence stretched while they watched and assessed each other. Both Bryony and McNamara recognised stubbornness when it lay before their eyes. Besides, McNamara found it almost amusing to see that slip of a girl matching him every step of the way. Yet, the look in her eyes compelled him to say something.

"Artair," he finally said, albeit reluctant to divulge his moniker. McNamara had kept his given name a secret for far too long, and habits were like a second comfortable skin for him. The inspector had had a few encounters with people's narrow-mindedness in the past, so he had chosen to introduce himself only with his last name.

"That's my first name," the man specified when he noticed her inquiring glance.

"Gaelic," Bryony observed pensively. "I like it. I think it suits you just fine. If I remember correctly, it means 'bear' or 'eagle'," Bryony observed and waited for him to confirm her supposition.

McNamara nodded briefly, yet he didn't voice a reply. The man had tensed, waiting for her to make fun of his first name. However, the woman merely smiled at him once more and gestured for him to follow her. With mixed feelings, the DCI followed the young woman to the kitchen.

The man recalled the kitchen as one of Bryony's favourite rooms in the house when it came to spending the evenings. So, it looked like things hadn't changed too much there since his last visit a few weeks before.

"Have a seat," Bryony gestured towards the table. "I've already made some coffee," she said and went to the coffee maker to bring the carafe to the table. "If I know you well, you'll need it."

"What are you saying?" he glared at her, his famous frown between his brows, which made the woman grin. After all, it looked good on him.

"Don't read too much into it," Bryony replied, waving her fingers to dispel his displeasure. "I only know that you like long work hours, and coffee surely helps you. From what I've seen, you practically live on that stuff, and work looks like your basic reason for existence," the woman shrugged as if she had explained the basics of life to him.

"Maybe not tonight, though," McNamara expressed his hope in a dry voice, accepting the coffee cup she had prepared for him. Sipping from the hot liquid, the man was delighted to note that she had remembered how he liked his coffee. After all, it was a good sign, and he was willing to take whatever the lass had to offer.

"So, DCI," Bryony mused, watching the man with hope and chewing her lower lip for a moment. "May I call you Artair, or should I stick to McNamara?"

"The cat's out of the bag now," the man grimaced with displeasure. "So, you don't need to continue calling me McNamara, but only when we're alone. I don't want others to feel like they would have leeway to use my first name," he mentioned. He could do without ironic grins and useless innuendos.

Bryony glanced at the man briefly and then lowered her eyes on the cup she held. To fill in the silence, she sipped from her coffee cup and said softly, "I wonder why."

Artair shrugged as if the answer hadn't been significant. The man didn't think he should go into the other reasons. Still, he believed that he should have clarified his position, "I prefer a certain distance in my relationships."

"So, I should be flattered, then," Bryony observed pensively, but a glance back at him told her that McNamara didn't like the direction of her thoughts. The man looked highly uncomfortable with her reasoning.

The young woman burst into laughter, touching his arm light-heartedly.

"Don't worry, inspector. I didn't imply that we have a special relationship. I was just making conversation. You know what I'm talking about. It's that social ritual... a thing people do when they get together... To pass the time...."

The man scowled at her, but it was just for show. McNamara wasn't so closed-minded that he couldn't understand that the girl merely made light of his worries. Yet, he felt slightly unbalanced because their interaction was far from what he had expected, and her words, no matter how well-meant they were, didn't make him feel more at ease. Nevertheless, the man decided to pass over the moment's awkwardness and looked for something to say.

"How have you been?" he asked, his eyes sweeping hungrily over her face and body. After all, McNamara had longed for having her close and talking to her.

The young woman looked as good as he remembered, and the man did remember well her dark blue eyes with long eyelashes and her rosy skin. With her hair, she made him think of a Scottish rose. A healthy and sunny Scottish rose. Still, that thought made him feel silly.

"Not bad," Bryony replied with a shrug and stood up. The woman waved her hand, noticing the mute question in the man's eyes. "I've just remembered I bought some shortbread and cookies this morning. I think they would go well with the coffee. Although…" she started to say but left the sentence unfinished.

"Although what?" McNamara inquired suspiciously, knowing that the lass could be unpredictable. He wasn't ready for any kind of surprises right then.

"I was just wondering…. Maybe you're hungry. You've come from work, haven't you?"

"You don't need to trouble yourself with that," the man dismissed her worries with a wave of his hand. "The cookies will do just fine," Artair assured her, not feeling like wasting the little time he could spend with her. It wasn't as if he had never gone hungry before.

"I'll bring the cookies, then," Bryony nodded and then went to take the cookies out of a cupboard and arrange them on a plate. When

Bryony returned to the table, McNamara noticed that the woman was biting her lower lip. She looked as if she had wanted to attack a specific subject but didn't know how to do it.

"You want to ask me something, so, go ahead," he said.

Bryony put the cookies on the white square napkin in front of McNamara. Then, she sat at the opposite side of the table. She looked straight at him with grave eyes and asked.

"Have you heard anything about Mr Thompson?"

That wasn't a question the man had expected. It wasn't a question he liked more to the point, and his displeasure gleamed in his narrowed eyes.

"Why the sudden interest in Thompson?" McNamara asked, stressing the man's name with derision. "You gave me the impression that you weren't interested in him," he pointed out, scowling at her.

The young woman stared at him wide-eyed, stunned that he had reached the wrong conclusion, and taken aback and couldn't say anything for a few moments.

The DCI took advantage of her silence and said, not without malice, "He won't be back soon.

You'd have to wait for him for a while if you sat your cap for him."

The bitterness in his voice wasn't lost on Bryony, and she hurried to set things straight. The woman slapped his arm and said, "I'm not interested in him, you loggerhead. I was just asking because of Alice. She's become somewhat reclusive lately. From what I can see, the only person she's been talking to is Mary Reid and that not very often. I saw Alice this afternoon when I came home, and she avoided me like the plague. She's been doing that since the case ended, and I'm a bit sick of it to tell you the truth. The idea is that I don't know if she blames me or not. Besides, I must say that she isn't looking good, either," the woman explained her worries.

"Well, Thompson's situation is irrelevant to her well-being. He is guilty and confessed his involvement with the underage prostitution ring and blackmails. He'll do some time. There's no other way... Anyway, I haven't heard of Alice's visiting him or anything, so I'd say she has already closed that door. I imagine that she just feels hurt and humiliated right now. You can't do anything to change that," the man added with cold indifference. McNamara didn't give a fig about Thompson's situation. Even though he somewhat pitied Alice, he didn't care about her either.

The inspector had learnt early not to get emotionally involved in any of his cases. However, he doubted that he could get emotionally involved in anything. His indifference and lack of emotion were neatly written in his genetic code. Besides, the man had never wasted energy or thought over such insignificant matters. Emotion, anger, or compassion only blurred the lines, and he liked to see everything with clear eyes.

Anyway, a policeman needed to be whole for the next case. One thing was sure: there would always be another case, as crime never slept in Edinburgh. McNamara knew that his job would never become obsolete. He didn't have to worry about that.

Nevertheless, the man had a short supply of empathy. He lived only by a rigid set of rules he had set for himself. It just happened that those rules coincided with society's legal and social code, which sometimes felt like a relief.

"Aren't you a little... too cynical?" Bryony wondered, raising her brows, and her question made the man glower.

"I don't afford the luxury of making friendly connections with the people I interrogate or arrest," McNamara retorted. Then, he mumbled, 'As if I'd want to make friends with them.'

The man intended that muttering only for his own ears. However, Bryony still heard his words. So, she asked, "Should I understand that I'm the exception to the rule, or should I read something different in your visit tonight? I thought… we were friends or… on the way to becoming friends… Was I wrong… Artair?"

McNamara realised that the woman used his first name to make a point and stared at her for a few long seconds, not knowing how to reply. The man looked undecided what to choose from the thoughts whirling in his mind, and the silence stretched until it became unbearable.

"Look," Bryony started in force, and her eyes showed him that his silence had hurt her. "I didn't mean to put you on the spot. We can go on without defining what… this… means," the young woman said, waving her hand between them.

Her half-hearted concession jarred Artair to react. He ran his fingers through his hair and stood up abruptly, looking at her with unreadable eyes. Then, the man took a few steps towards the window and stopped there. He looked out the window, even though his eyes didn't register anything. He didn't perceive the lights in the street or the two women talking in front of the Reids' house.

McNamara needed a few seconds to gather his wits so that he could reply to Bryony's mute reproach. When the man considered that he knew what to say and it was safe to answer, he turned his gaze back to Bryony.

"I haven't thought about that," he reckoned. "I think you're right, though. You're the exception to the rule because I definitely want the two of us to be friends. Close friends, if possible," he emphasised his intentions, and the curve of her spontaneous smile at his words pleased him. Yet, it worried him, as well. He was in serious trouble if the woman could touch him with only a smile.

With a wave of her hand, Bryony invited him back to the table to snack on the cookies, and once the man sat down, she led the conversation far away from his work. She also steered as far away as possible from his feelings for her. Before, the woman had noticed that McNamara didn't like to talk about that.

Bryony didn't know the man well. But she knew enough to understand that Artair would have been mortified to comprehend that he harboured any feelings. So, talking about those feelings would have been inadvisable.

***

The evening turned into night. However, Bryony and Artair still talked. Their conversation had been flowing almost without pause for a couple of hours now.

Now, McNamara was convinced that he had made the right choice for the evening. Bryony was precisely like he remembered. She had wit and humour, and she didn't play coy with him. The man appreciated her openness, and more importantly, the woman didn't annoy him. The time passed faster than he would have thought.

When his cell phone went off, interrupting the flow of their conversation, McNamara scowled and muttered a curse, which brought a wicked smile to his companion's lips. The policeman noticed it and glowered at Bryony.

Still, he reckoned that her reaction was represented the perfect response to his own.

The detective took the call, although he was reluctant to let the evening end. Yet, the man knew his duty and that it had to always come first in his profession. He listened carefully to the person at the other end of the line. He replied, "I'll be there in probably twenty minutes."

Disconnecting the call, the man turned to Bryony. A nearly imperceptible sigh left her lips when she saw the expression on his face, but it still reached his ears. The rumour that his eyes turned metallic and cold whenever he got news about a new case was not unknown to him. McNamara seemed unable to control it, although he didn't want the lass to know too much.

"I have to go," the man said without intonation.

Bryony nodded. "I know," she replied softly. "Be well, all right?" she urged him quietly, but the detective perceived the inquiry hidden in her voice.

"Aye, I will," Artair responded and turned to leave. He stopped in the hall and took his time to watch the woman while she took his coat out of the closet.

"I'll call you... as soon as I can," the man promised reluctantly, pressing his lips tight after the words came out of his mouth.

"I know, Artair... I suppose you're going to have a hectic period..." the young woman said with some hesitation, watching him fastening his coat.

"That's right, Bryony. I'll have a busy period. That's how it is when a new case comes up... Yet, I'll call you and find the time to come to see you, all right?" he repeated his earlier promise, staring her down for making assumptions.

Bryony nodded and, leaning forward, kissed his cheek. "One for the road, you know... Maybe you'll have luck," she smiled impishly.

The man's gaze searched her face avidly, and then, with a sudden decision, he leaned over her and kissed her lips hard. McNamara stared into her eyes for just a few more moments and then opened the door and went out into the night.

CHAPTER 4 – THE MISSING BODY

The detectives drew themselves aside and made room for the doctor to take a closer look at the gruesome scene. Yet, the head attached to the hydrant by its hair mesmerised everyone, and they warily kept stealing glances at it.

All the policemen at the scene had seen their share of bodies during their careers. Still, it was unnerving to watch the eerie faded violet eyes, which seemed to look straight through them. More than one detective shuddered under their intensity.

As the fog rolled in, the police people had the unsettling impression they were part of a horror movie set. They kept looking around, wary of what might have lurked in the forest's dark.

A sudden gush of wind stirred the leaves nearby, and Jo almost jumped out of her skin, moving closer to Mike, but not only for his body warmth. It was true that the nights were getting much chillier than the daytime now. That spoke of the end of September in Edinburgh.

That autumn had been quite a surprise for everyone, as it started with high temperatures. Even now, when they were drawing to the end of September, the days felt warmer than expected. The other night, the weather girl had announced the highest temperature on record for that time of the year. Most times, people would go out without wearing a coat. It became a common occurrence.

However, despite the warmth during the day, the evenings and nights were getting colder. The drop in temperature was steep, although it wasn't chilly enough to make people pile many clothes on them. That would come in a couple more weeks, though.

The detectives could hear the coroner droning on, lecturing the medical technician. They strained their ears, trying to listen to what the man was saying, but his voice was hushed, and they couldn't understand his words.

The medical examiner disliked sharing information in the early stages of an investigation. He didn't say anything before he had straight facts to give the inspectors. That didn't mean that the detectives were not curious to catch what the man said. After all, inherent curiosity was what had driven them to their profession.

Yet, the inspectors didn't try to get closer to the coroner, knowing from painful experience that the man loathed their intrusion. His temper was famous. It rivalled even McNamara's, given the right conditions. So, none of the detectives felt like being the target of the coroner's sharp tongue that night. He wasn't a man to trifle with, and his snarky comments wouldn't end that night. David Stewart had the unpleasant habit of reminding the inspectors of their mistakes even months later.

All the people at the scene glanced behind them when the sound of a car door slammed hard reached their ears. That announced a newcomer at the murder scene, and they had a pretty good idea who that person might be.

All of them, including the coroner, turned their heads. They watched the silhouette of a man taking a shortcut through the meadow. The fog drifting around amplified McNamara's height and dark appearance.

Mike elbowed Jo, and when she turned to him, he whispered. "Look out, he's mad, Jo. Just look at his gait. Something's got under his hat tonight. We're in trouble. Listen to me. You know how volatile the Chief is, and anything could happen when he's like that."

Jo glanced back at the man crossing the meadow and sighed. Unfortunately, Mike was right again. Her friend was a good judge of McNamara's moods.

It wasn't difficult to assess her boss's mood for herself that night, though. The woman understood that they were in for a long and arduous night. All the signs were there for them to see.

McNamara's anger simmered at the surface, and the man was nearly stomping on his way to his men. The rigid line of his shoulders showed that something bothered him badly.

The policewoman knew that the DCI didn't welcome being called to murder scenes as a rule because he had a genuine aversion to crime. Yet, that wasn't his usual behaviour when such a call occurred. After all, the man had had his share of calls, taking all of them in stride.

There was something more there besides the late hour. If the woman hadn't known better, Jo would have thought that the Chief Inspector had been disturbed while on a pretty exciting date. He wouldn't have cared a fig if things had been different.

The DCI was quite cavalier about his relationships, and Jo knew he had never had a serious one. The man had a phobia for commitment. He enjoyed women briefly and left them in haste afterwards. As far as Jo knew, McNamara hadn't even been on a date for a while now.

The DCI approached the people huddled together, and after a brief greeting, he turned to the coroner. "What have we got here, David? Any ideas you'd like to share?"

"You can look for yourself, lad," the coroner moved aside, and taking his gloves off, pointed to the hydrant.

Now, McNamara had a clear view towards the woman's head, and the metallic glint in his eyes betrayed his dismay. He immediately took note of the knot fastened to the hydrant and, without turning back to the others, said, "Shorty, be sure to take a photo of that knot. It doesn't seem ordinary and might tell us something about the killer's profession. I'm nearly certain it would have something to do with boats."

Shorty was about to assure him that he would do it when Mike chimed in. "If not his hobbies, boss. It might be somebody who likes sailing, not necessarily someone who makes a living on a boat," the man pointed out.

Jo nudged him hard, driving her elbow into the man's side. It was never a good idea to point out such things when the DCI was in one of his moods, and Mike should have known better.

McNamara noticed her gesture, and a sarcastic grin appeared in the corner of his mouth.

"Mike's correct, Jo, so don't bother to discipline him. None of you should be afraid to share your ideas with me. We have a common interest, after all, to solve the case," he pointed out harshly, turning to the coroner afterwards. "No body, David?"

"Not for the moment," the doctor answered, shaking his head. "Although we've looked around carefully. We've already covered the ground for about a fifty-four-yard radius. Anyway, Shorty has already sent a couple of teams out to cover some more ground. I hope they'll find the rest of the body, McNamara. Otherwise, I won't be able to tell you very much from that," the man continued, pointing his thumb back towards the human remains, still hanging from the hydrant.

"But you must have an idea, old man. You always do," McNamara insisted, his harsh voice pushing the old coroner to give him an answer. He did have a reason. The Chief Inspector knew what the man could do.

David Stewart possessed a very sharp mind and had acquired a lot of experience along the way. The man had been working as a coroner for over thirty years already. Besides, he had had his share of strange cases.

The man rolled his eyes at the Chief Inspector's insistence. Still, he replied, "I can tell you that she was definitely beheaded while alive. Considering what the old woman who found her said, I would say that the victim was murdered a maximum of fifteen or twenty minutes before the witness arrived here. You have a very agile and dexterous killer to catch this time, McNamara," Stewart added maliciously. He would have liked to see what the young Chief Inspector could do with what he got.

McNamara peeked back at the head and then at the doctor. The man was taking a cigarette from his pocket, ready to leave. "Why do you think he's agile?" the Chief Inspector's question stopped the man.

"Think, lad. It's not such a quandary. The attacker had to kill the woman and mount her head there in under fifteen minutes," the coroner indicated impatiently, pointing his thumb back to the hanging head again. "Otherwise, your old woman would have witnessed the deed. She wouldn't have been just the person who found the crime scene or part of the crime scene. You'd have had two corpses instead of one. Or a partial one, as it turned out....." The doctor mumbled the last part of his speech, but McNamara still heard him.

"You're right, David," the policeman admitted. "Have you finished here?" McNamara asked the doctor, waving broadly to encompass the surrounding area.

The coroner nodded and lit his cigarette meticulously, cautiously covering the flame of his lighter so the wind wouldn't quench it. Then the man said without addressing someone in particular, "They can take that head from there. I've got everything I need."

Stewart headed to the road, and after a few steps, he shouted back, "Of course, I need a body if you could find me one, lad. I'm not a bloody magician."

McNamara nodded, amused, following the doctor by sight. Then, the man shook his head and turned to his people, immediately noticing that Jo shivered. The wind had picked up within the last ten minutes or so, and the temperature had dropped another few degrees. The Chief Inspector glanced to the victim's head once more and then around.

"Shorty, start combing the area for everything we could use. If it's loose, bag it," the DCI said, failing to hear the forensic expert's upset mutters.

The man knew to do his job and didn't feel like getting instructions more appropriate for a trainee. Still, he didn't dare tell that to McNamara.

"Jo, where's that old woman I've heard about?" the DCI asked his subordinate, shifting his gaze to her.

"She's with James, sir. We couldn't keep the woman here. She was shaking like a leaf, and not only because of the cold," Jo explained apologetically. "Besides, she had a difficult time controlling her dog. From what I could gather, Missy -- that's the dog's name, was acting out of the ordinary and frightened the old woman."

"That's good to know, Jo, but where is she with James? I haven't seen anyone in the cars parked down there," McNamara asked with exasperation, making Jo cringe.

The DCI would always complain that she wasn't precise enough when she presented facts to him. She didn't want the Chief Inspector to be cross with her that night. He was far from his usual slightly grumpy mood, which now seemed like a ray of sunshine. She missed it. Now his disposition had taken a turn for the worse, and Jo knew she wouldn't be able to get on his good side with her typical tactics, so she settled for precision.

"James took the old woman back home. I have the address here, sir," the policewoman rushed to say and tapped a manicured finger on the top of her notebook.

Noticing the DCI's inquiring look, Jo opened the notebook quickly. She fumbled with the pages for a few moments and then showed him the spot where she had written the address.

McNamara glanced at the address scribbled in Jo's indecipherable writing and glowered. He couldn't make heads or tails of what the woman had written on that paper. He stared at her for a second and then glanced at Mike.

"Mike, you stay here with Shorty. Hopefully, he finds a body. You can wait in the car if you want, and Shorty will call you once he has any news. If they haven't found anything in the next hour, you are free to go home and get some sleep. I'll see you at the station first thing tomorrow morning. We'll take it from there."

Then, the Chief Inspector turned to talk to Shorty and realised that the man had already left the group, heading to the trees. His long stride had already covered a reasonably good distance. McNamara didn't feel like shouting and calling him.

He shook his head and turned back to his other people. "Mike, after I leave, you'll call Shorty and tell him he'd better let me know once he's found something. You'll also have to supervise the guys over there," he continued, pointing to the forensic team. "So, I'm afraid until Shorty returns, no warm car for you."

Mike nodded that he understood and tried not to show that McNamara's behaviour stunned him. The DCI was a good boss, but he never coddled his subordinates or expressed concerns for their comfort while on duty. The man's attitude bordered on indifference.

The DCI was full of contradictions that night, and Mike didn't like it when he didn't understand what was going on around him.

However, McNamara's voice shook him from his pensive mood. "You'll come with me, Jo. We have to talk to that old woman, and I can't read anything from what you wrote here. You'll have to show me the way," the man handed her the notebook back and gestured for her to lead the way.

Jo stuffed the notebook into her pocket, and then, she decided to burrow both her hands into her pockets. She was too cold and shivered in earnest now.

CHAPTER 5 – A CHAT WITH MAUDE

Maude lived in one of the three-floored townhouses in the village north of Edinburgh. The rows of white dwellings lined the lower border of the forest on one side and the Almond River on the other. Each floor accommodated one flat, making people wonder if the apartments were spacious enough.

Maude's flat lay on the ground floor with a view of the river. The old woman had been living there for decades. She felt comfortable in her two-bedroom and small kitchen flat. She was happy to have enough room to receive guests now and then and didn't yearn for more. A larger apartment would have been an inconvenience since some days the woman found it difficult to clean the entire house, as it was.

That night, Maude had a visitor she had never expected to see in her kitchen. Detective

Sergeant James was courteous and attentive to all her needs, yet the old woman felt like a fly under a microscope.

She had always been circumspect around police, a habit instilled in her as a child. Her parents had respected the authority that came with the function but had been reluctant in making friends with the village constable.

Weary, the old woman glanced at the clock on the wall. Midnight had already come and gone. She had never been awake so late, or, at least, not for the last two decades.

The woman didn't blame James for that. Maude knew she wouldn't have slept even if D.S. James hadn't been there. The image of the severed head was still vivid before her eyes, and she doubted that she would forget about it any time soon.

Maude wasn't fond of gruesome stories. She would read a regular crime novel, but nothing that would evoke ghastly images or go into details about gory things. The old woman preferred to keep her innocence when it came to some issues.

The woman knew she was like the proverbial ostrich with its head in the sand, but she liked her sleep free of nightmares. Her daily life was filled with enough aches as it was, so she prayed for peaceful nights. As a rule, one pill did the trick. However, Maude didn't believe that a drug would do the thing right then.

"Are you sure you don't want a cup of tea, young man?" the woman asked the detective. "I could use a spot of hot herbal tea," she explained, attempting to stand up. However, her knee joints ached after the sprint she had subjected them to that night.

"Sit down, Mrs Campbell," James stopped her with a light touch on her arm. "I'll make the tea for you. You'll see that I'm competent enough in the kitchen. I know you've had a terrible evening and need your rest," the man reassured the woman, tapping her shoulder.

James knew that she wouldn't be satisfied with his service, which was inevitable. So, he steeled himself against her reproachful eyes and words. The old people, stuck in their ruts, were never content when someone else would do things, even though they grudgingly admitted they needed help. Shrugging imperceptibly, the detective prepared the kettle under Maude's careful eyes.

Maude was afraid that the man would ruin the tea or chip her teapot. The old woman watched him like a hawk. Like most people of a certain age, who had lived alone for a long time, she was confident that no one could do things her way, and her system was always correct.

However, James impressed her, making only one mistake. He put the kettle on a kitchen towel instead of using the tray. The woman cringed but refrained from saying anything. The man was trying to help, after all. He proved competent enough, at least better than her niece, Maggie. That girl would drive Maude crazy whenever she came to visit. As stubborn as her aunt, the two women often came to blows during those visits.

As people often noticed, they were both a chip off the old tree. Maude's father had also been a very stubborn man.

He would go blue in the face claiming the sky was red if he had happened to make such a statement. The man never took his words back if he happened to make a statement, and he died because of that. He declared that the weather would undoubtedly improve, so he didn't need to postpone his trip or, at least, wear warmer clothes. Everybody else's words fell on deaf ears. However, the weather proved him wrong, and the man died three weeks later. Virulent pneumonia had ravaged his lungs, and the doctors were at a loss to help him.

D.S. James brought a cup and saucer to Maude and poured the tea for the old lady, noticing with dismay that she wasn't very pleased with his ministrations. The man smiled inside but kept a neutral appearance, unwilling to let her guess his thoughts. It was hardly a secret. The woman had pursed her mouth, signifying that she had clenched her teeth hard to keep her mouth shut.

The Sergeant had hardly poured the tea in her cup when someone knocked on the door. The detective signalled the woman to remain seated and headed for the front door himself. He didn't expect any trouble but preferred to err on the caution side and be thorough than sorry afterwards.

James glanced through the peephole and spied Jo and McNamara, so he turned to his hostess to reassure her, "It's just the police, ma'am, no worries."

Then, the man opened the door to face a sullen McNamara. The DCI disliked waiting even for a train. However, staying in front of closed doors was much more aggravating for his impatience.

"Any problems, James?" the man asked, reproachfully raising his left brow. The Chief Inspector had heard the Sergeant approaching the door and didn't understand why he had to take his sweet time to open it.

"No, there are no problems, Chief. Just reassuring Mrs Campbell that she didn't have anything to worry about," James explained, stepping aside to let them pass.

The DCI entered the hallway, and Jo followed, smiling kindly at James, "You've got everything under control, haven't you, Ainsley?"

Jo was one of the few detectives that used the Sergeant's first name. Most of his colleagues got used to calling him James and never strayed from that.

"Yes, everything's fine. Mrs Campbell is less frightened now," James stated meaningfully, and McNamara appreciated his thoughtfulness. The young man had a knack to put people at ease and make questioning easier. The DCI knew he could always count on James's common sense.

The DCI entered the old woman's kitchen and bowed his head slightly.

"Good evening, Mrs Campbell," he greeted her, sweeping the frail woman with his eyes. The woman's paleness was striking, and the man imagined that she must have been shaken to the core. Indeed, that head displayed for everyone to see wasn't a sight for those with weak hearts.

Even a more assertive nature would have felt uneasy, if not scared.

Maude raised her eyes to the Chief Inspector, and the man read strength and determination in her direct gaze. His demeanour softened, and his earlier bitterness and anger subsided.

"May I sit down?" the DCI asked quietly. Maude nodded and showed him one of the stools surrounding the kitchen table.

McNamara took off his coat and laid it on a nearby stool before sitting down and facing Maude. Then he asked her, "How are you feeling?"

Her eyes turned mutinous, and she retorted sharply, "How do you think I'm feeling, young man?"

The detective's eyes sparkled, and the corner of his mouth twitched. He liked the old woman. Maude might have been shocked earlier, but she had recovered enough to stand to him. Her slight appearance hid steel, and McNamara had learnt to recognise a kindred spirit.

"I suppose you're here to ask pertinent questions, not to make chit-chat," the woman continued in an abrasive voice, shamelessly taking the man's measure.

The Chief Inspector was a wolf, unlike the already tamed James. Maude had already concluded that a determined woman would run roughshod over the Sergeant.

As if he had read the woman's thoughts, McNamara grinned. He was man enough to find her impression refreshing.

"All right, Mrs Campbell. In your own words, tell us what happened tonight," the DCI invited her with a gesture.

"Hmm..." she murmured, glancing at him through her lashes. "You'll be disappointed," the woman said, shrugging gracefully, which surprised the detectives. "I haven't seen anything more than you did, although I'd have preferred not to...," the woman reckoned.

With a far-away look in her eyes, she paused for a few seconds, and McNamara considered it better not to interrupt her thoughts. Maude shivered and then returned her gaze to him.

"I went for a stroll with Missy," she said, pointing to the beagle sleeping peacefully on a pillow in the kitchen corner. "She's tired now," Maude remarked with sarcasm. "She wasn't so tired when she dragged me all over the forest," the woman scoffed with obvious exaggeration. "Well, we were just strolling peacefully when Missy started growling and snarling.... Then, she started running towards that blasted hydrant... As if it had gotten up and disappeared...."

Maude shook her head, still shaken because of the dog's behaviour. But then, her knees still hurt, and exhaustion claimed her body, fibre by fibre. The old woman knew she would forgive the dog eventually. More probable in the morning, after she had a good night's sleep. "Missy stopped only when she got there."

"Did you see anything?" McNamara inquired, leaning slightly forward.

Tiredness wrinkled the corners of the woman's eyes and was also visible in the pressed line of her lips. McNamara felt sorry for her but still had to ask her questions.

"When we got there, I didn't see anything," the woman shook her head. "I was just happy because the blasted dog had stopped. I closed my eyes in relief and tried to catch my breath... When the blood stopped roaring in my ears, I opened my eyes. I saw that..." she trailed off, pressing her shaky fingers over her lips, a sudden image of the severed head popping into her mind.

McNamara waited patiently. Tears threatened to spill over the wrinkled cheeks of the old woman, so he decided to show compassion even if it killed him. Maude had touched a particular chord in his heart.

Maude needed all her strength to keep her tears at bay. She never cried in public. Hell, the woman had never shed tears for the last two decades. Her tears had dried up when she witnessed her husband's mangled body dragged from under a car. A blasted tourist had forgotten to drive on the left side of the road and ran the man over at full speed.

The woman shook her head and turned her gaze to the detectives again, only to notice sympathy on Jo's and James's faces. Angered, Maude sneered. She didn't need their pity. Defiantly, she turned to McNamara. His face didn't reveal anything, and the woman welcomed the lack of empathy in the man's eyes.

"I saw that head and the hair knot... I saw the blood still dripping and pooling on the ground... I saw those violet eyes fading... And damned me if I can remember where I saw them before...," Maude muttered under her breath.

McNamara caught her mutters and leaned towards the woman. "Did you say that you saw those eyes before? Do you know the woman?" he asked sharply.

"No, I don't know the woman, young man," she replied crossly, a deep line between her brows. "I mean, I don't know her name or anything... Yet, I remember talking to her...."

"When and where?" McNamara asked punctually.

"I'd have told you if I'd known," the old woman snapped at him.

She knew that it wasn't the man's fault that she couldn't remember. Yet, Maude felt guilty for her forgetness but wanted to have someone else to blame. Her memory hadn't faded yet, so she should have been able to remember when and where she had seen that woman.

McNamara swallowed a harsh reply, realising that the woman was old enough to have memory problems. She was also shaken, and the last thing she needed was him, biting her head off.

"All right, Mrs Campbell. That's no hurry. When you remember, you'll let us know. Is there anything else you could tell us?"

Maude looked straight into McNamara's eyes and almost nearly shook her head. Then, she reconsidered and leaned forward as if she had wanted to impart a great secret. Her fingers skimmed the top of the table in hesitation.

"Aye, that blood, Inspector... It was fresh... I could see it was still flowing... I knew that woman had just been killed... And I think... the killer was still there.... Right then, when Missy was running towards the hydrant, the murderer must have been there... There were too many shadows, though, and I didn't see... a person... but... it was... And while I was calling 999, I felt someone watching me from the tree line... And you should know that I didn't imagine that thing, young man," she brusquely snapped at James.

With a deep frown on her face, the woman also turned to Jo to tell her a few things. Maude had guessed well because both James and Jo thought that the woman had imaged things because of fear.

McNamara had to bite back a smile at the woman's reaction. The man didn't believe that many would have angered her willingly. He liked Maude. Her honest behaviour was something he understood.

"I believe you are correct, ma'am," McNamara nodded to her. "The kill was fresh, and definitely, the killer didn't have time to scamper away."

"Then... shouldn't we have a guard on Mrs Campbell?" James asked, surprise seeping into his voice.

McNamara considered his words briefly, but then, he shook his head. "No, we won't leave anyone here with her. The killer might watch her. That's true. But if we put someone to guard her here, he'll think that she knows something. Right now, he might believe that she didn't see him, and he has nothing to fear," the Chief Inspector explained, looking straight in Maude's eyes. "Of course, we'll have someone watch from afar. You'll be protected if anyone tries to get to you, ma'am."

Maude agreed with him. She didn't need to put herself in danger's way if she could avoid it. Besides, she preferred to have the house to herself, not stumble upon someone else whenever she went to the kitchen or bathroom.

"Perfect," the woman replied. "Then you can leave now so that I can go to bed." Her harsh tone brook no argument, and McNamara stifled his grin. Maude turned out to be a tough old bird.

MCNAMARA SERIES BOX SET
BOOK 0NE & TWO

CHAPTER 6 – THE BODY ISN'T MISSING ANYMORE

McNamara leaned on the windowsill, crossing his arms over his chest. His eyes levelled on the coroner evenly. David Stewart had just come into his office and didn't seem in a good mood. McNamara's lips twitched in an ill-concealed smile at the thought that Stewart hadn't been in a good mood for most of the last twenty-five or thirty years. Maybe even as a lad, he had been the same cantankerous bloke as now.

The coroner was absently rolling a cigarette between his fingers. The DCI knew he wouldn't light it in his office. However, the inspector didn't doubt that the man regretted the old days when he could have done just that.

"Well, are you bringing any news?" the detective decided to ask the man. The waste of time bothered him. Pushing off the windowsill, he crossed the floor to his desk, plopping onto the chair behind it.

"Aye, some news," the old man offered reluctantly, but

he didn't continue. Lost in thought, Stewart stopped paying attention to the DCI, whose left brow hiked up his forehead.

A few moments later, sick of the silence stretching in the office, McNamara asked sarcastically, "So what should I do to hear that news?"

The inspector's tone made the coroner look up sharply. A blush powdered the top of his cheekbones, betraying the man's embarrassment. Stewart had been tired lately, and his mind wandered in the worst moments. "We found the body," the doctor blurted, hoping to cover for his absent-mindedness.

"Did you, now?" McNamara inquired quietly.

He already knew that the body had been located. Shorty had called him in the morning with that news. It had taken a while to be true. The killer had carried the body to the other side of the woods and thrown it into a ravine. He had discarded it as if it had been a pile of garbage.

A metallic glint flushed in the detective's eyes. The man had a problem with people that held low regard for human life.

In McNamara's eyes, Stewart read that the DCI already knew about the body but shrugged indifferently.

"Aye. It was packed in plastic... The killer beheaded the woman right on that plastic sheet...." Rolling his cigarette and driving the inspector crazy, he continued absently, "With an axe...."

McNamara needed a clear-headed coroner, and the man before him seemed to be in the clutch of his thoughts. His obsession with that cigarette grated on the detective's nerves.

"Just light the damned cigarette, David," he exploded. "What the bloody hell is going on with you?"

The doctor practically jumped off his chair, and McNamara almost regretted his outburst.

"Nothing..." Stewart mumbled, shaking his head.

However, McNamara couldn't fail to notice that the man wouldn't look him in the eye.

"David..." he said quietly, rising off his chair. Coming around the desk, the DCI stopped in front of the doctor. "We've known each other for some while... Quite a long while," he reiterated, touching David's shoulder to make the man keep his attention on him. "You can tell me what's going on," the inspector said more forcefully.

The DCI wasn't interested in people's lives. Still, he had a soft spot for some of his people. He didn't have friends, but David Stewart came close to that.

Stewart raised his gaze at him, and to McNamara's dismay, tears glistened in the old man's eyes. A wrenching feeling told him that things were terrible. The Chief Inspector hoped that the doctor wouldn't start crying because he didn't know what to do in such an event. Still, he insisted, "What is it, David?"

"Agatha," the man whispered, lowering his eyes to his lap, unable to look at the inspector.

Stewart's teary answer chilled McNamara to the bone. "What about Agatha?" the man asked with dread, expecting the worse. After all, the coroner wasn't given to bursts of melancholy every day.

"The doctors said that she might have cancer... They found a brain tumour... The hospital scheduled her for surgery this morning," the man hissed through quivering lips. However, he tried to maintain his composure. To break down in front of the DCI wasn't something he had dreamed of doing.

His words turned the inspector's face into stone. McNamara's fingers bore into the man's shoulder, even though he wasn't aware of his gesture. He hadn't expected to hear that. Suddenly, the man pushed away and, with deep anger in his voice, bellowed to the coroner, "What the bloody hell are you doing here? Shouldn't you be there, at the hospital? With her? She might need you when she wakes up, man."

"I had to finish the post-mortem," the doctor replied with eerie calm as if McNamara's fury had drowned his feeling of impotence. "I've finished the autopsy," he thought to be more specific.

"I don't give a damn about that post-mortem, David," McNamara smashed his fist on the top of the desk, and his shout reached the people on the other side of the door. Everybody in the squad room stopped from what they were doing and looked at the closed door, waiting feverishly to see what would happen next.

McNamara turned around, but he returned to the coroner after two steps. The DCI didn't think David Stewart didn't care about his wife. Nevertheless, the man couldn't understand what the doctor was thinking. "You should be there, David," he said softly.

"I will be there," the man whispered. "Agatha wanted me to do my job and go to her in the afternoon," Stewart continued in a stronger voice now. "You know it is not an easy surgery.... It takes hours," he informed the inspector, his eyes wandering in the direction of the window once more.

McNamara realised that the man repeated what Agatha had told him and that David had decided to respect her wishes.

"But you'll go to the hospital after we finish here," the DCI insisted, his gaze boring into the old man's face to drive his words through.

David nodded. "Soon enough, I will go... I have finished everything... I wrote the report...," he shrugged, explaining his thinking process.

"Do you want to add anything to that report, David?" McNamara asked in a calmer voice now.

The man seemed to consider his question a few seconds and then dismissed it with a shake of his hand. "No, everything's in there," he said, pushing the file toward McNamara and standing up. "I'm leaving now, lad."

His lips tight in a hard line, the detective merely nodded, unable to say anything.

When the inspector asked cautiously, David had already reached the door, "Isn't there any hope then?"

The coroner stopped with his hand on the door handle and hesitated a moment or two. Then, he turned to McNamara and said, "There is some... But, I'm afraid to hope against hope, you know?"

"And Agatha? What's she thinking?"

"She does hope," Stewart replied with a sad smile. "You know, she said she wouldn't leave me now. We've been together for far too long," the coroner shrugged.

"Then it might turn well," the inspector insisted, firmly believing that everyone could make their own fate.

"The odds are low," the doctor shrugged. "But maybe... just maybe... she'll be spared...," he said and turned to the door. A tear found its way down his cheek. The man didn't want to show weakness in front of his friend.

"Then, I'll think she will," McNamara replied with determination.

At the steel in the younger man's voice, the doctor couldn't do anything but smile and shook his head imperceptibly. As if the DCI could will the tumour to be benign! The man shook his head once more and silently left the room.

McNamara snatched the coffee cup off the desk, but his fingers smashed it before he could take a sip. The anger he had tried to keep at bay while Stewart sat in his office had free rein now. Agatha was one of the few people he not only tolerated but admired and liked.

A knock on the door made him growl. "Not now," the Chief Inspector shouted.

James's hand froze on the other side of the door in mid-air as he was just about to knock again. Silently, the Sergeant returned to his desk, wondering what had happened. McNamara was brusque and blunt at times, but James had never considered him volatile. The DCI's tone had just proved him wrong.

***

McNamara needed over half an hour to calm his raging thoughts. The man paced the room, his mind in turmoil, going through different scenarios.

When his anger subsided, the DCI sat down at his desk and grabbed the post-mortem report, scanning through the lines. Finishing with the account, he dialled an extension. "James, come to my office and bring Mike and Jo with you," he ordered. However, the Chief Inspector didn't wait for James's response but just put the receiver on the hook and leaned back in his chair.

He didn't have to wait for long. The three detectives filed into the room with reluctant steps in less than five minutes. Apprehension shaded their faces. Nevertheless, McNamara couldn't blame them, knowing that he had lost his temper for a moment there with David. His voice must have carried to the detective squad room.

The Chief Inspector showed them to sit in the chairs before his desk, and then, he pushed the post-mortem report towards them.

"As you can see, the woman was killed right there near the hydrant. The killer laid her down on a plastic sheet, and when he finished, he rolled the body in the sheet," McNamara explained. "Quite a good way of transportation," he continued, tapping his fingers on the top of his desk.

His anxiety had subsided but not wholly. It still hummed in his blood and forced him to cover it and speak faster. "The coroner found chloroform in the body. He had already tested the cornea before they found the corpse and found residues," he informed the detectives.

"That bloke must be strong," Mike said pensively. "He carried that body to the opposite side of the woods and fast enough. We'd have caught him otherwise," he pointed out.

"My point exactly," McNamara agreed with the detective's assessment. "So, we're looking for a strong man with a sailor's knowledge about knots and a fair hand with an axe. Not a squeamish one," he shook his head. "I imagine that it takes some cold blood to behead a woman," the inspector observed cynically.

"Aye, Chief. Not everyone could do it," James commented, raising his eyes off the post-mortem report.

"Any news about her identity?" the DCI asked Jo, to whom he had assigned that task that morning. The woman was good at ferreting clues.

"I'm afraid not, sir," Jo replied apologetically, shaking her head. "There's nothing in the system. No prints, no photos... We're still asking around to see if anyone had known her or about her."

"Maybe I can bring some light in this matter," James said quietly, leaning forward.

All eyes turned to the Sergeant, and his instinct made him squirm a little under the scrutiny. He needed his willpower not to let them see that he didn't enjoy being under the lights.

"Mrs Campbell called earlier," the man continued. "She remembered where she saw the woman," he informed the DCI.

"And you're only now bringing this news to me?" McNamara thundered, his eyes piercing the young Sergeant.

"I tried to talk to you when she called, but you said not to disturb you, sir," the man replied quietly, although he had to try hard not to wipe off his forehead. He felt the clammy fingers of sweat, and a drop had already fallen on his eyebrow, making him itch.

James didn't know why the DCI affected him, but the man was determined not to show any weakness. McNamara couldn't stand a man who shook in his boots at his slightest growl. That would have been worse.

"Aye, you're right," McNamara conceded and cursed himself. He never let personal concerns interfere with his duties. "So, what did she say?" he asked the Sergeant.

"Mrs Campbell remembered that she had seen that woman on the esplanade a couple of times in the morning. She recognised her violet eyes and mumbled something about being as violet as Liz Taylor's."

"Liz Taylor?" the detective frowned in concentration. He couldn't recall that anyone with that name was involved in that case.

"An American actress, Chief," Jo offered him her help. "Liz Taylor was a great actress, and she was renowned because of her violet eyes."

"Ah, all right," the DCI dismissed the matter with a gesture, as he had no interest in film stars. Then, the man turned back to James. "Did she talk to that Liz Taylor?"

"No, she didn't, but the old woman saw her talking to another woman from the neighbourhood. Mrs Campbell believes that the victim was probably asking for directions. She noticed that the other woman kept pointing a bony finger one way and the other," James concluded his explanation.

"I see," McNamara said, glancing at his watch. "It's almost two. I think that you and I will go on the hunt, James," the man said, standing up. "You two, continue to find out if there's anything about this woman somewhere," he turned to the other two inspectors.

Jo and Mike nodded their understanding and rushed out of the office, happy that they escaped in one piece. James thought to wait for McNamara, imagining that the detective would take his coat and leave with him.

"Wait for me in the squad room for a few minutes, James," McNamara told him, sitting down again.

Thoroughly confused now, James nodded and left the Chief Inspector's office, throwing a glance behind to make sure he understood the DCI's request.

MCNAMARA SERIES BOX SET
BOOK 0NE & TWO

CHAPTER 7 – BEWILDERMENT OVER A MERE RELATIONSHIP

The door closed behind James, and McNamara picked up his mobile phone to speed-dial Bryony's cell phone number. The man knew she would be at the shop at that hour.

The Chief Inspector had been thinking about the young woman with increasing frequency since the night before. Only through sheer will, had he been able to wait for so long before calling her. McNamara didn't care whether she was busy at work right then. He needed to talk to her. The inspector couldn't begin to understand his impatience to hear her voice. So, the man scowled while waiting for her to answer and willing his heart beating to slow down. For God's sake, he wasn't a teenager, and Bryony wasn't the first girl for whom he had ever shown an interest.

"Hullo," Bryony's soft voice suddenly broke into his thoughts, and heat spread through his chest, making the man brush his fingers over his heart.

"Hello," he replied with an unexplainable harshness. The surliness was directed to him, but Bryony couldn't know that. "It's me, McNamara," he specified and felt stupid for a moment. He expected the woman to recognise his voice. After all, she had talked to him just the night before.

"Oh, hello there, stranger. I didn't expect you to call so soon," the young woman replied, and he could say from the sound of her voice that she was smiling.

The detective was confused, and it wasn't a feeling that he liked. His own behaviour and expectations were part of the problem, and her response to hearing from him was the other part. In response, his mouth pressed into a tight line.

McNamara liked tidy things: tidy conversations, tidy reactions, and tidy relationships. He valued too much the control he had upon his life to allow anything to mess with that. If something erred from tidiness to something else, his world turned upside down, and the man lost his bearings.

"I said I would call you," the detective replied gruffly. His rebuttable may have sounded like a reproach but didn't have the expected effect. Just the opposite. It made the woman grin again.

"Well, you did. That's true. But you said that before, in the past, and you waited for a few weeks before doing it, so…," Bryony pointed out. Despite his displeasure, the man had to reckon that she was right.

"I'm calling you now, aren't I?" he retorted and instantly slapped his forehead. 'Scintillating conversationalist, McNamara. Way to go!'

"True," the woman agreed softly. "Anything on your mind?" Bryony asked as if she had felt his contradictory thoughts and feelings.

"I was just wondering…," the man said after a few moments of silence, uncomfortable with the woman's astuteness. She had read his mind before, and he hadn't liked it then.

His restless fingers kept browsing the papers in the file left on the side of his desk. The detective couldn't find his words, which baffled him.

"About what?" Bryony insisted when the silence stretched some more.

"If you'd feel like going out tonight," the man finally replied, after gnashing his teeth and scolding himself for behaving like a green man, wet behind his ears.

"Tonight?" the young woman laughed, slightly uneasy, and her bewilderment felt like a slap.

"Aye, tonight," McNamara repeated. "Are you having others plans, something to do?" he asked and strolled to the window, looking blindly at the square on the corner, determined not to care one way or the other. After all, if Bryony didn't want to see him, it wouldn't be the end of his world as he knew it.

"No, I don't have any plans, but don't you have a case to solve, Detective?" the woman asked playfully, and the laughter bubbling in her voice grated at him.

"I always have a case to solve," the inspector retorted sullenly. "So what?"

"Well, if I remember well... And believe me, I do. Whenever you have a case, you spend all day long until late into the night trying to solve it," Bryony noted gravely, all laughter gone from her voice. "I didn't believe that anything else would find a place in your busy schedule," she explained her reasoning.

McNamara knew that the woman was right. That was what he did. Yet, the man wanted her. However, he didn't know exactly what he wanted from her. His yearning was too intense. So, the Chief Inspector needed to find ways to go around work if that way he could have the woman on his side for a while.

"We can make do," the inspector muttered, but her baffled exclamation let him know she caught his words.

"How?" Bryony asked with bafflement.

"We could have a coffee or something in between," the inspector went on stubbornly. "Or, if you're not tired, I can come by your house later in the evening." The detective was willing to do whatever it took to make it happen.

Bryony kept silent for a few moments. Then, she said, "All right. Let's start with coffee. I suppose you'd prefer having coffee in the area where you investigate your case."

"If you don't mind," the detective replied softly, still stunned that the woman accepted his proposition.

"I don't. Just tell me where and when, and I will be there. Provided it's after five. I can't leave my shop sooner," Bryony explained.

McNamara didn't reply immediately but pinched the base of his nose between his thumb and forefinger. The man thought about the best time and place for a date with her. "Would you make it to Cramond Bistro by six?"

"In the Cramond Village?" she inquired.

"Aye, there. I know you drive," the man mentioned stubbornly, not to leave her a way to get back on her word.

"Of course, I drive. And I think I can be there at six," the woman agreed. After a brief pause, she inquired, "I suppose you would wait for me if I'm a little late. I can't know how the traffic will be at that hour. I don't take that route daily," she pointed out.

"Of course, I'll wait for you," the inspector replied. His exasperation came through his voice with clarity. "I'm not so rude," he defended himself, hurt that the young woman believed him capable of doing something like that.

Bryony laughed. "I wasn't saying that you were rude. But I know you're not a very patient person and...," she trailed off without finishing her thought.

"I'm not that way," his retort came hotly, but the man didn't continue because guilt nudged him. He could deny it, but he was impatient. Not all the time, but most of it.

"As you say," Bryony replied softly. "I'll try to be in front of the bistro at six. All right?"

"See that you do," McNamara answered gruffly. But then, he thought better and added, "And of course, I'll be waiting for you if you are late."

"See you then," the woman laughed again and disconnected the call.

The DCI listened to the dial tone for a few moments, and muttering under his breath, he turned off the phone, not very pleased with himself. He had planned to be polite and aloof while talking to Bryony, and instead, he had been rude, overbearing, and far from charming. The man reckoned that the young woman would have been in her own right to disconnect that call. She hadn't, though, which puzzled him. He had known the woman was more than met the eye. Now, he had the feeling that she was much more than he had thought.

Shaking his head, the inspector grabbed his coat and left the office. James still waited for him in the squad room, and undoubtedly, the man's curiosity was running wild now.

McNamara didn't doubt that the Sergeant wouldn't ask questions, but, sometimes, what remained unsaid stirred the waters more. With a frown, the DCI reminded himself that inflaming his subordinates' curiosity wasn't one of his goals.

MCNAMARA SERIES BOX SET
BOOK 0NE & TWO

CHAPTER 8 - MEETING THE GOSSIP OF THE NEIGHBOURHOOD

Striding quickly, McNamara crossed the squad room with a sign for James, and the DS fell in step with him. Without a word, the two detectives headed to the parking lot.

Still saying nothing, McNamara opened the car doors and just pointed to the DS to get into the car. The Sergeant sighed, and that grated on the Chief Inspector's nerves. The man gnashed his teeth with exasperation, unable to understand his officer's reluctance to share a car with him when the DCI was driving. After all, his driving wasn't bad at all. It wasn't sedate. That was true. Most of his officers would drag through the traffic, but McNamara wasn't one of them. In his opinion, traffic was something to be conquered and tamed.

The Chief Inspector didn't comment on James's sigh, even though he would have liked to blast the man's ears. He merely started the car and drove out of the parking lot, choosing the fastest route to Cramond.

***

McNamara stopped the car in a parking lot near the pier. With James in tow, the man headed towards the houses close to the Esplanade. James followed him, taking his little black book out of his pocket, getting ready to take notes. He also prepared the photo with the victim's head, which had already been Photoshopped. It wouldn't do to show a severed head to a civilian. The Sergeant didn't feel like calling in an ambulance, thus wasting time.

They stopped in front of the first dwelling. Two storeys high, the building seemed to house at least two flats, if not four. The white of the exterior wall wore the effect of time and the effect of the wind and humidity.

James rang the bell at the flat on the top floor first. When no answer came, he rang twice more, and only after another couple of seconds, a woman's high-pitched voice, shouting from inside, reached their ears.

"I'm coming. I'm coming now. Just hold on a moment." Muttered words followed her shout, but the two detectives couldn't make heads or tails of them.

Suddenly, someone pushed the door open. A sixty-year-old woman glowered at them with murdering eyes.

It didn't take long for the two detectives to understand her sulkiness. The woman had been sleeping when they called on her. It looked like her hair was in dire need of a comb, and she hadn't buttoned her dress properly. Her eyelids appeared swollen, and sleep was still visible on her face.

"We apologise for disturbing you, ma'am," McNamara said. However, his flat voice betrayed that he was anything else but sorry. "I'm DCI McNamara, and this is D.S. James. If you don't mind, we have some questions for you," the man continued. However, his demeanour showed clearly that the woman had better answer their questions then.

"Oh, I suppose it is about that woman you found near the ravine," their hostess said in a rush and immediately stepped back to allow the detectives to enter her flat.

The old woman wanted to know everything. "I've been thinking about that all day today. I asked questions around, but no one had seen the body and couldn't give me details," she continued, letting the policemen see her displeasure. Her lips pursed, and a frown nestled between her brows. "How was she killed? Is it true she was raped? Was there more than one killer?" the woman breathlessly asked, making James feel his head swirled.

McNamara smiled thinly and put up his hand, stopping the torrent of words. "Why don't we have a sit somewhere and talk about it?"

The DCI had no intention of giving the woman any details about the crime. Still, he was determined to make her talk and provide them with something useful.

The old woman invited them to sit in a musty sitting-room, crowded with furniture and clutter. McNamara turned his nose up at the smell in the room but didn't make any comments. He merely intended to ask his questions and be on his merry way as soon as possible.

The woman offered to prepare some tea or coffee for the detectives. Still, McNamara refused immediately, unwilling to spend more time in her flat than he had to.

"May we have your name, ma'am?" James asked, getting ready to take notes.

"Oh, I forgot to introduce myself," the woman said, slapping her hands in distress. "I'm Mrs MacDonald," she gave James her name.

"May I ask if Mr MacDonald is also available for a discussion?" James continued with his inquiries.

"Huh," she exclaimed. A thin smile appeared on her lips, and the woman shook her head. "He hasn't been available for about thirty years, young man. My husband died on the sea. You see, he was a sailor," the woman pointed out.

"Oh, I am sorry for your loss, ma'am," James said quickly, afraid that he had upset the woman, but she merely waved his concerns away.

"It is not a bother, lad. MacDonald wasn't much of a husband to begin with, so his passing away wasn't too much of a loss," the woman said very matter-of-factly, and McNamara grinned unwillingly.

The DCI always appreciated the honesty. The woman in front of his eyes seemed to have it in spades.

"The man even cured me of any romantic thoughts," the old woman continued, not paying attention to McNamara's sudden grin. "Much better to live on your own. That's what I always say. No one to ask questions... No one to participate in decisions... Marriage is a waste of time, young man. Believe me," she nodded vigorously, rubbing her hands together, satisfied that she had managed to present her point of view thoroughly.

James didn't answer but looked down at his notebook where he had noted only her name. He didn't know what to say or how to react to the torrent of her words.

Yet, McNamara didn't feel any compulsion to continue his investigation. He leaned forward and braced his elbows on his knees. He didn't give a fig if his posture wasn't very official.

"So, I understand that you heard about the crime," the Chief Inspector began. "Did you see anything last night, though?" he asked.

"I was told that the woman was killed around midnight," their hostess said. "I was long in bed at the time. I always go to bed between nine-thirty and ten o'clock. I never stray from my schedule," the woman shook her head. "If you have questions about my neighbours, I can help you there. I know everyone and everything. You see, I don't believe in discretion. One must know everything so that they don't have any bad surprises," she imparted her opinion with conviction.

"I see," McNamara said quietly. "Let's see if you recognise this woman," he continued and signalled James to show the photo to the woman.

James took out the photo and handed it to Mrs MacDonald, who took it in a rush. Her eyes searched the face in the photograph with avidity for a few minutes, and the silence got on McNamara's nerves.

"Do you recognise her, Mrs MacDonald?" the inspector asked impatiently when she didn't say anything.

"I'm thinking," she snapped at him in a cantankerous voice. "I don't know the woman, but I saw her. I'm trying to remember where, lad," she pierced McNamara with a dark look.

The DCI mused but didn't say a thing. He let her ponder her memories, hoping that she would come up with something in the end.

"Now, I know," she said, patting her lips with a finger. "It was a month ago... On a Tuesday... I think it was around six or seven in the evening. This woman was on the Esplanade, talking to my neighbour, Mr Wilson. He was waving his hand... I think he was giving her directions or something. I wanted to intervene and help, but she stared at me with those unnerving eyes of hers... I didn't like her," the old woman said, shaking her head. "I noticed that she despised me on the spot, and I don't know why," the old woman said, anger colouring her voice.

"I'm a MacDonald. But before that, I was a MacKay. My family meant something in this area in the past," the woman continued in a voice that with fury.

McNamara understood the woman's rage. It hadn't been easy for her to be dismissed like that. However, the circumstances of her dismissal were interesting. The victim seemed to have been an astute person. She had read the old woman like an open book, so she didn't trust her with anything.

"And that was the only time you saw her, ma'am?" James intervened in the discussion when he noticed that McNamara was lost in thought.

"I think I saw her once more, but I am not very sure. I was in a shop, two streets from here. I think this woman passed by the shop window, but I'm afraid I can't be very sure," she reckoned with a shrug.

McNamara judged that the old woman didn't have any more information for them, so he stood up. Nevertheless, he didn't like to leave anything to chance, so he handed her his business card. "If you remember anything about this woman, please, don't hesitate to call me," the Chief Inspector advised her.

Visibly pleased, the woman took the card. Her bony fingers stroked the shiny paper with awe. She couldn't recall when it was the last time she had held a business card in her hand. "I certainly will, detective. I will," the old woman said with eagerness and showed them to the door.

She didn't close the door immediately after they left but followed them with her gaze. McNamara felt her look boring holes in his back and had a few sweet words for her. The man didn't utter them loudly, but only because he didn't think that the old woman would like to hear them. He was on police business there and couldn't alienate witnesses, regardless of whether they were helpful or not.

MCNAMARA SERIES BOX SET
BOOK 0NE & TWO

CHAPTER 9 – LIZ TAYLOR'S MYSTERY ELUCIDATED

James rang the bell at Mr Wilson's door and waited patiently. However, the Sergeant was afraid the man was also in bed asleep if he was as old as Mrs MacDonald, but his assumption was proved wrong.

An old man indeed, Mr Wilson opened the door promptly and assessed the two officers with cold eyes. His demeanour showed that the man was as far from sleep as possible. After a brief but thorough perusal, Mr Wilson guessed that McNamara was in charge and addressed his words to him. "What can I do for you?"

"We're with the police, Mr Wilson," McNamara said. "This is DS James, and I'm DCI McNamara," he continued, taking out his ID and showing it to the old man.

"Important people from what I can see," the man noted, inviting them inside. "So, to what pleasure do I owe your visit?" he inquired while closing the door behind them and then showing the way to his sitting room.

"I suppose that you heard about the crime that took place last night near the ravine, Mr Wilson," James began to say on the way to the sitting-room, but the man stopped him abruptly, putting up his hand. The DS stared at their host with puzzlement.

"I didn't hear anything," the man shook his head. "I don't waste my time with gossip," he concluded, cutting the air with a sharp gesture.

Unphased, McNamara headed into the room, passing by the older man and taking his measure. The Chief Inspector wondered how the man spent his days if he didn't talk to his neighbours and didn't show any interest in what happened in the neighbourhood.

After sitting on a settee in the sparse sitting room, the DCI asked James to show the photo to the old man, hoping that maybe that woman might have attracted the man's attention.

Their host took the photo from James with shaking fingers. It looked like that even holding the picture in his fingers was a challenging endeavour. Apparently, age hadn't been very kind to him.

"Aye, I've seen this woman before. His gaze shifting to McNamara, the man exclaimed, "She's unforgettable," he shook his head. "Those eyes of hers reminded me of Cleopatra," he said in a voice full of longing.

Baffled, James stared at the man, wondering what Wilson was thinking and whether the man's mind might have already beaten other trails. When the Sergeant thought of Cleopatra, the image of a dark-haired, dark-eyed woman came to mind, and that description didn't match the victim at all.

"Cleopatra?" McNamara asked with bewilderment, wanting to make sure that he had comprehended correctly what the old man said.

"Not the real Cleopatra," the old man replied impatiently, waving his shaking hands in broad gestures. "I was talking about Liz Taylor's Cleopatra."

McNamara realised that it was the second time he had heard that name and decided that the time to verify what that meant had come. He hated it when people talked about things he had no idea about.

"In what way?" the inspector inquired. The DCI wasn't willing to show his ignorance in front of him. He hoped that the man would come with supplementary explanations.

"Her eyes," the old man pointed to the photo with exasperation. He couldn't comprehend what was so difficult to understand. "You can see that it's the same exquisite violet," he explained. "Liz's eyes could make a man forget about everything. I have an album for you to see if you want," the man offered eagerly.

Without waiting for the detectives' approval, he rose, pushing on the arms of his armchair with all his might. The man headed towards the escritoire hidden in one of the room's corners. The man opened a drawer and took out a thick album from inside. His shaky fingers stroke the aged cover of the album with love, and then, he returned to the detectives.

"Here," he said, pushing the album to them. "But have a care," he continued in a stern voice. "It's old and fragile. I want it back in one piece," Wilson told them in a commanding voice. However, that stern demeanour didn't match the fragility of his body, and the DCI lifted a brow inquiringly.

Wilson didn't return to his armchair to sit back down but remained standing next to the detectives, ready to snatch the album back from their hands if necessary.

McNamara hid a grin and opened the scrapbook. Pictures or articles cut out of magazines covered every page. Those violet eyes, everybody talked about, pierced the Chief Inspector from every photo. The man turned the pages carefully. After further inspection, he had to reckon that the colour of the actress's eyes matched the violet of his victim's eyes.

His mind wandered to Bryony for a moment, and McNamara made a note to ask her if she wanted to see one of the Liz Taylor films with him. Stunned to discover that he was thinking about the young woman in the middle of his investigation, the Chief Inspector shook his head with dismay.

Distracted, the man closed the album with more force than Wilson would have liked. The old man's glower predicted thunder, and indeed, he snatched the album from McNamara's hands and effectively growled. "Have a care, young man. My entire youth and adulthood are in there," he scolded the detective.

Knowing old people and their memories well, McNamara swallowed the words that came to the tip of his tongue. He wondered what he would be attached to in his old age as an afterthought. The detective shook those thoughts off and decided to let the old man's outrage go unanswered.

The DCI asked the man, "So, where did you see this young woman and when, Mr Wilson?"

A scowl firmly etched on his face, the man took his time to put the album away and then shuffled back to his armchair. He didn't bother to answer anything before resting his arms on the faded-coloured armrests.

"Probably a month ago," Wilson finally filled the silence, and his voice betrayed a sort of nostalgia. It was not difficult to believe that those violet eyes had caused Mr Wilson to be smitten.

"I believe you can do better than that, Mr Wilson," McNamara retorted with veiled sarcasm. One of his brows hiked high onto his forehead. "I'm sure you remember exactly when and where you saw her," he continued, and a delicate blush covered the old man's wrinkled skin.

The detectives expected a harsh reply from their interlocutor for a moment. Despite his blush, Mr Wilson's eyes thundered. The man hadn't liked McNamara's bold assumption. However, Wilson disappointed the detectives. Still scowling, the old man answered the detective's question without further ado. Yet, his tone of voice didn't disappoint. It was crisp, like a cold winter's morning.

"Aye, damn it. I know exactly when. It's not like my life is full of exciting events, is it now? Something like that would stay with me for a long time... It was exactly a month and a week ago to the day. I was walking on the Esplanade... I always walk there in the morning. And there she was... Pretty like a sunny rose," Wilson recalled in a softer voice. His eyes wandered off as if he had remembered something pleasant.

"I see," McNamara interrupted his reminiscence. "Are you sure?" he asked the man again. "I've heard you met her on a Tuesday, around six in the evening, a month ago," the inspector repeated what Mrs MacDonald had told them.

"I see my youth faux pas haven't been forgotten," the man replied with an ironic chuckle and seemed to sit straighter.

Both McNamara and James stared at him nonplussed for a moment. None of them comprehended what Wilson was talking about.

"I beg your pardon?" James inquired after a few moments of silence.

"I see you still keep your eyes on me. Even now," Mr Wilson explained with his specific broad gestures.

"I'm afraid we really don't understand what you mean, sir," McNamara decided to intervene, sick of playing the game.

"Don't take me for a sucker, Detective," the old man replied with anger in his voice. "It is clear that the police still have eyes on me. Even now, after over forty years," Wilson said forcefully but started coughing at the end of his tirade.

"I'm sure it would be fascinating to hear what you did forty years ago," McNamara replied with a tinge of sarcasm. "Unfortunately, we don't have time for that right now. We're looking for a killer," he pointed out. "And we..."

"Huh," the old man interrupted him suddenly. "Then, how did you know that I met the woman on a Tuesday a month ago? Only if I'm under surveillance...."

"Stop it there," McNamara ordered, putting up his hand. "It's not necessary to go into all that. It suffices to say that one of your neighbours offered us that information. You're not under any surveillance, Mr Wilson," the detective pointed out. Then, he muttered under his breath, 'Although you'd enjoy it, I'm positive.'

Mr Wilson leaned forward with his mouth in a perfect "O". With the wind out of his sails, the man looked like a wounded bird. McNamara felt sorry to ruin the old man's fantasies, but he didn't have the time to indulge him.

"I see," Mr Wilson said with visible disappointment. "Probably that woman told you. I think her name's MacDonald," he continued pensively. "Well, she wasn't wrong, but she wasn't right either," the man said with a shrug.

"What do you mean?" James intervened, confused.

"It's simple, young man. I met the woman for the first time in the morning a month and a week ago, and I met her a second time that Tuesday, in the evening," Wilson explained and shrugged nonchalantly.

The glimmering lights in his eyes betrayed his glee that he had managed to thwart his nosy neighbour's allegations.

McNamara could easily imagine what kind of boy Wilson must have been. He would have definitely enjoyed playing pranks on other kids and adults. It wasn't a wonder that he had done something forty years ago that might have put him under police surveillance.

"All right," the DCI agreed. "So, what did you talk about when you met for the first time?"

The old man shrugged again, and then, with an expansive wave of his hand, he said, "Nothing important. She just wanted to know if anyone in the area wished to sublet a townhouse or a flat."

'Nothing important indeed,' McNamara thought and felt the impulse to shake the man for all of his worth.

"And what information did you give her, sir?" he inquired calmly, although he used a lot of restraint.

Wilson seemed baffled that the detectives wanted to know that. However, he said, "I sent her to the grocer's shop, here, in the neighbourhood. I was sure that I had seen a note with a townhouse to sublet. I was looking to see if there was any notice about old cinema magazines. I collect such magazine because there's always a chance to see Liz in their pages," he wisely explained to the two detectives.

James shook his head imperceptibly and decided it was time to put his notebook and pen away. He didn't think Mr Wilson would give them any valuable information from that point forward.

However, McNamara wasn't done yet, so he signalled James to sit where he was and then turned to their witness. "And the second time, that Tuesday? What did she ask you? I understand you were pointing here and there as if you were giving her directions."

"Oh, yes, she wanted to get to a specific café, but she didn't have the correct directions. Strange, though, she had one of those phones in her hand. I noticed people use them to get directions, but she didn't want to," the old man mused as if just then, he had found that notion weird. "Anyway, I gave her instructions, and she left... I'd have liked to talk to her more... I even offered to show her to the café... Yet, she said she was in a hurry and would find it just fine."

"And that was the last time you talked to her?" McNamara asked.

"Aye, it was. I saw the young woman twice afterwards, though," Mr Wilson said and leaned back in his armchair with economical movements.

"Where?" McNamara ground out through his teeth. Discussing with the man was like pulling teeth, and the DCI's patience had reached its limits.

"Once, I saw her in the grocer's shop. She bought some of those instant foods," the man grimaced as if that had been a serious crime. "That's not food for such a young woman like her. Instant food is for men like me, who don't have anyone to come back home to," Wilson pointed out. "And the second time I saw her, she was driving. She didn't see me and drove inside one of those underground parking lots, which all those row townhouses have," Wilson waved his hand.

"Do you remember what parking lot?" James asked the man.

"Of course, I do, young man," Wilson replied in a quarrelsome voice. "I might be old, but my mind is still sharp," the man didn't forget to mention.

"And would you mind also telling us which one?" McNamara inquired sweetly. Apparently, too sweetly because both James and Mr Wilson turned to him instantly with expressions that betrayed their disbelief.

However, after a few seconds, Mr Wilson indicated which parking lot they should verify. Understanding that there wasn't anything more to be ferreted, the detectives left.

Mr Wilson's door closed behind them with a little more force than necessary, and McNamara grinned, biting his lower lip.

CHAPTER 10 - IDENTITY AND SURVEILLANCE TAPES

"That old man's something else," McNamara grumbled to himself, but James heard him, and the shadow of a grin appeared in the corner of his mouth.

James imagined that Wilson's behaviour had strained McNamara's patience somewhat, but that wasn't something new. Although he had to deal with all sorts of people on any given day, the DCI wasn't a man who liked such interactions, and his tolerance was often put on trial.

"Let's go to that parking lot first and see if they know who that woman was. Maybe they can tell us where she lived... You know what, maybe they monitor the underground parking lot and have some surveillance tapes that could help us," McNamara said, lengthening his stride.

However, James followed him with ease. He knew his boss's reactions when he finally had a lead and got used to the rhythm the man requested.

When they got to the parking lot, the detectives noticed that no one was there to take care of it.

The detectives found the explanation soon enough. People were supposed to present a magnetic card to the reader to drive inside. Otherwise, the immense automatic door wouldn't have opened.

The detectives followed the signs leading to the administration office. There, they found a thirty-year-old woman pouring over some ledgers.

Baffled, James wondered how it was possible that someone still worked with ledgers in the era of the computers but kept his mouth shut. If Jo had been there, James would have said something. The young woman would have enjoyed his remark. Anyway, McNamara wasn't interested in irrelevant matters.

"May I help you, gents?" the woman asked, standing up and pushing the ledger aside.

"We're with the police, ma'am," McNamara said, showing his ID. "This is DS James, and I'm DCI McNamara."

"My name's Lydia Abernathy," the woman introduced herself with a nod. "I'm in charge of the townhouses in the area," she continued, showing the detectives to a sitting area.

The policemen sat down on the sofa laid out for prospective visitors, but the woman didn't follow them immediately. She went to bring a carafe with coffee and cups, which she put on the coffee table before the detectives. She poured the black liquid and invited them to help themselves to sugar and milk.

Lydia Abernathy was a statuesque woman, well rounded in some areas. The men's eyes followed the woman's every move with close attention. Yet, what held their attention was her impressive stride and her fiery hair, which tumbled over her shoulders in an indefinite curly mass. The young woman seemed to be effectively gliding as if she had been on a fashion podium.

The detectives didn't know where to look first. Her office skirt stopped mid-thigh and displayed her long and rounded limbs. Truth be told, the garment left little if nothing to their imagination. The afternoon sun lit the woman's reddish curls and formed a halo around her head. The men were pressed hard to look all over the length of her body, but none of them believed that she would enjoy it.

McNamara admired what he had before his eyes. However, the man knew that Abernathy was a woman to be looked at but not invited out. Everything on her seemed too perfect and chosen with too much care. The young woman made him think of an exhibit on display, the kind one could look at but couldn't touch.

When the woman finally sat down, holding a cup of coffee, James exhaled a soft sigh, which reached McNamara's ears. The DCI grinned with visible satisfaction. At least, he had had the strength not to let anyone understand what crossed his mind.

When Ms Abernathy sat down and crossed her legs, the skirt rode up her thighs and exposed even more her round limbs. The Sergeant's eyes couldn't stray from there, no matter how much he tried. Now, James realised that he had felt relieved prematurely.

Luckily, Lydia Abernathy didn't notice or didn't care. 'Probably, it happens to her all the time,' James thought.

Nevertheless, McNamara noticed where James's eyes were riveted. He also observed with dismay that the Sergeant was not going to ask any questions soon.

The Chief glared at his subordinate, but James didn't see it. He had forgotten about McNamara and his job. Apparently, even about the petite, blond Claire McKay, the woman he had been wooing for a while.

It was McNamara's turn to sigh, even though just inwardly.

"So, Ms Abernathy, as I said before, we're on police business here. Apparently, we have a victim who sublet a house here, on your domain," the DCI started the interview in a pleasant voice. "We're trying to identify the victim, and I think you could help us in this endeavour," he added. The man leaned forward and absently picked up one of the cups, sipping some coffee. He noticed with satisfaction that the hot liquid seemed strong enough to help him go through the remaining part of his workday.

"If your victim sublet the house, I might not be able to help you," the woman replied apologetically. "Not everybody tells us when they sublet their dwelling," she explained to the detectives. "Right now, I know only of two sublets. Did the victim drive?"

"Yes, she did," McNamara answered.

"That might be helpful. We have the underground parking lot under video surveillance. We had a few problems a few years back, and the company decided to monitor the comings and goings," she told them.

"We have a photo if you could look at it. Maybe you have seen the victim," the DCI said, glancing pointedly at James.

James finally realised that he was out of line. He immediately jumped off the settee, taking the photo out of his jacket pocket to show it to Ms Abernathy.

The woman stretched her arm, and two perfectly manicured fingernails snatched the photo off his hand. The Sergeant's brows rode up to his forehead. He hadn't expected her to do that.

The woman looked at the photo and nodded. "Yes, she's one of the two I mentioned," she said, gazing at McNamara. "She was driving, and the man she sublet the house from wasn't. So, she needed a key card to get into the parking lot, which was why I met her. Otherwise, I don't think Mr Martin would have said anything about subletting his home for the summer," the woman reckoned.

"So, you know where she lived," McNamara concluded with hope in his voice.

"Yes, of course," she replied. "I suppose you'll want to see the house," the woman added, rising off her armchair.

The detectives followed suit at once. Ms Abernathy strode to her desk and opened a drawer. "This is a master key," she said, showing them a skeleton key. "I can let you inside," she added, heading for the door.

"We will need time inside, Ms Abernathy," McNamara didn't forget to warn her. "We need to go through the entire house, and unfortunately, without you," he added. "And, of course, we'd like the videotapes from the underground parking, as well," the DCI remembered to ask. "Do you need a search warrant for the house or the tapes?" he inquired.

"I don't see why," the woman shrugged. "There's no one living in that house if the woman is dead. Nothing is incriminating for our company on the videotapes. You can have a go both to the house and videotapes with my blessing," she said, displaying her professional smile to them.

"That's perfect," McNamara said. "We can gain a full day of work if we don't have to wait for a warrant tomorrow. I will send a policewoman for the tapes," he told Ms Abernathy.

MCNAMARA SERIES BOX SET
BOOK 0NE & TWO

CHAPTER 11 – A SEARCH WITH SHOCKING SURPRISES

McNamara and James waited in front of the townhouse where the victim had lived for the last month and a half if they were to believe Ms Abernathy. It was true that they didn't have any reason to doubt the woman's word, but the detectives were impatient to get inside and see what was there.

James had already called the forensic team at the location. The experts were supposed to be there any moment now. The trip there shouldn't take them more than fifteen minutes even if the traffic was heavy.

Another phone call had dispatched Jo to pick up the tapes from Ms Abernathy. McNamara told her to spend the following day watching them with Mike and see what the victim had done during her last days of life. The DCI hoped that the tapes would shine some light on their inquiries and offered them a line of investigation.

McNamara would have ordered them to start watching the videotapes right away, even though it was late in the afternoon.

However, the two inspectors had started work around nine-thirty that morning and needed a break until the following day. Besides, he needed Jo and Mike there in the house that afternoon to help with the search.

The DCI needed the detectives' help as he had a date with Bryony soon and couldn't stay until the team finished with the house. After all, more eyes at the scene meant a better chance to uncover all the clues, and they needed anything they could get.

McNamara threw a glance at his watch with impatience. He had less than an hour to be at the Bistro where he had invited Bryony, and the man hoped to be there on time so that the lass wouldn't have reasons to complain. Still, he also wanted to be at the victim's house when they went inside because he needed to gather his own impressions about the victim. His detectives were good, but the Chief Inspector knew nothing could replace his eyes. He preferred to draw conclusions by himself.

Now, McNamara felt a pang of regret that he had rushed and set a date with Bryony for that afternoon. If he had known that they would find the victim's house, the inspector would have asked Bryony out the following day.

Irritated, McNamara started pacing in front of the house, a frown deep between his brows. Absently, he waved a curious bee away and continued his absent-minded walk, his thoughts whirling around, trying to find solutions for his predicament.

James noticed that the Chief Inspector was deep in his thoughts and thought he had better leave him alone. He found the shadow of the only tree in front of the building and decided to take advantage of it.

His eyes wandered along the street, but nothing moved in his line of sight. The silence was eerie, and that baffled him.

The Sergeant would have expected to see children playing outside at that hour. After all, the school had already ended for the day. The man couldn't believe that no children were residing in that neighbourhood.

The humming of several cars coming up the drive drew the detectives' attention, and McNamara's relief at their arrival was almost tangible. James felt the angry pressure, which had built a little more with every passing moment of their wait, dissipate. The Sergeant breathed out slowly, satisfied that the tension had passed. He never liked it when the DCI was in one of his moods.

Steven Gilchrist, the man in charge of the forensic team, first got out of the car. His reddish hair competed with the sun's light for a moment, and McNamara grinned, his fingers playing with his keys inside his coat pocket.

The man's massive figure made it impossible for him to move with any degree of elegance. He hadn't even made it out of the car before he lit one of his ever-present cigarettes. Lisa, one of Steven's forensic team, came out of the vehicle immediately after him with a black case in hand. The tech carefully stepped around him, moving out of the smoke range.

That seemed peculiar to McNamara. The man had often had the chance to see her standing right next to Steven when he indulged in one of his bad-smelling cigars. The woman had never looked like she cared about second-hand smoking or the awful smell of Steven's cigars.

Steven Gilchrist wasn't known for his good manners. He let his displeasure be known immediately if something irked him, regardless of the person who had angered or tried to slight him. Nevertheless, the Chief Inspector had to admit that the woman's move had been so casual that Steven didn't seem to mind it an iota, which was something.

Lisa and her colleagues Tom, Joe, Georgie, and Ned had worked with Steven for over ten years. So, it wasn't surprising that the pretty brunette knew exactly how to move not to get into Steven's way or raise his anger.

James accurately read McNamara's thoughts and drew near him, whispering only for his ears, "Rumours have it that Lisa has finally got pregnant, Chief. After so many years of disappointment, she wouldn't inhale Steven's smoke."

With a thankful nod, McNamara showed his understanding. It wasn't like the Major Investigation Team hadn't had other good detectives. However, the Chief Inspector wanted to know why things happened, and James always took care of that. That was one of the reasons the man had always paired with him.

"So, you found it, lad," Steven came to McNamara, slapping him on the shoulder. McNamara wasn't much younger than him, yet the forensic expert always treated him as if the difference in their age was immense.

The DCI wasn't keen on Steven's familiarity. The man liked to keep a certain distance from people, but not because of his rank. That was who he was. McNamara preferred to look at people from a certain distance and didn't encourage friendships.

"Well, we've had a bit of luck," the Chief Inspector answered nonchalantly, glancing swiftly at his watch. McNamara noticed that he still had half an hour available for the search before leaving to meet Bryony. With a tilt of his head, the man led the team to the front entrance, where he opened the door with the master key received from Ms Abernathy earlier. They strode inside the house carefully, stopping just where the entrance hall ended.

As the ground-floor plan was open, McNamara could see beyond the sitting-room to the kitchen and also had a good view of the den, situated on the left hand of the sitting room.

Everything looked in place. McNamara didn't discern any sign that someone had searched the house or that a fight had taken place there. If the woman had been chloroformed there, she should have fought, at least for a minute or two, but the Chief Inspector couldn't observe any traces of a struggle.

Then, Steven dispatched his team members to investigate every room in the house. All of the people in the team covered their footwear with plastic. McNamara pulled a pair of gloves on his hands and headed to the den, where he found the desk's surface clean of clutter. He would have liked to see a computer or pad, but none laid in plain sight. The Chief Inspector tried to open the first drawer but noticed that it was locked.

"Steven, I have a lock for you to pick," the DCI called out, sitting on the chair behind the desk to wait for the man.

Steven strode into the den with heavy steps as if an elephant had trodden across the room, and McNamara struggled to stifle his grin. First, the forensic expert dusted the lock and collected the fingerprints. Only after finishing with all that did the man pick the lock. He pulled the drawer open, and his eyes widened in surprise.

McNamara noticed the change in Steven's demeanour and stood up to bend over the men's shoulder to look into the drawer. The inspector couldn't believe his eyes at what was waiting for him. Little soldiers in rows, a pistol, a knife with a rugged blade, three types of daggers, a garrotte, and a nunchaku laid neatly there. That improbable arsenal raised many questions, and the DCI was afraid that he wouldn't have liked the answers. Still, he needed them.

"We'd better unlock the other drawers," the detective said quietly, and Steven nodded briefly.

The burly expert made short work of unlocking the other drawers and invited the DCI to check its contents with an exaggeratedly broad gesture.

The second drawer from the top-down contained only an iPad, which was protected by a password, as they found out immediately. Steven placed it in an evidence bag and sealed it with a sigh.

"It's never simple," the man complained, shaking his head. "Why can't people have the courtesy to leave their password neatly written on a piece of paper on the desk? God knows how long it will take to the blokes from the tech department to uncover that bloody password."

McNamara didn't believe that Steven waited for an answer from him, so he didn't bother to provide one. The inspector pulled the third drawer, which sheltered two rows of small notepads. He lifted the one on top and flipped the cover. The first page featured only three lines:

N. C. – 42 – Cramond

Desired – accident – on October 1st

65 k (including expenses)

'It sounds like a hit, but I might be wrong,' the detective thought. Then, he turned the page only to find a map of Cramond, drawn by hand. An ominous X had been placed right next to a row of buildings near the Cramond Bistro. The following page offered a detailed schematic of the area near the Bistro, with thorough notes related to traffic and the shops' hours.

"James," McNamara called out to the DS, who hurried to join him next to the desk. "I want you to read this notebook and the others. But this first one, I wanted it to be read tonight, if possible," the inspector ordered. "Have a report ready for me in the morning," he added harshly.

James let the Chief Inspector know that he understood with a brief nod and placed the notebook in an evidence bag, which he photographed before putting it into his coat pocket. Still, his gaze followed McNamara closely. The DCI picked up the second notebook and opened it. The first page read:

ST – 27

Desired – kidnapping – garrotte

80 K (including expenses)

Done

The third notebook cemented McNamara's original idea. Those notebooks described hits. Their victim suddenly changed the status from a powerless victim to a hired killer.

Expressionless, McNamara signalled Steven to bag all the notebooks and waited patiently for him to place them in one of his ever-present evidence bags. Then, he pulled the last drawer, and his eyes widened.

"Jackpot," the DCI whispered, and noticing his reaction, both James and Steven drew closer to him to look into the drawer.

On top of some papers, four passports formed a neat pile right before their eyes. A fifth passport lay lonely aside. McNamara reached out and took one of the four passports, and a driver's license fell out of the pages. The names on the passport and the driver's license matched and belonged to Lucinda Danvers, age 36, hailing from Sussex.

McNamara placed the documents into the bag Steven was holding for him and snatched the second passport. Opening it, he noticed the woman's violet eyes, studying him seriously. Beneath the photo, her name read Amanda McCormick, originating from Edinburgh. The third passport paired the same woman with Elisabeth Burnaby from Sidney, Australia. The fourth sported the name Alice Markham from Hamilton, Canada.

After placing each passport into the proffered bag, the detective picked up the lonely ID document. The man found a driver's license always tucked between the pages as with the others. This one starred Joanna Livingston from London, UK.

"I think this is the woman's real name," McNamara showed James and Steven the driver's license. "It is just a feeling I am having," the inspector explained. "However, I think that's why she set it aside."

The DCI failed to see the other two men's approval nodding. He had already picked up the documents lining the bottom of the drawer, and now, he was reading them with undivided attention.

The first document showed that Alice Markham had rented a Volvo XC90 SUV a month and a half ago. The second document showed that the same woman had paid the rent for the house in full for the following six months.

"James, I want you to go to the parking lot together with two of the techs and impound that car. Take care to have it thoroughly searched. We already have Ms Abernathy's permission to search the premises, so you won't have any problems there," McNamara mentioned. Then, he turned to Steven. "Steven, you continue here with your team. I want you to take care and not leave a brick unturned. Anyway, you know your job and don't need me to remind you how to do it," the DCI said with a dismissive wave. "I'm leaving. I'm late somewhere," the man threw over his shoulder, leaving the house.

Wide-eyed, Steven and James watched the Chief Inspector getting out of the door. Steven's facial expression mirrored James's to the tee.

CHAPTER 12 – A BREATH OF FRESH AIR

McNamara walked to the Cramond Gallery Bistro. The traffic in the area had increased later in the afternoon. It wasn't worth taking the car as he couldn't be sure whether he would find a parking spot or not.

The Bistro welcomed him with a buzz of conversations. Small tables lined the façade of the restaurant. In a couple of weeks, the weather would probably not allow that anymore, so everyone seemed determined to take advantage of the mild autumn weather.

The early evening had brought many people out of their homes, and the Chief Inspector chastised himself because he hadn't thought of that beforehand. He didn't like crowds. Many labelled him a lone wolf, but the man didn't want to socialise in reality. Anyway, his genetic make-up didn't allow him to relate with other people beyond a shallow manner.

The detective glanced at his watch and, with a scowl, noticed that he was five minutes late. He prided himself with his punctuality, so the man muttered a few choice words under his breath.

McNamara's glance swept over the faces of the people gathered around the tables until his eyes found Bryony. The young woman was already staring at him, an amused grin forgotten on her lips.

Bryony had commandeered a table at the far end of the terrace. The woman had been afraid that the Chief Inspector was detained with some police work, but understanding the man's work, she wouldn't have blamed him. Probably, that was the only thing she clearly understood about him. Now, she waited patiently for him to make an appearance.

The young woman admired the man's long stride while her eyes perused the length of his body. When her gaze reached his eyes, the strange light shining there disconcerted her.

McNamara was the first man the woman had ever met that she couldn't read or understand fully. Every time Bryony thought she had him figured out, something else came up, and she found herself back to the beginning.

The woman had often wondered if that was why McNamara fascinated her. Baffled, Bryony shook her head slightly. When she hadn't deemed it worthy of giving anyone the time of day, she had been more than willing to drive all that way to Cramond and wait for him in a crowded café.

Shaking off her thoughts, the woman threw a broad smile to McNamara, saying softly, "Hello, there, Detective."

That soft voice played havoc on man's skin, feeling like a silky glove. Still, McNamara couldn't decide whether he liked that sensation.

"Detective?" the man scowled at her. "Yesterday, you wanted my first name, and now you call me 'detective' again?" he asked sullenly, that particular deep line between his brows present once more.

Bryony waved her hand to signify that it was of no consequence, and then, she said playfully, "First, take a seat, Artair. Then, you can start scolding me."

Unwillingly, McNamara's lips twitched, the man fighting a sudden grin. Only then, it hit him. That drew him to her and made her so different from the others. The woman didn't give a damn if she displeased him. and didn't try to be coy or surround him with vain and false pleasantries just to gain a moment of his time.

Trust had always come to McNamara with some difficulty. It was not a common commodity in his daily life, and the man rarely relied on people. Until then, women, in particular, hadn't proven to him that they were capable of being straightforward. Bryony represented the exception to the rule, which brought a rare genuine smile on the man's lips.

"I apologise, but I was detained," the Chief Inspector said, sitting on the chair across from her.

Nevertheless, the woman waved his apologies aside. "Don't worry about that. I know you are in the middle of an investigation, so I expect delays, if not absences," she assured him.

"I said I would be here, and I should have been no matter what," the detective retorted more forcefully than he wanted.

"That's... kind of you," Bryony replied, her brows hiking up. "Still, you should know that I don't expect you to leave everything aside to meet me if you are in the middle of something important, McNamara," she continued. "Work is work, and it always must come first," the young woman pointed out, drumming her finger onto the top of the table.

Speechless in front of a woman for the first time in his life, McNamara observed Bryony. From his experience, very few women would have agreed with her. "Are you serious?" the man managed to say, his eyes widening.

"Of course, I am," Bryony snapped back, her brows bunched in a frown. "Don't forget that I also work and although my work doesn't have the same... urgency as yours, sometimes, or nearly all the time, to be honest, I still have some work ethic," she assured the man.

Still mistrustful, the man's gaze studied her face carefully for a few more moments. Nevertheless, then, McNamara concluded that Bryony spoke the truth. So, he said, waving his hand, "Let's order something and not only coffee. I'm too famished to stay here, surrounded by all these smells and not try a soup or something."

Bryony burst into laughter. "I knew it. Don't worry, Artair. I've already ordered to save time. I told them to bring you the Cullen skink soup and a huge sandwich. I also ordered coffee and scones with clotted cream. Is it all right?" she thought to ask, squirming under the man's inscrutable eyes.

Leaning forward, McNamara replied quietly, "Aye, it's just fine." Without any warning, his fingers grasped hers, and the man turned her hand. His thumb started caressing the soft pad of her palm, his gaze following the movement intently. Bryony felt tingles in the weirdest possible spots and shivered imperceptibly.

McNamara's gaze rose and latched to hers. "So, what have you done today?" he asked, and from that moment on, the conversation flew with easiness.

Bryony told him about the most intriguing characters that had visited her small bookshop that day. The man encouraged her to talk because he couldn't tell her anything about the case. Not that he felt the need to say something. Yet, it was much more than that. The young woman had a natural talent for describing people and showed particular humour.

Bryony stopped only when their order came, and McNamara, surprised, realised that he had smiled during the conversation with her more than he had done in a month.

However, the man had just dunked his spoon in his soup when his cell phone rang off. He apologised to Bryony for the interruption and answered with a bark, "Aye."

"Sorry to interrupt you, Chief," James apologised over the line. "Still, I'm sure you'd like to know about this. We found the first crime scene. The victim undoubtedly had been taken from her car. We found signs indicating a struggle, and one of the lateral windows is cracked."

"Do you need me to come there?" McNamara asked, steeling himself against the regret already pulling at his heart. The man would have enjoyed finishing that soup first. He would also have liked to spend his date with Bryony. McNamara raised his gaze at Bryony and noticed that she had averted her eyes. The woman now looked at the water expanse before the Bistro and the swans floating somewhere in the distance.

"No, not necessarily," James replied, though. "We have only to document everything on film and bag the evidence gathered in the car and around it. We'll impound the car, of course. So, we'll probably know more about this story tomorrow," the DS explained, and McNamara congratulated himself for having such hardworking people under his command. They saved him a lot of time.

"All right, then, James. Tomorrow, first in the morning, we'll discuss your findings," the Chief Inspector said, disconnecting the call afterwards.

"I've got a reprieve," he said, turning back to Bryony.

"Does it mean you can stay?" the woman inquired, and trepidation lit her features.

"Aye, and have my dinner," the man murmured, although his thoughts were elsewhere. McNamara expected that some of her joy would vanish at his unfeeling words, but it didn't happen. They shared a good meal, seasoned with pleasant chatter and even a few laughs.

'She is good for me,' the inspector thought after a while. McNamara realised that his thoughts hadn't turned to the case once. That had always happened before, even while on a date.

When the last crumbs disappeared, McNamara paid the bill and invited Bryony for a stroll along the riverbank. The late afternoon had turned into evening, and the reddish of the sunset reflected in the water.

Later, the man trailed her car back onto Nightingale Street, leaving his near the curb while she parked hers in the drive. Bryony waited for him to join her and then invited him inside.

"Not tonight," McNamara replied with a shake of his head. The man wasn't sure how far he wanted to go in that relationship and needed time to think, far from Bryony. The young woman had a particular talent for muddling his thoughts.

"Maybe, some other time then," the woman murmured. "Have a safe ride home, Artair," she added, but he still didn't move. Her left brow raised on her forehead as if she had asked him what he waited for or wanted. McNamara leaned forward and touched his lips to hers for a flitting moment.

The detective needed his entire strong will to straighten up and say, "Goodbye, Bryony. I'll call you soon. All right?"

"All right," she answered softly, brushing her fingers along his tensed arm.

McNamara turned to his car and drove off, muttering under his breath. That chaste touch of her lips had been a mistake: he couldn't take her taste out of his mind now.

***

Bryony's eyes followed the lights of his car until they disappeared around the corner. Then, the woman shrugged to shake the indefinite loss she had felt at the man's departure and turned to go into the house.

MCNAMARA SERIES BOX SET
BOOK 0NE & TWO

CHAPTER 13 – MORE LIGHT SHADED UPON THE VICTIM

That day had started with a frenzy of activity, which demanded everyone's help. So, at around eleven o'clock, McNamara made some more coffee, needing to fuel his brain.

Steven's team had worked all night to analyse the evidence collected in the townhouse where the victim lived and in the garage. Logan MacGregor, the squad's computer guru, had already broken into the victim's iPad, revealing more files about various hits the victim had undertaken. It looked like that woman had been either quite a busy bee or one with an extreme bloodthirsty personality.

Dismayed, McNamara suspected that they would never be able to trace all the woman's crimes. The police didn't have all the victims' names because they had only initials to work with, so they needed to match those with crimes all over Great Britain. However, they deducted that some of the crimes had undoubtedly taken place abroad because nothing similar could be found in their database.

Still, one thing had become apparent. The victim was a hitman or hitwoman – McNamara wasn't sure whether that term existed. Still, the DCI was always careful not to undermine the feminist movement.

Anyway, the victim's chosen profession raised a lot of problems for the detectives. They still had to solve her murder, even though they passionately disliked the dead woman. Due to her homicidal endeavours, the pool of possible suspects was more expansive than anything they had ever seen before. Motives abounded and sprang all over the place. McNamara thought it would, in fact, be easier to determine who didn't have a reason to kill Joanna Livingstone.

At least, the detectives had established that Joanna Livingstone was indeed the dead woman's real name. They traced her origins to London. The daughter of a former army sergeant and a teacher, the victim, had shown a lot of promise. Nevertheless, to her mother's disappointment, the woman had chosen to follow in her father's steps. Joanna Livingstone joined the army at the age of eighteen and reached the higher apprenticeship level 4. She worked in real-time operations. Subsequently, the woman earned a Level 4 Diploma in Intelligence Operations, only to leave the army shortly afterwards.

Now, the police understood why the woman had resigned from the corps. She had decided to strike out on her own and put her new skills to work in a new 'job.' It looked like Livingstone had fallen off the grid once she hit civilian life. She still held some bank accounts, but only one of them was in the UK. Apparently, the woman preferred the Swiss and their penchant for secrecy and privacy.

The detectives succeeded in gathering little information about her. Livingstone died at the age of thirty-two, but no one could inform them about the woman's activities between the age of twenty-seven, when she had left the army, and thirty-two.

The police detectives in London had contacted her parents early that morning. Still, they didn't have any more luck than their counterparts in Scotland. The old couple hadn't seen their daughter in over four years, and they weren't even aware that the girl had bought a flat in London a few years back.

Finding out what she used to do for a living stunned them. Still, the woman's mother had stated that she couldn't accept what they were saying about their daughter. Her husband supported her opinion and had already threatened the police with a lawsuit for marring their daughter's memory. Nevertheless, McNamara knew that nothing would come out of that. The parents would subside in the end after passing over the shock.

The Chief Inspector poured coffee into his cup and returned to his desk without adding sugar or milk into the liquid. He preferred his poison black and strong. The man tapped his fingers on the top of the desk for a few moments, pondering on what he knew about the case, and then picked up the phone.

"James, everybody in my office now. Jo, Mike, Steven, and you, of course," the Chief said briefly, hanging up without waiting for an answer, as his habit was.

A couple of minutes later, his subordinates filed into his office silently, merely nodding towards the DCI. They sat down on the chairs he had set on the opposite side of the desk.

Only two weeks before, McNamara had requested to have two more chairs sent to his office. The man remembered the awkwardness of their previous meetings when some of the detectives had to stand around.

"Steven, I want you to begin with what you know," McNamara said. He had decided to start with the forensics, hoping that the team had unearthed more information than what he had read in the file they sent to him.

"We still have to make some more tests, Chief, but we know enough so that you can continue with the investigation," Steven began his account. Then, the man flipped a few pages in the book he held in his hand. "The woman was attacked in the car, boss. I think she was attacked while getting out of the car, to be more precise. The victim was chloroformed first, but she still fought for a few minutes... Considering the findings, I can say, without any doubt, that the woman wasn't a puny miss. If you know what I mean," the forensic expert remarked, raising his gaze to McNamara.

The detective nodded his assent. Then, the man tried to keep his amusement contained, noticing that all the others in the people in the room bobbed their heads in unison. With a brief wave, McNamara signalled Steven to continue with his account.

"The woman broke two nails in the fight. She didn't have long fingernails, but they were long

571

enough to get broken," he said, taking his eyes off the book for a few seconds and glancing at the DCI again. "That was a good thing," Steven pointed out with a decisive nod. "We found some skin traces attached to the nails and a drop of blood. We ran tests, and they showed that the DNA belongs to a man," he said. "At least, now, you know the sex of the murderer," Steven mentioned.

Then, the expert flipped another page in his book. The man read what he had written there and turned his eyes to McNamara once more.

"We haven't found any trace that would link the killer to a fishing boat or anything like that. No other piece of evidence to lead you directly to someone," the man said. After a few more seconds, Steven frowned and admitted, "No fingerprints, either. The man wore gloves."

Everybody kept quiet while Steven verified what he had noted in his book once more. Still, everybody watched him. It took the man about five more minutes to find something else to say. McNamara, already enervated, was about to turn to another one of his team when Steven finally spoke.

"The house showed no foreign fingerprints. However, we found some more hidden weapons: a pistol in one of the night table's drawers, a dagger mingled with the cutlery in the kitchen, another dagger hidden under a photo in the sitting room. The photo belongs to the person who sublet the house," Steven thought to specify. "We've uncovered a bloody arsenal, Chief," the man concluded, his eyes glistening with bafflement. "Anyway, you'll have everything summarised in my final report," Steven said, suddenly too exhausted to go through the entire list of weapons. "We've also found some weapons in the car," he added as an afterthought. "However, I don't understand what the woman wanted to do with the grenades," the man said, rubbing his chin pensively.

"Are you serious?" McNamara asked in a bewildered voice. "Really? Grenades?"

Steven nodded vigorously. "Aye, Chief. She had two in a flowerpot in the backyard and one in a box filled with cotton in her car trunk."

A strange humming filled McNamara's brain, and the man shook his head. He couldn't believe that someone would consider that grenades could make good home guarding weapons.

Steven hadn't finished, though. "By the way, you should know that we're analysing the mud on her rear wheels. We think that it might tell us where she drove before being attacked."

"Good job, Steven," McNamara praised the man. "You should take the afternoon off. Go home and rest. You deserve it. If anything else comes up, I'd prefer you take care of the forensic investigation, so you'd better take time off now," the Chief Inspector explained. "You'll need that rest."

Steven nodded, standing up with difficulty. The man's size and tiredness made him look like a bear with a severe case of gout as he strode out of the room with heavy steps.

McNamara's eyes followed his progress across the office, and once the door closed behind him, he turned to Jo. "Anything in the surveillance tapes?"

"We started watching the tapes from the last two hours before the murder. We decided to divide the pile of tapes in two afterwards because, otherwise...," Jo trailed off. "Anyway, boss, we saw the woman driving her car into the garage half an hour before her demise. She parked and did something in her car for a couple of minutes... We couldn't see what because of the camera's position. Just a few moments before she opened the car door, a shadow appeared in the frame... Clearly, a man's silhouette. The bloke hunched so that the victim wouldn't see him. He waited until the woman opened the car door.

When she tried to get out, the man hit her arm and put a compress over her face, pushing her back into the car. We couldn't see what happened inside... The camera, you know," she shrugged, looking straight at McNamara.

The Chief Inspector couldn't do anything else but nod.

"After a few minutes, the man got out of the car and looked around. When he made sure that the way was clear, the attacker pulled the victim out of the car and carried her to another vehicle parked in a nearly blind spot for the camera. We could observe only a part of the car, but not enough to make out the make or a number," Jo explained.

"How did the attacker look?" McNamara asked, bracing his elbows on the top of the table.

Jo shifted imploring eyes to Mike, who shrugged but gave in. "We didn't have much luck there, either, Chief," the detective reckoned. "The bloke wore a cap, pulled low on his forehead. We noticed some short sandy hair, but indescribable... Average height... God knows the age," he shrugged again.

McNamara didn't like it, but he knew he couldn't ask for results when there wasn't a way to get results. "I see," he said. "Anything else?"

"Something, aye," Jo replied. "We watched the tapes back in time and noticed a black car monitoring the garage. We spotted it a few times... Always in such a position that we couldn't make out the number. However, it was a Vauxhall Astra. In my opinion, it could be the same car that we saw in the garage."

"That's something," McNamara approved, nodding more enthusiastically now.

"The same car took advantage of someone else getting into the garage and followed closely," Mike said. "Just about forty-five minutes before Joanna drove in. Interesting though, the plates were splashed with mud," the detective continued, and Jo approved his telling with a nod. "I say it's interesting because the car was spotless. Only the plates were muddy."

"But muddy, Chief," Jo intervened. "We might have a chance to obtain part of the number. However, it will take a lot of work. I passed the tape to the techs. Maybe they can uncover the number or enough of it to make a case later," the woman explained wisely.

"All right, Jo. You and Mike take a couple of photos with the car and return to Cramond. Take Donna Blair and Angus Mackie with you and ask questions around. Someone might remember the vehicle," McNamara ordered. The two detectives hurried to leave immediately. "Now, James, how's it going with deciphering the notebooks from the victim's desk?" the DCI asked, turning to the Sergeant.

"Slowly," the man admitted. "I've managed to match the notes with nearly a dozen cases since last night. I'm waiting to hear from Interpol about a few of them... Anyway, I asked them for details only for the cases that took place during the last two years," he shrugged.

"Why only those?" the DCI asked with a frown.

"If it's revenge, Chief, I don't think the killer waited longer than that," James explained with a shrug.

McNamara pondered on the man's words for a few moments. Then the inspector noted, "Sometimes, revenge is a course better served cold, James." The man tossed his head, drumming his fingers on the desk. "The reason for this murder might lie in a case older than two years. Still, we have five years to consider. Of course, if we don't factor into other reasons," the DCI pointed out.

"For that, it will take time, Chief. A lot of time," James stressed out, widening his eyes. "It will take weeks to solve the case, boss," the man said, and McNamara nodded his agreement.

"Maybe even months, James. And that if we succeed in solving the case," McNamara admitted, stroking his chin pensively. The Chief Inspector never embraced defeat, but he had to consider that possibility now. Too many suspects were out of their reach.

"That's why I thought to focus on the last two years," the Sergeant admitted. If nothing comes out of that, boss, I will extend the research," James said, watching McNamara directly in his eyes.

"All right, James. What cases did you think might be related to this murder?" the detective inquired, leaning forward and folding his hands on the top of his desk.

"I actually considered four initially, but one doesn't seem to have triggered any revenge. The victim was an older man. From what I understand, no one liked him, and everyone was happy to see him gone. His fortune was divided between his children – two sons and three daughters. Any of them could have ordered the crime, or, more probably, all of them chipped in," the Sergeant shrugged. "The pay-out was high. According to Joanna's note, she got 85 k, including expenses, and she had to make it look like an accident, which she did. I passed the case to the major crime unit in the Clyde Valley," James noted, and McNamara approved his move.

"So, you have three cases left," the DCI observed, and James nodded.

"Yes, Chief. The first one is about a young couple... An ugly case," the man shook his head. "They just got married a week before they died. The fee for their 'accident' was 150 k, including expenses. Ms Livingstone made it look like an accident, as requested. The brakes on their car malfunctioned, and they ended up at the bottom of a deep ravine. The young man died instantly. The wife lingered for almost three weeks in a coma. Eventually, the family disconnected her from the machines," James recounted, and a glint of steel shone in his eyes.

McNamara understood perfectly. It was a terrible waste: two young lives cut short because of a whim. "The reason?" he asked.

"The male victim's brother inherited everything. A lot of money," James observed. "The victim had just won the lottery."

"Where did it happen?" McNamara asked, tapping his fingers on his desk.

"Highlands, in North-East," James answered.

"Have you notified our colleagues in the area? This case must be brought to light," the DCI remarked harshly.

"Yes, of course, boss. I sent them all the information," the Sergeant reckoned. Then, he emphasised, "The murderer might not exist anymore, but the crime instigator must be punished."

"Correct," McNamara agreed. "Now, who would want revenge?"

"The young man who died didn't have anyone else but the brother, who definitely ordered the murder. The young woman, though, left a sister and a mother behind. They might have wanted revenge."

"If they knew that it was a crime," McNamara pointed out.

"Aye, if they knew," James approved quietly. "I will have news from the DS there in a couple of hours. Then, I will know, without doubt, whether the revenge is related to this case."

"If it's revenge," McNamara muttered again.

Yet, James heard him. "Aye, if it's revenge. But what else can it be?" he wondered, shrugging and opening his arms.

"Maybe she asked for too much money...." McNamara speculated. "Or maybe she angered someone... Or she decided to blackmail someone..." the Chief Inspector enumerated a few possible motives.

"Aye, there might be other reasons," James acquiesced, pressing his lips in a tight line.

"Anyway, you said you considered four cases initially, and we discussed two. Which are the other two?"

"There is one case where she was supposed to stage a suicide," James said, after glancing at his notes. "A young woman... She was only twenty-two... And I think this is the most promising case, Chief. The young woman, Clarissa Ross, was depressed at the time... However, our colleagues in Dundee told me that the opinions about the woman's state of mind at the time differed vastly."

"Why?" McNamara inquired, raising his brows.

"The young woman was supposed to get married... She was even pregnant. Suddenly, the wedding was off, and the woman miscarried. Some said she caught the bloke with another woman and got upset. Clarissa told him that she wouldn't marry a two-timing piece of shit. Excuse my language, boss, but that's exactly what I was told. Those people said that the bloke's father had already warned him to put his life together. One mistake, and he was out of the house and the family business for good. His parents loved Clarissa and were hell-bent on having her as a daughter-in-law."

"I see," McNamara nodded, already understanding where the story was going.

"Anyway, those people also said that the bloke came over to speak with Clarissa. He beat her when she wouldn't take him back, and the woman miscarried. Afterwards, her state of mind was indeed dark. Part of the people that talked to the police believed that she had killed herself. The other part thought that he had her killed."

"I see," McNamara said. "And what did the police think?"

"Initially, the case had been ruled as a suicide. However…," James paused and frowned slightly.

"However, what, James? I see you took a page from Jo's book. You like to build suspense," McNamara tried to mock him into talking.

"Well, the bloke, Clarissa's former fiancé, was viciously killed a week and a half ago," James disclosed.

"Oh, really?" McNamara sat straighter in his chair. A pricking sensation ran across his neck, as always when he got a new lead.

"Somewhat similar to what we have here," James continued.

"How similar?" the DCI insisted, his brows bunched over his eyes.

"The man was found in a ravine... Not a pleasant sight," the Sergeant reckoned. "Someone had cut his legs and arms off and left him there to bleed to death."

After a moment of shocked silence, McNamara stated quietly, "You're right, James. This is the case." James nodded. That was what he thought. "Start looking into the girl's family and friends. And keep me posted," McNamara ordered. "I'm off to Cramond to assist Jo and Mike," the DCI said, rising off his chair.

MCNAMARA SERIES BOX SET
BOOK 0NE & TWO

CHAPTER 14 – BATTERIES MISSING IN A HEARING AID

McNamara still had a few things to do at the office, so the man caught up with his detectives only at around three in the afternoon. He had left his car in one of the free parking lots and enjoyed the walk in the fresh air. The inspector watched and admired the swans spotting the water on his way, noticing that the river glistened in the bright sun.

Suddenly, Bryony's face popped into his mind. The man remembered their stroll the previous evening, and the need to see the young woman again became overwhelming. So, he promised to call the lass that afternoon if he had a moment to do so.

By chance, the Chief Inspector stumbled upon Donna and Angus. They were questioning an older woman with an eye-catching demeanour. She held herself straight like a soldier, despite her fragile appearance. The DCI observed the wild bewilderment on the detectives' faces and the hint of anger present in their eyes.

McNamara hovered next to them for a few moments, considering whether he should make his presence known to his inspectors. However, the DCI couldn't hold his curiosity in check. He needed to find out what could have unsettled the even-tempered Detective Inspector Mackie. Although minted Detective Inspector only a little over a month before, he was renowned all over the force for his patient approach in all his dealings.

Soon, McNamara had his answer: the subject of their interview couldn't hear, even though the woman wore a hearing aid. Mackie had to shout his questions, and after each question, the man would look around, slightly embarrassed but also with a lot of concern. The type of investigation they conducted didn't need an audience, but that couldn't be helped in those circumstances.

"I was asking if you saw this car, ma'am," Mackie shouted from the top of his lungs once more, pushing the photo under the woman's eyes. It looked like he had done that several times already. The man regretted that he had approached the old woman in the first place. Mackie thought they should have found a better subject to inquire about that blasted car, but they hadn't known that at the time.

The old woman's birdlike appearance was striking. McNamara wondered how she could stand because her bones seemed so frail that he worried she would break in two if she continued to keep that haughty stance.

However, the man reckoned that a steely core existed under that fragile exterior. A glint of satisfaction shone in the woman's eyes when Mackie yelled his question, probably for the tenth time. Then, McNamara had the certitude that the woman was merely enjoying all the trouble she put his detectives through.

The DCI decided to intervene in the discussion before the shouting match went too far. He noticed that a couple of people were already watching from their porches. God knew how many others were enjoying the free show through their windows.

"Good afternoon," the Chief Inspector approached the group.

Donna and Mackie had been so focused on their query that they hadn't noticed that the DCI was there. Donna even winced, realising that the man was in attendance, and apparently, for some time now.

The old woman turned to McNamara and assessed him with calculating eyes. However, she didn't limit her assessment to his face. The woman perused his body from the top of his head to his feet and then back again. A sarcastic grin flourished on her lips, and McNamara couldn't say precisely why. Still, he had the feeling that she was satisfied to have someone else to torment.

"So, what seems to be the problem here?" the Chief Inspector inquired in an even voice. He didn't relish the thought that he would have to shout, as well, to make himself heard.

"She doesn't hear, boss," Mackie explained. "We should have found someone else to approach," the man confessed. "But we already asked her questions, and then, we couldn't get rid of her," the detective told the DCI aside, forgetting for a moment that the woman couldn't hear him.

The woman could not hear him, but she could read his lips just fine, and she scowled at him. McNamara noticed her glower immediately and understood that she had just had some fun with his detectives. The woman could have answered their questions just fine, but she probably was bored and needed the diversion, or she had a twisted sense of humour.

The detective told Mackie, "She might not hear your words, but she knows exactly what you're saying. She reads lips." Then, turning his sternest glance towards the woman, he said, "Isn't that right, ma'am?"

The old woman scowled again, understanding that her game had ended. Then, she shrugged as if his words had been inconsequential to her.

"What's your name, ma'am?" McNamara inquired, staring the woman down.

"Martha Anderson," she replied grudgingly.

"I apologise for my insensibility, ma'am," the DCI said in a voice that betrayed anything but an apology. "I see you have a hearing aid. Why don't you turn it on? It would be easier for everyone concerned," he remarked.

"It needs batteries, and I don't feel like buying any right now," the woman shrugged nonchalantly. "Besides, I've enjoyed my conversation with these detectives a lot," she added in a dry tone of voice, waving towards the two inspectors.

"I can see that," McNamara said in a deadpan voice. "Now, let's put the games aside," he said with authority. "We have a job to do and a killer to catch. I'm sure you can find something else to amuse yourself with," the man observed. "Have you seen this car?" he asked and pushed directly under her nose the photo he had grabbed from Mackie's hand.

"I've seen lots of cars like that, young man," the woman scoffed, not even bothering to glance at the picture a second time. "The roads are full of them. No one would be able to tell one car from another, especially if they had this photo as a comparison." She pushed the photo aside and stared straight into McNamara's eyes.

The DCI gnashed his teeth but calmly said, "I know this type of car is very common around here, Mrs Anderson. However, I hoped you might see something that would make you remember about a certain person or place."

Martha Anderson gazed at him with her unnerving look for a couple of seconds. Then she snatched the photo from his hand and looked at it carefully. Her forehead wrinkled, proving her concentration.

The old woman took her sweet time to analyse the photo. Only after a few minutes, she muttered, "What strikes me, it's the absence of a license plate."

McNamara waited patiently, thinking that the woman might recall something related to the plate.

Martha didn't disappoint. "I remember that I saw a car like that a few days ago... Across from the underground garage at the end of this street... Don't ask me exactly when," she snapped, upset with herself that she couldn't recall. The woman rubbed her forehead and closed her eyes, trying to focus on her hazy memory. Her memory had shown disturbing losses for the last couple of years, which she didn't like.

McNamara was about to leave, thinking they had exhausted that avenue, when the woman put her hand up to stop him.

She said, "Aye, now I do remember. I saw an older man washing the plates of a similar car. Aye, it was the same day, I think. The car was parked somewhere on that street," she pointed to the north. "I'm talking about the street that intersects the one with the grocer's shop. I was coming back from my friend Elisabeth's... Now, I remember," she beamed. "It was Elisabeth's birthday. She and I went to school together and got married the same year... We even had children the same years..." she reminisced with a faraway look in her eyes.

"Anyway," Martha came back to the present. "That's not here or there. What I wanted to say was that we talked all afternoon and evening... Well into the night," she nodded, pursing her lips. "I left her place at around midnight, I think. It's faster to come down that street. I saw the man and the car in the driving alley of a house. He was cleaning the plates."

McNamara smiled gratefully at her and asked, "Do you remember the house, Mrs Anderson?"

"Huh! They all look alike. I can't remember, young man, how could I?" she scoffed at him.

"What's Elisabeth's date of birth? Do you know?" McNamara tried another question.

"Of course, I know, young man. I might not remember what happened yesterday, but I certainly remember my best friend's birthday," the woman bristled.

Mrs Anderson told them Elisabeth's birthdate. The date coincided with the day of the murder. Apparently, the woman had indeed seen the murderer.

"Did he see you?" Donna inquired. Nevertheless, the detective thought the woman wouldn't have made it to the morning if the man had seen her.

"No, he didn't," Martha replied, shaking her head. "I was walking on the side with a lot of trees. It's little light there, and the shadow is thick. He was on the other side. The moon shone right there," she remembered.

"So, you saw him very well," Mackie concluded.

"Huh!" the woman replied. "Not much to see, young man. He was of average height, sandy hair... Probably because of his age," she mused.

"His age?" McNamara inquired, raising his brows.

"Aye, his age. He was younger than I am but much older than you. I suppose, ten if not twenty years older," Martha said. "His face was common," the woman shook her head, unable to give any details. "There's nothing particular to mention," she shrugged.

"Would you be willing to accompany the detectives to headquarters to work with an artist? If possible, we would need a portrait," McNamara tried to persuade her. "Of course, we'll drive you home afterwards," he pointed out so that the woman wouldn't think that they would make her waste her time and leave her to find her way back by herself.

Mrs Anderson took her time to ponder his invitation. However, after a few minutes, she accepted with a vigorous head nod.

McNamara said to his subordinates, "Take Mrs Anderson with you and try to obtain a sketch." Then he turned back to Mrs Anderson. Looking straight into her eyes, the detective inquired, "Is it possible to obtain some batteries for your hearing aid, ma'am?" The woman raised a brow, so the detective thought he should explain why. "It would make things easier at the police station."

The old woman grinned and replied, pointing to her house, "If we go inside, I can replace the batteries in a moment, young man."

McNamara couldn't help it, and the man smiled at her shrewdness with a shake of his head. However, the two detectives grimaced. They had wasted a lot of time and composure over a simple matter like a change in batteries. Now, they felt silly.

Anyway, Donna and Mackie accompanied Mrs Anderson into her house after handing the photo with the car to McNamara. The DCI strode to the next door to question the residents.

CHAPTER 15 – A NEW CRIME SHADOWS THE NEIGHBOURHOOD

"I haven't seen anything, Detective," the young woman said hastily, both her hands clutching the front door, ready to slam it in his face. She eyed the inspector nervously, and McNamara couldn't discern if the woman reacted that way because she knew something or was a fearful bird.

Suddenly, the noise of something breaking inside reached the front door. The woman turned her head towards the inside of the house. "Ian, I'm going to skin you alive, you wretch. What have you done now? Rose, come downstairs and mind your brother," she shouted so sharply that the windows shook.

For the last fifteen minutes, McNamara tried to talk to Mrs Muir, a young housewife with a large brood of children. However, the man didn't get any results. Between her frequent shrieks and headshakes, the woman sorely tried his patience. Her answers varied from 'I don't know anything' to 'I haven't seen anything.'

Besides, the young woman would stop mid-sentence and yell to one of the children inside. When she returned to the Chief Inspector, Muir would repeatedly state that she had no knowledge about what happened, as no rumours had reached her ears.

After a few words, Muir also stopped to check her hair or apron. A few times, the detective noticed with dismay that the woman was perusing her fingernails, which was quite a feat with her fingers firmly attached to the door. McNamara concluded that he had a very self-aware woman before his eyes.

"I've told you, Detective, I don't recognise the car, and I don't know anything about that woman whose photo you showed me," Muir said. Then, without breaking her stride, she bellowed, "Michael, if I get to you, you'll be sorry."

McNamara had to admit defeat, convinced that he wouldn't get any information from that woman. He only got was a headache. The pain throbbed behind his eyelids, and the man hardly suppressed the need to rub his temples.

"Thank you for your time, ma'am. I'll leave you to your children. You seem to have your hands full," he said, a shadow of a sarcastic grin on his lips.

The DCI didn't feel like smiling, though. He also felt like breaking something, and the man envied Ian. At least the lad got to break something, even though he would probably be the receiver of an unpleasant reward for that. Mrs Muir didn't seem to be the forgiving type and meant business.

McNamara strolled up the street, his mind a little muddled. His headache had worsened and now claimed the temples and the back of his head. Rubbing his temples once more, the inspector thought of the last evening's date with Bryony, recalling how peaceful and relaxing it had felt.

Impulsively, the man took his cell phone out of his pocket to speed dial her number. The lass already had key 'one' assigned to her, which somewhat confused and disturbed the man. McNamara hadn't realised that she had become so important to him, but he must have thought that unconsciously.

"Hullo, stranger," Bryony answered the call softly with her usual greeting.

"Question," McNamara said briefly. "That's how you greet everyone, or...."

The woman burst into laughter., which should have hurt the man. Whenever he had a headache, the inspector couldn't stand piercing sounds. Yet, her merriment didn't, but surprisingly, it felt good.

"Of course, I won't greet everyone like that, Artair," Bryony replied, laughter in her voice. "But I know your number by now, so I can greet you that way," the woman explained.

"All right then," the man said, his joy reflected in his voice. "Would you like to get together tonight, or is it too soon?" McNamara asked.

"It's not too soon, and I would like that," the woman answered in a small voice, and the man's heart swelled. He had dreaded Bryony's possible answer for a few seconds.

"That's good. However, it would be a bit later," the inspector explained. "It's one of those days... Information comes from everywhere, and there's a lot to do... What are you saying about eight-thirty at Mr Brown's pub? I wouldn't think to make you come back in town again at that hour," the man clarified.

"Dinner or only drinks?" she asked in a matter-of-fact voice.

"I was thinking both," he replied.

"Great, then I'll see you there," Bryony agreed. "I suppose you're still busy now and don't have time to chat," she surmised.

"Unfortunately, aye," the man said regretfully. "But we'll talk tonight. All right? Should I come and get you at eight-thirty?"

"Yes, of course. At eight-thirty then, Artair. See you," Bryony replied, disconnecting the call.

Feeling a little better, McNamara pushed the phone back into his coat pocket and chose to try the first house on the right. The Chief Inspector had just started climbing the front stairs when his phone rang, so he checked the caller ID to notice that Mike was the one calling. The detective answered the call, going back down the stairs at the same time.

"Yes, Mike, what is it?"

"Chief, we have another murder here," the inspector replied dryly.

"Another one?" McNamara inquired with bewilderment. The man wouldn't have imagined a similar second murder in that investigation, as that killing method wasn't a common occurrence.

"Aye," Mike replied. "We've just found a woman. She's barely beheaded, though."

"How come?" the Chief Inspector retorted briskly. "Either she's beheaded or not."

"I'd say she's partly beheaded," Mike explained apologetically, not knowing how to better explain what he had before his eyes.

"Give me the address, and I will come there," McNamara barked into the phone, at the same time, taking out a small notebook from his pocket to write the address down. "Have you called the coroner, Steven Gilchrist, and the rest of the team?" he asked Mike after replacing the notebook into his pocket.

"Yes, sir, they're on their way. I also called James. I thought you'd like him here as well. Should I call Donna and Mackie?" the Detective Inspector inquired, but the DCI didn't have time to reply. Jo's impatient voice came from somewhere in the background, "Mike, come here."

"Aye, tell them to come as well if they don't have another lead, and then, go and see what Jo wants. She seems ready to take your head off," McNamara ordered before disconnecting the call.

The Chief Inspector took his bearings for a moment and then started up the street with long strides. A boy, who was just walking his dog, noticed the scowl between the man's brows and decided it would have been safer to cross on the other side of the street.

***

Everybody was busy at work when McNamara shadowed the townhouse's front door where the second murder occurred. That wasn't a clean murder. The DCI noticed the techs bagging evidence, and it looked like the killer had left a lot behind, which didn't rhyme with what the Chief Inspector had observed with the first crime. Whoever had done the present one hadn't taken any precautions as if they hadn't cared about leaving a trail behind.

McNamara noticed that the coroner on duty was David Stewart and glared. He hadn't expected the doctor back at work so soon. "How's it going, David?" the Chief Inspector inquired once the doctor straightened up.

Stewart had already finished with the preliminary examination and started gathering his instruments. The Chief Inspector's voice made David turn to McNamara, a greeting smile on his lips. Traces of the man's ordeal during the last few weeks marked his suddenly old face, but he still looked somewhat better than the last time the Detective Inspector had met him. "Duty, you know," David Stewart answered, waving his hand nonchalantly.

"Is everything fine?" McNamara inquired, lifting his famous left brow, and his question attracted the baffled eyes of the people in the room. The DCI never asked about people's lives, and, definitely, his question didn't refer to the victim.

"Oh, lad, aye. Everything's fine," the doctor replied with a firm nod, getting closer to McNamara. Then, he whispered, "Martha's fine. They successfully removed the whole tumour, and the subsequent tests showed it was benign. Feel like celebrating, McNamara? Next Saturday? You can bring your lady with you. Rumour has it you have one now," Stewart grinned the detective, wriggling his brows.

"Such news, David, require a celebration, indeed," the detective replied earnestly, tapping the coroner on the shoulder with more enthusiasm than he had ever shown before. Even a broad grin appeared on his lips, making his people wonder what had come over the man.

As a rule, they had already noticed that McNamara didn't care about people. The DCI's interest lay in his work and little else. Yet, the

Chief Inspector cared about the Stewarts. And more than he had ever cared about any other of his co-workers. He felt them close, like family.

"And I'll ask my lady to come too," McNamara added quietly, thinking that Bryony wouldn't refuse to meet the Stewarts. The lass didn't seem too high in the instep, and she genuinely cared about people.

The people around pretended to be busy at work, but they still threw casual looks at McNamara. They couldn't hear what David Stewart was saying, but the two men's behaviour spoke volumes. People had known the DCI had a closer relationship with the coroner than he had with any other of them, but they hadn't known the two men were so tight that they shared secrets.

"Well, David, what are we having here?" the DCI turned to professional matters after exhausting his interest in Stewarts' issues.

"We've got a murder, McNamara," the coroner replied dryly. "I would say it's the garden-variety one," he added.

"I understand that the victim was partly beheaded, David," McNamara countered, raising his brows. "I don't see anything of the garden variety here. Besides, this crime hits closely to the one we're already working on," he observed.

"Not if you look closely," the doctor contradicted him, shaking his head stubbornly. "This is a copycat, detective... In my opinion, it's a pretty bad one," he added after a few seconds. "First, the killer struck the victim in anger with that big knife over there," the coroner pointed to a big butcher knife the techs had already labelled.

One of the forensic experts was just placing it in a paper bag to preserve DNA and fingerprints.

"The first strike came on the side of the neck," the coroner showed him the spot on the victim's body. "I'd say that was instinctual. It was a crime of passion... or of a certain passion," he added after reflecting on his words for a second.

"Then, once the woman died, which happened quite fast, considering that the principal artery got nicked, the killer thought of throwing us off the trail. That's why the attacker tried to behead the victim, which, of course, it isn't an easy thing to do. Apparently, the murderer found that out soon enough and forgot everything about completing the beheading... I suspect the killer may be a woman, and this is probably, her first attempt to murder someone."

"Why would you think that?" the detective asked for details.

Stewart pointed his thumb to the techs behind him. "The lads found the spot where the killer got sick at the back door."

"I see," McNamara said and felt somewhat sorry for the tech who had to bag that. However, with a shrug, he waved the thought away. Each agent had to do their job, after all.

"Well, they can take the body now," the coroner added. "I'll do the post-mortem tomorrow."

"All right, David," the Chief Inspector acknowledged the man's words. "Then, I'll assign Jo and Mike to this case. I trust your instincts, and if you say it's a different case, I believe you."

The doctor nodded, leaving after a noisy round of goodbyes. McNamara's gaze followed the man until he left the house and then turned to the murder scene. The inspector thoughtfully analysed the crime scene before him for a few moments and then called Jo, "Jo, come here."

The woman hurried to come to the Chief's side, and McNamara told her, "You and Mike will handle this case now. The doc says it's clearly not related to the case we're already working on. However, I want you to verify and ensure there's no connection. Do we know anything about this woman?"

Jo nodded, saying, "Aye, boss. She lived here. Married with one child, a toddler. Her mother took the child with her in the morning, wanting to spend the day with the boy. Anyway, we called and asked the husband to come back from work so that we could talk to him."

"All right, Jo," McNamara said. "Send a few uniforms to inquire around and see if anyone visited the woman in the morning. Do you have a name for her?" the inspector asked, sick of saying 'the woman' all the time.

"Aye, sir. Her name was Dana Luther. Age twenty-seven, housewife," Jo gave him all the details, and speechless for a few moments, the DCI stared at her. The detective had sounded like a tape, reciting the facts like that.

Then, the man shook his head and noted, "Good. Investigate the husband and neighbours. Doc says it's a crime of passion or rage, so the woman might have upset someone terribly."

Jo let the Chief know that she understood his orders and then signalled Mike to come to them. Coincidentally, James stepped into the house right that moment, wiping off his forehead with his fingers. The day seemed unusually warm for that time of the year. Unfortunately, such weather didn't agree with the Sergeant too much.

Both James and Mike reached the DCI and Jo at the same time.

"Another murder, Chief?" James inquired, looking around, trying to get an accurate idea about the situation.

"Aye, James, but I don't think it's related to our case. Jo and Mike will take care of this one," the DCI explained, glancing at Mike, who nodded his understanding. "You and I will take over the first case with Donna's and Mackie's help. Any news from Mrs Anderson?" he asked.

A flitting grin lit James's face, but then he answered gravely, "Still working on the portrait, sir... I don't think Josh will ever be the same," the Sergeant added with a shake of his head.

"Who's Josh?" McNamara asked with bewilderment, drawing a blank. Usually, he was better than that to remember people's names.

"The artist, sir," Mike reminded him, raising a brow.

"Oh, I see," McNamara nodded and grinned. "I should understand that Mrs Anderson is giving him fits," he continued.

"Something like that," James acquiesced, pursing his lips, knowing that the Chief's statement was an understatement.

"Let's hope that Josh will succeed in drawing the portrait, though," McNamara shrugged. "It would help us a lot. Anything new about Clarissa Ross's relatives and friends? Anyone ringing a bell, James?" he inquired.

The Sergeant shook his head. "Not just yet, sir. I'm still looking. I decided to wipe off the list anybody who had an alibi for both murders, the murder of Clarissa's former fiancé, and our victim here."

"Good thinking, James. You should continue with the list. I will see if anyone here saw anything on that street that Mrs Anderson mentioned earlier. With everyone involved in something else, I can spend a couple of hours doing the rounds," McNamara said with sarcasm. "We'll have a meeting tomorrow at nine in my office, and everyone must be present there," he ordered, looking around. "You too, Steven," he warned the forensic expert, and Steven waved his hand, letting him know that he had heard his command.

CHAPTER 16 – ANOTHER TYPE OF BATTLE

McNamara walked Bryony home from the pub. A state of good feeling had enveloped him since the beginning of their dinner, and he still felt good. That was why it had taken the man a few moments to realise that he had been holding the woman's hand.

Bryony never pushed and never asked uncomfortable questions. To his surprise, the young woman never wanted to know more than he was willing to share, and she understood his reticence to speak about a case he was working on.

Those were rare qualities, and the DCI had never found them in anyone else. That was why his appreciation for the strawberry-blond woman, who reached just to his shoulder, increased more and more.

It was past ten o'clock already, and the two young people were strolling leisurely along Nightingale Street. The time had simply flown away in Bryony's company for McNamara, and he would have liked to spend some more time with her.

The lass made him laugh and wasn't bent on talking only about herself all the time. When Mr Brown came to their table to share a glass of ale with them, Bryony didn't get upset because someone else interfered in their time together.

McNamara knew when he had something good before his eyes. Yet, he was also afraid. The man was almost thirty-eight and had never felt such a pull from any women. He casually dated them a couple of times and discarded them as soon as the novelty had worn off.

McNamara had already accepted his lot in life. Maybe the man hadn't understood what he meant when he was diagnosed with Asperger's at seven. But he understood later.

The DCI wasn't like other men and didn't yearn for a happily ever after. His company wasn't easy going, and he didn't want to saddle any unsuspecting woman with such a dour man.

And yet, with Bryony, things looked different, and his wishes changed.

"I forgot to ask you," the man suddenly said, remembering David Stewart's invitation. He halted their stroll, and his green eyes fixated on her. "Would you go with me to a barbeque next Saturday?"

"Of course, I'd love to," Bryony replied, leaning forward on tiptoes and kissing McNamara gently on the cheek.

Her innocent gesture shocked and, at the same time, aroused the man, who suddenly felt like a fish out of water. He squeezed her hand involuntarily, and surprised, she gasped.

"I apologise," McNamara said and immediately released her hand. "I didn't mean to hurt you," he explained.

"You didn't," she replied. "I was just surprised," the young woman explained, her fingers closing over his. Her dark blue eyes looked straight into his, and McNamara noticed that she wasn't lying. That brought relief.

The detective might not have been the best man around, but his policy was to never hurt a woman physically. McNamara knew he had probably bruised a few hearts when he stopped seeing them without too much of an explanation. However, the man had never caused them any physical harm.

Bryony stopped in front of her dainty little house and turned to him, looking at him expectedly. "Would you like to come in?" she asked with an inviting smile.

McNamara looked at her intently and then shook his head. "No, not tonight. It wouldn't be a good idea."

The detective had accepted such invitations, even after a first date. So the man didn't know why he had refused her. Maybe McNamara did it because he felt so raw and aroused that he needed time to think about everything. Or maybe, he didn't trust himself to make the best decision right then.

The inspector tilted his head and kissed her lips hard. He swallowed her gasp, and the young woman put her arms around his neck and pulled him closer.

When he pulled back, their breathing was laboured. McNamara looked at her reddened lips, and a faint smile claimed his mouth.

"I'll call you tomorrow, then," he said. "Maybe come by tomorrow evening," the man continued.

"I'd like that," Bryony replied and stroked his chest with her fingers.

McNamara stepped back to remove himself from the path of temptation. Then, his eyes fell on a shadow at Mrs Stevens' window. "Cerberus is watching us," he whispered.

Bryony burst into laughter and slapped his chest playfully. "She's not so bad," she told him.

"No, she's worse," he replied cynically. "She'll probably come out to bother you," the man continued, and now, anger rang in his voice.

"Don't worry," Bryony tempered his anger. "She can't dictate me what to do, which she knows it."

"Are you sure?" McNamara inquired, and a flicker of doubt shone in his eyes.

"About what?" the woman asked, her voice filled with bafflement.

"That she won't change your mind, and you'll continue to see me," he specified an intense light in his eyes.

"Be serious," the young woman replied. "What is between the two of us, what we have, it's not her business. Of course, I won't even consider doing what Mrs Stevens says or wants," she continued in a voice that didn't broach any argument.

The detective stared at her for a few more moments and then nodded. "All right then. I'll call tomorrow and tell you when I will be here." McNamara leaned forward and kissed her briefly, not just to annoy the old bat, who kept watching them from her window. Then, he climbed into his car and drove away. Bryony's eyes followed him until he went right at the end of the street.

With a dreamy smile on her lips, Bryony turned to go inside when Mrs Stevens opened her window and called to her, "Bryony, just a moment, love. I want to talk to you."

Bryony grimaced inwardly but went to Mrs Stevens' window.

"Hullo, how are you? Why are you awake so late?" the young woman asked, although she had a good idea why the old woman was at the window and not in her bed.

"I noticed when that man parked his car, lass," Mrs Stevens chided her. "I told you he's not good for you," she continued without caring for the frown that now marred Bryony's face.

"I see," the young woman answered. "And I remember telling you that I won't accept advice about him," she said softly, but her voice didn't invite an argument.

Still, Mrs Stevens waved her words away negligently, "You're too young to know better, so you should listen to me, Bryony."

"I'm not so young, Mrs Stevens," she replied.

Bryony knew that she looked anywhere between twenty and twenty-five, but she was, in fact, closer to twenty-nine. People had a hard time believing it, and she couldn't do anything about that. However, her neighbour knew her age very well. Besides, the young woman wouldn't stand for interference in her personal life, even though Mrs Stevens was very dear to her.

"And even if I had been," Bryony said and put up her hand to stop the other woman's words, "it wouldn't have mattered. I don't share your opinion of McNamara."

"He's a policeman," the old woman snapped.

"So what? Policemen are people. They live and think like us. It's not like the man's an alien species, for God's sake," Bryony almost shouted. She took a deep breath and then said, "Mrs Stevens, we are friends, good friends," she stressed out. "Let's agree to disagree in this matter. However, please understand that my relationship with Artair is not your business."

"Artair?" the old woman asked, confused.

"He has a first name as everyone," Bryony snapped at her older friend. "Anyway, I'm going to bed. Have a good night," she turned to leave.

"So you'd quarrel with me because of that man," the old woman reproached in a waspish voice.

Bryony turned back to her and looked her straight in the eyes. "I wouldn't if you were reasonable. McNamara is not open for discussion," the woman stated again and then, she went home.

The old woman needed a few moments to realise that her mouth was hanging open. Nay, she didn't like that man at all. Because of him, Bryony had turned against her.

Yet, the old woman knew that she had to accept the detective if she wanted to keep her friendship with her younger neighbour. That didn't mean that she had to like or trust him.

CHAPTER 17 – A MEETING WITH SURPRISES

The entire team met in a conference room at nine sharp as McNamara had asked. Initially, the DCI wanted to hold the meeting in his office, but it wasn't enough space there for everyone.

Mackie came into the room, carrying a carafe with coffee. Meanwhile, Donna followed with recyclable cups and a sugar, sweetener, and milk bag. Jo had already laid a box with tea cakes on the conference table. Everybody was happy to partake in the impromptu snack. They wouldn't have dared to do that in the Chief Inspector's office.

McNamara entered the room and was taken aback for a moment. People talked loudly, passing cakes and coffee cups one to the other. However, noticing his arrival, everybody stopped talking, staring at him wide-eyed, which baffled the Chief. They should have known he would come.

The DCI assessed the detectives for a couple of moments and then said gruffly, "Prepare your coffee and take your cakes so that we can start working."

"Would you like a coffee, sir?" James asked.

"Why not?" the DCI answered. "You know that's my poison," he said with a significant gesture, and a few dared to laugh. Once he had a cup of coffee in hand, he turned to more important matters. "So, anyone, any news?"

"I think Jo and Mike should start, boss," James suggested, and McNamara glanced at him inquiringly.

"Their case has already been solved," James explained.

"Oh, is that true?" McNamara turned to the two detectives, somewhat vexed that he had to find out about that during the meeting when he should have been informed before. Being in charge of the Major Crimes Unit, he needed to know everything that happened.

Jo didn't dare look at him. The detective found something interesting in her tea cake to stare at and analysed the piece as if she had had it under a microscope.

"We've just finished with everything, sir." However, that was water under the bridge already. Mike also knew that they had made a mistake not calling McNamara before the case's conclusion.

"Tell me," McNamara ordered in a stern voice.

"Well, we started around seven this morning," Mike explained. "We wanted to have something to contribute to this meeting," he continued with broad gestures. "We went back to the house, thinking w would catch the neighbours before going to work."

"That's nice and good," McNamara said. "But what did you find out? I don't need a play by play now, that everything ended," he pointed out.

Mike scolded himself for letting his mouth run and then presented everything as succinct and quick as possible.

"The woman wasn't liked in the neighbourhood. She was not only the worst gossip possible but also mean-willed. We talked only with four neighbours, but all mentioned that she liked to bully, especially women. Something interesting, though. Her husband supported her in such endeavours. People have learnt to avoid her. If they weren't fast enough, they would have been verbally harassed, or she would spread rumours about them. Anyway, around eight-fifteen, the dispatch called us to come back to the headquarters because a young woman had come and confessed to the murder. Her name is Aileen Dunbar. She's only twenty-two. The victim had told her husband that he'd married a tart, and he was the laughingstock of the street. The victim told him that she'd seen many men paying visits to his little wife while he was at work. They'd just moved there in that neighbourhood, and the man didn't really know what Mrs Luther was capable of. He still doesn't. Aileen and her husband quarrelled a lot and, in the end, the husband left. Aileen was not only heartbroken but also broke. She doesn't have a job, and he left her to deal with the lease and everything. Mrs Dunbar was furious. She still is, I should say," Mike pointed out. "Anyway, she heard about Ms Livingstone's murder and decided to kill her nemesis exactly the same way. Dunbar thought the guilt would shift onto someone else. She didn't know what killing meant and, more to the point, what beheading someone implied. Her first strike was pure luck if you want to look at it like that. She hit the artery. Mrs Luther fell down and died in no time at all. Now, Mrs Dunbar tried the beheading thing, but she got sick and had to run out of the house. After Dunbar finished throwing up, the enormity of what she had done hit her. The woman ran home and cried for hours... Of course, that's what she says. Anyway, sometime during the night, she decided to come forward."

"Did you match her story with the evidence?" McNamara asked. He knew that crazy people came forward to confess a murder or another crime most of the time.

"Yes, the prints on the knife correspond to her prints, and the techs used the vomit to determine DNA... They said something about throat epithelia, I think. Anyway, the DNA matches as well," Mike shrugged.

"All right then, you have your culprit," McNamara approved. "Don't forget the paperwork," he warned Mike, knowing very well that he was a hell of a detective, but he didn't like that side of his job.

Mike nodded, "Aye, boss. No worries, I'll do it."

"Now, about the other case," the DCI turned to the others. "What do we have?" he inquired.

"I've eliminated most of Clarissa's friends and family members," James said. "I still have to check on an estranged grandfather and a former boyfriend who still has strong feelings for her."

"Estranged grandfather?" Donna wondered.

"Aye," James said. "I understand that her grandmother was supposed to marry a lad, yet he enlisted in the army without a word. She was pregnant at the time. He came back after five years, but the woman refused to have anything to do with him. However, the granddaughter accepted the old man."

"How old are we talking about?" McNamara inquired.

"Quite old. Around sixty-five, I think," James specified.

"Probably too old to have murdered the woman, but let's verify him anyway," McNamara decided. The DCI had had surprises in the past and wasn't willing to pass over any credible information.

"Anything about the portrait?" he asked Donna.

"Oh, aye, Josh managed to draw the portrait. After he spent a few hours in the company of the battiest woman in Scotland, I must say," Donna answered, and exasperation rang true in her voice. "Josh implored me not to bring such people to him any time soon."

"I'm sure he survived," the DCI observed in a dry voice. "So, where's the portrait?"

Donna opened a file and handed a sketch to McNamara. The detective took the paper with mild interest, but his eyebrows shot up when his eyes fell on the drawing.

"James, have you seen this?" he asked quietly.

His tension was conveyed to the others, and they exchanged baffled looks. James, sitting next to McNamara, turned aside to have a clear sight of the paper.

"Do you remember him?" McNamara asked.

James nodded, at a loss of words. Neither of them could believe it.

"See what you can find out about the grandfather, James," McNamara urged. "You have ten minutes," he warned the Sergeant. "In fifteen minutes, we'll leave. You, too," he turned to the other detectives in the room.

MCNAMARA SERIES BOX SET
BOOK 0NE & TWO

CHAPTER 18 – APPEARANCES MISLEAD

Four cars stopped in front of the building, which made Mrs MacDonald, the biggest gossip of the street, appear at her window. Her eyes widened, betraying disbelief, probably, the effect of the two cars marked Police. She had never seen such a sight on their tiny street.

The woman's eyes fell on McNamara and James, who exited from one of the unmarked cars. She wondered why the detectives had returned there with such an impressive backup.

The DCI and the DS entered the building, followed by four other people dressed in plain clothes and two constables.

Mrs MacDonald immediately ran to her front door. She opened it with not too much finesse — it hit the wall effectively. She didn't care about that, though. The noise didn't stop her to eavesdrop on what happened on the stairs, either.

She listened to the detectives' steps until they stopped on the landing below in front of the flat door. Hard knocking on the wooden panel echoed on the staircase.

With the purpose of a hunting dog, the old woman strained her ears until she caught the voice of a man greeting the detectives. Her brows raised in befuddlement, and she scowled. 'Why are the detectives visiting that insipid man?'

"Good morning, Detectives," the man said. "I thought I told you everything I knew," he remarked idly, slightly puzzled to find McNamara and James darkening his door once more.

"Not everything," Mrs MacDonald heard McNamara's harsh voice. "Why don't we go inside and talk without supplementary ears around?" McNamara proposed, pointing to the landing above where he had heard MacDonald's door slamming into the wall earlier.

A faint blush spread over the woman's cheeks, and she tiptoed back inside her flat. This time, Mrs MacDonald closed the door behind with much care. She knew she wouldn't be able to hear them if they went inside the flat, and the detective seemed determined not to talk out there in front of the door.

On the landing below, the man invited the detectives inside with an expansive and somewhat mocking gesture, "By all means, be my guests, Detectives."

The policemen followed him into his sitting-room. Still, despite his invitation to sit down, they chose to stand, their eyes fixed on the man before them. They knew he was dangerous, even if only from the traces of the crime he had committed, and they had already seen. But then, they had also found out about his training with SAS, and, despite his age, his latest exploits proved that he still could hold his own. The policemen had no intention of tempting fate.

The man began speaking softly, waving his shaking hands exaggeratedly. "So, Detectives, to what do I owe the pleasure of your new visit? I see you've brought more people with you this time," he mentioned just in passing. Still, McNamara didn't miss the sarcastic glint in the man's eyes.

"You shouldn't bother acting the role of an old and frail man anymore, sir. The shaking hands... and the rest. We know the truth...." McNamara said with derision. "By the way, you forgot to tell us about your granddaughter's murder and especially about your murdering Ms Livingstone," McNamara added, in a voice more suitable to discuss the weather,

"Ms Livingstone?" the older man inquired, feigning surprise.

"Mr Wilson," McNamara said. "Acting won't help you now. We already have all the evidence we need."

"I didn't know the victim's name," Mr Wilson shrugged. "You never told me."

"How inconsiderate of us," McNamara snapped. "Look here, we know who you are, and we have evidence and witnesses connecting you to the crime. Whether you choose to say anything or not, you're done."

Mr Wilson assessed the detective openly and spared a few glances to the others, as well.

"I've never imagined I'd continue with my life as it is," the man shrugged. "I did what needed to be done. Vermin must be exterminated. I'm pretty sure that there are a few people out there who'd show their gratitude," he observed flatly.

"There might be some truth in your words," McNamara replied. Noticing the slight nods of agreement from the others, the Chief Inspector scowled at them and then returned to the murderer.

"Yet, it's not your place to judge and condemn. You should have gone to the police," the detective continued in a harsh voice.

"Huh," Mr Wilson exclaimed and then laughed mirthlessly. "I told those nitwits that my sweet Clarissa hadn't killed herself. I couldn't go further because they invited me to ease on the booze and on mystery novels," he continued bitterly.

"I understand you must have been angered..." McNamara began to say, but the man's shout interrupted him.

Mr Wilson had practically roared. Even Mrs MacDonald heard his words from her apartment.

"Angered? Angered, you say?" His voice was getting more forceful. "I was damn enraged, Detective," the man boomed. "How would you have felt? They dismissed me as if I had been nothing and let that piece of garbage go free," he ended his tirade, slamming his fist in the wall next to him.

"You could have insisted, sir," James remarked quietly.

Mr Wilson's outburst prompted the policemen to step closer to McNamara, ready to overpower the old man. Their move amused Wilson for a second, but then he became serious again and answered James's statement, "To whom, lad?"

Silence reigned for a few moments. McNamara pondered the old man's words. He wanted to say something, but the man waved his hand dismissively. "You have me now, so it doesn't matter anymore. My Clarissa had her revenge, and those two won't darken the world again."

"We'll have to put the cuffs on you, sir," McNamara observed. "It's the rule."

The old man just shrugged and showed them his hands. James handcuffed him and asked him to follow them downstairs.

"One question, DCI," Wilson stopped before McNamara. "Would I be allowed to take my Liz Taylor album with me?"

EPILOGUE

McNamara had called Bryony twice that day. The first time, he phoned to tell her that he was about to tie all the loose ends in his murder case. The detective had known the lass would be waiting for his call, and he wasn't sure he would be able to get to her house very soon. Apparently, the man had been right. She did wait for his call. The second time, he called just half an hour ago to tell the young woman that he was leaving the police station and was on his way to her house.

The man parked his car in her driving alley and picked up the chocolate box he had bought on his way there. It had seemed a good idea at the time. Now, he wasn't so sure anymore.

McNamara fortified himself against the ridicule and defiantly got out of the car, anxiously squeezing the box with his fingers. He didn't realise that the chocolates might get smashed as well.

Mrs Stevens' window opened, and she sternly called out to him, "A word, young man."

"Not now, maybe later," McNamara dismissed her without breaking his stride. However, he added in his mind, 'Maybe never, if I can help it.'

"Now," she barked, thumping a cane on the floor.

"I don't have the time," the man negligently waved the hand unencumbered by the chocolate box and climbed the few steps in front of Bryony's house.

"We need to talk about Bryony," the old woman shouted after him. "You can't take advantage of her," she declared,

A scowl firmly etched between his brows, McNamara knocked on Bryony's door louder than he would have intended. The detective didn't bother to answer the old bat anymore but muttered a few choice words under his breath.

Bryony opened the door and stepped back, startled. His frown didn't promise a good time.

"What's the problem?" she asked, her blue eyes prodding his.

"Oh, just that old bat," McNamara grumbled. Then, her recoil at seeing him registered in his mind. "Are you afraid of me?" he asked the young woman with displeasure, not expecting such a reaction from her. The detective had thought that Bryony had started knowing what kind of man he was.

"Don't be silly," she replied, slapping his arm. "Your scowl surprised me, that's all. And you shouldn't care about Mrs Stevens," the lass added. "She has no saying in our relationship, Artair. Come in." She took his arm to pull him inside.

Her eyes fell on the chocolate box, and a smile fluttered on her lips. It looked like the box had suffered a fatal accident already.

"Bryony, I need to speak to you," Mrs Stevens' voice rang from behind the detective.

Bryony looked around McNamara and noticed her neighbour almost hanging out of the window.

"Hullo, there, Mrs Stevens. I haven't seen you," the young woman said sweetly, even though she shook her head in disbelief. "I do apologise, but I have guests tonight. We'll talk tomorrow. All right?" she added with a friendly wave for her neighbour.

Then, Bryony pulled McNamara forcefully into her house, not caring for Mrs Stevens' outraged gasp. She closed the door behind him and sighed. "Don't pay any attention to her, Artair. So, would you like some coffee, some dinner, or…?"

The man thrust the smashed chocolate box into her hand and said, "I brought you this."

Bryony smiled and looked at the box. "My favourite chocolates, did you know?" she said, trying hard not to shake her head at the sorry sight of the box.

"I'll remember," the man replied in a dry tone of voice.

"Give me your coat and come into the kitchen. How long are you going to stay?"

McNamara took off his coat and handed it to her. When Bryony turned back to him, he grabbed her shoulders and kissed her, his hard mouth stealing the gasp off her lips.

"Until morning?" the man said, asking for her permission.

"I'd like that," she replied softly, striking the side of his face.

EXCERPT FROM THE NOVEL
AN IMMIGRANT

The echo of hasty steps coming from the direction of the Gigue reached his ears. Victor lifted his head and stared unblinkingly into the night with trepidation.

Anxiety and fear nudged at him, and he pushed hard with his palms into the ground to move. Each inch he covered brought more sweat and aches. Pain instantly radiated everywhere in his back, but resolute, gritting his teeth, he tried to crawl under a tree. It felt as if he had moved through molasses.

'At least I'm alive,' Victor thought. 'But not for long, if I don't move out of this darn trail,' he groused and pushed harder, gritting his teeth to contain his grunts.

"He fell somewhere here," a solid male voice shredded the silence.

"Are you sure? I can't see anyone," a throaty female voice replied with evident doubt.

Victor stopped any movement and tried to become one with the ground. He knew he was in the shadow, and they couldn't see him.

"I can hear him," the woman said with enthusiasm, and Victor grimaced.

'How the heck can you hear me?' he wondered, and his eyes widened. His fingers dug into the floor of the grove as if he had wanted to anchor himself.

'I'm not saying jack,' he thought. 'I'm not so out of my mind that I'm talking without being aware of that, aren't I?'

"Yeah, I hear him too," the man's voice replied. "He's kept his humour, so he mustn't be in a terrible shape," he noticed drily.

Victor's eyebrows shot up his forehead. 'Who the heck are these people? More importantly, what the heck do they want with me?'

"I don't hear anyone around," the woman said. "Take out your flashlight," she ordered.

'She's like a drill sergeant,' Victor mused, listening intently to every sound they made.

***

Victor gave up any pretence when the light swept over him. He didn't know those people, but there were only two options — either they came to save him or finish him. There wasn't any way around that.

He lifted his head, and gnashing his teeth, he turned to the light. The flashlight blinded him, and this time, he couldn't hold a groan.

"He's there," the man said and rushed to kneel next to Victor. "Hey, buddy, are you still with us?" he asked, and Victor sensed the smile in his voice.

Victor grunted and nodded once. He didn't know whether he still had his voice. His eyes searched the man's face. Satisfied he had never seen him before, he laid his head on his folded arms again and closed his eyes.

"Is he still alive?" the woman's voice asked.

"Yes, he is. What should we do now?" the man inquired, rousing Victor's curiosity.

'Why would he ask for her advice?' he thought, and the next moment, the man's laughter filled the air.

"Because she's the boss now," the man replied with good humour.

His words shocked Victor, and he just froze. His eyes zeroed in on Axel. He couldn't even blink.

"Now look what you've done, Axel," the woman chided her companion. "You scared him."

"He'll survive," Axel answered matter-of-factly, and Victor had the distinct impression that the man shrugged with nonchalance.

"Who are you, people?" Victor croaked, unable to keep his mouth shut one second more.

He felt as if he had fallen into a strange dimension. This time, he was sure he hadn't voiced his question.

The woman's cold hand brushed his hair off his forehead, soothing his increasing fever.

"I'm Leah MacKay, a detective, and this is my boyfriend, Axel Arnett," she replied in a kind voice. "I'm going to call an ambulance for you," she continued.

She tried to stand up, but the man's fingers closed over her wrist with surprising strength.

"No police," he groused.

He bit his lips. The sudden move had sparked arrows of pain along his spine and lower body.

Arnett burst into hearty laughter. The sound gritted on Victor's nerves. If he had had the strength, he would have knocked the man down.

"Sorry, pal, the police are already here," Axel explained with cheer, making Victor lock his teeth again.

Leah pried his fingers off her wrist gently and took her cell phone out of her pocket. She dialled 911 and explained to the operator who she was and that she needed an ambulance and her team at the Sarabande.

Defeated, Victor sighed and laid his head on his arms again. He'd seen a commercial once with a tiny hedgehog coming out of a hole just to be hammered down once more. Now, he was the hedgehog. He had lost control of his life. 'Eh, it's not for the first time,' he mused.

Axel Arnett leaned over him and whispered, "Everything will be well, don't worry. She's the best."

"That's what I'm afraid of," Victor grumbled, prompting Axel to chuckle.

Axel liked the man and felt satisfied that they got to him in time. Hopefully, he would survive.

Axel felt the strength in him and counted on his build. He wasn't a man that could be quickly taken down.

MCNAMARA SERIES BOX SET
BOOK 0NE & TWO

AUTHOR'S BIOGRAPHY

Roxana Nastase enjoys writing and baking - these two work very well hand in hand. She also enjoys spending time with her dog - or at least most of the time, as he is a hellion.

One trip to Scotland made her lose her heart to a beautiful country and extraordinary people. That is why she chose a Scottish detective to promote some of her crime stories.

BOOKS BY ROXANA NASTASE

Mayhem on Nightingale Street – McNamara Series – Book One

Scents and Shadows – McNamara Series – Book Two

McNamara Series – Box Set (Book One – Mayhem on Nightingale Street & Scents and Shadows)

Relative Bonds – McNamara Series – Book Three

Surprise on the Links – McNamara Series - Book Four

MCNAMARA SERIES BOX SET
BOOK 0NE & TWO

A Suitable Epitaph – MacKay - Canadian Detectives Series - Book One

An Immigrant – MacKay - Canadian Detectives Series – Book Two

MacKay - Canadian Detectives Series – Book Set (A Suitable Epitaph & An Immigrant)

A Churchgoing Woman

Payback Is a Bitch

The Man in the Elevator

Team Building with a Twist

A Change of Heart – MacKay Canadian Detectives Series – Book Three

Conversations with My Dog – Pseudo-Essays

Forthcoming:

Stay on Track – Josh Aldridge – PI Series – Book One

Thank you for taking the time to read McNamara Series, Book One in.

If you enjoyed it, please consider telling your friends or posting a short review. Word of mouth is an author's best friend and much appreciated.

Thank you,
Roxana Nastase.

To hear about future releases, please, subscribe to my newsletter on:

www.roxananastase.com.

No other type of emails will be sent to you.

MCNAMARA SERIES BOX SET
BOOK 0NE & TWO